BATTLE ATERNUS

THE ATERNIEN WARS BOOK #5

G J OGDEN

Copyright © 2023 by G J Ogden
All rights reserved.

No part of this book may be reproduced in any form or by any electronic or mechanical means, including information storage and retrieval systems, without written permission from the author, except for the use of brief quotations in a book review.

These novels are entirely works of fiction. The names, characters and incidents portrayed in it are the work of the author's imagination. Any resemblance to actual persons, living or dead, events or localities is entirely coincidental.

Illustration © Tom Edwards
TomEdwardsDesign.com

Editing by S L Ogden
Published by Ogden Media Ltd
www.ogdenmedia.net

ONE
CONCLUDING BUSINESS

MASTER COMMANDER ROSE stepped off the Galatine's cargo ramp, and the sharp clack of his boot heels striking metal was replaced by the soft crunch of them treading dirt and stones. His reason for returning to Gliese 832-e was two-fold. Firstly, Carter had to learn the fate of his XO, Major Carina Larsen, who had been infected with the Aternien virus and placed into Nathan Clynes' care. As the mastermind behind the Longsword program, and the only man to retain technology from before the first Aternien war, Clynes had been Carina's only hope for a cure. Secondly, regardless of the outcome of the first, Carter had to secure Nathan Clynes' assistance in his plot to attack the Aternien home world, whether the genius scientist wanted to help or not.

Brodie Kaur, Carter's re-commissioned Master-at-arms, had used the Galatine's plasma shield to scorch clear the terrain close to Nathan's underground complex, providing Amaya with a clear landing site. Brodie was now at his side, once again in his battle uniform, to provide backup in case any more of the scientist's synthetic creations decided to leap out at them. The passage of time had not affected his officer's square-jawed good looks, and Brodie was still built like a battle tank. If anything, he looked even more intimidating than he had done the last time he'd worn the uniform.

Carter's senses climbed, distracting him from thoughts of how his crew had barely changed in over a century, and forcing him to scour the terrain beyond the charred landing site. A centaur trotted through his field of view, taking a few moments to regard them with curiosity, before continuing on its way. It was one of Nathan's many synthetic creations, most of which were belligerent in nature, though Carter was relieved to discover that the centaur was indifferent to him. Then there was the ear-splitting creak and groan of a tree trunk being bent and eventually snapped, and Carter spun around to see a dinosaur pushing through the forest some distance to their rear. He grabbed his 57-EX revolver and looked to Brodie to back him up, but his Master-at-arms appeared unconcerned.

"Don't worry, MC, that ain't a threat," Brodie said, turning his back on the dinosaur.

Carter scowled. "That thing must be three metres tall, and heavier than an elephant. How can it not be a threat?"

Brodie shrugged. "It's an Iguanodon; a veggie-saurus," he replied, casually. "We're not on the menu." The Master-at-arms then noticed that Carter was still scowling at him, though now with one eyebrow raised. "Hey, I like dinosaurs. A man's gotta have a hobby, right?"

"I thought your hobby was wearing demon masks and beating up criminals?"

Brodie grinned. "I have a diverse range of pastimes."

Just then, a faun trotted across the clearing, headed in the same direction as the centaur. It spotted them, jolted back in surprise, then sprinted into the trees and was gone in the blink of an eye.

"Though I have to say, Nathan Clynes' hobbies are a little on the weird side," Brodie added.

Carter huffed a laugh. "Wait till you see what else he has stashed in his underground warehouse."

Carter took point, using his cutlass to hack through the undergrowth and clear a path to the scientist's lair. Brodie watched his back, carefully observing the natural ambush points in the dense forest, while also occasionally watching – but never being distracted by – more of Nathan's inventions. One such creation, which had also caught Carter's attention, appeared to be a horse crossed with a kangaroo, allowing it to hop or gallop, depending on its mood. After ten minutes of continuous hacking and slashing under the hot Gliese 832 sun, Carter finally cut through into the clearing where Nathan Clynes' stripped-out C37-B Mule Light Transport ship was gathering moss.

"I won't be sorry to leave this planet behind for good," Carter said, sheathing his sword. He mopped his brow with his sleeve, more because he felt like he should be sweating, rather than because he actually was. His augments and bio-engineered physiology meant that he was able to regulate his temperature without the need to excrete liquids as a method of thermoregulation.

Suddenly, Carter's senses spiked and he drew his 57-EX, pointing it toward where his augmented sixth-sense told him that danger was lurking. However, before he could fire, or even spot the target, Brodie had drawn and energized his Scottish claymore sword. The fizz of Aternien particle energy racing around the razor-sharp edge sounded like an arc welder on overdrive. Brodie thrust the blade into a thicket and there was a startled yelp, followed by an agonized wheeze as whatever creature had been impaled exhaled its last breath. Brodie lifted the sword out of the thicket, and Carter saw that a rodent-like beast had been skewered like a giant kebab.

"I've seen some rats in my time, but this one takes the cake," Brodie said, bringing the Frankenstein creation closer to his scrunched-up nose.

"Nathan was out here on his own for more than a century; he had time on his hands," Carter commented, also scrunching up his nose at the beast, which looked like a furless capybara, but double the size. "That's far from the worst thing I've seen on this planet."

He noticed that the creature's skin, which had started out as a greenish-brown, had changed color to blend in with Brodie's battle uniform. His Master-at-arms then slung the beast into the forest, disengaged the blade of his claymore, and returned it to his back-scabbard.

"Isn't that Rollo Jay's sword?" Carter asked, recognizing the weapon that had belonged to Damien Morrow's traitorous Master-at-arms.

"Yeah, but I like it," Brodie said, referring to the weapon as if it were something as commonplace as a pair of sneakers. "My old plasma broadsword was still in the armory, but the claymore has more heft. Plus, the golden energy looks kinda cool."

Carter lifted an eyebrow. "Don't like it too much, or Admiral Krantz will think you're being lured to the goldies' side."

Brodie laughed. "No chance of that, MC, not after those

bastards killed Kendra. The only thing this Aternien sword is killing, besides rodents, is Aterniens and their sympathizers."

Carter nodded and continued past Nathan's old C37-B, toward the entrance to the underground lair, while trying not to think about his deceased Master Engineer. Kendra had died on Venture Terminal, at the hands of Damien Morrow, and while he'd exacted his vengeance upon the traitor in brutal fashion, his grief was still raw. Clearing his head, Carter kept his 57-EX in hand as he descended the ramp, while Brodie covered their rear with a plasma sub-gun, which was his preferred weapon.

"It's still unlocked, which is surprising," Carter said, hauling open the slab-like door to sub-level one of Nathan Clynes' underground complex.

"I guess that means we're invited?" Brodie said, uncertain.

Rose grunted a similarly unsure reply. The fact that Nathan had left the door open for them made him feel uneasy, and he was reminded of how little he trusted the man, though this was not without good reason. When they'd last met, Carter had intentionally infected Nathan Clynes with the Aternien biogenic virus, in order to incentivize the scientist to find a cure. His decision to expose Nathan was partly – probably a large part, he admitted – driven by his desire to save the life of his XO, Major Carina Larsen. In retrospect, he could hardly blame the scientist for wanting to kill him, which was why it felt off that Nathan appeared to be making no attempts to do so.

"Stay on your toes in here," Carter said, drawing his cutlass as a second line of defense, but not engaging the blade. He didn't want to draw unnecessary attention to himself.

"You're right, this guy has some weird hobbies," Brodie said, sticking close and aiming the barrel of his sub-gun at the synthetic monsters and beasts that looked the most dangerous and threatening.

Carter's senses had dipped since Brodie had skewered the chameleonic rat, yet they remained at an elevated level. It wasn't helping that every synthetic being in the warehouse was watching him as he progressed. The bodies and heads of the creations, ranging from mythical creatures to hideous human-animal hybrids, remained still, but their eyes followed him like a shadow. He expected the monstrous creations to jolt into action and charge at any moment, so it was with as much surprise as it was relief that he made it to the exit unchallenged.

"That was a lot harder the last time I was here," Carter commented, trying the door to sub-level two, and also finding it open.

"Don't knock it, MC," Brodie replied, following Carter through the door. "This place is going to give me nightmares, even without having to fight these things."

The door at the bottom of the stairs also opened without any complaint, and a gust of hot air blasted his face. The hydroponics level was even hotter and muggier than the surface of the planet, and no less dangerous.

"Watch your step in here too," Carter cautioned his Master-at-arms.

Brodie scoffed at this. "I think I can handle a few tomatoes and carrots, MC."

"Don't be so sure," Carter hit back, remembering the plant that had stung him with a venom so potent it even managed to overwhelm his robust biology. "There's as much in here that's liable to eat you as there is on the level above."

A flicker of movement caused Carter to stop and signal his Master-at-arms to hold position. Then a spherical bot approached from across the far side of the room, liberally spraying some of the crops with an atomizer held in its mechanical clutches. The bot then froze, suddenly realizing it was not alone, and the atomizer dropped to the ground with a coarse clatter.

"Hello Farmer," Carter said to the bot.

He recognized it as one of the two gophers that Clynes had squirreled away on his C37-B at the end of the war, before the artificially-intelligent machines were outlawed. The other bot was called Fixer, who was likely to be somewhere on the workshop level below. Farmer narrowed its single red eye at Carter, then blew a crude raspberry at him, before zooming away and disappearing through a porthole-shaped door in the wall.

"Something tells me that bot doesn't like you very much," Brodie said.

"No," Carter grunted. "I think it's holding a grudge. Hopefully, Nathan is a little more understanding."

His Master-at-arms laughed at this, since he knew all too well that Nathan Clynes was not the forgiving type. Carter then continued on through the hydroponics level, taking care to avoid anything that looked like it might sting, poison or try to eat him, and arrived at the door to sub-level three without incident. Like the other doors, it was unlocked.

"I know it sounds strange, but I'd almost prefer it if Nathan was making this hard for us," Carter said as the door slid into its housing.

"No, MC, I totally get you," Brodie replied. "From what

you've told me, Nathan is bound to want some kind of payback, so the warm welcome doesn't sit right."

He grunted an acknowledgment, but continued down the stairs, flexing the fingers of his weapon hand to keep them limber and supple. The truth was, even if by some miracle Nathan Clynes wasn't plotting to kill him, the scientist soon would be once he learned of his plan.

Carter entered the workshop level, though while the scientist's second bot, Fixer, was conspicuous by his absence, the rhythmic clatter of machining tools told him that someone was inside. He advanced with caution and was pleased to find the labor bot hard at work, repairing what looked like a regular kitchen kettle. Considering that the labor bot had tried to kill him on his last visit, Carter's warning alarms should have been ringing out loud, but he sensed no threat. The seven-foot humanoid robot then spotted him and downed tools, before offering Carter and Brodie a welcoming wave.

"Friend or foe?" Brodie asked, as Carter approached the machine.

"I'm not sure yet," he replied, honestly.

"Hello, Master Commander Rose. It is pleasant to see you again, and under better circumstances." The bot's tone was perfectly amiable, but Carter wasn't sold yet. The machine's eyes then fell on Brodie. "And who is your companion?"

"This is Master-at-arms, Brodie Kaur," Carter said.

"A soldier," the labor bot replied, with a shocked, fearful tone. It recoiled and held up its hands in surrender. "There is no need for violence; I mean you no harm. Though I understand why you may find it difficult to trust my word."

Carter expected his Master-at-arms to have reacted with

more circumspection, but the man's relaxed expression and body language told him that Brodie didn't feel the slightest bit threatened by the labor bot. Due to the nature of their roles, the augments and training that a Master-at-arms received honed their senses of danger to sensitivities even above his own near pre-cognitive abilities. If Brodie was comfortable in the bot's presence, Carter was confident it was not a danger.

With the bot's arms still raised, Carter then noticed that the majority of the damage it had sustained during their fight had not been fixed. There was evidence of some minor repairs, which had perhaps been necessary for the bot to function properly, but anything cosmetic had been neglected.

"How come you haven't fixed yourself?" Carter asked, moving closer to the workstation that the bot was occupying. "You have all the tools and materials right here."

Despite its expressionless, mechanical features, the bot somehow still managed to appear forlorn. It lowered its arms and its chin fell to its chest.

"Nathan does not consider my physical condition to be important," the bot replied, scuffing the metal sole of its right foot across the floor as it spoke. "So long as I can complete my tasks, he is content to let me remain this way. He says it is a punishment for failing to stop you reaching his private living quarters."

To his surprise, Carter realized he felt pity for the bot. Even during the height of the Union's pre-war technological power, AIs had never been officially considered sentient, though Carter had believed otherwise. He had always treated JACAB as an emotional, conscious being, and he knew that the rest of his crew felt the same about their gophers. labor bots, on the other hand, had always been smart, but he'd never met one that he'd considered alive, until that moment.

"It sounds to me like you're not happy here," Brodie cut in.

"Happy?" the bot said, somewhat wistfully. "I have never had cause to consider my own happiness."

"Why not?" Brodie shrugged. Being direct, sometimes to the point of rudeness, was the only way his Master-at-arms knew how to be.

"I have no choice but to be here, and to do what I am directed to do," the bot replied, mimicking Brodie's shrug. "Whether I am happy are not is therefore irrelevant."

"What if you did have a choice?" Brodie went on. He glanced over at Carter with expectant eyes; it was the sort of look he got when he wanted or needed something. "I mean, we could use a hand in engineering, and it looks like you're good at fixing stuff."

The bot's glowing orbs shone bright and its chest appeared to physically swell, despite the fact its rigid metal chest plate made this impossible. Now it was not only his Master-at-arms, but also the labor bot that was looking at him with hopeful eyes.

"Generally, crew appointments are made by the ship's commander," Carter said, returning Brodie's eager expression with an admonishing look. "And generally speaking, I don't recruit people, or bots, that have previously tried to kill me."

The machine's shoulders sank, and Carter felt guilt stab his insides.

"I understand, Commander Rose," the labor bot said, its voice actually cracking with emotion. "However, the sub-core block that Nathan installed to override my protocols has been destroyed and can no longer direct my actions. I have since made modifications to ensure this could never happen again."

Carter sighed, suddenly feeling like the biggest shit-bag in the galaxy. He noticed that Brodie was still watching him with a sad face, like a kid in a toy store, clinging to an action figure and desperately willing his mom or dad to buckle under the weight of emotional pressure, and take it to the cash desk.

"So, if you had the option to switch jobs, would you?" Carter grunted. He saw Brodie beam a smile at him but pretended to ignore it.

The bot stood tall again, as if had been fitted with a fresh power cell. "That sounds… fun!" it said brightly. Then the light in its glowing eyes faded again. "But I belong to Nathan Clynes, and he would never allow it."

"You belong to no-one," Carter said, with feeling. He didn't believe that bots were property, even if the Union, and Nathan Clynes, did. "Look, if you fancy a change of scenery then meet us outside. You've got some work to do to prove you won't murder me in my sleep, but I'm willing to give you a chance."

Brodie leapt on him and hugged his shoulders, jostling him like they were teammates on a football squad, and Carter had just scored a touchdown. However, the Master-at-arms quickly realized that he'd overstepped, hustled away, and stood to attention, trying to pretend the incident had never happened. Carter cleared his throat and addressed the bot again.

"I take it that Nathan is in his living quarters?" Carter asked.

The bot shrugged. "I am not allowed in the living quarters, but I assume so."

Carter blew out a sigh. He was hoping that the labor bot could answer the question that had been churning his insides since arriving at Gliese 832-e – was Carina still alive? As it was, he'd have to find out for himself, and he resigned himself to descending the final flight of stairs to sub-level four.

"Catch you on the flipside," Brodie said to the bot, slapping the machine on the back as he strode past.

The bot gave Brodie a thumbs up signal in return, then resumed fixing the kettle that he'd been working on. His Master-at-arms caught up with him a few seconds later, and found Carter staring at the door, blankly.

"Something wrong, MC?" Brodie asked, accessing his comp-slate to scan the door. "I'm more of a demolitions guy than a locksmith, but I can give this a go, if you like?"

"It's okay, Brodie, it's not locked," Carter said, waving him off.

Brodie frowned then understood the reason for his hesitation. "Hey, I'm sure it'll be fine, MC. Like you said, Nathan has a well-developed sense of self-preservation. He won't have cured himself and let the Major die, because he knows what you'd do to him if that happened."

Carter nodded. "Of course, it's possible that Nathan died from the virus too."

Brodie scrunched up his brow and poked his tongue out of the corner of his mouth. "Crap, I hadn't thought of that." He clicked his tongue then hit the button on the door's frame, causing it to slide open. "Only one way to find out," he added, inviting Carter to go first.

Carter didn't appreciate Brodie making the decision for

him, though to be fair, it was better than procrastinating, which was what he would otherwise be doing. He blew out another sigh, then walked into the living area. The sound of classical piano music floated through the open-plan space, and he could hear the sound of voices, chatting in a sociable manner. Heading left, he came upon the kitchen and found Nathan and Carina sitting at the solid-wood dining table, sharing a meal. The major had a glass of wine in hand, and appeared to be enjoying Nathan's company, which only made the already bizarre scene seem more unreal. He opened his mouth to speak but found that nothing came out. It was like he just walked into the lunch hall at high school and found his crush sitting with someone else. He cursed the human part of himself for succumbing to such frivolous and ridiculous feelings of jealousy and pulled himself together.

"What's on the menu?" Carter said, then cursed himself again for such a cheesy opening line.

Carina's eyes widened and she rocked back, sloshing the wine around the large burgundy glass as she did so. "Well, shit… You're actually here!" she said, beaming a smile at him. "What the hell took you so long?"

"Oh, you know, the traffic was awful," Carter replied, playing along. "Plus, there's that annoying war thing still going on."

Carina laughed, set her glass down on the table, and sprang up to greet him. Despite himself, he almost hugged her, but was glad he managed to resist the urge. Longsword officers were hard to kill, but they could still die of embarrassment. Suddenly, Carina flung her arms around him and squeezed so hard that he actually gasped. A couple of seconds later, she released him, and took a step back, hands pressed to her hips. Her cheeks were flushed, though Carter figured that could have been because of the wine.

"Thanks for saving my ass, Carter," Carina said. She then flashed her eyes at him and grinned. "You're my hero..."

Nathan coughed loudly from his seat at the dining table, and waited until all eyes were on him before he spoke. On this occasion, Carter didn't balk at the interruption, since it spared his own blushes.

"I'm quite certain that I played a somewhat significant role in the major's recovery, and yet, I seem to have been overlooked for my contributions yet again," the scientist said, with a hint of annoyance in his voice. "Story of my life," he snorted. Nathan then stood up and pressed his hands to the small of his back. "Now, I'd appreciate it if we could conclude our business, so that you can get the fuck off my planet, and never come back."

TWO
UTILITARIANISM

CLYNES HAD a knack for rubbing Carter up the wrong way, but it was still remarkable that the scientist had managed to piss him off within seconds of his arrival. That Nathan's comments had poured water on the happy discovery of his XO still alive and well made it all the more jarring.

"I'll deal with you soon enough, Nathan, don't worry about that," Carter said. He came across with more hostility than he'd intended, on account of his sour mood, and Nathan recoiled at the veiled threat, but the man was not about to be pressured into silence, at least not without a fight.

"I upheld my end of the bargain, Carter," the scientist proclaimed, before pointing to Carina. "As you can see, your major is alive and well, so just give me the fucking data I was promised and be on your way."

Carter could feel his pulse climbing, but while he was battling the urge to grab Nathan's shirt collar and slap some manners into him, Carina interjected and deflated the situation with her charm.

"What Nathan means to say is that he's impatient to restart his work on human soul transference," his XO said, subtly positioning herself between the pair of them, while facing the scientist. "Why don't you grab the capsule with the serum, and while you're doing that, we can get working on the data transfer?"

Nathan scowled at Carina then at Carter, who scowled back, in what became a Mexican standoff of hostile facial expressions. Nathan, whose wilted flesh and partly-cybernetic appearance was disagreeable at the best of times, caved in first, huffing and muttering to himself as he headed to an area at the far end of the kitchen. Carter watched him carefully, noting that there was something new in the scientist's living space that had not been present during his last visit. It looked like a shop mannequin blanketed by a dust cover and it immediately made him anxious and suspicious.

"He's actually been quite an amiable host," Carina said, as Nathan continued to search for the capsule containing the serum. It seemed that while the man was a bona-fide genius, he was far from organized. "He's a bit of a sleazeball though. You know, wandering hands…"

Carter felt his blood boil and his fingers tightened around the grip of his cutlass. Carina noticed this, smiled, and patted him on the chest.

"Don't worry, I put him in his place," she said, perhaps worried that he was about to remove Nathan's 'wandering hands' with the swing of a sword. Brodie then strode up beside them both, plasma sub-gun in hand, and a workman-like expression on his face. Carter had been so distracted by

Nathan's obnoxiousness that he hadn't even realized his Master-at-arms had run a security sweep of the living space.

"There's nothing too scary in here, MC," Brodie said, now watching Nathan like a hawk. "A few of the mannequins and statues are actually automatons, like the freaky stuff on level one, but they appear to be inactive."

Carter nodded, remembering that one such mannequin of a Samurai warrior had attacked him during his last visit, and that the Samurai had been replaced by a sword-wielding knight in medieval armor.

"Thanks Brodie but keep an eye on them. These things can spring into action when you least expect it."

Brodie nodded, then turned back to Nathan, who was now cursing out loud, while tossing tools and other small objects out of a drawer and onto the kitchen worksurface.

"I'm Carina, by the way," Major Larsen said, making it clear that the lack of an introduction had been a discourteous oversight on Carter's part.

"Crap, sorry, I forgot you two haven't met" Carter said. Carina still looked a little put out, so he clarified his statement. "What I mean is that you're so much a part of the crew now that I forget you weren't with us a during the first war, a century ago."

"Well, in that case, you're forgiven," Carina replied, and Carter breathed a sigh of relief, feeling quite smug for digging himself out of a hole.

"Brodie Kaur, meet Major Carina Larsen," Carter said, continuing with the formal introduction. "Brodie is our Master-at-arms."

"Nice to meet you, XO," Brodie said, shaking Carina's hand and beaming a smile at her. "The MC has told me a lot about you. For a normie, you seem pretty badass."

Carina raised an eyebrow, but continued to smile, taking the somewhat backhanded compliment in the spirit it was intended.

"Finally!" Nathan barked, before slamming the drawer shut and spinning around. He had a silver capsule, not dissimilar to a nano-stim container, in his right hand. "I'm normally more methodical, but as you're aware, there was quite a tight deadline for producing this serum."

Carter fully accepted that it had been a dick move on his part to infect Nathan with the Aternien virus in order to ensure that man found a cure in rapid fashion, but he still felt a measure of cruel satisfaction at the fact his plan had worked. The slight smirk that curled his lips was evidence of this, and it didn't go unnoticed by the scientist.

"Laugh it up, Carter," Nathan snarled. "But one day, you'll regret what you did to me."

"Don't threaten me, Nathan," Carter replied, the smirk wiped off his face. "And don't think for a second that this makes us even for you selling us out."

Nathan wisely bit his tongue then handed the serum capsule to Major Larsen, passing it over at full arm's length, so that he could stay as far away from Carter as possible. "I don't know what use this serum will be to you, since the Union lacks the necessary equipment and expertise to reproduce it," Nathan added, taking a couple of paces back from Carter. "Even so, I have included instructions on how to replicate it, using the sort of technology available to present-day scientists." The man then sneered, "I included this information at no extra cost, out of the goodness of my own heart."

"Well, that just shows what a stand-up good guy you are," Carter replied, thick with sarcasm.

"The Union had this sort of tech before, and they can learn it again," Carina cut in, trying to stop the conversation from being derailed and descending into a slanging match. "Though it will take time to put into production, and that's time a lot of people don't have, so we should get going."

"Speaking of time, you're wasting mine," Nathan said, rapidly losing what little patience he had left. "Now give me my data."

Carter was about to warn Nathan again for giving him orders and making demands, when the tarpaulin covering the mannequin at the rear of the kitchen slipped, and billowed to the floor, revealing the synthetic body of a human male. The body was completely naked, which in itself was quite startling due to its anatomical correctness, but it was who the mannequin resembled that really got his attention.

"You built a replica of yourself?" Carter asked, pointing to the body. Revulsion colored the tone of his voice, which Nathan picked up on right away.

"Yes, of course I did," Nathan snapped, irritably gathering up the slipped tarpaulin. "You know that's why I want your data on the Aternien imposters. I'm hoping it will give me the answers I need to finally complete my work and transfer my consciousness into this synthetic form."

"You could have at least put some pants on the damned thing," Carter said, trying not to look at the body's synthetic appendage.

"It's just flesh, Carter, don't be such a fucking prude," Nathan snapped. The scientist tossed the tarpaulin back over the body, which succeeded in covering its modesty, though the mannequin's feet and ankles were still visible, like someone who was really bad at hide and seek.

"Did you make your manhood the same size or bigger on Nathan two-point-oh?" Carina cut in, fighting back a smile.

"Really, Major, I expected better, at least from you!" Nathan replied, shaking his head.

Brodie was shaking with laughter, which only added fuel to the scientist's burning hot embarrassment. However, for what he had to say next, he needed Clynes calm and amenable, so Carter raised a hand and gave his two officers a stern look, and they both took the hint and piped down.

"With the data you owe me, I can perfect my neuromorphic brain, and finally achieve my goal of becoming truly post-human," Nathan explained. "Now, without wishing to sound rude…" Carter couldn't help but snort at this, "…you have your officer and your serum. Now give me my data and, in the nicest possible way, fuck off."

"I just have one more thing to discuss, before we leave," Carter said, causing Nathan to blow out his cheeks with exasperation and roll his eyes. "It'll be quick, and also likely of interest to you, as well."

Nathan shook his head then threw his arms out wide. "Fine, what is this other matter?"

Carter collected his thoughts, suddenly regretting having caused Nathan so much aggravation, in case it affected his willingness to cooperate further.

"Some time ago, an Overseer told me that her essence was permanently linked to something called the 'Soul Crypt' through the conduit of spacetime," Carter began, and immediately Nathan took notice of what he was saying. "Immortals and lower-status Aterniens are backed up at intervals, or restored from their physical soul blocks, so it's only the senior ranks that have this link. I was hoping to tap into it, and wondered what you knew?"

Nathan's muddy-brown eyes narrowed. "You're thinking of using this spacetime conduit to somehow attack or infect the Soul Crypt?"

"So, it's true?" Carter said, feeling a burst of adrenaline rush through his veins. "This conduit exists?"

"First tell me why you want to know," Nathan replied. The scientist was making demands again but Carter kept a lid on his anger, reminding himself that he needed the man's willing cooperation.

"I'm considering it as a possible line of attack, yes," Carter grunted. He'd tried to make it sound like attacking the Soul Crypt was just one of many possible avenues he was exploring but in truth, Carter was hinging everything on the possibility of hijacking the Aternien link to their immortal souls. Without the Soul Crypt, any Aternien that died would be truly dead. And that was a factor that could change the dynamic of the entire war. Nathan was also playing his cards close to his chest, weighing up the risks of telling Carter what he knew, versus the risks of withholding that information and angering him. He reminded himself that Nathan Clynes had no interest in helping the Union win the war. To him, the Aterniens were the superior race.

"Markus and I discussed this idea of a soul repository a long, long time ago." Nathan eventually answered, surprising Carter with the truth. "The concept was analogous to cloud storage, but instead of housing inert data, the Soul Crypt stored living consciousness itself."

"And you know how this works?" Carter asked. He was buoyed to have gotten a positive response and was keen to follow it up and see what else he could learn.

"It is as you say," Nathan replied with a shrug. "High-status Aterniens are fitted with solid-state warp field generators, which synchronize their souls to the crypt through miniaturized spacetime conduits."

Carter was about to pursue the topic further, and in particular his idea of using the conduit as a means to disrupt or even destroy the Soul Crypt, but Nathan raised a hand to stop him.

"But you can't access this link, nor can you disrupt it," the scientist was quick to add. "So, I'm sorry to say that your idea is a non-starter."

"And you know that for certain?" Carter asked, suddenly annoyed. "You've already tried?"

"Of *course* I tried, it was a key area of my research during the first war," Nathan snapped, feeding off Carter's irritation and projecting it right back at him. "But you seem to forget that Markus Aternus is the most brilliant and ingenious being to have ever lived. He anticipated this potential flaw and ensured that only Aternien soul data could pass through the firewall. I attempted for years to break down that wall to no avail but you can waste time trying, if you like."

Carter had to resist the urge to pummel the scientist into a more compliant form, like kneading dough, but Carina again stepped in to offer a calmer and more measured brand of diplomacy.

"Won't you at least consider trying again?" Carina asked. "I know you don't care for the Union, but billions of lives are at stake. Surely, your past grievances aren't more important than the survival of an entire species?"

Carter appreciated his XO's interjection, but he'd already gone down this road with Nathan Clynes, and knew it led to nowhere.

"If humanity is destined to survive then nature will decide," Nathan replied, with the pomposity of a tenured professor who'd been challenged by an audacious college freshman. "Call it an evolution of Darwin, if you like. The strongest species survives." He shot Carina a cruel smile. "That's the Aterniens, in case you were wondering." To Carter, he added. "Now, if that's all, can I please get my data?"

Carter knew he'd gotten all he was going to get from Nathan Clynes, at least willingly. He had held out a sliver of hope that the scientist would cooperate and give him a crucial piece of information, which would prevent him from having to do what came next. However, Nathan had been disappointingly predictable, and that left him no choice.

"You'll get your data, but not yet," Carter said. Nathan's face fell and blood drained from what little natural flesh remained. "You're coming with us, Nathan. If we can't destroy the Soul Crypt using the conduit then I'll destroy it the old-fashioned way, with guns and missiles."

"You're insane!" Nathan yelled. He'd flipped and all pretense of politeness vanished. "Even if you knew where New Aternus was, and no-one does, you can't destroy the Soul Crypt. It's madness to even suggest such a thing!"

Carter glowered at the scientist and advanced on him, forcing Nathan to retreat until his back was pressed against the wall, next to his synthetic alter-ego. The scientist bumped up against it and the tarpaulin again slid to the floor.

"You're coming with us to Old Aternus," Carter growled, peering down at the man. "Somewhere on that world is a clue to where those bastards fled. And since you know more about the goldies than anyone living, you're going to help me find New Aternus, whether you like it or not."

"Fuck you!" Nathan raged, shoving Carter in the chest,

though the impact didn't budge him even by a millimeter. "I already said I won't help you, and that goes double now that you've cheated me!"

Carter grabbed the man's shirt collar and lifted him ever so slightly closer. "I don't care if I have to drag you out of here, but you're coming. I'm sorry, truly I am."

"Bullshit you are!" Nathan hit back. "You're an asshole, Carter, and you'll never leave this planet alive. I'll set all of my creations onto you. Just wait and see!"

The scientist was incandescent with rage, bellowing his threats into Carter's face, showering him with spittle as he did so. Carter allowed it, because the truth was, he deserved to be on the receiving end of the man's tirade. He'd broken his word to the scientist, which was something he never did lightly, but he didn't have the luxury of allowing Nathan to refuse. There was too much at stake. Perhaps, even that didn't justify forcing the man's hand, but if it was to be a stain on his honor, then so be it.

"I know this is a shock, so let me spell out your two options," Carter said, still pinning the man to the wall in case Nathan tried to squirm away and run. "One, you come with us, help me to locate New Aternus, then get dropped back on Gliese 832-e with all the data you could ever want, and you live happily ever after."

Nathan continued to struggle, but once it was clear he was going nowhere, he gave up and relented. "And what's option two?" he snapped.

"Two is you continue to bust my balls and refuse to cooperate, leaving me no choice but to take off in the Galatine and bomb your compound to dust."

Nathan struggled fruitlessly again and growled from

frustration. "You could choose to just honor your original bargain, you duplicitous bastard!"

Carter released Nathan and took two steps back. The scientist briefly considered trying to run, but thought better of it, partly because Brodie was still zeroed in on him like a bloodhound that had caught a scent.

"Think of it this as an opportunity," Carter said, trying to sprinkle some sugar on the shit-sandwich he'd just served up. "There might be some tech or data on Old Aternus that can help you figure out how to ascend. I mean, what better place in the galaxy is there to look?"

Nathan raised an eyebrow at this, and suddenly appeared less like cornered prey, and more like his old self. Carter realized that he'd piqued the scientist's interest. *Maybe I should have started with that…* he thought. "You can even bring Nathan junior," he added, pointing to the naked body. "Think of it as a scientific expedition."

Nathan mulled this over for a few seconds, but it appeared that Carter had finally coerced the man into agreement. "Since I appear to have no choice, very well," he replied.

"Good, Brodie will see to your accommodations and make sure that you're comfortable and secure, though not necessarily in that order," Carter said. His Master-at-arms advanced, and Nathan shrank into the corner again. "Just remember that this isn't a pleasure cruise. You're coming along for a reason."

"Yes, yes, I know," Nathan crowed. "I can't promise I'll find anything, though. Markus was always very good at covering his tracks."

"For your sake, Nathan, you'd better hope he left a trail

of breadcrumbs, otherwise you'll find yourself without a home."

Brodie escorted Clynes away, the man muttering curses and promises of retribution under his breath as he went, all of which Carter heard clearly because of his augmented hearing. He let them slide, however, on account of the morsal of guilt he was feeling for forcing the scientist's hand.

"I kinda feel sorry for him," Carina admitted, as Brodie manhandled the scientist through the door. "I mean, he *is* an asshole, but still."

"I didn't want to force him, but needs must," Carter said. He looked over at his XO, who seemed as strong and vibrant as ever. The cure that Nathan had created had cleared up all signs of her infection. "But don't feel sorry for that asshole. If it suits his purpose, he'll murder you in a heartbeat and not give it a second thought. He doesn't give a damn if the Union burns, so long as he gets what he wants."

Carina nodded. "The best action is the one that results in the greatest good for the greatest number of people…"

Carter frowned at his XO. "Is that Sun Tzu or something?"

"Utilitarianism," Carina answered, smiling. "It's a moral justification for the dick move we just pulled off. I thought it might make you feel better about doing it."

Carter considered this, but the morsal of guilt he felt had already begun to disappear. "Is it wrong that I don't really feel all that bad about it?"

Carina laughed and slapped him on the shoulder. "You're a tough old bastard, I'll give you that."

His frown deepened into a scowl. "Less of the old…"

"But you *are* old…"

"Maybe, but I don't look it, silver beard aside," Carter said, feeling oddly affronted.

Carina laughed again, then her thoughts seemed to wander, and her eyes fell onto the synthetic body of Nathan 2.0. "I once asked my aunt about Old Aternus, but she didn't know where it was," Carina said, suddenly weighed down by the enormity of the task ahead of them. "Apparently, only the president has access to that information. It's sealed in a data vault, and behind miles and miles of red tape. I can't see us getting those coordinates any time soon."

"I know where Old Aternus is," Carter grunted. He didn't think revealing this would shock his XO, but the bombshell almost knocked her off her feet, and she had to take a step back to steady herself.

"When were you going to tell me that?"

"I wasn't keeping it from you," Carter said, annoyed by the implication he was being guarded with her. "It's one benefit to being old, I suppose. The Union considered striking Aternus during the middle part of the first war, but they'd already upped and left by the time we sent recon drones to scout the planet. The coordinates are still in the Galatine's core block."

Carina nodded and cocked her head slightly to one side, appearing to accept his explanation. "So, do you think this could really work?" she asked.

Carter was under no illusion that his plan was based on scant knowledge and plenty of assumptions, but he didn't see a better option. They couldn't defeat the Aterniens in open warfare, nor could they win with subterfuge or diplomacy. Their only hope, as he saw it, was to take away the one thing that defined the Aterniens – their immortality.

Then the rules of the game would change, and perhaps change in their favor.

"Somewhere on Old Aternus is a clue to where they went, Carina, and I intend to find that clue," Carter said, mustering all his determination to make his statement sound as convincing as it needed to be. "We're going to find New Aternus and destroy their Soul Crypt. We're going to take their immortality, Carina. Then, when dead really means dead, we'll see if Markus Aternus still has the stomach for a fight."

THREE
HELPING HANDS

CARTER AND CARINA waited in the warehouse level, watching Brodie supervise Nathan, who had insisted on bringing crates of equipment with him that the man had deemed vital to his research. And since Carter had sold Nathan on the idea that visiting Old Aternus might help unlock the secrets of mind-transference, he'd begrudgingly agreed to take on the cargo. The labor bot that was considering a career change was doing the heavy lifting, literally, while Brodie followed Nathan around, keeping his plasma sub-gun pointed at him at all times. Both Brodie and Carter knew this was unnecessarily draconian, but it kept the scientist on his toes, and reminded him that he was under close scrutiny.

"So, how do you feel?" Carter asked his XO, partly to make conversation, but also because he was understandably invested in her recovery.

"Honestly, never better," Carina replied, shooting him a reassuring smile. "As you've probably noticed, Nathan is falling apart at the seams, and has spent a considerable chunk of his time in exile perfecting the medical skills necessary to keep himself alive. He didn't only cure me he gave me a pretty good tune-up too." Carter raised an eyebrow, and Carina scowled. "Not that sort of tune-up, you dirty old man," she added, impishly.

"Well, I'm glad to hear you're okay," Carter said, choosing to ignore his XO's jibe since he was just happy to have her back.

"I meant it earlier when I said you're a hero," Carina continued, a little more earnestly.

"You said, 'my hero', if I recall correctly..." Carter cut in, giving as good as he got.

Carina laughed. "I did say that, didn't I?" There was a pause, during which time she became reflective again. "But truthfully, you went out of your way to save my ass, Carter. I appreciate it, and I won't forget it."

Carter nodded. "Just doing my job, Major." He could just have accepted the compliment, but Carter always found it difficult to receive praise, especially when it was given with heartfelt sincerity, and also deserved.

"I heard about Kendra," Carina added, her tone turning glum. "I'm so sorry. I didn't know her for long, but it was long enough to realize she was special."

Carter felt his gut churn and cursed his augments for failing to protect him from the surge of emotion. As a younger man, he could process loss in same the way a computer processed calculations; methodically and dispassionately. Yet while age had not dulled his wits or withered his powers, it had mellowed his sensibilities, and Kendra's death – *no, Kendra's murder,* he corrected himself – still weighed heavily on him.

"She died doing her duty, which is what she'd have

wanted," Carter said, sucking it up and giving the answer expected of a Master Commander. "She didn't deserve it, but who does? It's war, and the truth is that we Longsword officers aren't exempt from suffering."

Carina watched him for a time, perhaps considering whether to say more, but in the end, she simply smiled and returned to observing Brodie chase Nathan around the storage area. Carter was grateful for this, and also impressed that Carina had recognized he'd said all he'd wanted to say on the matter. He cared little for games in general, but he'd always thought he had a decent poker face. His XO was proving that assumption wrong.

The deck beneath his feet began to shudder with a rhythmic beat, which alerted Carter to the imminent arrival of the labor bot. The machine powered through the door from level two moments later, carrying two large storage trunks, one stacked on top of the other. It was an impressive feat of strength, and one that Carter suspected even he would struggle to match. A few seconds later, Nathan 2.0 walked through the door, thankfully now dressed in a navy-blue boiler suit. However, while the synthetic body, moved and looked perfectly human, its eyes were dead, like those of a boiled fish head.

"That thing creeps me out more than any of the crazy shit inside this storage area," Carina said, watching the zombie-like progression of Nathan 2.0 as it followed the labor bot.

"I know what you mean," Carter grunted.

It wasn't just the soulless eyes and procedural gait of the body that bothered Carter, but the fact it was a replica of Nathan Clynes – a replica that the man intended to fill with his own soul. The scientist had cheated death and lived longer than any human being, Carter aside, but there was a limit to how many organs and chunks of flesh the man could replace. Clynes was dying, and the synthetic body was his last and only chance at immortality. Like Markus Aternus before him, Carter wondered to what lengths Nathan would go to secure everlasting life. Suddenly, he felt his senses climb and his eyes were drawn to where Nathan was standing, mid-way along the opposite wall. The man had his back turned and appeared to be working on something.

"Hey, what are you doing?" Brodie called out. His Master-at-arms had also become suspicious.

Carter frowned and began to make his way over, but Nathan refused to answer Brodie's question and began working more furtively.

"Nathan, don't do anything stupid," Carter called out, wrapping his fingers around the grip of his 57-EX.

A hidden passage in the wall then opened and Nathan ducked inside, before peering back into the storage room through the narrow gap where the door was still ajar. "This is your fault, Carter!" he yelled. "You brought this upon yourself!"

Brodie ran at Nathan, but the door had closed before he could reach him. The Master-at-arms pounded on the wall where the passageway had been, but while his fists dented the metal, he was unable to break it down. The door leading to level two also slammed shut, and a heavy shutter dropped across the main exit leading outside, blocking them in. For a second, none of them moved or spoke, then all the lights were killed.

"Stand ready!" Carter cried out, drawing and igniting his plasma cutlass.

The flickering glow from the blade, combined with the

light from their luminescent battle uniforms, barely cut through the darkness. Brodie jogged up beside him, shadows dancing across his face, and took aim into the gloom with his sub-gun. A few of Nathan's synthetic creations were visible ahead of them, faces white, like ghosts in a graveyard. Then there was the shuffle of feet and hooves on the ground, followed by the eerie moans and guttural growls of the many and varied monsters they'd been trapped with.

"Stay behind me," Carter said to Carina, who was unarmed. "I only just got you back, and I'll be damned if I'm going to lose you now."

Brodie unslung his plasma sub-gun and held it out to the major. "Here, take this," he said, thrusting the weapon upon Carina.

"What about you?" Carina answered, taking the sub-gun and passing the sling over her head.

Brodie stepped back then drew his two-handed claymore sword out of his back scabbard. He energized the blade, which flooded the area immediately surrounding them in golden light.

"Never mind, I think you're covered…" Carina added.

Brodie charged toward the oncoming horde, striking his first blow two-handed, and cleaving a trio of synthetic abominations in half. Carter also didn't hold back, hacking down four-armed humanoids and bizarre, man-animal hybrids with his usual brutal efficiency. Blasts of plasma raced between him and Brodie, burning golf-ball sized holes into monster and beast alike, but those that fell were merely trampled on by others advancing from deeper inside the warehouse, and the onslaught continued.

"Stand your ground!" Carter called out, still swinging

with all his might. "We have nowhere to run, and no help coming."

No sooner had he spoken the words than a powerful beam of light cut across the room, so intense that it dazzled the synthetic creatures and forced them to reel back, hissing and growling and covering their eyes. Carter squinted and tried to see the source of the light, but all he could make out was a faintly humanoid shape, powering toward him at breakneck speed. Carter raised his guard and prepared to defend himself but the shape stomped past and smashed through the synthetics with the power of an avalanche. The light then dimmed and as his eyes adjusted, Carter saw the labor bot standing in the center of the belligerent mob, dinner-plate-sized hands closed into fists.

"I will assist you," the bot said, calmly. The seven-foot-tall giant then swung its fists and clobbered a troglodyte so hard it was knocked clean across the room, its scaly, clawed feet not touching the ground until it slammed into the corner and landed in a ragged heap. Other synthetic creatures piled in, but the machine continued to whirl its fists like giant medieval morning stars, sending man, beast and monster crashing to the ground.

"Brodie, Carina, cover me!" Carter called out, backing away so that he could access his comp-slate and call for help.

"You got it, MC," Brodie answered, shoulder-tackling an elven warrior, before severing one of the heads off a hydra.

Carina used the considerable bulk of the Master-at-arms as a shield, from behind which she continued to pulverize the synthetics with plasma blasts.

"Amaya, do you read?" Carter called out through his uniform's comm system, while also trying to raise the

Galatine on his comp-slate, but the signals were being blocked. "Amaya, respond!" Still no reply.

He let his mind race in an effort to find a way out, but he was barely allowed a second to consider their predicament before a minotaur charged directly at Carina. She saw the creature and dropped to a crouch, hammering shots into its muscular chest, but the beast kept coming. Carter accelerated and everything besides the minotaur became a blur. He collided with the beast at full speed, propelling it into the throng, but the mass of bodies cushioned its fall, and the creature recovered quickly. It snorted like a raging bull and charged again, but Carter held his ground, aiming the point of his cutlass at the monster's heart. The minotaur ran into the blade which sank into its synthetic flesh, hilt deep. Carter dug in his heels, but the beast still managed to push him back, raining blows onto his shoulders and neck with enormous, leathery hands. Thinking on his feet, he dropped low then rolled out from beneath the creature, yanking the blade from its flesh in the process and causing the minotaur to fall flat on its face. The beast roared and thumped its fists into the deck, ready to charge again, but Carter acted fast and swung hard, decapitating the Minotaur with a single, savage strike.

"We need a way out of here," Carter called out, directing the statement to the labor bot, who was spinning on the spot, flattening creatures left and right like a whirling dervish of death.

"I have an idea," the bot replied, using the palms of its hands to crush the skull of a synthetic man like crashing two symbols together. "Please clear a path to the far-east corner."

Carter nodded to Brodie, who didn't need telling twice. The man stormed ahead, blade flashing through the air like streaks of golden lightning, felling anything in his path. Carina remained close – but not too close – picking off any beast or monster that tried to flank them, then Carter drew in behind his XO, covering their rear. Before long, they'd reached the corner, and the labor bot joined them, tearing goblins off its body and stomping them underfoot as it did so.

"I require sixty seconds," the bot said, crouching and pulling a panel off the wall. "Please protect me."

"I think we can manage that," Carter said. Then he wished he hadn't spoken so soon.

A red-skinned, horned-head demon standing eight-feet tall was approaching, tossing anything that got in its way aside with frightening ease. Carter wasn't a superstitious man, and he certainly didn't scare easily, but even he had his limits, and the demon struck preternatural terror into his heart. Brodie, however, was a man without fear, and he had also been a demon himself. Blazing claymore sword held out to his side, the Master-at-arms met the demon's advance, teeth gritted and bared. The malevolent entity drew back its clawed hand, ready to rend Brodie's flesh from his bones, but Brodie was faster and thrust the claymore through the demon's chest. The entity howled and grabbed Brodie's shoulders, and his Master-at-arms released the claymore, leaving it impaled into the monster's red flesh, before wrestling the demon to its knees with unconquerable strength. Then with a punch that could have cracked the planet's crust, he caved in its horned head and put the thing down for good.

"Holy shit, and I thought Carter was a brute!" Carina said, staring wide-eyed at the mass of red flesh lying inert on the deck.

"Thanks, I think?" Brodie replied, wiping synthetic demon gunk of his hands.

Suddenly, the lights in the warehouse switched back on, and all of Nathan Clynes' synthetic creations stopped moving, fixed in their last positions. Some, which had been running or were in mid-flight after a jump, thudded to the deck, knocking others over and causing a domino effect, but none reacted. It was as if they'd all been frozen in time.

"I have disabled the wireless access relay," the labor bot reported, rising to its full height again. "Nathan will no longer be able to control these synthetics."

"Good work," Carter grunted, disengaging the blade of his cutlass and sheathing the weapon. His senses also told him the danger had passed. "I don't suppose you can open the door too?"

"Yes, of course," the bot replied, as cheery as ever. "Please follow me."

They all followed the machine, Carter limping a little from a bruised thigh, then waited as the labor bot crouched in front of the warehouse door and dug its fingers underneath the lower lip. Then the powerful machine straightened its legs, gears whirring and motors screaming, and tore the slab-like barrier off its hinges. It clattered to the ground moments later, and the blaring hot Gliese sun poured inside.

"Maybe we should have thought about doing that first?" Brodie said, a little sheepishly.

"Hmm," Carter grunted, not wanting to acknowledge that he'd also overlooked the most obvious solution to their predicament.

"You have to admit, he's pretty handy to have around," Brodie continued, cocking his head in the direction of the labor bot. "We could sure use him. And he seems to be on our side."

Carter couldn't argue with the assessment his Master-at-arms had made. He looked at Major Larsen, who simply nodded her agreement, giving her tacit approval of their potential new recruit.

The labor bot then dusted down its hands, in a strikingly human-like manner, and turned to face them. "Are you all undamaged?"

"Thanks to you, yes," Carter replied. "So, I was thinking about what we talked about earlier, about you changing jobs. How would you feel about joining my crew?"

The bot's eyes brightened and it seemed to smile, even though its fixed metal jaw made this physically impossible in practice. "I would love to become a member of your crew!" it exclaimed with gusto. The bot then straightened to attention and threw up a very proper and correct salute.

Carina and Brodie smiled, and Carter even allowed the corner of his mouth to turn up a fraction, but he was cautious not to make light of the gesture, since it had been meant sincerely.

"You don't have to salute me, but you do need a name," Carter said. "I mean, we can't just keep calling you, 'labor bot', can we?"

The machine considered this, tapping a finger to the corner of its non-existent mouth as it did so.

"Though colloquially known as a 'labor bot', my official designation is Heuristic Advanced Remote Power and Engineering Resource, Model Seven, Variant Three-Alpha."

"That's a bit of mouthful," Carina said, also tapping her finger to the corner of her mouth as she thought. She then clicked her fingers in an "ah-ha!" moment. "Wait a second, it's right there in front of us! Heuristic Advanced Remote Power and Engineering Resource. HARPER!"

The bot clapped its hands together. "Yes! Yes, I like that name very much, thank you, Major."

"HARPER it is, then," Carter agreed. He offered the machine his hand. HARPER, confused for a moment, finally took it, and they shook, warmly. "Welcome aboard, HARPER. I know you'll do us proud."

FOUR
REUNIONS AND REMINISCENCES

CARTER HEADED out of the underground storage area, followed by Major Larsen and the newest recruit to the Longsword Galatine, Nathan Clynes' former labor bot, HARPER. He was expecting to have to hunt down the scientist, who had slipped through a secret door before setting his synthetic creations onto them but was pleased to discover that a chase wasn't necessary. Amaya Reid was walking toward them, pushing Nathan ahead of her at the barrel of a plasma pistol.

"I think someone got a bit lost," Amaya said, giving the scientist another sharp jab to the small of the back for good measure.

"I think 'ran away' is a more accurate description," Carter grunted, grabbing Nathan by his shirt collar. "But thanks, Amaya, you saved me from having to chase him down." He peered deeply into the scientist's eyes. "And that would have really pissed me off…"

"What did you expect?" Nathan blurted, struggling to free himself from Carter's grip, without success. "You bullied me into this with threats of violence, and you didn't think I would resist?"

Carter sighed and let go of Nathan's shirt, causing the man to momentarily lose his balance. The scientist briefly considered running for a second time, but there was nowhere for him to go. He was boxed in on all sides by Carter, Brodie, Amaya and Carina. HARPER was not far behind, and to Carter's perceptive eyes, the machine appeared to be enjoying the downfall of his cruel former master.

"Honestly, Nathan, I don't blame you," Carter said, stunning the scientist and freezing him to the spot. "Everything you've said is true. I did go back on my word, and I am forcing you into this, so you've every right to call me an asshole and whatever other names you'd like. But non-cooperation isn't an option, not when billions of lives are at stake."

Nathan scoffed. "Oh, please! Spare me the holier-than-thou, 'I'm doing this for the greater good' bullshit. You're a tyrant, pure and simple."

Carter took the verbal tirade on the chin, since he was being honest when he told Nathan that he deserved it, but the fact was it didn't change anything. And the scientist needed to understand that.

"Now you've got that off your chest, it's important that you get something into your slowly-rotting skull," Carter said. His tone was firm, but he was trying not to sound aggressive. "You've had your little escape attempt, and I'll let it slide. This time." He pointed a finger at Nathan, who scowled at him in return. "But try anything stupid like that a second time, and I will dramatically alter the terms of our arrangement. I need your help, Nathan, and by God I'm going to get it. You can either help willingly, and be comfortable, or keep fighting me, and be my prisoner."

Nathan laughed and shook his head, reading between the lines. "So, torture you mean? I didn't think you'd stoop so low."

Carter leaned in close again and the scientist's cockiness evaporated. "I'll do what I must in order to win this war," he said, plainly. "You know I will."

To his credit Nathan considered his next words carefully, instead of speaking in the heat of the moment and making matters worse. Whether this was the man genuinely accepting the inevitability of his situation, or a calculated effort to make Carter think he was cooperating, remained to be seen.

"Have it your way, Carter," Nathan finally replied. "But don't expect me to be polite company."

Carter huffed a laugh. "When were you ever polite company?"

"Fuck you," the scientist snorted. He gave him the middle fingers of both hands, before turning his back on him.

Carter nodded to Brodie, who took charge of their involuntary guest, and began leading him toward the Galatine. Carter then caught movement in his peripheral vision and turned to see Fixer and Farmer, Nathan's two gophers, creeping out of the underground storage level.

"Hell no!" Carter said, drawing his 57-EX revolver and pointing it at Fixer, who was the foremost of the two bots. "You two can get back inside."

"But I need them!" Nathan protested. "If the point of this ridiculous venture is to learn the location of New Aternus, how do you expect me to help without my bots?"

"Not a chance, Nathan, we have bots on-board the Galatine who can help, and I trust them with my life." He waved his revolver at Fixer and Farmer. "I wouldn't trust either of those two to pour water on me if I was on fire."

Talk of the Galatine's bots suddenly reminded Carter of RAEB, and he felt like he'd been sucker-punched in the gut. An image of Kendra Castle's coffin floating through the void intruded on his thoughts, and all he could think about was her loyal bot, who had sacrificed himself to join Kendra on her final journey. Somewhere in deep space the bot was still alive and functioning, and he wondered what could possibly have been going through its artificially-intelligent mind at that moment.

"Well, I trust my own equipment, and I'm telling you I need them!" Nathan yelled. The man's whiny tones sounded like a mosquito buzzing in his ear, driving him crazy, but at least they had the effect of snapping Carter back to the moment.

"There's not a chance in hell I'm letting them aboard my ship," Carter said, sticking to his guns. "So, the answer is no, and that is final."

Nathan looked ready to explode into another tirade, but the man suddenly thought better of it, cursed under his breath, and continued to be led away by Brodie.

"You two, back inside," Carter said, approaching the bots. "Go water the tomatoes or feed the griffin or whatever, I really don't give a shit." Fixer and Farmer both warbled and screeched angry protests, but since Carina and Amaya were also now aiming their pistols at the gophers, they had intelligence enough to know they were beaten. Reluctantly, and while still squawking objections, they skulked back inside Nathan's bunker.

Once he felt sure the bots were not about to race out and follow them, Carter continued on toward the Galatine, and the journey was mercifully without incident. There were occasional sightings of dinosaurs, mythical creatures and beings that frankly defied explanation, but they all turned out to be benign, and simply ignored the group. Carter even saw the faun that he'd startled on the outward leg, and this time the strange half-human, half-goat creature stopped to give them a wave.

They reached the clearing just as the red dwarf star began to descend toward the horizon, painting brushstrokes of ruby red across the sky. The cargo ramp of the Galatine whirred open and thudded into the dry ground, then Brodie marched Nathan inside. The scientist was followed by his synthetic alter ego and HARPER, who was again carrying the man's ridiculous quantity of luggage. Carter was also about to climb the ramp when his comp-slate chimed an urgent alert. He lifted his left wrist to check the screen and saw that it was JACAB calling. Amaya had left the bot in command of the ship.

"What's up buddy?" Carter asked, trying to tap into his senses through their link, but there was nothing triggering his internal alarm system.

JACAB warbled and bleeped and the translation appeared on the screen. It made him question whether his augmented sensitivity was malfunctioning.

"JACAB says that a ship just jumped into orbit," Carter announced, switching to a scan readout, which was being relayed from the Galatine. However, the data was still populating.

"Aterniens?" Carina asked, her voice tight.

"It has to be." Carter replied, coming to the only logical

conclusion. He turned to Amaya, his senses sharpening. "Hurry to the bridge and get her started. We'll have bug out of here in a hurry."

Amaya nodded. "Aye, aye, skipper," she replied, then raced up the ramp at a full sprint. Carter and Carina followed, but at a brisk march, since he still needed to be able to read the comp-slate clearly.

"Maybe they realized we found Nathan, and are worried about what he knows?" Carina suggested.

"Perhaps..." Carter grunted. He wasn't discounting any possibility, but since the Union didn't know where Nathan Clynes was, it left few options other than the Aterniens.

A sonic boom then shook the air, and Carter stopped just short of the cargo ramp, and looked up. Carina also peered skyward, but his augmented eyes were sharper, and he located the mystery craft straight away.

"It's a shuttle of some kind," Carter said, before waiting for the object to get a little closer so he could see it in more detail. "I can't tell exactly what it is, but it's definitely not Aternien."

His comp-slate updated with the scan readout of the vessel and Carter felt a wave of relief wash over him. He finally recognized the craft, though he was still none the wiser as to why it had arrived at Gliese 832-e.

"It's looks like a Union shuttle," Carina said. The vessel was now large enough in the sky for even her regular human eyes to discern. "And I'd say it's a civilian craft too." She scowled and scratched the back of her head. "You know, I've got the weirdest feeling of déjà vu."

"There's nothing weird about it, Major," Carter replied, smiling at her. "It just means that you're perceptive."

Carina was now frowning at him instead of the craft. "You recognize that ship?"

"It's the shuttle that Cai Cooper used to escape from Terra Six," Carter replied. "Not just the same model, the exact same craft."

The scan readings from his comp-slate had confirmed the ship's registry ID, but even if it hadn't, Carter recognized the shuttle's unique markings.

"Cai is here?" Carina said.

"It certainly looks like it." Carter could understand why his XO was having a moment of brain-freeze. He was as much at a loss to explain his Master Operator's sudden appearance as anyone. His comp-slate chimed another alert, but this time it was an incoming message from the shuttlecraft. Carter copied-in his crew's comp-slates then answered the call.

"Cai, is that really you?" Carter asked.

"Ah, Master Commander, I'm glad that I didn't miss you," Cai replied. His tone was casually apologetic, like was he saying sorry for being tardy to a lunch appointment. "I had worried that you might have already left."

Carter huffed a laugh. "Cai, no offence, but what the hell are you doing here?"

"I'm here to serve, sir," the Master Operator replied, without hesitation. "Permission to dock and resume my duties."

―――

The shuttle conveyor ferried Cai's ship to shuttle pad two in the docking garage, where it was set down and secured by mooring clamps. The rear hatch hissed open a few seconds later, and Cai emerged, somber faced and serious, as was his manner. "Permission to come aboard, sir?" he asked, straitening to attention.

"Permission granted," Carter grunted in reply.

Cai stepped off the ramp then Amaya immediately launched herself at him and pulled him into a tight embrace. His Master Navigator and Master-at-arms had both come to meet Cai off his ship, while Major Larsen held down the fort on the bridge.

"I've missed you, Cai," Amaya said, still hanging off the man's neck like a medallion on a chain.

"You too, Amaya," Cai replied. He was smiling, though also clearly embarrassed by the attention.

Brodie then went to greet the Master Operator, but Carter raised a hand to delay him.

"Is our 'guest' safely locked up?" Carter asked. He didn't want the crew so distracted that Nathan would have another opportunity to screw them over.

"He's secured tighter than the lid of a pickle jar, MC," Brodie said, appearing supremely confident in his assertion. "I've put him in Rosalie's old room but disabled the internal control systems and cut the hard line to the computers, so Nathan can't access anything outside his little box."

Rosalie had been their Master Medic during the first war, but had died from a Trifentanil overdose in 2356, aged eighty-one. He'd mourned her loss after he'd learned of her death, but the mention of her name re-opened the wound as if it had happened yesterday.

"I've also boosted the locks and added a surveillance system to the room, on a private network, isolated from any other," Brodie continued, oblivious to Carter's wandering thoughts. "Besides, I've got Taylor keeping an eye on him."

Carter nodded, satisfied with the report his Master-at-arms had given. All of the precautions were warranted, but the simple fact that Brodie's gopher, Taylor (also known as a Tactical Assistance and Logistics Operations Bot - Master-at-arms) was tasked with keeping an eye on Nathan was enough in itself to give him peace of mind.

"I'm glad you managed to put Taylor back together," Carter said.

Brodie beamed a smile. "It was actually the new guy, HARPER, that did it. Taylor was in pieces in the armory, but it took our latest recruit no more than ten minutes to fix him up. Even Kendra would have been impressed."

As a demolition and surveillance specialist, Taylor would not only prove extremely useful in the mission ahead, but the bot also packed a serious punch, thanks to an integrated plasma cannon. As a result, Taylor was twice the diameter of the volleyball-sized gophers, JACAB and ADA, largely so that it could accommodate the extra power cells it needed. Brodie's mention of HARPER then made him realize he hadn't seen the former labor bot since they'd boarded the Galatine and been waiting for Cai to arrive.

"Where is HARPER, anyway?" he asked his Master-at-arms, who was also the ship's security officer. "I know he's been on our side, but we need to keep close tabs on him too, until we're a hundred per cent sure he's not a trojan horse that Nathan might take control of at any moment."

"Relax, MC, I'm on top of it," Brodie said. "I installed a tracker, with HARPER's consent I might add, and gave him some resources to digest. Ship protocols and Union military rules, that sort of thing. Plus, he only has limited access to engineering at the moment, so he can't do any serious damage."

To a casual observer, Brodie might have sounded arrogant, but Carter knew better. His Master-at-arms may have come across as overly laid back, but he was meticulous in his work. Even so, no-one was infallible, as Carter knew better than most, considering how Nathan had so easily gotten the better of him only an hour earlier.

"Good work, Brodie," Carter said, patting his Master-at-arms on the back. "Let's keep an eye on HARPER, but I have a good feeling about him."

"Me too, MC," Brodie replied. He cocked his head toward Cai, who was locked in conversation with Amaya, and from the troubled look in her eyes, it appeared that they'd already gotten onto the topic of what happened on Terra Six.

"Go ahead, Brodie, you two have a lot to catch up on," Carter said, finally releasing his Master-at-arms so that he could greet the new arrival.

Carter watched from a distance as Brodie and Cai shook hands then began talking, Cai in a reserved manner, and Brodie punctuating his words with animated flourishes of his hands. He was again struck at how natural they were together, despite the huge gulf in time that had separated them since the end of the war. It wasn't quite a full family reunion, however, and Carter's thoughts again turned to Rosalie and Kendra. He had learned how to adjust to their absence but, like losing a limb, it would never quite be the same again. And speaking of family, he was also acutely aware of the reason why Cai had not rejoined his crew in the first place. It was a topic he couldn't ignore, and as Cai and the others walked toward him, laughing and smiling, he figured there was no time like the present.

"It's good to see you again, Cai, but I can't pretend that

Terra Six didn't happen," Carter said, stopping the Master Operator in his tracks. "What about your family?"

The man straightened to attention, appreciating the significance of the question. "My daughters are being well looked after on Terra Prime," Cai answered. "I spoke with Admiral Krantz, and she agreed to shelter them, along with my brother, and his in-laws, so that I could resume my post."

"You should be with them too," Carter said.

It sounded harsh, considering the man had only just arrived, but he had to be sure that Cai had fully thought-through his actions.

"I can't just sit on my hands and do nothing, sir," Cai replied. "I've been following the progress of the war, and based on my own investigations, and what the admiral was willing to tell me, it's clear that the Union can hold out for perhaps another two-weeks, a month a most. Learning this, I had to come."

"How did you even find us?" Amaya asked.

It wasn't the most pressing question, but Carter had to agree it was a conundrum that had been gnawing at the back of his mind, ever since he'd confirmed the ID of Nathan's shuttle.

"Admiral Krantz mentioned you were looking for Nathan Clynes, so I scoured the archives, searching for any and all mentions of the man," Cai explained. "Then I cross-referenced the data and came up with a number of possible locations for his self-imposed exile. Based on the range of his C37-B transport vessel, and what I knew of how the man's mind worked, this seemed the most likely destination."

Brodie laughed and slapped the man so hard on the back it jolted him forward by a step. "You always were one smart son-of-a-gun!"

Cai smiled at Brodie, but Carter scowled at him instead, which encouraged his Master-at-arms to refrain from any further interruptions.

"In simple terms, sir, this ship and her crew are our only hope," Cai continued. "I can't be selfish anymore. I need to do everything I can."

Carter narrowed his eyes at the man, but Cai didn't flinch or even blink. It seemed that his mind was made up. Even so, Carter had to test him further, to make absolutely sure there wasn't even a micro-fracture in his resolve.

"Honestly, we've got this covered, Cai," he lied. "You don't need to risk your neck. Out of all of us, you have something to live for."

Brodie and Amaya could have taken offence at the suggestion their lives were meaningless outside the pursuit of duty, but both understood what Carter was trying to do. Cai likely did too – Carter was terrible liar and a worse bluffer – but he responded appropriately.

"I understand why you have to ask, sir," Cai said, back still as straight as a two-by-four. "But you can be assured that I'm all in. I have a duty to perform, the same as you, and I will not abandon it. I have to fight, not only for the sake of the Union, but for the sake of my children too. While the Aterniens are a threat, they'll never be safe."

Carter scrutinized the man and stroked his silver beard, trying to convey a sense that he was still deliberating, while in truth, he was as sure of Cai's resolve as he was his own.

"Walk with me, Cai…"

Carter and his Master Operator strode side-by-side down the long corridor that ran from bow to stern inside the blade-shaped vessel. En route, he informed Cai of his plan to find New Aternus and destroy the Soul Crypt, where the consciousness of every Aternien was stored. His Master Operator considered it a somewhat radical plot but agreed that drastic times called for drastic measures. Carter also covered the reason why Nathan Clynes had been forcibly brought aboard and warned Cai of his slippery nature. His Master Operator absorbed everything like a sponge, while asking thoughtful questions, and providing insights that Carter had sorely missed during the man's absence. As much as he felt guilty for keeping the man away from his family, he couldn't deny that having Cai back provided a massive boost to their chances of succeeding.

En route to the bridge, Carter stopped at the armory. He unlocked the door then slid a neatly-folded battle uniform off a shelf just inside the entryway and offered it to Cai.

"Last chance to back out," Carter said, drawing the uniform back just as Cai was about to take it from him.

"No thank you, sir," Cai replied, taking the battle uniform into his hands in a ritualistic manner. "With your permission, I'll get settled in my quarters, change, and meet you on the bridge."

"Agreed," Carter said, allowing himself to smile.

Cai was about to leave but hesitated as if he'd forgotten to ask something important. His look of consternation then cleared and he turned back to Carter, bright-eyed again. "Is Kendra down in engineering? I'd like to say hello, before I do anything else."

The smile fell off Carter's face and a sick feeling threatened to overwhelm him. He rested a hand on his Master Operator's shoulder and met his eyes, even though he'd rather have looked away.

"Cai, there's something else we need to talk about…"

FIVE
REUNIONS

THE STARFIELD SHIFTED and the rusty orange of Gliese 832-e vanished from the viewscreen and was instantly replaced by the more familiar, aqua blue of Terra Prime. Station Alpha was front and center on the screen, silhouetted by the bright planet, but the Union's principal military outpost was far from the only object in space. Hundreds of Union battleships prowled close by, and dozens of them were baring down on the Galatine, like sharks descending on the corpse of a whale.

"Something tells me that the Union is a little jumpy at the moment," Brodie commented from his position at the tactical station to Carter's rear.

"It's understandable, given the situation," Carter replied.

"Perhaps I shouldn't have jumped in so close?" Amaya said, hands poised to enact evasive maneuvers, should any of the Union ships fail to identify friend from foe.

"No, you did right, Amaya," Carter replied. He stood up and walked to the center of the bridge, ready to contact

Admiral Krantz. "But let's make sure we're broadcasting our ID loud and clear."

"You got it, MC," Brodie said. "I'm pretty much yelling at these guys to back the hell down."

Carter waited for a few more seconds, carefully observing the squadrons of destroyers and battlecruisers for any sign they might attack, but soon the ships adopted a less aggressive posture.

"Destroyer squadron fifty-two has requested that we follow them to Station Alpha," Cai said, from his position at the crescent-shaped operations station. "We have apparently been cleared to dock at upper-pylon six."

"Your aunt doesn't hang around," Carter said, casting a sideways glance at Major Larsen, seated to the right of his own captain's chair.

"She's a busy a lady," Carina shrugged. "I imagine she's keen to get an update on our progress."

"And she's probably keen to make sure you're okay too," Carter added.

On reflection, Carina was probably right that the admiral would focus on operational matters primarily, before a personal matter. To that end, Carter figured that it would be potentially useful to bring Clynes along too. The scientist had developed the serum that counteracted the Aternien bio-genic virus, and while the man had also created a guide on how to replicate it, Carter felt sure that the Union scientists on Station Alpha would welcome a chance to quiz Nathan in person.

"Brodie, go fetch our guest, and make sure he understands he needs to be on his best behavior," Carter said, turning to look his Master-at-arms in the eyes as he gave the order.

"You got it, MC," Brodie replied. "Taylor will make sure he doesn't cause any trouble, because if he does, he'll get zapped in the ass."

Carter considered ordering his Master-at-arms to adopt a less heavy-handed approach, before reminding himself how much of a danger Nathan had been. He decided that being zapped by the massive tactical bot might do the man some good.

"Commander, if I might offer a suggestion?" The question had been asked by HARPER, who had occupied Kendra Castle's engineering consoles at the rear of the bridge. The bot cut an imposing figure with his its bright yellow cladding, and Carter was pleased to note he had conducted the necessary repairs to himself that Nathan had previously forbidden.

"Go ahead," Carter replied, curious to learn what the labor bot had in mind.

"While we are docked at Station Alpha, I believe some routine maintenance to the nano-mechanical systems could increase our armor value by seven percent," the bot continued. "Additionally, a simple adjustment to the linear magnetic accelerator will increase plasma cannon yield by six percent."

Carter raised an eyebrow at the bright-yellow bot. "That sounds like a plan, but we won't be at Station Alpha for very long."

"It will require only a few minutes," HARPER replied, calmly.

Carter's eyebrow lifted up even higher. "Okay, do your worst." Carter was about to turn away from the machine, before feeling an urgent need to clarify his statement. "What I actually mean is, 'do your best', in case that wasn't clear?"

The bot cocked its head to one side. "After so long in the company of Nathan Clynes, I am highly familiar with the human concept of sarcasm. However, there is no need to doubt my abilities. As a pre-war Heuristic Advanced Remote Power and Engineering Resource that has been actively learning for over a century, my skillset has become quite sophisticated."

"And he's so modest with it," Carina said, grinning at the bot.

"Ah! More sarcasm," HARPER replied, cheerfully. "Bravo, Major."

"You're approved to proceed, Mister Harper," Carter said. "Cai will assist you."

The bot bowed slightly. "That is not necessary, but I welcome the company."

Carter had a good feeling about HARPER, but the bot was still largely an unknown entity, which was why he'd asked Cai to assist. However, HARPER was smart enough to read between the lines and understand that Cai was really there to keep an eye on him. Thankfully, this didn't seem to have offended the labor bot, which Carter took as another good sign he was genuine about earning their trust.

"Amaya, you're in charge while I'm gone," Carter said, pointing to the Master Navigator as a way of passing the baton.

He began marching off the bridge with Brodie and Major Larsen in tow, but he caught HARPER looking at him, as if he wanted to ask a question. Quite how Carter came to this conclusion, given that the machine's face was a single, machined block of metal that was incapable of expression, he had no idea. Nonetheless, there was still *something* about the bot that conveyed its emotions through its inflexible exterior, and made it seem alive.

"Is there something more you wanted to say, Mister Harper?" Carter asked, hovering by the exit.

"Yes, there was one thing," HARPER replied, a little nervously. "I wanted to say thank you for this opportunity, and that I will not let you down, boss."

Carter was unprepared for how powerful the use of a single word could be, but when HARPER called him 'boss' – the honorific that Kendra had always preferred – he felt electricity race down his spine.

"Don't mention it," he grunted, containing his emotions. "You're one of the crew now."

HARPER nodded then Carter took his leave, marching down the long central corridor of the Galatine toward the armory, where the silver capsule containing the serum was stored. Brodie detoured to collect their honored guest, and they all met at the docking hatch, just in time for Amaya to pull alongside and latch on. The precision maneuver was completed in less than half the time that it should have taken a ship the size of a Longsword-class Battlecruiser to dock, and it had been done entirely on manual control too.

"Amaya likes to show off," Carter said, smiling at his XO, who was clearly impressed.

"Yes, yes, very notable," Nathan Clynes droned from behind them. "I wonder if your superiors will be so impressed with the fact you threatened and abducted one of its citizens."

Taylor zapped Nathan in the ass with a focused jolt of electricity, causing the man to leap off his feet and yelp like a puppy.

"I'm sorry, did you say something?" Brodie asked the

scientist. Nathan gritted his teeth and considered talking back, but in the end, common sense prevailed, and he bit his tongue. "That's what I thought," Brodie added, maintaining a steely-eyed and hard-nosed expression.

The docking umbilical pressurized then the inner hatch unlocked. Carter pulled it open then stepped through, leading the party toward the exit onto upper pylon six of Station Alpha. The pressure door station-side opened as he approached, and Carter saw that Admiral Clara Krantz was already waiting for them, with an entourage of armed guards.

"Master Commander Rose, good to see you," Admiral Krantz said.

Normally, such a greeting would have been accompanied by a firm, but friendly handshake, but the admiral kept her distance, and when Carter continued to walk toward her, the guards thrust their weapons in his face.

"Something wrong?" Carter asked, taking the hint and halting his advance.

"My apologies, Commander, it's just new protocol,' Krantz replied. "I have to make sure that you are who you say you are, before allowing you onto the station."

Carter nodded, understanding the need for caution. The issue of Aternien infiltrators who were able to pass for human beings still loomed large over the Union, creating a culture of suspicion and fear.

"We have an updated tool that can accurately detect Aternien spies," Krantz went on. Her eyes were constantly flicking toward Carina, but her expression remained stoic. "It won't take more than a couple of minutes."

One of the guards lowered his weapon then held up a device that was slung around his neck like a satchel. At the same time, Krantz rolled up her sleeve and held out her forearm. Carter watched as the guard pressed the device to her flesh, which snapped like a staple gun then hissed as if a can of soda had been opened. He observed the admiral's eye twitch and cheeks muscles flinch and could tell that the procedure had caused her pain. The device was then removed, leaving a button-sized bruise behind. He noted that a dozen other such bruises were present on her forearm, all at various stages of healing. A few seconds later, a panel on the side of the device turned green, and the guard nodded to the admiral, as if to say, "it's okay, you're still human…" Krantz pulled down her sleeve and lowered her arm, resisting what must have been an unbearable urge to rub the injection site. It was an unnecessary display of her 'toughness', though Carter guessed it was for the benefit of Nathan Clynes, more than himself or his officers.

"I'm afraid this test isn't pleasant but it's the only way to be sure who is human and who isn't," Krantz added, while the guards tested themselves, displaying the clear green result each time.

One guard then approached Carter with the test device, though somewhat tentatively. "I'm afraid there are no exceptions, sir…" the officer said.

Carter detected an undercurrent of animosity in the soldier's voice, and in the way the man had looked at him. It was a reaction he was used to receiving from people who still had an aversion to *what* he was. To be fair to the guard, the man had concealed it better than most.

"Make it quick," Carter replied. He rolled up the sleeve of his battle uniform and held out his forearm, then purposefully tensed his muscles as the device was pressed against his skin, turning his flesh to steel. The device thudded and hissed, before generating two angry bleeps. The screen flashed white, and the guard removed the device to find the injection module bent out of shape. Carter's arm remained unpunctured.

"Oops," Carter said, smiling at the guard, who was able to do nothing other than gawp at him with a stupefied look on his face.

"Don't worry, Lieutenant, I'll vouch for the Master Commander and his crew," Admiral Krantz cut in. She then turned her attention to Clynes, whose cybernetically-enhanced body was arguably closer to Aternien than it was human. "Though I don't quite know what the test will make of you. I assume you are Nathan Clynes?"

The scientist bustled forward, but only managed to draw level with Carter before Brodie caught him by the shoulder and prevented him from progressing any further. The man struggled and protested, but Brodie could have held back a bull simply by grabbing a horn, making the scientist's attempts to free himself comically pointless.

"Yes, I'm Nathan Clynes, and I wish to press criminal charges against Commander Rose for kidnapping, vandalism and theft!" Nathan raged. "He abducted me from my home, destroyed my property, and stole an extremely rare and valuable labor bot!" The scientist then aimed an accusatory finger at Carter. "I want him arrested and thrown in a cell at once!"

The man was irate, and Carter guessed he'd been bottling up his anger for some time, waiting for his moment to explode. However, if Nathan thought that Admiral Krantz would offer him a sympathetic ear, he was sorely mistaken.

"You're considered dead, Mister Clynes," Krantz said, straight-faced. "Dead men can't press charges."

The admiral nodded to the lieutenant, who had replaced the injector module in the testing device while they'd been talking. The officer seized Nathan Clynes' arm and pressed the detector device to one of the few patches of available organic flesh. The scientist yelped with pain and snatched his arm away, but the device had already taken a sample. A few seconds later, the screen flashed yellow.

"What does that mean?" Nathan said, pressing his hand to his forearm, where the injector had penetrated his skin.

"It means I don't know what the hell you are," Krantz replied. "You're not Aternien, but not exactly entirely human either."

"What does it matter?" Nathan snapped. "I was a valued member of the Union, who developed vital technology that ensured our victory over the Aterniens." He slapped the back of his hand to Carter's muscular chest, as if revealing one of his latest synthetic creations. "Here is an example of my work."

Carter grabbed Nathan's hand between thumb and forefinger, adding enough pressure to make the man yelp once again, and removed the hand from his chest.

"Don't touch me, Nathan," Carter said, still adding enough pressure to make the man squirm. He leaned in close and, with feeling, added, "Don't ever touch me again…"

Carter released the scientist, who snapped his hand away and cradled it, as if it had been badly burned in a fire. Admiral Krantz had already lost interest in Nathan, and was working on her comp-slate, dealing with the never-ending stream of communiques that she was inundated with on a daily basis.

"Am I to infer that you'll do nothing about this?" the scientist asked.

"You can infer whatever the hell you like," Krantz replied, head down and still working. "All I need from you is an understanding of how this serum works, and how it can be replicated." She looked up. "Actually, my chief scientific advisor and his team need to know. Personally, I couldn't give a damn how it works, so long as it does, and so long as we can reproduce it."

Nathan folded his arms across his chest. "I will not assist you, not without a promise that justice will be served."

Admiral Krantz sighed. For a woman with barely a nanosecond to spare in her schedule, one of the worst crimes anyone could commit was wasting her time.

"Mister Clynes, you are no longer a citizen of the Union. You forfeit that right over a century ago."

Clynes opened his mouth to protest, but Krantz raised a finger and he clamped up tighter than a drum.

"The Master Commander has broad authority in this matter, so for your own sake, I suggest that you comply. However, do this, and I assure you that you will be treated fairly, and are sufficiently compensated for your losses and any inconvenience we have caused."

Nathan Clynes snorted his disgust at the admiral's response, but as on other occasions, he knew when he was beaten. He'd taken his shot and missed.

"This is the serum," Carter said, plucking the silver canister out of a pocket in his uniform and offering it to the admiral. "It works, though it might be hard to reproduce."

Krantz took the capsule, then her eyes briefly landed on Major Larsen, and for a fleeting moment, she smiled, before her expression resumed her normal, ultra-professional mien.

"Walk with me, Commander," she said.

The group left the lounge at upper docking pylon six and

hustled through Station Alpha to a vast medical and scientific laboratory, which seemed to occupy the entire deck. That it was on the same level as pylon six was clearly the reason the admiral had chosen that particular docking port, Carter realized. She led them into one of the labs and handed the capsule to a mid-fifties man with wavy, 'mad scientist' hair that was half gray, half brown. Krantz explained what it was, then introduced the Union scientist to Nathan Clynes. The two boffins conversed energetically for several minutes, under the attentive gaze of Brodie. Taylor had remained within zapping range, but the two scientists were so deep in conversation that Nathan didn't even notice the beach-ball sized tactical bot looming over his shoulder, cattle prod extended.

While this was happening, Carter briefed the admiral on his plan to learn the location of New Aternus and destroy the Soul Crypt. As he described the mission to an attentive, if undeniably skeptical-looking Admiral Krantz, he became acutely aware of how implausible it sounded, and how it was based on exactly zero hard evidence.

"It sounds like you're taking an awful risk, Commander," Krantz said, once Carter was finished. "Are you sure you can trust this former Overseer, Monique Dubois? What if she is misleading you on purpose, and all that awaits you at Old Aternus is an ambush?"

Carter had considered that possibility, along with a dozen other equally plausible scenarios that ended with the destruction of the Galatine at the hands of the Aterniens, but it didn't change the fact it was their only choice, beyond standing and fighting. And in that situation, against the Aternien fleet and two fully-restored Solar Barques, the Union had no hope of victory.

"I know it's a risk, Admiral, but it's the best shot we have," Carter said, choosing to condense his thoughts into a simple, straightforward answer. "Immortality is their not-so-secret weapon, but if we take that away then the game changes."

Krantz sighed again, then was briefly distracted by various new updates on her comp-slate, which were followed soon after by summaries delivered by one of the officers in her entourage.

"Very well, Master Commander, you are authorized to proceed," the admiral said, once the officer had stepped away. "You'll leave as soon as Mister Clynes is done patronizing my chief scientific advisor."

Carter grunted a laugh. "We could be here for quite some time."

Krantz smiled then her eyes flicked across to Major Larsen again. His XO had hung back, not wanting her personal connection to the admiral to get in the way of business. However, since it seemed that everything was in order, Carter decided to excuse himself, and give aunt and niece a chance to catch up.

"If you'll excuse me for a moment, Admiral, I need to contact my Master Operator," Carter said, faking an incoming call on his comp-slate.

"So, Cai Cooper did find you?" Krantz asked.

"He did," Carter replied. "And thank you for sheltering his family."

"It was the least I could do," Krantz replied. She then took Carter's hand and squeezed it gently. "And thank you, for what you have done," she added, again glancing at Carina.

Carter felt his throat tighten but simply nodded a reply. It was a rare glimpse of the admiral's human side, and it affected him more than he expected. With pride swelling inside him, he decided it was a good time to take his fake call from Cai.

"Shout if you need me, Admiral," Carter said.

He stepped away and turned his back on the admiral, in the hope that she would avail herself of the opportunity to catch up with Carina. There were a few awkward moments and barely-exchanged glances, then finally Krantz approached her niece, and the two women slipped inside the office of the Union's chief scientific advisor. After a minute or two, Carter couldn't resist the urge to look, and he turned his head just in time to see Krantz pull her niece in for a deep embrace, while Carina squeezed her eyes shut, forcing back tears. He smiled and watched for a few second longer, allowing the joy they felt to fill him up too, before looking away to give them back their privacy.

Suddenly, alert klaxons sounded and red lights pulsed in the corners of every wall. Admiral Krantz and his XO came running out of the office, and were soon joined by Brodie, his hand firmly gripped around the collar of Nathan. However, Carter didn't get any sense that the troublesome scientist had been the cause of the alert. It was something else. Something dark and ominous. He could feel it, like an approaching storm.

"An Aternien fleet has just warped into Terra Three," Krantz said, receiving the news both on her comp-slate and from her aide. "I must go at once." To Carter, she added. "Continue with your mission as planned, Commander. It may be our only chance to stop them."

"Admiral, if the Galatine isn't on the front line at Terra Three, Markus Aternus will wonder why," Carter said, interjecting before the admiral could hurry away. "We need to at least show our faces, to make sure they don't suspect something is wrong. Then once the battle is done, we'll jump directly to Old Aternus."

Krantz nodded, immediately seeing his point. "The Dauntless will lead the defense of Terra Three, under my command," she said. "The Galatine will focus on any Aternien Solar Barques, and the transport vessel carrying the bio-genic weapon."

Carter nodded. "Understood Admiral."

"Then get to your ship, and good hunting," Krantz added, before quickly extracting herself from the lab and charging down the corridor, with her entourage in hot pursuit.

SIX
UNTO THE BREACH

BY THE TIME Carter and the others had returned to the Galatine, and safely stowed Nathan back in his quarters, the Dauntless had formed up at the head of six taskforces and was preparing to jump. The fourth fleet was already en route to Terra Three, plus whatever other ships the admiral could spare, without leaving the rest of Union undefended.

"Amaya, do we have a course locked in?" Carter asked, dropping into his captain's chair. JACAB was in his cubby to Carter's left, and the bot bleeped cheerfully as he sat down. Carter rapped his knuckles gently against his gopher's spherical shell, by way of a hello.

"Aye, aye, skipper, we're spun up and ready," the pilot and navigator called out. ADA was docked to the station alongside her. "Say the word and we're out of here."

The Dauntless disappeared through a fold in space, followed moments later by the taskforces under Admiral Krantz's direct command. It was like watching marbles fall into a pool of thick-black ink; for a brief moment, they hung on the surface, then in the blink of an eye they were gone.

"Brodie, take us to battle stations," Carter said, and immediately the lights dipped and floor-level red lighting ran around the bridge.

"Battle stations, aye," Brodie replied, before looking toward the pilot's console. "Amaya, are you ready to hook up?"

"I thought you'd never ask," Amaya replied, a mischievous twinkle in her eye.

This had been a running joke between the two Longsword officers during the first war. Despite how it sounded, Brodie wasn't propositioning the navigator, but asking permission to link to her console, and by definition, her mind. This allowed gunner and pilot to coordinate their actions at a subconscious level. Amaya would fly and get them into range of a target, then temporarily relinquish control to Brodie to line-up and take the shot. It could all be done without a single word spoken between them, though because neither Amaya nor Brodie were exactly the quiet types, they still liked to chat. Carter didn't mind, so long as the job got done, and Amaya and Brodie in tandem always got the job done.

"HARPER, did you manage to complete those upgrades to the nano-mechanical armor and plasma cannon?" Carter asked, turning to the yellow labor-bot at the aft engineering stations.

"Yes, boss, I did," the bot replied, sticking with the honorific that Kendra preferred, in homage to her. "In fact, plasma cannon yield was increased by nine-point-seven percent."

"Good work, HARPER, we'll be needing the big guns for this one," Carter replied, thumping the arm of his chair in readiness. "Keep the cannon juiced up and see if you can't squeeze out some additional power for the plasma shield, while you're at it."

"Already done, boss," the bot replied, while working on two stations simultaneously. "Shield effectiveness is up ten percent, and total shield power has increased by five percent."

"Now, you're just showing off," Carina said, smiling at the machine. "But keep doing it, I like to be impressed."

"It is my pleasure, Major. It is nice to be appreciated, for once," HARPER answered, with a bow of his head.

"Cai, your job once we arrive is to locate the biogenic weapon ship," Carter continued, grateful to have an operations officer back on station. "That's our primary target. As soon as we tag it, we need a plan to take it down. Likely, it will be heavily guarded."

"Yes, Master Commander," Cai replied, before turning to TOBY to discuss strategy. Or it could have been poetry, or philosophy, Carter admitted; it was hard to know with Cai and TOBY.

"We're all set, people," Carter said, glancing at his XO, who nodded her agreement. "Amaya, punch it…"

The soliton warp drive spun up to a crescendo, sounding even more fluid than usual, which Carter considered was again likely on account of HARPER, then the Galatine vanished through a hole in the veil of spacetime. The starfield shifted and Terra Three appeared directly ahead. Without paying close attention to the layout of the continents, anyone could have easily been mistaken for thinking the planet was Terra Prime, such were the similarities between the worlds. However, the key difference was that an Aternien war fleet was threatening to eradicate all life on Terra Three, while Terra Prime remained – for the moment – unchallenged.

"The bulk of the Aternien fleet is amassing in orbit above New Cambridge," Carina reported, reading the data that was streaming onto her chair's comp-slate. "That city alone has a population of twenty-million."

Carter nodded, but he was keenly aware that twenty million was only the tip of the iceberg. Terra Three had a global population of 1.2 billion people.

"Amaya, slot us in alongside the Dauntless and take us in," Carter said to his pilot, before turning to his Master-at-arms. "Brodie, what's the composition of the Aternien fleet?"

"It's sizable, but to be honest, I was expecting more of them." Brodie sent an analysis to the main viewer and Carter shuffled forward in his seat, keen to see what they were up against. "I'm reading three-four-three Epsilon-Class Gunboats, niner-eight Khopesh-class Destroyers, not including seven Royal Court vessels, plus the Solar Barque Senuset," Brodie continued.

Carter noted that the enemy forces were arranged in multiples of seven, which was the Aternien lucky number – another one of their curious superstitions adopted from ancient Egyptian custom. He then noticed that the Khopesh destroyers were all launching what looked like fighters or shuttles, two apiece. He zoomed in and tracked one of the vessels, but it was something he hadn't seen before, in the current war, or the last.

"Brodie, any idea what that is?"

"The flagship just classified them as Griffin-class combat interceptors," Brodie said, adding a tactical scan of the new ship to the viewscreen as an overlay. "They're bang-on seventy-meters long from nose to tail, and I'm picking up two Aternien particle cannons on the wingtips. I'd say they have limited warp capabilities, but the thrust-to-mass ratio is high, which means they're much faster than anything the Union has, us aside."

Carter studied the new vessel. The Griffin's wedge-shaped wings were angled forward like a sparrow in flight, and the craft was small enough to require a crew of perhaps two or three at the most. However, the short, stubby body hinted at another purpose, and Brodie was quick to confirm his suspicions.

"My guess is that each one of those Griffins is also carrying maybe fifty or sixty Immortals," the Master-at-arms continued. "They're raiders, MC. I'd advise that the fleet keep their distance, or they'll quickly find themselves getting boarded."

"Make that recommendation to the flagship, Brodie, but until we locate the weapons ships, our focus is the Senuset and its Royal Court escorts."

"You got it boss," Brodie replied, actioning the order while continuing to analyze the enemy fleet. "Planetary defenses have engaged the enemy, but we're mainly talking about missile batteries, and the Aterniens aren't struggling to shoot them down."

That was to be expected, Carter realized. The Union hadn't enhanced its planetary defenses for decades, since it hadn't seen the need to. While they had worked well enough to deter any pirates that were foolish enough to prowl the inner colony worlds, no-one in the Union had the foresight – or common sense – to consider that scoundrels and ne'er-dowells might not be the only threat that humanity would face in the future.

"Cai, any luck locating the biogenic weapon?" Carter asked, turning his thoughts to their primary target.

"Negative, Master Commander, but I am continuing my scans," Cai replied.

Carter frowned. He'd expected the weapon ship to be easy to find, considering its size, and the likelihood that it would be protected by a sizeable portion of the fleet. That it was missing was concerning.

"Cai, tie us in to all the sensor relays and satellites in orbit of Terra Three," Carter added. "Something's not right here."

"What exactly am I looking for?" Cai asked.

Carter thought about this, knowing that his Master Operator lived in a quantifiable world of fact, which made vague requests difficult for the man to process. However, he couldn't be more precise, and so had to rely on Cai's indefatigable ability to uncover the truth.

"I don't know exactly, Cai. Just look for something that's trying not to be found…"

Cai raised an eyebrow at this. At one time, he might have sought further clarification, but the new Cai Cooper – the one who had fallen in love and had a family – clearly enjoyed a good mystery.

"Admiral Krantz is on the line for you," Carina said. "It probably has something to do with us being two minutes away from a pitched battle."

Carter smiled. "Put her on."

The image of Admiral Krantz appeared on the viewscreen and her penetrating, chisel-edged stare almost cracked it in half.

"The second and fourth fleets will handle the Epsilons and these new Griffin-class vessels, while I take six taskforces against the Khopesh destroyers," Krantz said, as ever getting straight to business. "See you what you can do about the Senuset and the Royal Court vessels. Beyond that, any help you can give us would obviously be vital."

"Understood, admiral, but we have another issue," Carter replied. "We haven't been able to locate the biogenic carrier ship."

"I noted its absence too," Krantz said, her eyes narrowing a fraction. "We can't explain it, other than to assume the Aterniens intend to take Terra Three the old-fashioned way, with an orbital bombardment followed by a ground invasion."

Carter considered this, and it was a possibility, but there were no troop carriers amongst the Aternien armada. It was possible they were waiting at a staging area, ready to turn up when the Senuset gave the signal. However, for now, they could only deal with what was in front of them.

"Cai is still looking, so we'll update you if we find anything," Carter said. "Good hunting, Admiral."

"You too, commander, Dauntless, out."

The viewscreen cleared and Carter refocused it onto the Senuset, the Grand Vizier's ship. The Solar Barque and its Royal Court escorts were heading right for them, but there were squadrons of Epsilons and Khopesh destroyers between the Galatine and its Aternien counterpart. Carter accessed the comp-slate built into his chair, but now that he had a complete bridge crew, he could also make use of JACAB. The bot used its holo projectors to create a tactical map of the targets. Carter could reach into it and manipulate the display like a chess board made from light. He marked two dozen targets that the Galatine would initially take care of, and synced the data with the flagship, so that Krantz knew to take the rest. With that done, he locked in an attack pattern and handed it over to his officers to execute the attack.

"Brodie, Amaya, you know what to do…"

"Aye, aye, skipper," Amaya said. "Brace for gravitational maneuvering in ten seconds." Her gaze was locked ahead, as if Amaya was staring blankly into space, but in reality, his Master Navigator had become one with the ship. She was no longer seeing through her own eyes, but through the Galatine itself.

"All weapons are hot," Brodie reported.

"Power generation is at ten percent over standard," HARPER chipped in, showing off again.

Carter tightened his grip around the arms of his chair. "Then let's give them hell…"

The Galatine surged toward the enemy, using its unique gravitational maneuvering capabilities to carve a path through the void with the nimbleness of a fighter-bomber flying in atmosphere. The Aternien warships fired at them, but their particle blasts cut through space where the Galatine no longer was. Arcing back toward the leading squadron of Epsilons, Brodie opened fire with the 120mm guns, pulverizing ten ships with nano-adaptive armor piercing shells, which adjusted to the armor profile of their targets to ensure maximum effect. The Aternien ships were torn apart, some listing aimlessly into the dark, while others exploded with violent force, sending wreckage slamming into the hull of the Galatine, but it was like bugs splatting against a windshield. The opening onslaught was devasting, but the

Galatine was only just getting started. Carter selected the next target group – two squadrons of Khopesh-class destroyers – and deferred the attack pattern to his Master-at-arms. He didn't turn to look at Brodie, but he knew that this decision would have made the man smile.

"Amaya, let's do the chevronater," Brodie called out.

"Don't you think we've used that a little too often?" Amaya replied, eyes still locked ahead.

"Whaddya mean? We haven't done it for a century!" Brodie hit back. "Besides, the Aterniens always expect us to do something clever, and it always trips them up when we do something dumb instead."

Amaya shrugged then gave him the thumbs up signal.

"What's a chevronater?" Carina asked, keeping her voice low, perhaps because she was embarrassed for not knowing the maneuver in question.

"Basically, Amaya tacks the ship from side to side, like a continuous chevron pattern," Carter explained, using his hand to illustrate the zig-zag maneuver that Amaya was now executing. Carina scowled, no longer confused, but certainly unimpressed. "I know, it's pretty dumb, but with gravitational steering it makes us really hard to hit. And Amaya is right; Aterniens think it's a prelude to something more sophisticated, and by the time they realize it's not, they're usually burning in space."

Carina appeared to accept this explanation, but even if she'd had more questions, the sudden shift in the Galatine's position made it impossible for her to ask them. A zig-zag maneuver didn't sound particularly sporty, Carter agreed, but when it involved riding curvatures in spacetime at tens of thousands of kilometers per hour, it was certainly enough to get even his pulse racing. His XO, on the other hand, was bracing herself against the back of her seat, as if she was riding the downward section of a rollercoaster. *At least she held onto her lunch this time…* Carter thought, recalling his familiar expression of being thankful for small mercies.

"Plasma cannon standing by," Brodie said. "Amaya, give me control in five…"

Particle blasts from the Khopesh cruisers raced past, but the Galatine was simply too nimble. The sword-like ship pierced the ether like the point of Amaya's rapier, then Brodie took control, and suddenly the space ahead was filled with burning plasma.

Each shot was aimed with improbable accuracy, like an archer rapid-firing ten arrows in quick succession and bulls-eyeing each one. Ships exploded and the Galatine's point defense cannons shredded the wreckage in order to clear a path toward their real target – the Solar Barque Senuset. Within seconds they were through, and the Dauntless and her escorts were left to pick off the dregs.

"Part of the fourth fleet has broken off to attack the Royal Court ships," Carina said, keeping her eyes on the wider conflict.

"Damn it, that's suicide," Carter grunted. "This is no time to be a hero."

"The admiral has called them back, but it's too late," Carina added, shaking her head.

The ship's XO put the engagement onto the viewscreen and they watched as the Solar Barque ripped through the Union taskforces with terrifying effectiveness. Restored to full power, the Senuset gleamed golden in the light of Terra Three's sun, while its engines and weapons systems twinkled like jewels. Intense particle blasts, some delivered as pulses and others as continuous cutting beams, ravaged two Union squadrons in seconds, before the Senuset bore down on a trio of heavy battlecruisers and obliterated them in a merciless display of unstoppable firepower.

The ships that hadn't yet retreated returned fire, pounding high-explosive cannon shells into the majestic-looking craft. Detonations rippled along its hull, from its axe-shaped rear quarter to its broadhead nose. Two of the blade-like superstructures that sprouted from its central mass were damaged, and the Aternien hieroglyphs were pockmarked with burns and shallow scars, but the Senuset withstood the onslaught with the imperiousness of a redwood standing firm against a raging storm. The Royal Court destroyers then swooped in to finish off the remaining Union vessels, and together the elite warships resumed their course toward the Galatine. As Carter watched, he could see the damage to the Senuset repairing itself in real time. In every way conceivable, the Solar Barque was the Galatine's equal, except for in one aspect – his crew was superior.

Carina's comp-slate chimed and she took on a look of surprise. "The Senuset is calling us," she said, turning to Carter. "The Grand Vizier would like to speak to you."

Carter adopted a similar look of surprise, which then morphed to one of concern. He hadn't expected any communication from the Aterniens, and the fact the Grand Vizier – the god king's right-hand man – was calling gave him cause to worry.

Do they know what we're planning? Carter wondered. *Has Nathan Clynes somehow managed to tap into our systems to alert them? Or was it the Overseer, Monique?*

He put these questions to the back of his mind and stood up. Whatever the Grand Vizier wanted, he needed to present an air of calm. In other words, it was time to test his poker face.

"Put him through, Major," Carter said.

SEVEN
POKER FACE

MAJOR LARSON'S console chirruped as she accepted the comm-link from the Senuset, then the image of the Grand Vizier filled the viewscreen, larger than life in more ways than one. Some of the highest-ranking Aternien nobles had transformed their bodies so dramatically that they no longer looked human, and the Vizier was a prime example. The man's long neck swayed with a swan-like grace, while his sinewy frame, covered in scale armor, made him look part-dragon. The chest section of the armor bore the Ankh of Aternus – the symbol of the Royal Court inner circle.

"What can I do for you, Vizier? You can see I'm a little busy destroying your brothers and sisters in arms…" Carter began. He always liked to start a conversation in the manner he understood best, which was to say, 'aggressive.'

"So busy that I have not seen you for some time, Master Commander," the Vizier replied, already hinting that he suspected something of their secret mission. "I almost expected to not find you here, participating in this futile defense of Terra Three."

"Maybe you should ask Damien Morrow where I've been," Carter replied. "Or Fleur Lambert, or Shime Akeno. Perhaps Rollo Jay?" He smiled, watching as each of the names he rattled off caused the Aternien's perfect mouth to twitch with anger. "Oh, that's right, you can't, because they're all dead."

The Vizier composed himself and a synthetic-looking smile appeared in place of the snarl. "It's curious that you found your way to Venture Terminal, seemingly from out of nowhere," the Vizier said. "Our spies and recon drones could not find you for some time prior to that."

Carter shrugged. "Then get better spies and recon drones. I'm not hard to find, Vizier. Maybe the real problem is you."

The Vizier feigned a look of surprise. "Really? And what might I ask is the problem with me?"

"You've been ducking a fight ever since you got that fancy Solar Barque back together," he teased. "I defeated it, and you, once before, and I think you're worried I might take away your precious sun ship again."

Carter let that sink in, watching the Vizier closely for his reaction. The Aternien had called with the intention of pressing him for information, but by appealing to the Vizier's ego, which was vastly more inflated even than it had been before the man ascended, he was changing the narrative. If the Vizier was angry and spoiling for a fight, Carter figured he would stop asking difficult questions.

"You are too far beneath me to be worth the effort, Master Commander," the Vizier said, his snarl returning. "The Royal Court will deal with your pathetic Longsword, while I am content to watch."

Carter made his next smile as provocative and derisive as

possible. "You know what I think, Vizier? I think you were a chickenshit a hundred years ago, and that you're even more of a chickenshit now."

Rage flashed behind the Vizier's glowing eyes, and his perfectly-elegant jaw clamped up. "You are unwise to say such things…"

"And you're a coward," Carter hit back, further stoking the fires inside his enemy. "If you want to prove me wrong then tell your Royal Court cronies to back off, and you and me can throw down, one-on-one."

Carter was a master at winding people up the wrong way, and he knew exactly when to speak and when to let his words marinade. He could have gotten in a few extra jabs, but there was no need. For all their talk of being superior, the Aternien neuromorphic brain was merely a copy of the original human mind, replete with its fears, anxieties and weaknesses of character. He'd beaten the Vizier before, and that was a century-old wound that had never healed. Suddenly, the Vizier raised a hand, and the Royal Court ships slowed. At the same time the escorting squadrons of Khopesh destroyers and Epsilons broke away and pursued new targets.

"Major Larsen, kindly inform the flagship to steer clear of the Senuset," Carter said, while still peering into the Vizier's eyes, which were alive with azure energy. "The Vizier has accepted a challenge, and we want to be good sports and observe the rules."

"Aye, sir," Carina replied, sending the message.

The two commanders continued to wait, facing each other across hundreds of kilometers, as if they were a pair of eighteenth-century duelists, about to take ten paces then turn and shoot. His comp-slate updated, and JACAB bleeped too. Carina leaned across to his chair and looked at the holographic map that Carter's bot was projecting. It showed that the Dauntless was holding position at their rear, ahead of a squadron of battle cruisers. It seemed that Admiral Krantz had chosen to act as his second.

"Are you sure you don't want to chicken out?" Carter said, getting in one final jab. "Sorry, I mean, 'concede graciously'?" he added, rubbing salt into the wound.

The Grand Vizier glared at him then cut the transmission at the source.

"I guess that's a no?" Carina said, smirking.

Ordinarily, Carter might have allowed a smile to curl his lips too, but the truth was that a dogfight with a Solar Barque was no laughing matter.

"Amaya, Brodie, are you ready for this?" he said, as the two ships began closing to combat range.

"Don't worry, MC, we'll smoke this golden bastard, pardon my French," Brodie replied.

Carter turned to face his Master-at-arms, shooting him a look that made the man straighten to attention. Brodie often came across as cocky, despite never actually falling into the trap of becoming overconfident, but on this occasion, he needed to make sure the man was one-hundred-percent on his game.

"Don't underestimate the Senuset, or the Vizier," Carter said, also turning to look at Amaya, who had disconnected herself from the Galatine in order to listen. "We beat them in the last war, but this is an upgraded Solar Barque, and a Vizier with a score to settle. That might make him rash, but it'll also make him fight like a demon. I want to remind that sonofabitch what a Longsword can do. I want to remind him what the Galatine can do."

"Aye, sir," Brodie said, for once forgoing his usual honorific, MC.

"Understood, sir," Amaya added.

Carter nodded then took his seat and gripped the arms tightly. "Let's kick their ass…"

The Galatine accelerated, moving under gravitational propulsion. The Senuset matched their maneuvers, also gliding along the edges of spacetime, like a surfer riding the inside of a wave. A particle beam raked through space, lashing them on the aft, port quarter, then Brodie returned fire with the 120mm cannons, battering the mid-section, dorsal armor of the golden ship.

"Minor damage, armor is regenerating," Carina called out, as the fight continued apace.

The Senuset turned sharply – more sharply than Carter or Amaya expected – and unleashed a storm of particle blasts at the Galatine's long belly. Brodie engaged the plasma shield barely in time to soak up the bulk of the energy, but sections of their armor were depleted and their hull temperature climbed.

"Swarm missiles away," Brodie announced, as a cloud of projectiles billowed out from the Galatine and raced toward the Senuset.

The Solar Barque engaged a shield, which soaked up the explosive impact of every single missile, but Brodie wasn't concerned. He and Amaya were already a step ahead and in perfect sync.

"Coming about… ready the plasma cannon," Amaya said, pulling the Galatine into a swooping, high-energy turn that sent his head spinning, and caused Carina to temporarily black-out.

Carter caught his XO and pulled her back into her seat,

but there was no time to check on her condition. More blasts were hammering into their armor, and their plasma shield was still regenerating.

"Locked on... firing!" Brodie said, spitting blazing hot shards of plasma at the Senuset.

The Solar Barque tried desperately to evade, but Amaya had outmaneuvered them, and the Aternien ship took heavy damage to its axe-like aft section, opening up its hull. Two of the vessel's powerful engines flashed out, and nano-machines raced to the damaged areas to make hasty repairs.

"We've got hull breaches on deck five, all along the port side from sections F to I," Carina reported. She was back in command of her senses, but her skin was clammy and her hands were shaking. "Emergency seals are in place."

"Brodie, let's finish this!" Carter said, sensing that they had the upper hand.

"Amaya, give them the old one, two..." the Master-at-arms called out.

Amaya nodded, then threw the Galatine to starboard, evading a streak of energy from the Senuset, before angling their nose at the vessel, and riding spacetime into what appeared to be a collision course. Brodie opened fire with the cannons, striking the Senuset hard. The Aternien took evasive action, but Amaya held her course, racing over the top of the Solar Barque so close that their grav-wake buffeted both ships. Blasts from the Aternien's aft cannons punched more holes into the Galatine, then Amaya swung hard to port, a mirror-image of her earlier maneuver. With perfect timing, Brodie unleashed the plasma cannon and hit the Senuset on the side opposite to where the cannon rounds had landed. It was a left-right combo that sent the Aternien ship reeling.

"We've got a dozen red lights, but nothing we can't handle," Carina said, hands still shaking though it could have been from adrenaline, Carter reasoned. She then turned to the yellow labor bot at the engineering stations. "See what you can do, HARPER. We need to keep her together for another sixty seconds."

"Repair drones are en route, and nano-machines are repairing the hull breaches at forty-percent above usual efficiency," the bot answer. "In short, we will hold."

The Senuset spun away from them, flames licking a dozen parts of the ship's split-open hull. Particle blasts lashed out at them, but it was clear that the Vizier was firing blind.

"I've got you, you bastard," Carter said, thumping the arm of his chair. "Brodie, Amaya close in for the kill!"

Both officers acknowledged the command, but Major Larsen was looking concerned, and not just because of the debilitating effects of gravitational maneuvering.

"What's up, Carina?" Carter asked. His senses also told him that something was wrong.

"The Royal Court destroyers are closing in," Carina replied, working her comp-slate.

Carter looked at the tactical display that JACAB was projecting and saw that his bot had already updated the image to show the new threat. He looked at the numbers and cursed.

"We can still get the Senuset," Carter said, determined not to let his adversary slip away.

"We can, but we risk getting our ass handed to us by those Khopesh destroyers," Carina replied. "We've also taken a beating. The plasma shield is down to fifty percent, and we've more holes in our armor than a sieve."

Carter pounded the arm of his chair again, this time in frustration. "HARPER, can you give us more speed?"

"Yes, boss, I think I can give you enough," the bot replied, "but it will be close…"

Carter was about to order the attack when Cai spoke up. The Master Operator had been silently consumed with his task of locating the biogenic weapon ship, and Carter had not forgotten him.

"Sir, I've found something," Cai said, quickly sending his report to the viewscreen. "There's a vessel on the blind side of Terra Three, exactly opposite to our position. It is powered down and coasting using its existing momentum only, which is why it had not shown up on initial scans. However, there is a faint energy signature that I was able to detect."

"Is it the weapons ship?" Carter asked.

"Yes, sir," Cai replied.

There was no, "probably…", or "I think so…" about the Master Operator's answer, and Carter did not need to ask if the man was sure. If Cai said it was the weapons ship, then Carter trusted him.

"Can we orbit the planet in time to intercept?" Carina asked.

"Negative, XO, we're almost out of time as it is," Amaya replied.

Carina cursed, but Carter wasn't beaten yet. There was one way to reach the ship before it hurtled through the planet's atmosphere and sprang its deadly trap. However, to say it was an option he did not relish was an understatement.

"Amaya, spin up the drive and prepare to jump through the planet," Carter said. "I need you to bring us out in front of that weapons ship, or this world is dead."

"Aye, aye, skipper…"

If Amaya's response had sounded a tad tentative, it was for good reason. A short-range jump through a planet's gravity well was no mean feat. In many ways, it was as risky as jumping beyond the red line, into uncharted parts of the galaxy. Perhaps, even more so.

"Jumping through a planet sounds like a fine way to get us killed," Carina said.

"Amaya can do it," Carter replied, confidently. "That's why you get the big bucks, isn't that right?"

Amaya snorted a laugh then affected shock. "Wait, am I supposed to get paid for this job?"

Carter and Brodie laughed, and even Cai cracked a smile, but Carina was less than impressed.

"Honestly, of all the times you could pick to make jokes…"

"Don't worry, Major, our Master Navigator works best when she's relaxed," Carter said. "We each handle stress in different ways. Brodie talks big, Cai goes quiet, and Amaya needs to laugh it off."

Carina cocked her head to one side and seemed to accept this, then she too smiled. "And how do you handle it?"

Carter held up his hand, straight and level. "Does it look like I get stressed?"

Carina frowned then held up her hand beside his, though hers quivered like a plate of jello sat on top of a laundry machine. Carter smiled and Carina balled her hand into a fist in an effort to stop it shaking.

"That's not fair, you're augmented," Carina complained.

"And you needed a distraction," Carter replied, still smiling. "Feel better?"

There was a pause, then his XO said, "No…" though her eyes were smiling.

"We're spun up and ready, skipper," Amaya called out.

Carter and Carina both pressed their backs into their chairs, and Brodie gripped his station to steel himself against the disorientating jump.

"Do it, Amaya…"

The starfield shifted and the Senuset vanished from view. Next, they were spinning, like water gushing down a plughole, and for a moment they were lost somewhere between their universe and whatever existed beyond it. Then the Galatine burst back into space on the opposite side of the planet, and alarms rang out.

"Aternien weapons platform, dead ahead," Brodie called out. "It's seen us and is powering up."

"Don't let it, Master-at-arms," Carter said.

"You got it, MC…"

Suddenly, every weapon on the ship was brought to bear. Nano-adaptive armor-piercing shells, plasma blasts, swarm missiles, and even every defensive weapon they had all unloaded simultaneously. It was enough firepower to level a city, and more than enough to dispatch the Aternien biogenic weapon, which erupted into an inferno of blinking fire. Carter punched the air, and his excitement filtered over to his other officers. All except Cai.

"Target destroyed, sir, but fragments of the ship will still enter the atmosphere," the Master Operator reported.

"Won't they just burn up?" Carter asked, but the look on Cai's face gave him the answer.

"Most will, sir, but my scans indicate that some virus cannisters will survive entry intact," the Master Operator said. "I estimate they will pass though the stratosphere before breaking up and releasing the carrier drones."

Carter let out a heavy sigh and rubbed his hand down his face, suddenly feeling every one of his hundred and seventy plus years. "Just give it to me straight, Cai."

His Master Operator understood the question, but ran some additional calculations before giving an answer, to make sure it was his best and most accurate response.

"Terra Three will be exposed to the virus, but the effect will be limited to sections of the north-eastern continent, and a cluster of populated islands," Cai said. "Containment protocols should prevent it from spreading further."

"A number, Cai," Carter said, softly. "I need a number."

"Seventy million will die, if we're lucky. Two hundred if not."

Carter's head fell to his chest, but Carina refused to be deflated.

"That's a lot better than a billion dead, Carter," his XO said. "And we have the serum now. There's hope. This is a victory."

Carter sighed again and grunted. He understood what Carina was saying, and she was right, of course. He was just getting tired of small mercies.

"Signal the Dauntless that the weapons ship is destroyed and inform the admiral of the situation on the planet," Carter said. "Then we prepare to leave for Old Aternus. I'm done with always being on the back foot. It's time we took the fight to our enemy.

EIGHT
CLASSIFIED INFORMATION

THE GALATINE REMAINED at Terra Three to monitor the Aternien forces as they withdrew, no doubt to plot their next attack. Carter suspected that it wouldn't be long before the god-king moved again, which made their already hollow victory seem all the more insignificant in the grand scheme of the war. Even so, Carter tried to see the positives, as his XO had encouraged. The virus had been confined to a section of Terra Three, rather than being spread planetwide, and he had to admit that giving the Senuset and the Grand Vizier a thorough pasting had felt good too.

The number of people exposed on Terra Three currently stood at eighty-four million, mercifully on the lower end of Cai's estimate. The Union authorities had scrambled to contain the threat, locking down all planetary and off-world travel, and quarantining the regions affected, but it wasn't an exact science, and the risk of the infection spreading was very real. Saving Terra Three was now a race against time. Without the ability to deploy Nathan Clynes' serum en masse, the engineered virus would eventually find its way to every corner of the planet. Carter could only imagine how the people of Terra Three felt at that moment, trapped and at the mercy of an insidious, relentless, engineered pathogen that would not stop until every human being on the world was dead.

That was a problem for Admiral Krantz and the Union to solve. Carter's job was to make sure that Markus Aternus didn't get another opportunity to attack Terra Three or, as was now more likely, turn his attention to Terra Two or even Terra Prime. To do that he had to find New Aternus and destroy the Soul Crypt. Carter was then roused from his musings by the entrance of Brodie Kaur into the mission planning room. Amaya, Carina and HARPER were already inside with him, but Brodie had been waylaid, dealing with their persistent annoyance of a guest, Nathan Clynes.

"What did His Lordship want this time?" Carina asked.

Judging by the maddened expression on Brodie's face, the Master-at-arms looked like he had come close to strangling Nathan, assuming he hadn't done it already.

"He needed an analgesic cream to help soothe some sore patches of skin on his arms and neck," Brodie said, sounding singularly unimpressed by this. "It was apparently my fault that he forgot to pack it in the first place, because I rushed him out of the door."

Carina and Amaya smiled at each other but knew better than to tease the Master-at-arms. This was partly in sympathy because Brodie had landed the job of babysitting the scientist, but also because teasing Brodie might mean that Carter divvied the job to them instead, as a punishment. In truth, as much as his Master-at-arms hated the duty, Carter wouldn't give it to anyone else. Nathan was a slippery eel, and there was no-one better equipped to deal with the man than his burly and cunning Master-at-arms.

"Now that we're all here, I wanted to show you the location of Old Aternus, so we can work out the best plan of attack, as it were," Carter said, skipping over the subject of Clynes.

He accessed the comp-slate integrated into the briefing room table and projected a star map above it. One star was highlighted by a spinning gold circle, and everyone in the room gathered around a little closer, frowning at the display and trying to mentally picture where in the galaxy it was.

"Don't worry if you don't recognize these stars," Carter said, knowing that none of them would be able to. "They're what you might call, 'off the beaten track', at least in terms of where the Union has travelled to."

"And that's the Old Aternus system?" Amaya asked, pointing to the highlighted star.

Out of them all, she was naturally the most curious, given that she lived and breathed star charts, and Amaya was clearly vexed that the highlighted system was unknown to her.

"That's it," Carter confirmed. He then zoomed in on the star to display its planetary system and tapped the third of seven planets. The spinning golden ring was transferred to it.

"Its official designation is MOA-2011-BLG-028L, but since that's a bit of a mouthful, the Union simply designated it 'Aternus'," Carter continued. "It's an Earth-like world, but only if Earth was perpetually ravaged by electrical storms, gale force winds and near-freezing temperatures. Humans can technically live on Aternus, but you wouldn't want to."

Brodie huffed a laugh and folded his arms across his

chest. "So, the Union stiffed Markus with a bum planet, huh?" the Master-at-arms said. "One that we didn't want?"

Carter nodded again, a little more ruefully this time, since he understood Brodie's mildly defensive reaction. The fact the Union had exiled Markus and his flock to such an inhospitable planet was hardly conducive to ongoing cordial relations between the two cultures.

"Aternus, or Old Aternus as we now call it, has Union-standard gravity, breathable air, and an abundance of in-system resources, and since Aternien synthetic bodies hardly need a tropical paradise to survive in, the Union figured it suited."

"The most surprising thing about it was that Markus didn't protest the decision," Carina added.

"I think it was actually more surprising that the Union never wondered why that was," Carter added. Carina was their resident expert on Aterniens, but she lacked his first-hand knowledge, as someone who had lived through that time. "And once the Union realized it was because the god-king had no intention of staying there, it was too late. He basically ravaged the planet and others in the system for resources to build his new empire, then skipped out."

"So, when did the Union finally figure out they'd gone?" Brodie asked. His Master-at-arms never had much patience for history; he focused on the here and now.

"The honest answer is that we don't know for sure, but we believe the migration to New Aternus happened sometime between 2280 and 2290." Carter worked the comp-slate, and the map zoomed out to show the positions of Old Aternus and Terra Prime, relative to one another, then added in the diplomatic outpost, sited on what became the demarcation line. "The initial clashes between humans and post-humans that led to the creation of the Aternien Act happened between 2262 and 2266, before I was born," he continued. "At that point, post-humanism effectively became illegal, and Markus went voluntarily into exile on the planet shown on this map, on the understanding that he and his flock would be left alone. That's why the diplomatic outpost was established, so that a dialogue could be maintained. The Aterniens never sent anyone, of course, so the Union ignored their wishes and sent drones anyway."

Carina looked shocked. "That was never mentioned in any of the documents I saw?"

"There's a lot you won't have seen, Major," Carter replied, with the same rueful tone and expression he'd used with Brodie earlier. "The Union got away with spying on the Aterniens for a while, monitoring the establishment of their city, and their new fleet of ships."

"And none of that rang alarm bells?" Brodie cut in.

"According to the records, it all looked innocuous," Carter said, with a shrug. "The vessels were either mining ships or freighters and the like. There were no warships, or so the Union believed. Then, all of sudden, the probes went dark."

"All at the same time?" Brodie asked.

Carter nodded. "Yes, and that's when the Union asked for a meeting, and actually got one."

Carina nodded. "That was the infamous twenty-second parley of 2280. It was a message from the Aterniens, broadcast loud and clear for every Union world to hear."

Carter grunted as the memory of the event sprang into his mind, as if it were yesterday. "I was eighteen years old at the time, and the image of that Overseer, and the content of her message, has stuck with me forever. It was why I joined up with the Navy, because I knew even then that these people were bad news."

It was then that he noticed HARPER had tentatively raised a hand. The bot had been so quiet, Carter had almost forgotten he was in the room.

"Excuse me, boss, but I am not aware of this message," HARPER said. "I was built specifically for Nathan Clynes and first activated whilst on Gliese 832-e. As such, I am somewhat 'out of the loop'."

Carter looked to Carina, figuring that she might want to educate the bot, given her enthusiasm and knowledge of Aternien history, and she eagerly took up his unspoken offer.

"The twenty-second parley was the name given to the message addressed to Fleet Admiral Antonia Rodriguez by an unnamed Aternien, likely a High Overseer," Carina said. "The message only lasted twenty seconds because what the Overseer had to say was short."

The bot waggled its fingers like an excited child who had just been shown the cookie jar. "And what did this Overseer say?" HARPER asked, his words dripping with anticipation.

Carina smiled then cleared her throat and stood straighter, like an opera singer who was about to deliver a performance. Then, in what Carter considered to be an overly-dramatic voice, she recounted what the Overseer had told Admiral Rodriquez, word for word.

"Aternus is sacred. Any attempt to visit or monitor this world will be considered an act of war. Leave us in peace and we will do the same. Heed our warning. There will be no further communication between our peoples. Aternus is Immortal. Aternus is Forever."

HARPER rocked back and Carter thought he saw the bot

shiver, as if a chill had raced down his metal spine, though he could have imagined it.

"I guess it's fortunate that the Union heeded the warning and stopped sending drones to Old Aternus," Carina added, resuming her usual voice. "If we hadn't done then the war could have flared up much sooner."

Carter winced, scrunching up his eyes and nose. He rubbed his hand down his face in an effort to hide this, but the ever-observant XO has already spotted his reaction.

"We didn't send any more drones, right?" Carina asked, anxiously.

"I'm afraid we did," Carter admitted. "I'd recently been promoted to Lieutenant-Commander, so this was still way below my paygrade, but word leaked out that the Aterniens had gone, and soon everyone knew, though officially the government denied it."

"When was this?" HARPER asked, hanging off Carter's every word.

"That was in the summer of 2290 on the Terra Prime calendar," Rose replied, massaging his beard. "The first Aternien war began seven years later, and I was on the front line, commanding a warship, from the very beginning. It wasn't long after that I put myself forward for the Longsword program."

Everyone was silent for a time, and Rose understood why. The official history was that the Aterniens had been the aggressors, but the truth was that the Union had provoked them, not once but twice, first with the Aternien Act, then by spying on their sacred home world.

"So, if I've got this right, you're saying that the first Aternien war was the Union's fault?" Brodie said, breaking the silence. "I mean, they told us to stay away, warned us what would happen if we didn't, and we did it anyway."

Carter sighed and gave a half-shrug, half-nod. "Maybe it was the Union's fault, and maybe the Aterniens would have come for us no matter what, just as they have done now. In the end, it makes no difference." He worked the comp-slate and refocused the display on Old Aternus. There had been a reason for the history lesson, and he was about to get to it. "Officially, the armistice at the end of the war in 2332 reinstated the condition that neither side spies on the other, but the Union managed to gather some intel via a long-range telescope dropped into deep-space close to the planet before anything got signed." Carter zoomed the image and focused on an object orbiting the distant world. "This is why every probe ever sent to Old Aternus was destroyed."

The image was fuzzy, but it was enough to make out a star-like, five-pointed shape, containing an Aternien particle cannon in its center of mass. He then pulled back and hundreds of the objects, each circling the Aternien's original home planet, were highlighted by spinning golden circles.

"The Union designated these as Star Cannons," Carter continued. "Each one is armed with a particle cannon, but that's about as much as we know. We don't know exactly how many are in orbit, or how powerful they are, but it's safe to say they're a problem."

"Given that Old Aternus was abandoned a hundred and forty plus years ago, it's possible they're no longer functional," Brodie said. Understandably, the Master-at-arms had taken a keen interest in the orbital weapon. "But I'd suggest it's likely that the Aterniens are still maintaining the grid. After all, they did say the planet was sacred."

"We have to assume that they're active, and a credible

threat," Carter concurred. "As such, the best course of action is to warp to Old Aternus at a safe distance, so that we can run a detailed scan. The downside to that strategy is that it gives these planetary defenses more time to react and potentially alert the Aterniens."

Amaya was the one now taking a keen interest in the planet. She accessed the desk comp-slate and zoomed out the map, adding the location of Old Aternus, relative to Terra Three, which was their current location. She scowled at the image and rubbed her chin. Carter could guess why – the planet was more than 24,000 light years away.

"That's a hell of a jump, skipper, even for the Galatine, especially without up-to-date star charts," Amaya said, still rubbing her chin. "It must have taken the Aterniens multiple jumps over a course of weeks or months to even reach the planet in the first place." She then highlighted a pulsar midway between Terra Three and Old Aternus. "This pulsar is well known, though, and I could jump there easily. From the pulsar, I can update our navigation charts and make the jump to Old Aternus with much more accuracy, to ensure we arrive beyond the range of these Star Cannons. It would certainly help if you happened to have any data from the probes the Union sent?"

Carter raised an eyebrow, suddenly conscious that Major Larsen was scrutinizing him closely. "I may have kept a copy of that data on the core block I stole from the Galatine, before it was decommissioned," he admitted. Carina smiled but chose not to make a sarcastic comment. "That means it'll be in the ship's database already. I just need to dig it out for you."

Brodie's personal comp-slate then chimed, and the Master-at-arms wasted no time in checking the display, in case it was a security alert, or an update from central command about another Aternien attack. However, his angry, impatient growl and rolling eyes suggested it was a problem of a very different, if no less troubling kind.

"Yes, whaddya want?" Brodie snapped.

"What do I want?" Nathan barked back over the comm channel. "I want something fucking edible to eat, that's what I want!"

Everyone in the room rolled their eyes, while HARPER face-palmed instead, since he had no eyeballs to roll.

"Also, the lavatory is blocked…" Nathan added, almost as an afterthought.

"It's because you're so full of shit," Brodie hit back, before making a silent apology to Carter for the swear.

"Just bring me some food," Nathan barked. "You can't expect me to work if I'm wasting away in this bourgeois little cabin you locked me in."

Brodie looked ready to punch his comp-slate but he reined in his anger and took a deep breath. "I'll bring you some caviar and champagne in a few minutes. Brodie out…" The Master-at-arms closed the connection, cutting off whatever Nathan was about to say in response to his pithy remark.

"How come I got this duty, MC?" Brodie complained. "It's literally a shit job."

"I'm sorry, Brodie, but he's your problem, until he's not," Carter replied.

"If we're done here, skipper, then I'll work on the calculations for the jump to the pulsar, and wait for your data," Amaya said, looking to skip out, before Carter decided to lumber her with Nathan-duty instead.

"And I have some… erm… paperwork to do," Carina added, shuffling after Amaya as quickly as possible.

HARPER was slower to cotton on, but eventually he hooked a metal thumb toward the door. "I should check on the soliton warp drive," the bot said. "To make sure that it is…" the bot hesitated, clearly unaccustomed to dishonesty, before adding, "…still spinning."

Carter cracked a smile. *At least I now know that HARPER is a terrible liar…* he thought.

Brodie sighed loudly, his shoulders sagging. "In that case, I supposed I'd better go find a toilet plunger somewhere in the stores," he said, sloping off toward the exit. "And a gas mask…"

NINE
FIXING PROBLEMS

"JUMP COMPLETE," Amaya called out from the navigation station. She nodded to Cai, who linked to her console to assist with the delicate calculations required to progress their journey. "I'm plotting our second jump to Old Aternus now."

"Let me know when you're ready," Carter grunted. "And if anyone needs to pee, I'd suggest you go now, because it might get a little tense from here on in."

"I think I can hold it," Carina replied, grinning. The sight of the pulsar wind nebular on the viewscreen then distracted her from being her usual sarcastic self. "Is that what a pulsar actually looks like?"

Carter nodded, then reconsidered and half-shrugged. "Yes and no. They're not exactly easy to see with the naked eye, so the viewscreen is showing us a blended image, taking optical, radio, IR, UV and x-ray data into account to create the picture you see on the screen."

"So, it's sort of like an artist's impression?"

Carter thought this to be somewhat accurate. "I suppose

so, if you consider the artist to be a shipboard supercomputer based on long-lost technology."

"I think we've got it, skipper," Amaya said, glancing at him over her shoulder. "We can spin up and jump to Old Aternus whenever you're ready."

Carter cast a sideways glance at his XO. "You sure you don't want to pee?"

Carina laughed and shook her head.

"Okay, Amaya, spin her up," Carter said to his pilot, before briefly turning his attention to Brodie. "And take us to battle stations. Let's be prepared."

"Battle stations, aye," the Master-at-arms replied. "If we get a less than friendly welcome, we'll be ready."

"Soliton drive spinning up now," Amaya reported, though Carter could already hear the familiar beat of the engine building through the deck plates. "Jumping to Old Aternus in five… four… three… two…"

Suddenly, the beat through the deck plates reduced, and Carter could hear the changing pitch of the drive as it rapidly slowed.

"Warp system malfunction," HARPER said, from his station at the rear of the bridge.

Carter pushed himself out of his seat and stared at the bot in disbelief. "HARPER in all my years commanding this vessel, do you know how many times we've experienced a malfunction of the soliton warp drive?"

HARPER considered this question for a moment, steepling his metal fingers in a contemplative repose. "My estimate would be zero, boss," he finally answered.

"That's right," Carter said. "Not once. Ever. So, what the hell is going on?"

HARPER returned to his stations, working on two

separate consoles simultaneously. "According to my initial analysis there is nothing wrong with the soliton warp drive," the bot began. "The only deduction I can make is that the drive was disabled manually."

Carter felt his senses spiking. "That can only be done from inside the warp chamber itself."

"Correct, boss," HARPER replied. "The logical conclusion would therefore be that we have an intruder in the warp drive chamber."

Carter turned to Brodie, who was furiously working his console. The man looked angry and was shaking his head.

"Security systems aren't reading a goddam thing in the warp chamber, MC," Brodie said, clearly maddened by the result of his security sweep. "If there's something down there then it knows how to evade our scanners."

The operations console chimed a musical alert, and Cai rocked away from his station, holding up his hands as if to say, 'that wasn't me…'. "Sir, we just dropped a warp comms buoy," he said, resuming work on a different area of his console. "A space-fold was opened and a transmission has been sent."

"A transmission?" Carter repeated. Like Brodie, he was becoming flustered and was rapidly losing his temper. "I need the contents of that message, Cai, and who it was sent to."

"Working on it, sir," Cai replied, using the right hemisphere of his console, while his gopher, TOBY, interfaced with the opposite side in order to assist. "The message was encoded using a protocol that I am unfamiliar with. TOBY is attempting to extract any information he can, but I do know the destination. It was Union Outpost Two, close to the demarcation line."

Carina also stood up. It was clear that the problems they were experiencing were not the result of simple malfunctions, but the work of sabotage.

"Outpost Two is under Aternien control," she said, her voice tight. "They use it as a staging area for strike squadrons to launch raids on smaller Union targets, forcing us to pull ships off the line and keep us spread out."

Carter cursed under his breath. He no longer needed TOBY to crack the message, because he already knew what it said. "That means that whoever dropped the buoy just let the Aterniens know exactly where we are," he said, fists clenched at his side.

More alerts rang out from all stations, and a general warning klaxon sounded.

"Silence that damned alarm," Carter called out, and the blaring siren stopped a moment later. "All stations, report!"

"Engines just went down, skipper," Amaya said. "We have zero propulsion."

"Life support has also been disabled," Cai added. "All we have is the air and heat that is already trapped inside the Galatine."

Carter wasn't especially concerned about that. The ship was big, and they had their head coverings for additional oxygen if needed.

"Weapons are also offline, and internal security systems just failed across all decks," Brodie chipped in, from the tactical station. "The armory has a safety protocol, so it's secure, but every other door on the ship just unlocked."

Carter turned to his Master-at-arms. The implication of what the man had just said was as clear to Brodie as it was to everyone else on the ship.

"Clynes…" Carter hissed. "Find him and stop him. If my

hunch is correct, that slippery bastard will be high-tailing it to the shuttle bay."

"I'm on it, MC," Brodie said. The Master-at-arms hustled off the bridge, with his tactical bot, Taylor, close behind.

"Cai, you have the bridge," Carter added, turning to his Master Operator. "The major and I are going to the warp chamber to find our saboteur. Amaya, I need you to stay in the hot seat, in case we have to get out of here in a hurry. I suspect we will."

"Aye, aye, skipper, but right now we're dead in space," Amaya replied. "If the goldies do show up, we're an easy target."

"Understood," Carter replied, heading off the bridge. He then saw HARPER with his hand in the air and stopped in his tracks. "Do you have something?"

"I believe I can help to restore engines and life support directly from engineering," the bot said, tentatively approaching Carter as he spoke.

"Good, then do it," Carter grunted, setting off again.

"Boss, I do not have full access to engineering," HARPER called out, stopping Carter dead for a second time.

Carter glanced at Cai, who had been acting as HARPER's chaperone, while they evaluated whether or not they could fully trust Nathan's former labor bot with the keys to the ship. However, he needed his Master Operator on the bridge, which meant he had to make the call now. The possibility that HARPER was working in cahoots with the scientist, and was therefore the direct cause of the malfunctions, had crossed his mind already. Yet, as he stared into the bot's unblinking eyes, which peered back at him with a yearning that belied the machine's synthetic origins, there was no doubt in his mind that HARPER was on their side.

"Cai, upgrade HARPER's security clearance," Carter said, while still staring into the bot's eyes.

"Yes, sir," Cai replied, without hesitation or concern.

"I won't let you down, boss," HARPER said.

Carter nodded. "I know you won't. Now hurry, we don't have a lot of time."

The labor bot accelerated and was through the door, even before Carina had made it to the threshold. Carter caught up with his XO, and together they hustled along the ship's long corridor in the direction of the soliton warp chamber. The chamber and warp drive itself occupied nearly a third of the Galatine's internal area, which meant that it didn't take long to reach an entry point. However, the size of the space also made it the perfect place for a saboteur to hide.

"You go first, I'll cover you," Carter said in a low voice, 57-EX in hand.

Carina nodded, sucked in a breath of the rapidly cooling ship's air, then expanded the buckler on her left forearm. She signaled to Carter, who opened the door to the chamber, on Deck Four, Section E, which brought them out at the topmost sector of the massive warp chamber. Carina darted inside, pistol raised, covering the angles, and Carter followed a heartbeat behind. Plasma blasts raced toward them out of the darkness and Carina ducked behind her buckler, absorbing two shots. Carter held his fire, wary of causing damage to the very system they desperately needed to fix, then the angle of the blasts changed, and Carina was exposed. Rushing in front of her, he absorbed a plasma blast to the back, then used his own buckler to cover them both. He aimed a careful shot into the darkness and missed, but it was enough to force their hidden assailant to shift positions.

"Did you see who it was?" Carina asked, as they both moved deeper into cover.

Carter shook his head. "No, but they're shooting plasma, which means it's not an Aternien."

Carina frowned at the smoldering section of Carter's battle uniform. "Are you okay?"

"I'm fine, the blast wasn't that powerful," Carter replied, shrugging off the hit. "It was similar to what JACAB can deliver, so painful but not deadly, unless it's a headshot."

Carina checked her comp-slate while plasma blasts thumped into the deck, walls and structural supports surrounding them. Carter loosed off another shot to keep their attacker at bay, careful to ensure that the armor-piercing bullet didn't end up lodged into anything critical.

"I'm not picking up a damn thing," Carina said, as more shots landed, each one closer than the last. "What the hell can shoot plasma, but stay hidden from our sensors?"

They looked at each other, wide-eyed, both coming to the same conclusion, at the same time. "Fixer…" they both said, in unison.

"Or it could be Farmer, or even both of them," Carina added. "Though how the hell Nathan snuck them on-board is anyone's guess."

"He's nothing if not resourceful," Carter grunted. Then he had a thought. "Cover me, I have an idea…"

Carina and Carter shifted positions, and their movements were greeted by another volley of plasma blasts, which his XO fended off with her buckler. Returning fire with her energy pistol, there was a brief flash and squawk, then the shadow of a spherical bot whizzed out of view.

"I think I clipped him," Carina said, pulling back into cover. "But he's fast, and has the whole damned chamber to hide in."

"Which means we need air support," Carter replied. Tapping his comp-slate, he opened a direct channel to JACAB. "Hey buddy, I need you. Get to the warp chamber, deck four, section E, and watch your step. One or more of Nathan's bots is on the prowl."

JACAB warbled and bleeped a response, which very much sounded like the monotone equivalent of "sonofabitch!" to Carter, then the bot acknowledged the command, and the channel closed.

"Do you think JACAB can take him?" Carina asked.

Carter smiled. "Gophers are very protective, and don't take any shit, especially not from rogue bots. If it is Fixer or Farmer in here, then JACAB will get him."

A succession of plasma blasts interrupted their conversation, and forced them to move, shielding their heads with their bucklers. Carter was hit again and Carina took a blast to the leg, toppling her as if she'd ran through a tripwire. Carter returned fire, catching another fleeting glimpse of Fixer in the process, but the nimble bot rocketed out of sight, before he could get a clean shot.

"Damn, that stings," Carina said, pulling herself up, while clutching her thigh. Her battle uniform had been partially melted through, but it had spared her from a serious injury. "It's times like these I could really use your healing factor."

"My advice is just don't get shot," Carter grunted.

Carina patted Carter's shoulder, which was still smoldering after an on-target shot from Fixer. "You were saying?" she said, eyebrow raised.

Suddenly, the rogue bot's energy blasts were redirected toward the door, and Carter saw JACAB swoop inside the chamber, returning fire as he did so. His gopher zig-zagged then ducked into cover and accelerated toward Carter at ground level.

"Right on time, buddy," Carter said, as JACAB arrived, ahead of another volley of plasma from Fixer. "As you can see, we have a bot problem."

JACAB let out a rude-sounding string of warbles, mixed in with deeper tones that sounded guttural and angry.

"The major and I will run along the port side of the drive shaft, and draw Fixer out," Carter said, ducking as a plasma blast flew inches above his head. Fixer was rapidly zeroing in on them. "Then you head around the other side and give this asshole a taste of his own medicine."

JACAB bleeped and nodded, then a compartment in its spherical shell snapped open to reveal a plasma cannon. Carter nodded to Carina, who raised her pistol and got ready to run. He counted down from three on his fingers, then when his hand closed to a fist, he made his move. Plasma blasts chased him and a shot glanced his shin, but he kept on running. Carina returned fire, hammering blasts into the darkness with little hope of actually hitting Fixer. Then she was struck to the knee and sent crashing to the deck. The shot was repelled by her battle uniform, but the fall left his XO dazed, and she was forced to take cover. Carter stopped and made himself a tempting target then JACAB darted out of the shadows right on cue and hammered two blasts into the rear of Fixer's shell. The bot screeched and shifted position, moving so fast that even Carter struggled to keep pace with it. The two machines continued to exchange fire, and plasma blasts crisscrossed the drive chamber, sending sparks flying. It was like a truck-load of fireworks had accidently been set alight, and Carter had to shield his eyes from the glare. Then JACAB took a hit and the bot spiraled low, pursued by Fixer, who continued to rain shots at the gopher, like a fighter aircraft going in for the kill. For a moment, Carter lost sight of his bot, then JACAB shot up like a rocket and pummeled Fixer with two accurate blasts, one of which smashed the machine's glowing red eye. The rogue bot lost control and bounced off the wall, but JACAB was unrelenting. Three more shots split open Fixer's armor and the bot crashed to the deck, out of sight.

"Are you hurt?" Carter asked his XO, now that the immediate threat was gone.

"I'm more embarrassed than hurt," Carina replied, accepting Carter's help to stand. "Where's JACAB?"

"I think he got his man," Carter said, nodding to where Fixer had gone down. JACAB had followed soon after, perhaps to confirm his kill. "Here, I'll help you."

Carina waved him off. "It's okay, I can walk. Though if you fancy pumping me full of nano-machines, I wouldn't mind."

Carter huffed a laugh. "The hangover wouldn't be worth it. Come on."

As they approached the area where Fixer went down, Carter picked up the sound of metal striking metal, like someone was hammering a pipe to get their attention. 57-EX in hand, he crept closer then found JACAB sat atop Fixer, bashing the remains of the broken gopher with his extendable arms. It was the bot equivalent of a UFC 'ground and pound' attack.

"Hey, buddy, I think you got him," Carter said, though he was admittedly enjoying watching his bot smash Fixer to pieces. JACAB warbled and bleeped, bashed Fixer again for good measure, then hovered to his side. "Can you get her spinning again?" Carter asked, resting his hand on part of the enormous warp drive enclosure.

JACAB nodded then flew to a control station at the midsection of the drive. He interfaced with it then a few seconds later the warp drive initialized, and the familiar beat of the spinning internal mechanism filled the chamber.

"Good work, buddy," Carter said, giving his bot the thumbs up. He then accessed his comp-slate and dialed up his Master Navigator on the bridge. "Amaya, warp should be coming back online. Please confirm."

"Confirmed, the drive is spinning," Amaya replied. "But I still have no engines."

Carter tapped his comp-slate to expand the connection to all hands. "HARPER, what's your status in engineering?"

He was greeted with the sound of plasma blasts in response, before HARPER's voice was heard over the racket.

"I have run into a minor difficulty, boss," the labor bot replied. "Farmer is causing me some challenges, and your assistance would be appreciated."

"Hang tight, HARPER, we're on our way," Carter said, parking that particular problem for a moment to get an update on another. "Brodie, what about Nathan?"

"I've got him, MC," Brodie replied. The sound of muffled cries and the scuff of boots on deck plates could be heard in the background, as if Brodie was dragging the scientist along behind him. "He was trying to steal Cai's shuttle, just like you said. I'm about to toss his sorry ass into the brig."

"Good work, but once you've done that, get to engineering," Carter replied, already heading for the nearest exit. "We have another bot problem."

An alert interrupted them and stole the focus of his comp-slate's screen. Cai's voice came through an instant later.

"Sir, seven Aternien Khopesh-class Destroyers have just warped into the vicinity of the pulsar," the Master Operator reported. "We were fortunate that they arrived some distance from our location, but I estimate seven minutes until they are within optimal weapons range."

Carter scrunched his eyes shut and rubbed his face. "Understood, Cai… Brodie, belay my previous order and get to the bridge. The major and I will restore engines and weapons."

"You got it, MC…" his Master-at-arms replied.

"Stay alert, everyone. We're going to have to shoot our way out of this," Carter added, entering the long corridor and changing course toward main engineering. "But first, we actually need some weapons to shoot with."

TEN
UNDER PRESSURE

CARTER ARRIVED at main engineering to the sound of plasma blasts reverberating inside. He snuck into the entry archway and peered inside, spotting HARPER, hunched over behind a partition wall, his yellow armor scorched black in a dozen places. Carina arrived a few moments later, hobbling from the effect of the injuries to her legs. She was escorted by JACAB, who had stayed back to watch over her.

"What have we got?" his XO asked, flexing her aching knee.

"Farmer looks to have dug in on engineering level two, behind the reactor casing," Carter said. He nodded in the direction he was indicating, though this wasn't strictly necessary, because the constant streams of plasma blasts gave away Farmer's location.

"Sneaky little bastard," Carina said, peeking around the archway.

Carter understood his XO's sentiment. The Galatine's reactor core ran from deck three to five, spanning all three main engineering levels. It was heavily shielded, so that even a bullet from Carter's 57-EX wouldn't penetrate through, which made it perfect cover for Farmer. More importantly, the reactor was surrounded by all the control systems they needed to counteract the lock-down, which meant that any attempt to access those controls required running the gauntlet. And, judging by HARPER's scorched coverings, the bot had tried exactly that a number of times already and been beaten back.

"We need to reach HARPER, and find out what he knows," Carter said. "Go, and we'll cover you."

Carina nodded then steeled herself against the pain in her legs and hustled through the door. Farmer popped out of hiding to take a shot, but Carter unloaded his 57-EX and forced the bot back into cover, before sprinting for HARPER too. JACAB followed, spraying the area around where Farmer was hiding with plasma blasts to ensure the bot remained hidden. Thanks to his augmented speed, Carter managed to arrive at the same moment Carina did, which was barely more than a second before the onslaught of plasma blasts resumed.

"I am sorry, boss, but Farmer hit my secondary motor core, which has rendered my legs useless," HARPER said, which explained why the bot was frozen in place, half hunched over. "It knows my systems quite well, I'm afraid."

"Can you be fixed?" Carina asked.

"Yes, it is a simple fix. JACAB or TOBY could easily assist me."

"We'll get to that later," Carter said. Right now, fixing the ship – not HARPER – was his primary concern. "We have Khopesh destroyers inbound, so I need to get our engines and weapons back online. I'm hoping you have some idea about how to do that?"

"I know exactly how to override the lock-out," HARPER replied. The bot pointed in the direction of the starboard engineering station on the second level gallery. "Farmer has installed a diagnostic device into the console and forced the computer sub-core that manages the engines and weapons system into a looping diagnostic cycle. Remove that core block, and all systems will come back online." The bot then gestured to his non-functional legs. "I attempted to reach the engineering station myself but was unfortunately thwarted."

Carter's comp-slate chimed and he answered the call from Cai on the bridge.

"Sir, the lead Khopesh is hailing us," the Master Operator reported. "They are demanding to speak with you."

"Stall them, Cai, I'm a little pre-occupied right now," Carter replied, ducking instinctively as blasts from Farmer peppered the partition wall, which was now on fire.

"Understood, sir, I will do my best," Cai replied. "All seven ships have achieved weapons locks and are slowing to a full stop at optimal weapons range."

"Just keep them talking for a couple of minutes," Carter said, flinching as sparks from a blast burned his face. "And tell Brodie to be ready to unleash hell."

Carter closed the link then turned to his XO, who recoiled, regarding him suspiciously.

"You've got that look in your eyes again," his XO said.

"What look is that?" Carter replied. To his knowledge, he hadn't adopted any particular expression.

"It's the 'I'm about to do something heroic and dumb' look," Carina answered. "It's the same look you got when you scaled the barracks wall on Terra Six, then flung us both over the other side."

Carter shrugged, realizing he'd been busted. "Okay, so

maybe you're right, but we don't have time for anything better."

"Better than what?"

"You'll see," Carter replied, somewhat unhelpfully, but he also didn't have time for specifics. "Just be ready to take out that bot as soon as it shows itself." Then to JACAB, he added, "Buddy, stay here and repair HARPER. In about two minutes, we're going to need him mobile again."

JACAB warbled and tossed up a sharp salute, using the same mechanical arm that the bot had been using to beat Fixer with earlier. It still had flakes of the other gopher's paint stuck on it. Carter then activated his head covering and his buckler, which had only partially regenerated after the pounding it had taken from Fixer, and drew his plasma cutlass, keeping the blade deactivated.

"I don't even want to know," Carina said.

"Then just watch," Carter hit back. "And shoot…"

Swinging himself around the partition, Carter ran toward the starboard side of the engineering section, eyes locked onto the console on the level two gallery, five meters above him. Farmer darted out of cover and began raining blasts down all around him. Carter shielded them as best he could, but he was taking hits faster than he could dodge them. At the same time, Carina opened fire with her energy pistol, but her shots ricocheted off Farmer's spherical shell, and the bot continued its assault.

With his sensation blockers working on overdrive, Carter kicked off from the deck and launched himself toward the gallery, clearing the railings in a single, super-human bound. Farmer moved further out of cover, risking itself in order to prevent Carter from reaching the console. More blasts thumped into his body then a shot hammered into the back of his head, making him see double, but he gritted his teeth and rammed his cutlass into the core block that Farmer had installed, prizing it from its mounting. Another blast hit his head, melting the covering and sending him down. Disorientated, he dragged his body into cover, and reached for his 57-EX, before remembering that he hadn't reloaded it. He opened the cylinder, ejecting the spent cartridges, but his eyes were still blurry, and he fumbled while trying to slide in fresh rounds. Cursing, he crawled deeper beneath the console as shots chipped away at his cover. Then he heard a familiar voice, calling out from below.

"Hey, asshole!" Carina said. Through the gaps in the grated deck plates, Carter could see Major Larsen standing on the level below, waving her arms at the bot. Her pistol was still in her hand, but it wasn't aimed at Farmer. "Here's another target for you to shoot at!"

Thanks to his cotton-wool head, Carter saw two Major Larsen's. He didn't know which one to warn, but as it turned out, he didn't need to do anything, because Brodie's bot, Taylor, appeared out of nowhere and ambushed the enemy bot. Thanks to Carina's distraction, Farmer was completely blindsided, and Taylor's powerful plasma cannon reduced the bot to smoldering rubble in the blink of an eye.

"Engines and weapons are back online, sir," Cai said over the comm-link. Carter wished he was as calm as his Master Operator sounded. "But the Overseer has given me an ultimatum. If he does not speak to you in the next sixty seconds, we will be fired upon."

"Then I'll be there in fifty-nine seconds," Carter replied, hitting himself with a nano-stim at a twenty-percent dose. The agony consumed him for a couple of seconds, during which time he couldn't speak or barely even think. "Brodie, ready the plasma shield and all weapons. We'll only get one chance at this, so we have to hit them hard and fast."

"You got it, MC," his Master-at-arms replied, displaying glacial coolness under pressure.

The boost of nano-machines cleared Carter's head and made him feel stronger than ever. Pushing himself up, he leapt over the railings and landed beside Carina with a resounding crash, like a metal fence being rammed by a truck. His XO practically jumped out of her skin, and gave him a fierce look, which he admitted was likely warranted. However, there was no time for apologies. He had less than a minute to avert the next disaster.

"Let's move," Carter said, hustling toward the exit. HARPER walked out from behind the partition, flexing his legs, and Carter aimed his sword at the machine. "Are you good, Mister HARPER?" he asked as he jogged past.

"Good as new, boss," the bot replied.

"Then crank up the reactor and give us enough power to destroy a planet."

If HARPER had replied, Carter didn't hear it, because he was already sprinting along the corridor. Carina was left in his wake, but he had no choice but to leave his XO behind. Air streamed past his face causing his eyes to water, and the bridge door approached with the speed of a bullet train about to enter a tunnel. Carter pumped the brakes, managing to stay his forward momentum by enough to enter the command section at something a little less than breakneck speed.

"Put the Overseer through," Carter said, leaping over Brodie's tactical console and landing, sure-footed, two meters in front of his chair, just as the Aternien's pristine, golden-skinned face appeared on the screen.

"Having a little engine trouble, Master Commander Rose?" the Overseer said, sneering at him.

"You know what these old ships are like," Carter replied, countering the Overseer's bullish arrogance with a thick dollop of sarcasm. "It seems that we have a gremlin in main engineering. Two actually."

"How terrible for you," the Overseer said, still appearing incredibly pleased with himself. "Then it is perhaps fortunate that I am here to make you an offer."

"Really? And what offer is that, exactly?" Carter feigned surprise, while also checking his comp-slate. The reactor output was climbing steadily and was already at twenty percent above standard. Whatever HARPER was doing, it was working.

"The god-king offers your lives in return for your unconditional surrender," the Overseer answered. "We will take the Galatine as a prize and tow your crippled ship back to Union space as a symbol of their inevitable defeat. With their most powerful vessel under our control, the Union will realize the futility of their fight and surrender. Your humiliation will serve the greater good, speeding the end of the war and avoiding unnecessary suffering. You will then be sent to New Aternus, where our scientists will study your augmentations for ways to improve our own."

Carter stifled a laugh, while still watching his comp-slate. The reactor was now one-fifty over standard, which was dangerously high.

"You find this offer to be humorous, Master Commander?" the Overseer said, taking the fact that Carter was ignoring him to be a grave insult. "I assure you that the alternative is even less amusing. Instead of helping to end the war, we will vaporize your ship where it stands, then annihilate the remains of humanity with all the cruelty that war can offer."

Carter decided to stop looking at his comp-slate when the reactor hit one hundred and sixty-nine percent above standard, at which point Major Larsen entered the bridge, red-faced and blowing hard from the effort of sprinting the length of the ship.

"No, I'm sure your offer is really generous, Overseer, but I'm afraid I won't be able to accept," Carter said, nodding to Carina then catching Brodie's eye. He could see that his Master-at-arms was ready.

"So be it," the Overseer said. "But you will die knowing that you could have prevented the suffering of billions." The Aternien glanced to his side then the viewscreen cut off.

"The enemy ships are preparing to fire," Brodie announced.

Carter pressed his hands to the small of his back. "Engage plasma shield."

All seven Khopesh destroyers fired their particle cannons, but each vessel only shot once, perhaps believing that there was no need for anything more excessive. Carter wished he could have seen the expression on the Overseer's perfect face as his blasts were utterly absorbed by the Galatine's shield. And he wished even more that he could see the Aternien's expression, just before he blew his ship out of the ether.

"Master-at-arms, lower shield and fire at will…"

The Galatine's twin array of 120mm cannons unloaded first, striking the second and third ships in the V-shaped formation and tearing the destroyers to shreds. The lead

Aternien vessel tried to maneuver away, but it was already too late. Their plasma cannon fired on overdrive, launching a ball of energy that was so ferocious in magnitude that it caused the entire ship to tremble. The mass of plasma pulverized the lead Khopesh then continued on, striking the destroyer at the rear of the formation too, and melting its hull into a shriveled mass of slag. The vessel exploded violently, bombarding the two remaining Aternien vessels with molten debris that tore through their hulls and sent them listing into the dark. Finally, swarm missiles erupted from all around the Longsword-class battlecruiser, snaking away to their targets and reducing them to dust.

"All enemy vessels have been destroyed," Brodie confirmed, delivering the confirmation with the calm, confident detachment of a professional soldier.

"Stand down from battle stations, but stay ready," Carter said.

"Stand down from battle stations, aye," Brodie replied, and the red hue on the bridge evaporated like steam from a boiling kettle.

"Cai, coordinate with HARPER in engineering and run a diagnostic check on every system," Carter added. "I want to make sure that Fixer and Farmer didn't mess with anything else."

"It is already in progress, sir," Cai replied. "I must admit that HARPER is quite efficient."

"We might need to find him a can of yellow paint, though," Carina added, slyly. "He's looking a little worse for wear right now."

Carter huffed a laugh, then was reminded of what – or more specifically who – had instigated their latest crisis. He found his pulse starting to race and took a few deep breaths to calm himself down. "Brodie, you have the bridge," he said, turning to leave. "Major, you're with me."

Carina's face fell. "What? I only just got here!"

"The exercise will do you good," Carter replied, unsympathetically. "Now keep up, we have to pay a visit to a special inmate."

———

Carter and Carina walked into the brig to find Nathan Clynes sitting on the hard cot bed with his head in his hands. The scientist prized open his fingers enough to peek through them, then groaned and covered his eyes again.

"Not happy to see me, Nathan?" Carter asked, though his question went unanswered.

Taylor, Brodie's burly tactical bot, hummed through the door a moment later, carrying the remains of Fixer and Farmer in his powerful mechanical arms. He dropped Nathan's two bots in front of the cell bars then hummed away. The sound of junk metal piling up outside his cell encouraged Nathan to take another peek. The realization of what the wreckage was took several seconds to fully take hold in the man's mind, then the scientist jumped off the bed and landed hard on his knees, reaching through the bars to gather up what remained of his gophers.

"You murdered them!" Nathan cried. "You sadistic fuck! You killed my bots!"

Carter reached through the bars, grabbed Nathan's shirt collar, and lifted the man to his feet. The remains of Fixer and Farmer slipped through the scientist's fingers and clattered against the deck plates again.

"*You* did this, Nathan," Carter said, growling into the

man's ear. He pulled the scientist closer, squashing Nathan's face against the cold metal bars. "I warned you what would happen if you pulled another stupid stunt, and these are the consequences."

"We're done!" Nathan hit back, struggling to force the words through lips that were pressed hard against the bars. "I won't help you now! You can go to hell!"

Carter pushed Nathan away and the man landed on his backside, next to the stainless-steel toilet and washbasin that shared the cell with him.

"Do you hear me, Carter!" the man raged, scrambling to his feet. "We're done!"

"I hear you, Nathan," Carter replied, calmly. He reached over to the control panel outside the cell and hit a sequence of buttons. Alarms rang out then the rear wall of Nathan's cell split open and retracted to reveal a pressure door behind it.

"What is this?" Nathan said, staring at the door where the wall to his cell had once been.

"If you won't help me then that's fine," Carter said, continuing the arming sequence. "I'll do this without you."

Another alarm sounded then a second set of doors slid across the inside of the cell bars, sealing it off from the rest of the ship. This door had a porthole window in it, and Nathan's face appeared at the glass, wide-eyed with panic.

"You can't do this!" Nathan cried, his fractured voice now coming through a comm system. "You need me!"

"You had your chance, Nathan," Carter said. "And you chose this."

A computerized voice announced, *Cell A, arming sequence complete. Ready for decompression and prisoner ejection…*

"No, wait!"

Carter stopped with his finger over the button that would open the rear pressure doors and blast Nathan into the abyss.

"Okay, you win, damn it!" the scientist cried. "I'll do what you want!"

"Have you done anything else to compromise this ship's systems?" Carter asked, finger still over the button.

"No!" Nathan answered.

Carter considered this then shook his head. "I don't believe you…" he said, then activated the ejection countdown.

Decompression in five seconds and counting… four…

"I'm telling the truth!" Nathan screamed, hammering his fists against the porthole.

Three…

"Please!"

Two…

"I'm begging you!"

Carter pressed the button again, halting the countdown at one, and Nathan slid to his knees, sobbing openly.

"This is your room now, Nathan," Carter said, closing the blasts doors and returning the cell to its prior condition. "But let me be crystal clear. I so much as hear a whisper of complaint escape from your lips, and I will blow you into space, whether I need you or not."

"I understand…" Nathan sobbed. "I'm sorry."

Carter shook his head then turned to leave. He'd scared the living crap out of Nathan enough to believe that his answers had been truthful, but he didn't believe for one nanosecond that the scientist was done causing him trouble.

ELEVEN
STAR CANNONS

CARTER LOOKED into the bathroom mirror in his quarters, which were just along the main corridor from the bridge, and inspected the damage to his battle uniform. The nano-mechanical fibers were self-repairing far more slowly than usual, which he put down to simple age, and wear-and-tear. The garment was over a hundred years old, and to say it had lost its sheen was something of an understatement. He stepped outside the bathroom and opened his wardrobe, chancing upon another battle uniform that he had left there.

"Good thinking, Carter," he muttered, jokily congratulating himself for having the foresight to hang the uniform up a century earlier, in readiness for that moment.

He returned to the bathroom and removed his damaged jacket, folding it neatly and setting it down next to the sink. His tank top, which was another nano-mechanical wonder, was in good condition, as was his skin. Age may have depreciated his battle uniform, but it seemed that his body had maintained its resilience, despite the passage of years.

The burns to his back and shoulders were gone, and his brain no longer felt like a wet sponge.

His sterling silver beard, on the other hand, was looking a little raggedy, and he ran his fingers through it, allowing the wiry bristles to massage his fingertips, before resolving to give it a trim. He had time to kill, since they were still holding position close to the pulsar wind nebula, while Cai and HARPER finished running the extensive suite of diagnostics to make doubly-sure that Nathan's bots hadn't sabotaged any other systems. So far, everything was clear, but it had still turned out to be a worthwhile exercise, allowing the resourceful and eager-to-please former labor bot to work his magic all across the Galatine, increasing the efficiency and output of a dozen more systems in the process. Then while he was rooting around for a set of beard trimmers in the drawer beneath the sink, the door chime sounded.

"Come…" he called out, before finally locating the tool and removing it.

The door opened and Major Larsen walked in, though his XO's confused expression suggested she had not yet figured out where he was.

"I'm in here, Major," Carter grunted, while snipping away at his beard.

Pieces of hair as tough as iron filings dropped into the sink with a soft clatter. Due to his augmented biology, the protein filaments that comprised his beard fibers were extraordinarily strong. Carina poked her head around the door while he was snipping, then jerked back and made a show of shielding her eyes.

"You could have warned me that you were half naked," Carina teased.

"I hardly think pants and a tank top qualifies as 'half naked', Major," Carter replied, gruffly.

Carina stopped shielding her eyes then pushed open the door fully and lounged against the cabinet to the side of his mirror, arms folded and with a smile curling her lips, as if she were up to no good.

"Something I can help you with, Major?" Carter said, while continuing to trim his wiry bristles.

"I did have a reason for stopping by, but I've been distracted by your personal grooming regimen," she replied, still smirking.

"Well, feel free to call back in when you've remembered," Carter hit back. "You know where the door is."

"It's okay, it'll come to me," Carina said, picking up some of the trimmed beard fibers from the sink and rubbing them between her thumb and forefinger. "Jeez, you could scour a skillet with this stuff. I bet you get through a lot of pillows."

She peered outside at his bed, perhaps expecting to see the sheets torn to shreds, then ducked back inside, looking disappointed, since his bed was intact, and also perfectly made.

"It's only my beard hairs that are especially tough," Carter said, continuing his work. "The hair on my head is more like nylon thread."

"Personally, I'm always getting split ends," Carina said, grabbing a tuft of her hair and shoving it so close to his face that it tickled his nose. "It's hard to get good haircare products on a warship designed for superhumans, though."

Carter finished trimming his beard, set the tool down and turned to face his XO, arms folded. "I don't suppose you've remembered why you're here yet?" he asked.

"It's on the tip of my tongue." She then squeezed his

muscular bicep and winked. "Do you have a license for those guns?"

Despite trying his best to remain gruff and surly, Carter laughed, handing his XO a victory. Clearly, she had been trying her best to make him break, and now that she had, he figured his XO might actually get to the point.

"Do something useful and grab me the jacket from that wardrobe outside," Carter said, slipping past Carina and into the main cabin of his quarters. "Then perhaps you'll have remembered why you stopped by."

"Oh, it was just to let you know that Cai and HARPER have finished the diagnostics," Carina said, rooting around in his wardrobe. "Cai is also confident that the Khopesh destroyers didn't send a warp transmission prior to us obliterating them, and there's no sign that any more ships are going to drop in."

Carter stepped up to the wardrobe and fished a jacket off a hanger himself, since it was apparent that Carina was merely nosying around his personal effects, rather than actually doing what he'd asked.

"Sometimes, the Aterniens' arrogance works in our favor," he said, slipping on the spare jacket, which despite being just as ancient as the previous one, looked and even smelled new. "That Overseer probably thought we were his ticket to the Royal Court, and so didn't inform anyone else what he was doing."

"A bit of light reading?" Carina asked, while flicking through a copy of *The Analects* by Confucius.

"You should try it sometime," Carter grunted, snatching the book off his XO and setting it back down on the shelf inside the wardrobe. "You might learn something."

Carina scowled at him then folded her arms in a

defensive posture. "Won't this Overseer just get 'reborn' with all his memories and tell the others where we are?" she asked, finally moving onto a relevant topic.

"It's a possibility," Carter agreed. "But we don't know how quickly they are integrated into their replacement bodies. And even if this Overseer did remember, I doubt he'd volunteer the fact that he had his ass handed to him so easily."

Carina considered this then shrugged. "He may not have a choice. I doubt that Markus Aternus is big on people keeping secrets from him."

"All the more reason why we need to reach Old Aternus, sooner rather than later." He extended a hand toward the door to his cabin. "After you, Major."

Carter and Carina took the short walk to the bridge together and entered to find the rest of the crew ready and waiting. This included HARPER, who had also used the interval to replace his damaged motor core and give his coverings a fresh lick of paint. Like Carter with his trimmed beard and replacement jacket, the bot was looking good-as-new.

"Course laid in to Old Aternus," Amaya said, as commander and XO took up their seats. "We'll arrive well outside of orbital range, as you ordered."

"Very well, take us to battle stations and jump when ready," Carter replied.

"Battle stations, aye," Brodie answered, and the bridge lighting adopted a menacing red hue that foretold of battles still to come.

"Jumping in ten seconds," Amaya reported.

Carter listened to the beat of the soliton warp drive,

which was building stronger and faster than he'd ever heard before.

"Five seconds…"

Carter sucked in a breath then let it out.

"Jumping…"

The starfield shifted and the pulsar vanished, then a new star and a new world appeared in front of the Galatine, but unlike the bright blue orbs of Union worlds, it was a dirty mass of grey-brown, cloaked in clouds that shivered with lightning.

"Jump complete," Amaya reported. "Welcome to Old Aternus…" His pilot and navigator delivered the line with a theatricality that befitted the striking, dramatic-looking planet.

"Give me a full scan and tactical report," Carter said.

His Master Operator and Master-at-arms called out their acknowledgments, and Carter checked his comp-slate while he waited. JACAB was also busy processing the data, and building up a holographic map that the bot was projecting to the left of Carter's chair. From the initial scans, it was clear that the orbital plane of Old Aternus was chockablock with satellites.

"I've located the primary city," Cai Cooper said, announcing his findings first. "It is difficult to be accurate from this range, but I am picking up a power signature."

"Brodie, is there any reason we shouldn't approach closer?" Carter asked.

"I can give you about ten-thousand reasons, MC," his Master-at-arms replied, channeling Amaya's earlier theatrical tone. Brodie worked the tactical console then an object appeared on the viewscreen, and also on the holographic projection from JACAB. At first glance, it looked like a giant starfish in space, but as the image resolved and became defined, it took on a more angular, man-made appearance.

"Star Cannons…" Carina said, speaking the words as part of one long, exhalation of breath.

"And a lot of them, too," Brodie added.

Carter narrowed his eyes as he read the analysis. Each Star Cannon was fourteen meters in diameter, or roughly the size of a large water wheel, though it wasn't the size of the object that he was interested in but the weapon in the center of its mass.

"Brodie, can you estimate the yield of that particle cannon?"

"It's hard to say for sure, MC," the tactical officer replied, while still working. "But judging by the energy they're putting out, and the fact they're basically flying guns, I'd say that each Star Cannon will hit with the same power as one Khopesh-class Destroyer."

Carter rested his chin in his hand and grunted a sigh. One or even half-a-dozen Star Cannons wouldn't be much trouble, but more would quickly become a problem, and with ten thousand to spare, even the Galatine would struggle to run the gauntlet. Even so, he had little choice but to try.

"We won't get anywhere by sitting on our asses out here," Carter said, making his decision. "Amaya, ahead slow. And stay alert, people."

The Galatine's engines drove the ship forward and Carter remained in his seat, chin in hand, massaging his neatly-trimmed beard. The soft beep and chirrup of the consoles on the bridge only added to the tension, sounding like the sonar ping of a submarine, cruising the dark depths of an ocean with a hunter-killer on its tail. Finally, after a solid twenty minutes without incident, Brodie's tactical console chimed an alert.

"We're being scanned by one of the Star Cannons," Brodie announced. "The defense grid is coming online."

"Hold your course, Amaya," Carter said, immediately cutting off any suggestion that they would run at the first sign of trouble. "Brodie, talk to me…"

"We have two Star Cannons on an intercept course, moving fast," the Master-at-arms updated.

"Really fast, actually," Amaya chipped in. "Their acceleration curve easily matches what the Galatine can pull."

Carter rubbed his beard, weaving that new piece of information into his thinking. That the Star Cannons were fast was important, especially if they needed to outrun them. "Maintain heading and ready all weapons," he ordered. "We need to test how hard these things hit, and how much it takes to put them down."

A minute later the two Star Cannons were on them, and particle blasts erupted from their centers. The Galatine was struck, but the impact barely resonated through the hull.

"Direct hits, armor is holding," Brodie called out.

"Return fire with the one-twenties only," Carter ordered.

"Aye, sir, locking on with the one-twenties," Brodie replied. Carter could hear the man's fingers sliding across his console. "Targets acquired… firing…"

The port and starboard side cannons targeted the two Aternien Star Cannons independently, and both were struck cleanly and destroyed.

"Targets neutralized…" Brodie confirmed.

"That was easy," Carina commented, though she didn't

sound pleased by this. If anything, she was suspicious, and so was Carter.

"Maintain our speed Amaya," Carter said, feeling his senses begin to climb. "Let's see what else they throw at us."

"Aye, aye, skipper," his pilot replied, though like Carina, there was an edge to her response that suggested doubt in her mind.

"We now have seven new Star Cannons on an intercept course," Brodie said. "It looks like they're testing us too."

Carter nodded. "Then let's make sure we pass the test. Amaya, try to avoid us getting hit, if you can."

His pilot acknowledged the order then appeared to zone out, as she connected to the Galatine through her neural implants. He then recognized the sound of the soliton warp drive spinning up, which meant that Amaya was preparing for gravitational maneuvering.

"Suck it up," Carter said, grinning at his XO. "This is where it gets interesting."

It took Carina a few seconds to understand the meaning behind his comment, then she cursed and braced herself hard against the back of her seat.

"Targets in range," Brodie said.

"Fire at will…"

The Star Cannons broke formation and tried to surround the Galatine, but Amaya made this difficult by weaving the Longsword in a chaotic path that forced the defensive weapons to constantly adjust. Even so, the Star Cannons proved highly accurate, and by the time Brodie had destroyed them all, the Galatine had taken a dozen hits.

"Damage report," Carter said, resuming his anxious beard-rubbing.

"We got hit pretty hard, but no serious damage," Brodie

replied. "For the most part, our armor held, though it's down to the bare thread in about six percent of the ship. Nano-machines are working fast to patch the holes."

Carter nodded then the tactical console chimed again, and JACAB relayed the report to his holographic map. He cursed through his teeth as twenty-eight more Star Cannons split out of the grid and accelerated toward them.

"Based on how hard the last seven hit us, twenty-eight could seriously spoil our day," Brodie said. "I recommend we reverse course and rethink our approach."

Carter considered this, fighting the urge to plough ahead regardless, and listening to his rational side. "I agree," he grunted, grudgingly. "Amaya, all stop. Let's see if holding position is enough to make them back off. If not, we'll need to put the pedal to the metal."

"Reading all stop," Amaya said. There was a tense wait, before she added, "…but the Star Cannons are still coming."

Carter thumped the arm of his chair. "Come about, then ahead flank. Brodie, don't wait for those things to shoot first."

His officers acknowledged the commands and the Galatine began to power away from Old Aternus, but despite their massive engines the Star Cannons continued to gain.

"Swarm missiles away…" Brodie called out.

Carter watched the hundreds of projectiles snake away to their targets, taking out half of the cannons. The remaining weapons returned fire and their engines were hit.

"Engine output just dropped by ten percent," Amaya called out. "At the rate the cannons are gaining, we'll be overrun in seconds."

No sooner had she finished speaking than the leading

Star Cannons pulled alongside and began hammering the Galatine all along its body. Amaya threw the ship into a series of hard gravitational maneuvers, shaking them off and allowing Brodie to bring their one-twenties and plasma cannon to bear, but by the time the machines were destroyed, the Galatine had taken a walloping.

"Hull breaches, sections G12 to H13 on decks four and five," Brodie announced.

"HARPER, patch those holes, and get our engines back to full performance," Carter said, addressing the vibrant yellow bot at the aft stations.

"Structural repairs underway, boss, but the engines cannot be repaired while they are operating," the labor bot replied. "We will need to reach a safe distance and power them down first."

The tactical console then practically screeched an alert that was so shrill it made Carter's eyes twitch.

"More weapons are breaking away from the orbital grid," Brodie said, quickly compiling the data. His master-at-arms uttered a curse under his breath. "Three-four-three Star Cannons inbound and closing fast."

Carter spun around in his seat. "Three hundred and forty-three?" he repeated. "I just wanted to make sure I heard you right."

"You heard right, MC," Brodie sighed. "I hate to say it, but we need to bug out, and fast."

Carter's senses were now on full alert and his heart was pounding hard in his chest, preparing him for battle, but this was a fight he couldn't win. "Amaya, spin-up the drive and warp us to a safe distance," he said.

"Aye, aye, skipper, but we won't be ready to jump before that new cluster of cannons can get shots off."

"How soon, Amaya?" Carter asked. He was so far forward on the edge of his seat, he almost slid off it.

"This is uncharted space, so I need two minutes, skipper," Amaya replied. "Unless we blind jump, but I wouldn't recommend it. We could end up anywhere in the universe."

Suddenly, blasts hammered the ship and he felt their engines lose even more power, but more concerning was the fact he could no longer hear the soliton drive spinning.

"That last hit took the warp drive out of alignment," HARPER called out. Even the bot sounded fraught. "I will need to reset it manually from inside the chamber."

Carter jumped out of his seat so he could look the bot square in its glowing eyes. "How long will that take?"

"At least an hour, boss," came the bot's solemn and apologetic reply.

"Options…" Carter said, looking into the eyes of all his crew members in turn. "We can't outrun them, and we can't outgun them. We need a third choice."

The next few seconds felt like an age, then Cai spoke up, his voice bright and hopeful. "Sir, do you still have the blue lapis lazuli stone that the former Overseer, Monique Dubois, gave to you?"

Carter cursed himself for not thinking of it sooner. Monique had said that the stone could unlock doors that were previously closed to them, and interfaced with the Galatine it could be used to identify them as a friend instead of foe. He reached into his jacket pocket, before realizing that the lapis lazuli was in the jacket he'd taken off in his quarters. He looked at Carina, and she took on a ghostly visage, as she realized it too.

"HARPER, Amaya, give us as much speed as you can,"

Carter said, his voice almost a shout. "I don't care what you do but get me another two minutes."

The replies from his bot and his pilot were lost in the whoosh of air that was rushing past his ears, as he charged off the bridge in the direction of his quarters. The shockwave from his sudden acceleration knocked his XO backward, but he was already off the bridge before she recovered her balance. Carter reached his cabin door a few seconds later, and practically tore it open, before bustling inside and darting into his rest room. The ship was rocked hard again, and he had to brace himself against the doorframe. Lights flickered and the gravity on the ship fluctuated, though Carter couldn't tell if this from damage they'd sustained, or from another feat of gravitational maneuvering by Amaya. Searching the jacket, he grabbed the stone then accelerated again, bouncing off the walls of his cabin and into the corridor outside, like a dodgem car hitting the bumpers at the side of the track. He powered onto the bridge and threw the stone at Cai with the speed of a bullet, but his Master Operator's augmented reflexes were equal to the task.

"Thirty seconds until those Star Cannons reduce us to dust," Brodie called out, as ever calm under pressure.

"I have already created the necessary program to integrate the stone with our transponder and will require another twenty seconds to complete the interface," Cai answered.

"Don't feel like you have to cut it close for dramatic effect," Carina said, still finding time for sarcasm.

"Trust me, Major, I abhor drama…" the Master Operator answered.

Cai's hands were moving so fast across his console that Carter thought he could see smoke rising from the keys.

TOBY was also hard at work and it was then he realized the bot had been adapted to function as the receptacle for the stone. This was brilliant on the part of his Master Operator, since TOBY had previous experience working with Aternien computer systems, and understood their language, at least in part.

"Ten seconds…" Brodie said, his voice ever so slightly firmer. "Five seconds…"

"There! Done!" Cai called out, rocking back from his console, hands in the air.

"Brodie, report!" Carter added.

"Star Cannons are…" he paused, scowling at the display. "… disengaging and withdrawing."

Carter threw his head back and breathed a sigh of relief, while his XO had to sit down before she fell down.

"Great work, Cai. What did you do?"

"As you know, the stone is a key, of sorts, encoded with the authority of an Overseer of Aternus," Cai began. He sounded cool, and quite pleased with himself. "With TOBY's help, I used this authority to recode our ship's transponder ID with that of an Aternien vessel that was contained within the stone's databanks."

"Which ship?" Carter asked.

"The Star Cannons believe we are the Aternien Solar Barque Kagem-ni." Cai may have claimed to not like drama, but there was an unmistakable air of mystery about the way he spoke the name of the Aternien vessel.

"Didn't we destroy the Kagem-ni during the first Aternien War?" Carter asked, recalling the name from the depths of his memory.

"Yes, though the Aterniens always denied that it was lost; right up until the end of the war, they maintained that it was merely missing," Cai replied. "They did not believe it possible we could have vanquished it."

"Smart…" Carina said, smiling at the Master Operator. "Cloning the ID of an active ship or one that was destroyed could raise alarms, but the Aternien security systems can't know for sure we're not who we claim to be."

"Then the Kagem-ni we are," Carter smiled. "Let's hope she has a welcome homecoming."

TWELVE
ATERNUS CITY

CAI STEPPED out of the shuttlecraft, holding the Aternien keystone delicately between thumb and forefinger, then approached Carter and dropped the lapis lazuli into his waiting palm. "All done, sir," the Master Operator said. "As far as the automated systems on Old Aternus are concerned, this shuttle will appear to be a Griffin-class Combat Interceptor."

"And the Galatine still appears on sensors as the sun ship Kagem-ni, even without this little rock on-board?" Carter asked, shaking the stone in his hand.

"I re-programmed our transponder, so the stone won't be needed again," Cai replied. "So long as a ship crewed by actual Aterniens doesn't show up and take a look at us out of a window, the Galatine will be safe in orbit."

Carter nodded and pocketed the stone. His Master Operator had reassured him as best he could, but the prospect of an Aternien scout returning to their sacred world was still a distinct possibility, meaning that they had to work fast while on the surface.

"Last call, everyone heading to Old Aternus, get on board now," Carter said to his crew, who were all assembled in the shuttle bay.

Cai returned to the shuttle along with TOBY, followed by Major Larsen and HARPER, who had to duck low to avoid banging his armor-clad head. Brodie then arrived, shoving Nathan Clynes ahead of him at the point of an energy pistol. For once, the scientist didn't complain, though he shot Carter a look of thunder as he stepped on-board the craft, followed by the Master-at-arms and his bot, Taylor.

"The ship is yours, Amaya," Carter said, turning to his Master Navigator. "I'm sure JACAB and ADA will look after you."

Both bots bleeped their reassurances and hovered to the navigator's side to show their support in person.

"I'll be fine, skipper, don't you worry," Amaya replied, confidently. "Besides, with JACAB in the command chair, how could we not be?"

JACAB chirruped then saluted with one of his mechanical arms.

"You'll do great, buddy," Carter said, while drumming his knuckles gently against JACAB's spherical shell. "Just remember to keep your eyes peeled and put the pedal to the metal at the first sign of trouble."

"Understood, sir," Amaya said. "Should the Aterniens arrive, under no circumstances will we attempt a daring and heroic rescue." She smiled at JACAB. "Isn't that's right?"

JACAB nodded, but the bot was also stifling a chuckle, which made Carter strongly suspect that the pair of them had already cooked up a rescue plan, should things go South. He could have ordered them explicitly not to try anything so foolish, but he knew it would be pointless to do so. If it was him in their position, he'd ignore such an order too.

"I'll see you soon," Carter said, smiling and touching Amaya on the shoulder, before turning on his heels and slipping into the shuttlecraft with the rest of his crew.

The door to the craft closed and sealed, and Carter made his way through the passenger compartment and into the cockpit, where his XO was waiting for him in the co-pilot's seat.

"I thought that you'd probably want to do the honors, and take us down," Carina said. "Though considering you crashed the last shuttlecraft you piloted, I don't mind doing the driving." This last comment, made with smiling eyes, was merely an attempt to wind him up, rather than a genuine offer of help, and he was annoyed to discover that it had worked.

"Thank you, Major, but I think I'll manage just fine," Carter replied, petulantly.

He initiated the launch sequence and the shuttle was swallowed by the deck and dropped into the launch tube. Seconds later, Old Aternus loomed large beneath them, its violent atmosphere still crackling with electrical storms. More ominously, a Star Cannon hung in space to their starboard side, but the water-wheel sized weapon was aimed into deep space, and showed no sign of turning toward them.

"The Star Cannon has scanned us and registered our reprogrammed ID," Cai confirmed, linking to the shuttle's systems via his comp-slate. "We are clear to proceed to the planet's surface."

"Copy that," Carter grunted, and steered the craft on course.

The Galatine slipped past outside and Carter took a moment to admire the majestic battleship, which was still pockmarked with scars along its hull from the dozens of Star Cannons that had attacked them. He could see the nano-mechanical armor knitting back together, in the same way their battle uniforms self-repaired, and felt confident that his ship would soon be back to full strength.

"I've locked in the coordinates of the primary city," Carina reported, working her controls in the second seat. "Atmospheric interference is messing with our scanners, but it looks like Aternus City is entirely surrounded by a fifty-meter-high wall. I'm also detecting a major structure in the dead center of the city, but I can't yet make out what it is."

"I have the co-ordinates," Carter said, steering the shuttle into an entry angle. "And as for what lies beneath this murky veil, we'll find out soon enough."

The shuttle hit the upper atmosphere and shuddered like a horse and cart driving over cobblestones at speed. Visibility dropped to zero as flames engulfed the ship, and improved little as they hit the mesospheric and stratospheric cloud layers of the planet's icy lower atmosphere. Finally, after what seem like hours of being buffeted around like a feather in a hurricane, the shuttle pierced the tropospheric clouds, and the air cleared enough to get an unrestricted look at the surface of the Aternien city. The view did not disappoint.

"I'll say one thing for the Markus Aternus; the man has style," Carina said, craning her neck to take in the vista of Aternus City.

Carter didn't pass comment, but he was impressed too. Aternus City was a vast walled metropolis that gleamed gold, despite the limited sunlight that managed to reach the surface of the dingy world. The design of the buildings was clearly influenced by ancient Egyptian architecture, as was so much of the culture that Markus Aternus had created. Grandiose structures, built using hefty blocks of stone, towered above perfectly straight roads. Many of the buildings were clad in golden Aternien metal and featured intricate carvings and ornate decorations. Obelisk-like monuments were placed at even points around the city, which was a model of symmetrical, axial planning. Most striking of all was the central pyramid, which put any of the pyramids of Giza to shame, both in size and in the intricacy of its ornamental coverings. Smaller pyramids were built in line with it at each of the four corners, adhering to the city's rules of symmetry, which only added to the central structure's aura of majesty and mystery.

"I think I've worked out why they built the walls so high," Carina said, snapping Carter out of the moment.

"Why?" Carter grunted, before he too spotted what his XO had seen. "Scratch that, I think I understand," he added, eyes wide.

After his experience fighting dinosaurs, werewolves and other manner of strange beasts on Nathan Clynes' planet, Carter thought he'd seen it all. However, the kaiju-like monster that was roaming free beyond the walls of Aternus City was wilder than anything the scientist's vivid imagination had managed to cook up. It looked like a giant sea anemone, but moved like a slug, sliding over the rocky terrain outside the city walls and probing the structure with its tendrils. Suddenly, dozens of particle blasts flashed toward the monstrous creature, both from guard towers on the walls, and from the obelisk-like structures inside. The creature let out a shriek that knocked Carter back in his chair like he'd been punched in the face, then slued away, leaving an iridescent glop in its path, and with smoke rising from its blackened and burned tendrils.

"I am detecting the desiccated remains of many similar creatures beyond the city walls," Cai said. "However, there are relatively few still alive, at least within scanning range. I would surmise that the Aterniens hunted them to near extinction."

"At least we now know that the city's defenses are still operational," Carina added. "Though I'm not sure whether that's a good or a bad thing."

Carter believed it was both. The active particle cannons meant that the city still had power, which boded well for finding an intact computer archive that might reveal the location of New Aternus. On the flipside, it also meant that other security systems would likely be active too. And while their shuttle may have appeared on scanners to be a Griffin-class interceptor, it was obvious that neither he nor the rest of his party were native to the Aternien world.

"You're the Aternien expert here, Major, so where do you think we should land and look first?" Carter asked, looping the shuttle around the city in a holding pattern, like an airplane waiting to get its runway slot.

"It sounds obvious, but the central pyramid would be my first choice," his XO replied. "Likely, that would have been the palace where Markus Aternus lived and ruled." Carina then worked the shuttle's comp-slate and highlighted another structure, due North of the main pyramid. "In my expert and humble opinion, though, I think that is worth a look too."

Carter steered the shuttle lower and did a fly-by of the building that his XO had marked. It was a rectangular structure with a shallow-angled gable roof and ornate pediment, surrounded by majestic stone pillars. The building sat in the center of its own small, walled compound, accessed through a gate marked by two more large pillars. Carter agreed that the structure looked important, but so did many others in the city, and he couldn't understand why it had captured Carina's attention.

"Go on then, impress me," Carter said, inviting his XO to stun him with her cutting insight. Carina smiled and duly obliged.

"That building looks like the library of Alexandria from ancient earth, or as close to it as historians could imagine," Carina said. "And since libraries are repositories of information, I figured, what better place to start looking?"

Carter rocked back a little giving away his surprise. "That's actually pretty smart," he admitted.

"Well, don't sound so shocked," Carina hit back. "In any case, the library, if that's what it turns out to be, is directly across from the central pyramid, so if it turns out to be a bust, it's a short walk to our next destination."

"I'm sold, so unless anyone else has a better idea, I'll set down in the square between the pyramid and the library," Carter said.

"I have a better idea," Nathan Clynes spoke up. Carina rolled her eyes, and Carter would have done so too, had it not been risky from a piloting perspective. "You could take me home and carry on with this fool's errand on your own."

The scientist's predictably snarky remark was met with an equally predictable nudge and glower from Brodie, and Nathan quickly shut up again. Since no-one else had a serious alternative, Carter went with his XO's plan and landed the shuttle mid-way between the two structures of interest. The engines wound down and Carter opened the rear hatch, allowing the howling, rain saturated wind to whip inside.

"Nice place," Carina commented, squinting as icy droplets of water attacked her face and eyes. "I may book a vacation here."

"And you wonder why the Aterniens hate your fucking guts?" Nathan said, never one to miss an opportunity for a sniping comment. "You exiled them to this shithole and expected them to like it?"

"Hold your tongue or I'll pluck it out," Brodie said, shoving the scientist down the ramp and onto the rain-soaked stone street.

HARPER began to thud down to ramp next, but Carter was quick to halt the bot's progress. "I need you to stay with the shuttle," he said. "We don't know what might still be active in this city, and I don't like leaving the ship unguarded."

Nathan scoffed loudly. "But you'd entrust it to that traitorous machine?" the scientist snarled. "Big mistake, Commander. That bot is as yellow as its coverings, and will leave us stranded here without its tiny, unsophisticated brain giving it a second thought."

"HARPER has already proved himself, unlike you," Carter hit back.

"HARPER!" the scientist laughed, shaking his head. "You've even named it. How quaint."

"Do not concern yourself, boss, I will not leave any of you behind," HARPER said. The bot then slowly turned his head to look at Nathan. "Perhaps with one exception…"

Carter laughed and patted the hefty machine on the back, while Nathan cursed and shuffled away, both embarrassed and humbled from losing the battle of wits with his former indentured worker.

"Cai, you take the lead once we're inside," Carter said, trudging through the wind and rain toward the library. "The Aternien keystone should hopefully give us access to their repository, but we first have to figure out how their tech works. Use Nathan to help you."

The scientist looked ready to rebut any suggestion he would be of help, but Taylor's forbidding presence by his side compelled the man to hold his tongue. Soaked through and freezing cold, Carter passed through the gated entry to the library compound then traversed the courtyard and climbed the steep stone staircase to the main building. The roof, which was supported by gold-clad, stone pillars, extended a few meters over the terrace, finally offering the group some respite from the vicious Aternien weather.

"Cai, you're up," Carter said, brushing water off his uniform and squeezing it from his hair. "See if you can get us inside without tripping any alarms."

The Master Operator acknowledged the order and approached the tall, wooden doors, which were showing significant signs of wear, due to the incessant rain and cold temperatures. He scanned the doors with his comp-slate, pacing up and down in front of them, seemingly looking for something. Then he stopped and waved Carter over.

"I believe this is a keyhole," Cai said, pointing to an oval-shaped indentation in the door's Aternien metal surround.

"Luckily, I have a key," Carter said. He removed the blue stone from his pocket and pressed it into the hollow. Aternien hieroglyphs lit up on the lapis lazuli, shifting position and changing like they were projections beamed onto its surface. Heavy locks then thudded open, and the howling wind pushed the door ajar.

"Weapons out, people," Carter said, drawing his 57-EX. "We might have a key to the castle, but we're certainly not invited guests. Stay close and stay alert."

The door creaked as Carter pushed it open further so that he could move inside. His senses were heightened, but that was simply because of the situation he found himself in, rather than any specific perceived threat. Snooping around on what was once the homeworld of your sworn enemy had a way of getting the pulse racing, he realized. The inside of the building was as elaborate and ornate as the outside, with golden columns rising from floor to ceiling, separating rows of workstations, organized into a neat, symmetrical grid.

"I'm sure this is a library or archive of some kind," Carina said, tiptoeing inside behind him, pistol held ready. "It actually bears some resemblance to the current Bibliotheca Alexandrina on Terra Prime."

"Yes, well, naturally Markus was on the Board of Trustees for the Bibliotheca Alexandrina," Nathan said, sauntering inside with Brodie and Taylor hot on his heels. "He funded many major projects related to ancient Egyptian archeology and culture."

Carter and Carina glanced at each other, both thinking the same thing. *Jackpot…*

"Cai, see if you can find a working terminal, and use the keystone to gain access," Carter said, handing his Master Operator the lapis lazuli. He then turned to the scientist, who was already looking distinctly bored. "Nathan, go with him and try to be useful." The scientist narrowed his eyes at Carter and held his ground. Sighing, he added a strained, "Please…"

"See, that wasn't too hard, was it?" Nathan said, trudging after Cai. "Though this is a waste of time, of course. If you believe that Markus Aternus stored the location of his secret other world in a public library, you are even more stupid than you look."

Carter gritted his teeth and took a deep breath, fighting the urge to rise to the bait, and give Nathan Clynes a piece of his mind, or a punch in the face, whichever came first. However, he didn't want to give the scientist an excuse to withdraw his consent to help, so he let the insult slide.

"I'm going to have a look around, while Cai does his thing," Carina said, heading off toward a statue in the center of the great library. "After all, how many times do you get to walk around an alien city?"

"The Aterniens aren't aliens, Carina, they're just humans with golden rods stuck up their asses."

Carina laughed, and the sound filled the enormous space, which had the acoustics of an opera house. Carter begrudged feeling impressed by anything the Aterniens had built, even the formidable Solar Barques, but he couldn't deny that the library was a majestic work of art. While they were walking, Cai waved to them, almost frantically. Carter hooked his XO's arm and guided her toward the station where his Master Operator and Nathan were working.

"I have access, sir," Cai said, sounding like he'd surprised even himself with the speed at which progress had been made.

Each station had a golden figure of Markus Aternus, standing with his hands outstretched, perhaps to signify the god-king imparting his wisdom onto the users of the library. Cai had placed the lapis lazuli into the figure's hands, which had caused the keystone to again glow with hieroglyphs and activate the terminal.

"It will require some time to access and interpret the data, but with TOBY's help and Mister Clynes' knowledge of the Aternien language, I should be able to construct a translation matrix," Cai continued.

"See how he calls me, 'Mister Clynes', and treats me with a modicum of respect?" the scientist said, still trying to goad Carter into a response. "At least one of you has some manners."

"Focus on the location of New Aternus," Carter said, trying his best to ignore the scientist. "I realize this library is a potential treasure trove of valuable intelligence, but I don't want to hang around on this planet any longer than necessary."

"Understood, sir," his Master Operator replied, with a courteous nod.

It was only after Carter turned away from the library station that he realized his XO was no longer by his side. He then saw Carina standing by the statue in the center of the library and went over to join her.

"Ugly bastard, ain't it?" Carina said.

Carter looked at the striking statue, which stood four meters tall on a trio of spiked, spider-like legs. It had the torso of an Immortal – the warrior class of the Empire – but a faceless head that was smooth like a golden egg. In one hand the statue carried a spear, not unlike the war spears that the Overseers wielded, except larger, while in its other hand was a tall shield.

"An Aternien deity, perhaps?" Carter suggested.

"Perhaps," Carina said, shrugging. "The ancient Egyptians had many gods, but we've never seen evidence of this in Aternien culture, where Markus Aternus appears to rule supreme."

Carter scowled at the statue then scanned it with his comp-slate. It was constructed from an alloy similar to that used in Aternien scale armor, and its limbs appeared to be articulated, with evidence of gears and motors too. Then he scanned the head and alarm bells began to ring.

"This thing has a neuromorphic brain," Carter said, taking a pace back. "It's not as sophisticated as the Aternus brain, but it's the same tech."

Carina also took several paces back, and he could hear her heart begin to beat faster, while his own senses were climbing too.

"Commander, be careful, that object is in the library archives," Cai called out from his library station. "Its name roughly translates as 'Destroyer Immortal' and it is some kind of guardian. I strongly suggest that you do not expose it to scan radiation."

"Now you tell us…" Carter said, running his hand through his still-wet hair.

He held his ground, watching the Destroyer Immortal for any sign it was about to activate. For a fleeting moment, he thought he'd gotten away with it, then two eyes lit up inside the statue's smooth, golden head, and the Aternien guardian came to life.

THIRTEEN
SEEK AND DESTROY

CARTER DREW his 57-EX revolver and slowly backed away from the Destroyer Immortal. The monstrous Aternien guardian was not yet aware of them, and appeared dazed and confused, as if it were waking from a long slumber. Then its gleaming eyes finally saw him and sharpened, before the sentinel snarled like a guard dog confronting a household intruder.

"Nathan, find somewhere to hide, and stay there," Carter called over, though the scientist hadn't needed telling, and was already cowering beneath the workstation Cai was operating.

"Back away, slowly," Carter said to his XO, who remained close by his side, energy pistol drawn and ready. "Maybe if we don't act like a threat, it'll just go away."

The Destroyer Immortal continued to snarl, making a guttural sound like the growl of a bear. It bashed its spear against its shield then took a step toward them, angling the foremost of its spear-tipped mechanical legs at Carter.

"I'm pretty certain it already considers us a threat," Carina replied, with her usual dry sarcasm.

"Sir, do you need my assistance?" his Master Operator called out. Cai was already two paces away from his console, pistol in hand.

"No, keep working to retrieve the information we need," Carter replied, eager that they not waste the opportunity, since it might be their only one. "You'll know if we need help."

"How will he know?" Carina asked. She sounded insecure, as if she was unaware of a secret, telepathic link that existed between Longsword officers, but Carter had not intended to imply anything so sophisticated.

"He'll know because we'll be sprawled out on the floor, bleeding to death," Carter replied, dryly.

Carina snorted a laugh. "I wish I hadn't asked…"

Carter and his XO continued to back away then he saw Brodie and Taylor stalking closer on his right side. His Master-at-arms was aiming his plasma sub-gun at the destroyer, while Taylor had its cannon aimed at the machine's head.

"I say we shoot first, and figure out if it's friendly later," Brodie suggested. "But my money is on 'not friendly'."

"I don't think I'll take that bet," Carter replied.

The Destroyer Immortal continued to inch forward, covering its body with the long shield. Whether the machine was sentient or possessed only an animalistic intelligence, as its rasping vocalizations suggested, it was clearly smart enough to recognize they were a danger. As such, Carter decided to take the advice of his Master-at-arms, and attack first.

"On three, we hit this thing with everything we've got," Carter said, taking aim. "Shoot for the head but hit the damned thing anywhere you can."

Carter began the countdown but the Destroyer Immortal appeared to sense something was coming, and by the time he reached 'one', the machine had pulled its body almost entirely behind its tall shield. He emptied his 57-EX, the report of the overpowered revolver drowning out the fizzes and pulses from the energy weapons, but while his armor-piercing bullets dented and pockmarked the shield, they didn't penetrate it. Likewise, the energy blasts, even from Brodie's powerful sub-gun, were all repelled. Suddenly, the Destroyer lashed out with its war spear from behind the shield, using its height and reach advantage to sweep the weapon at them like a scythe cutting hay. Because of their augmented reactions, Brodie and Carter were able to duck under the shaft as it came at them, but Carina was caught flush in the gut, and thumped across the library floor, like a hockey puck sliding across freshly-polished ice. Cai abandoned his station and rushed to her aid, but Carter couldn't think about his XO at that moment and had to hope that her battle uniform had hardened quickly enough to protect her vulnerable 'normie' insides.

"Looks like we'll have to do this the old-fashioned way," Brodie said, slinging the sub-gun and pulling his claymore sword from his back scabbard.

"The harder they come…" Carter said, holstering his revolver and drawing his cutlass; his buckler expanded a moment later. "…the harder they fall."

The fizz of the energized swords igniting acted as a clarion call to the Destroyer Immortal, which surged forward and thrust the lance-like spear at Carter. He parried, measuring the guardian's strength at the same time, and finding it equal to his own, before darting forward and slashing his cutlass at the machine. The blade scraped across the destroyer's shield, then Brodie attacked, trying to slip past the sentinel's guard, but it deflected his thrust with a spear-tipped leg, then shield-bashed his Master-at-arms to push him away.

Carter and Brodie regrouped, both with considerably more respect for the Aternien Destroyer Immortal. Taylor then swooped in from behind and hammered blasts into the back of the machine's head, causing it to let out an angry howl. The spear was slashed at the bot, and Taylor barely managed to evade, before blasting it again. The damage was minimal, and with each shot that Brodie's bot landed on-target, the Destroyer Immortal became even more wild with fury.

Brodie rounded on the destroyer and launched a flurry of strikes, which were blocked or parried, but his onslaught allowed Carter to land two hard blows to the destroyer's back and rearmost leg. More howls of fury split the air, and the machine staggered away, finally having suffered enough damage to impede its movement. Without even looking in his direction, the Destroyer Immortal whirled the spear beneath its arm and thrust it at Carter. Despite his heightened awareness, it caught him off-guard, and he only partly blocked the strike, which cut open a gash across his ribs beneath his armpit and sent him crashing to the floor. Brodie tried to exploit the machine's shift of attention and landed a heavy blow that carved open the guardian's chest, exposing the Aternien machinery at its core. Even then the Destroyer Immortal was not halted, and Brodie was hammered through a console by a bone-crushing punch from the machine's tall shield.

Taylor bellowed a thunderous electronic growl and closed in on the destroyer, pummeling shots into the machine's body and neck, but in its desire for retribution, the bot left itself open to counterattack. The shaft of the spear connected with the resonant crack of a baseball bat striking a home run, and Taylor was sent crashing through a partition wall with a canyon-like depression across its middle. Brodie cried out with fear and anger, watching helplessly as his gopher trundled across the floor then came to rest on its dented side, lights barely blinking. Gripping his claymore in both hands, the Master-at-arms charged the destroyer and swung with all his might, slicing through the lower half of its shield and severing its foreleg at the knee. Using its spear as a crutch, the immortal hit back immediately, battering Brodie to the polished stone floor alongside Taylor, but in so doing it had turned its back on Carter.

Mustering all his strength, Carter leapt onto the Destroyer Immortal's rear leg then impaled the machine through its back, driving his energized cutlass hilt-deep. The machine roared and swiveled its body to face him, tearing the sword out of his hand in the process, before driving him back against the wall. The impact stole the breath from his lungs, then he saw the spear tip coming at him, aimed at his heart. He caught the shaft of the weapon in both hands and stopped it from piercing his flesh, but the warrior machine continued to apply pressure, pitting itself against Carter in a battle of strength. The destroyer pulled itself closer, peering into Carter's eyes, their faces mere inches apart, but as much as he tried, he couldn't overpower the machine.

Then he saw Brodie climb to his feet and gather up his

sword, and he knew he only had to hang on for a few more seconds. Sword held in a reverse grip, his Master-at-arms drove the weapon into the guardian's neck, and the machine howled and kicked like a bucking bronco, striking Brodie and again sending the man skidding across the floor, but in the process the Destroyer Immortal had also released Carter. Reaching the handle of his cutlass, he pulled the weapon free of the machine's chest and swung hard, cleaving the guardian's head from its thick neck, and finally putting the machine down. Breath heavy from the effect of being slammed into the wall, Carter watched as the destroyer's glowing eyes faded to black, then its damaged body collapsed in a heap. He disengaged his blade and rested forward using his thighs for support. Brodie limped alongside a few seconds later, his battle uniform cut open in a dozen places to reveal rapidly-healing, blood-red wounds.

"That's the hardest fight I think I've ever had," Brodie admitted, offering Carter his hand, which he accepted.

"Then you must be losing your touch," Carter replied, chest heaving. "I thought that was easy."

He delivered the line deadpan, but Brodie wasn't fooled, and soon they were both were laughing and embracing, in the way that only brothers- and-sisters-in-arms are able to do; their shared experiences bonding them more tightly than any weld or glue. A distorted warble alerted Carter to the approach of Taylor, Brodie's tactical bot. The machine was hovering under its own power, but it looked like it had been through a war. Brodie took his gopher in his arms and inspected the damage. His Master-at-arms was a hard man, but even Brodie's chiseled jaw trembled at the prospect of losing his friend.

"Give me a damage report, Taylor," Carter said, anxious

to learn how badly impaired the tactical bot was. Taylor warbled a response and Carter checked the report on his comp-slate, but the distorted characters and broken sentences were enough to confirm that the damage was significant. "Can you take yourself back to the shuttlecraft?" Carter added. "HARPER will be able to patch you up."

The bot complained bitterly, and Carter didn't need to read the translation of its squawks and bleeps to know that Taylor was refusing to leave their side.

"That's an order, buddy," Carter said, not taking no for an answer. "The rest of us can take it from here. You're no use to me as scrap metal, understood?"

Taylor growled his acceptance then hovered out of Brodie's arms and headed toward the exit. Carter gently rapped his knuckles against the bot's dented shell as he passed, and the gopher let out another warbled complaint, before continuing to obey his command.

"He'll be alright," Carter said to his Master-at-arms. He didn't know that for sure, of course, but even the hardest men needed someone to support and comfort them from time to time.

Cai and Carina then arrived, his XO grimacing and holding her ribs, but all told, she looked in better condition than he felt.

"I vote that we stay away from giant, three-legged killer machines from this point on," Carina said. The experience had clearly not robbed the woman of her glib humor.

"Motion seconded," Brodie said, placing a reassuring hand on the Major's shoulder.

"Motion carried," Carter grunted. He inspected the damage to his battle uniform, and tutted as he discovered each new hole and cut, but the garment was at least repairing rapidly.

"I brought an extra-supply of nano-stims, if you need one?" Brodie said, offering Carter a stubby silver cannister.

"I'll be fine, thank you, Brodie," Carter said, declining the offer. It hadn't been that long since he'd pumped himself full of nano-machines, and another hit so soon after would be like driving a cattle prod into his eyeballs. Brodie nodded then turned the dial of the cannister to forty per cent and injected it into his blood steam. If the agonizing side-effects of the extra nano-machines caused his Master-at-arms any discomfort, the man did not show it.

"There is some good news," Cai cut in, more concerned with his data and discoveries than the condition of his crewmates, at least on a surface level. "While you were fighting the Destroyer Immortal, I learned that the location of New Aternus was purged from this library's archive during the time of the exodus."

Carter frowned at his Master Operator. "How the hell is that good news?" he grunted.

"I also learned that all information pertaining to New Aternus was removed to the god-king's personal archive, in his chambers inside the great pyramid," Cai explained. "I have downloaded a significant quantity of data to TOBY's memory core, which should allow us to locate the records once we are inside. My worry is that the Overseer's keystone will not have sufficient clearance to access Aternus's data vault, so a brute force approach may be required."

"Now you're talking my language," Brodie said. The Master-at-arms flexed his sizable deltoid and trapezius muscles, as if readying himself for another brawl, but the Master Operator was quick to add a clarification.

"I do not mean that kind of force, but the sort that breaks through computer security," Cai continued, and Brodie's shoulders sagged with disappointment. "It will almost certainly require Nathan's assistance. No-one understands more about the Aternien computer language and architecture than he does."

Carter suddenly felt a shiver race down his spine. He looked around the library building, but Nathan Clynes was nowhere to be seen. "Where the hell is he, anyway?" Carter asked.

Cai ran back to the terminal he'd been using and looked beneath the workstation. "He's gone," the Master Operator confirmed. "And he's taken then Aternien keystone."

Carter cursed under his breath. "Then he'll be headed to the pyramid. There's only one thing Nathan wants out of this trip, and that's the knowledge and technology needed to ascend. And if that's anywhere, it'll be in Aternus' palace."

The group ran outside the library and saw Nathan sprinting across the rain-sodden stone street toward the great pyramid. He, Cai and Brodie took off first, leaving Carina in their dust, but even with their incredible sprint speed, Nathan's head start was too great, and the scientist had already reached the palace before they arrived.

"Nathan, stop!" Carter called out, drawing and reloading his 57-EX, while Nathan aimed his plasma sub-gun at the scientist. "We have no idea what might be inside that pyramid. We need to run scans first to make sure we don't awaken any more Destroyer Immortals."

"I've waited long enough!" Nathan hit back. He was standing in front of a monolithic golden door, which was carved with Aternien hieroglyphs and had a four-meter-tall Ankh of Aternus in the center. "Everything I've ever wanted is inside this pyramid, and no-one is going to stop me from going in!"

Brodie brandished his gun. "Say the word, MC, and I'll drop him on the spot."

After the trouble he'd caused, the last thing he wanted to do was kill Nathan before the troublesome academic had even been of use, but he was seriously considering Brodie's option. Then the door began to glow and the blinding brightness compelled him to shield his eyes. Next, the sound of heavy gears, chains and pullies operating boomed through the air, louder even than the constant rumbles of thunder from the planet's violent atmosphere. Bolts thudded open like the report of cannon fire, then the massive door stopped glowing and began to trundle open.

Carter ran up the steep stairs to find Nathan on his hands and knees, disorientated by the dazzling light. He grabbed the man and dragged him to his feet, before spotting the Aternien keystone in a pedestal to the right of the door. It was shining with hieroglyphs, but now the Ankh of Aternus was present in its center, where it had been absent before. Then he heard the rhythmic stomp of heavy boots marching in formation, and he saw seven soldiers advancing toward him from inside the pyramid.

At first, he was relieved that they weren't Destroyer Immortals, but nor were they the regular Aternien foot soldiers he was used to fighting. These warriors were over two meters tall, and had scale-armored bodies, but instead of human faces, they had jackal heads. Each of them carried a crook and flail crossed over their chests, the same as depicted on Tutankhamun's golden coffin. He had no idea what to call them, but he knew they were trouble. Then the warriors uncrossed their arms and brandished their weapons, and Carter responded in kind. He didn't relish another fight so soon after the ordeal with the Destroyer Immortal, but he'd come too far to be stopped now. Whatever dangers still lay ahead, he would face them head on until he got what he came for.

FOURTEEN
THE ANUBI

CARTER AND NATHAN LOCKED EYES, and he could see that the scientist was contemplating something reckless. The smart move would have been to turn away from the pyramid guardians and run like hell, but Nathan's obsession with discovering Markus Aternus' secrets had blinded him to reason. Instead, the scientist made a mad dash through the open door, but Nathan's slowly-rotting body had neither the speed nor the strength to make it past the guards. The frontmost of the jackal-headed warriors lashed the scientist across the chest with its flail, sending the man skidding out of sight beyond the door.

"Damned fool!" Carter called out, cursing the man, despite the fact he was likely already dead.

The palace guardians continued to march toward him, maintaining a strict diamond formation, and Carter backed away until he was side-by-side with Brodie and Cai. Carina arrived a few moments later but judging from the look on her face at seeing the Aternien warriors, Carter guessed that she was regretting leaving the relative safety of the library.

The frontmost guardian then began calling to them in a booming, monosyllabic voice, uttering what Carter assumed was a warning in the Aternien language to stay clear of the sacred palace.

"Cai, was there anything about these warriors in the library archive?" Carter asked his Master Operator, who had one eye on his comp-slate and the other on the guardians.

"Yes, they are called 'Anubi', named after the Egyptian god, Anubis," Cai replied, deftly managing to tap away at his comp-slate while still holding his Celtic short sword. "The library refers to them as protectors of Aternien royal temples and palaces. They are automatons that do not contain transferred human minds, but they are also intelligent, and deadly."

The Chief Anubi continued to utter its warning, speaking louder and more forcefully each time, then suddenly it stopped and its squad halted behind it. The guardian raised its crook, holding it perpendicular to the ground, and Carter could see that the face of Markus Aternus was molded into the curved handle. Suddenly, a blast of focused particle energy flashed from the handle of the crook, shooting from Aternus' likeness, as if it were the god-king himself trying to strike them down. Carter reacted swiftly, blocking the shot with his buckler, which melted under the intense heat and power of the blast.

"Take cover!" he called out. He dove to avoid a second blast from the crook, then scrambled into shelter behind one of the titanic stone columns that made up the colonnade in front of the grand pyramid entrance. More blasts hammered into the columns, chipping away at the stone and forcing dust and grit into his face and eyes. The seven Anubi then broken formation and moved to surround them.

"The crook is a particle blaster, similar in power to an Overseer's war spear," Cai reported, continuing his analysis of the guardians, despite them coming under fire. His Master Operator was nothing if not thorough. "The flail is an energized melee weapon, and I would estimate that the Anubi wield it with at least the skill of a Warden Immortal."

"Their armor looks too strong for plasma pistols, so we'll need to fight them sword-to-flail," Carter replied, glancing at the analysis on Cai's comp-slate.

"I think I'm a little out of my depth when it comes to sword-fighting," Carina cut in. "What can I do to help?" It was understandable that his XO was not taken with the prospect of fighting an Anubi hand-to-hand, and for good reason. Not only was her human body too fragile to withstand an attack from an energized flail, she also didn't have a sword to fight with. Thankfully, Carter had other plans for her.

"Major Larsen and TOBY will break left and use the colonnade as cover to harass the Anubi with weapons fire," Carter said, flinching as a chunk of rock the size of a house brick was blasted from the column and sped past his face. "If you can keep them distracted, we'll do the rest."

"Copy that," Carina said, nodding to TOBY and preparing to move.

"And Major…" Carter added, stopping her in her tracks, and extracting a frown from her. "Try not to get yourself slapped half-way across Old Aternus this time, okay?"

Carina raised a sarcastic eyebrow at him. "Good advice, sir, I'll be sure to follow it…"

Brodie and Carter gave covering fire as TOBY and Carina moved out, forcing the Anubi to scatter like scarab beetles. At the same time, the Aterniens swung their energized flails in a circular motion, whipping the beads so swiftly that they became a blur, like helicopter blades. Brodie's plasma blasts and even his armor piercing bullets were repelled by the whirling shields, and not a single shot landed. The Anubi quickly regrouped, then Carter, Cai and Brodie separated, each of them darting behind separate columns in the colonnade. Plasma blasts rained down on the Aternien position, and Carter saw TOBY circling above, hitting the Anubi from a high angle. The bot lacked Taylor's firepower and the blasts did little more than scorch the Aternien's golden scale armor, but it succeeded in diverting their attention. Carina also opened fire, catching the Anubi in a crossfire, and Carter saw his opportunity to advance. He didn't need to signal Cai and Brodie or inform them which targets to take down. They had fought side-by-side so many times before that their actions were instinctual, like soldiers who'd performed the same parade drill time and again.

Carter charged, covering the short distance between him and the Anubis' position before the guardians could react and return fire with their crooks. He had intended to take on the leader first, but that warrior had sunk into the pack, perhaps conscious that it was the primary target. The Chief Anubi began chanting orders to the others, which moved out to meet the charge head on, their jackal eyes burning red. Carter swung his cutlass at the first guardian, which blocked with its crook and counterattacked with its flail. He pulled his cutlass back to parry the weapon, but the flail's beads whipped around the edge of his sword and struck his shoulder. The pain was numbed, but the hit destroyed a section of his battle uniform and scorched his skin black.

A second Anubi joined the assault and Carter was forced onto the defensive, careful not to take another hit from the powerful melee weapon. His augments kicked into a higher gear, sensing on a primal level that he was in a fight for his life, but even with his insane speed and agility, the Anubi defeated his guard and struck his chest, cracking his breastbone like a biscuit wafer. This time not all the pain was suppressed, but Carter greeted the burning sensation like an old friend and allowed it to fill him up. Bioengineering and cybernetics could only take a person so far, and there was nothing quite so powerful as the human instinct to survive.

The first Anubi's flail whipped over his head, cracking the air like a rifle shot, and Carter threw all his weight into a counterattack that split the guardian's thick torso in half. The energized beads of the second Anubi's flail snapped past his face a split-second later, burning a groove across his left cheek, like searing a steak. He struck back, severing the beads from the weapon and sending them spinning into the colonnade, where they detonated like grenades. The Anubi attacked again, cracking his ribs with the head of the crook and knocking the breath out of him, before attempting to angle the molded face of Aternus at his chest and blast him to pieces. Carter grabbed the staff of the weapon and twisted it just in time to send the stream of particle energy flashing past his eyes and into the roof of the courtyard structure. Stone dust rained down on them, and the Anubi bared its golden teeth and growled words at him in its unintelligible Aternien language, but Carter was now the fiercer animal. He tore the crook from the guardian's hands and beat the Aternien with it until its knees buckled and it fell to all fours. Then with a savage strike of his cutlass, he sent the jackal's head tumbling down the stone staircase to the rain-soaked street at its base.

The victory was like a shot of adrenaline to his heart, and

Carter turned to the Chief Anubi, who was guarding the pyramid entrance as its last line of defense. From the way the jackal-headed warrior was looking directly at him, it was as if it the Anubi had not taken its red eyes off him even for a second. A single blast from its crook could easily kill him, and unlike the Overseer, or Damien Morrow, who could be goaded into a one-on-one duel, the Anubi had no ego to defend, so his approach had to be cautious. If it saw a chance to put Carter down, he didn't doubt for a second it would do it.

As Carter stalked toward the pyramid entrance, he observed Brodie and Cai out of the corner of his eye. His Master-at-arms had drawn upon his augmented ferocity and unparalleled skill to destroy the first Anubi in his path with a relentless cascade of blows from his energized claymore. Perhaps aware that it stood no chance against the two-handed sword, the second Anubi fell back and opened fire with its crook, but Brodie was like a shifting storm, impossible to tie down. At least as tall as the Aternien guardian, and even more powerful, Brodie made the jackal-headed warrior automaton look ordinary. Then with another blistering burst of speed, he caught the Anubi by its neck and drove the claymore through its chest, before savagely twisting the blade and withdrawing it.

The guardian crumpled at his feet, but Brodie wasn't complacent. Eyes as sharp as needles, his head snapped to where Cai was fighting his final opponent. The Master Operator had destroyed one guardian by hammering blasts into the back of its head at close range, but the second warrior had gotten the drop on him. Cai was down, and desperately trying to fend off repeated flail strikes, but even with sword and buckler, his battle uniform was scorched and melted all over. Only TOBY, his loyal bot, was preventing the Anubi from striking the killing blow, by constantly harassing the warrior with shots as it circled around its jackal head.

Carter was about to aid his Master Operator when Brodie caught his eye and an unspoken understanding passed between them. Brodie accelerated out of cover and swung the claymore so fast that the blade pierced the sound barrier, before it then split the Anubi in half from shoulder to hip. Seeing Brodie in the clear, the Chief Anubi aimed its crook at his Master-at-arms, and Carter saw his opportunity to strike. He charged the final pyramid guardian before it could open fire on his Master-at-arms, and cutlass and flail clashed, each of them striking and parrying with blistering speed. Then the bead of the flails became entangled around his sword, and the chief improvised, hammering the crook into his face and knocking him to his knees. The weapon was spun around and Carter found himself staring at the face of Markus Aternus, molded into the head of the particle weapon. He released his cutlass and grabbed the Anubi's wrist, deflecting its aim and causing the blast to scorch the side of his arm, instead of melting his skull.

Carter had fought enough battles to know that the outcomes of most fights were decided in moments such as this. No matter the skill of the fighters involved, all it took to lose was one wrong move or one misjudged attack, and the Anubi had just made its fatal error. Carter quick-drew his 57-EX and pumped all five rounds from the over-powered revolver into the base of the chief's chin, drilling though its skull like a jackhammer through asphalt. The warrior collapsed on top of him and Carter tossed the body aside, before collecting his cutlass and disengaging the blade.

Brodie and Cai regrouped with him, both still wary of other ambushes, but Carter's senses told him that they were safe, at least for a short time.

"Hey, MC, over here…" Brodie had made his way into the pyramid, and was looking off to the right, just inside the door.

Nathan Clynes… Carter thought, remembering how the foolhardy scientist had gotten himself flailed before the Anubi had attacked. Carter and the others followed Brodie inside and found Nathan lying on the floor with his eyes closed. The man's ribs were exposed, some bone, some metal, and the synthetic flesh covering his chest was bubbled and warped like melted plastic. A compartment inside his chest cavity seemed to house his vital organs, some of which were also synthetic in nature. By rights the man should have been dead, but he could still hear Nathan's shriveled heart beating.

"He's alive, but he won't be for long unless we get him to a med bay," Cai said. Efficient as ever, his Master Operator had already run a bioscan.

"We don't have time to get him to a med bay," Carter said, kneeling beside the scientist and removing a nano-stim capsule. "That's twice we've barely escaped with our necks, and who knows how many other Anubi and Destroyer Immortals might still be inside this pyramid."

"A nano-stim could kill him as easily as save him," Cai cautioned. Carter already knew this and didn't care. He needed the scientist, and risking a nano-stim was the only option he had.

"Then we roll the dice and see what happens." He turned the dial to fifty-percent and injected the nano-machines directly into Nathan's exposed chest cavity. The effect was immediate, with the scientist exploding back to life, as if reanimated through an act of dark magic. Carter held him down with one hand, as agonized spasms and convulsions tortured the man and horrific screams were forced through his thin lips. Then the scientist's ordeal was finally over and, incredibly, the man's heart was still beating.

"Remarkable…" Cai commented, speaking like an academic reviewing the results of his latest experiment.

"Don't forget that Nathan was already semi-augmented," Carter said, releasing the scientist and standing over him. "Nano-machines have been present in his system for longer than they have in any of us, me included."

"Still, he should be dead," Cai added.

"Yes, he should," Carter grunted. "But clearly some higher power, be it God, gods or just pure dumb luck, has other plans for Nathan Clynes."

FIFTEEN
TOMB OF THE PHARAOH

CARTER PICKED up one of the Aternien crooks and tore the mold of Markus Aternus' face off the handle. The weapon crackled and hissed, shooting sparks into the air like a firework, until finally it fizzled to nothing and died. Turning to Nathan he then offered the injured scientist the broken weapon to use as a crutch.

"Here, this should help you to walk," Carter said. The man eyed the crook with suspicion, then turned his distrustful eyes to Carter. "I've disabled it, so don't get any crazy notions about blasting me in the back."

"No, that's not what I was thinking," Nathan replied, as if Carter had further injured him with his hurtful words.

"Then what?" Carter grunted.

"I'm just surprised, that's all," the scientist explained, examining the crook as if it were a true ancient Egyptian relic. "I hardly merit such an act of kindness."

"I'm not being kind, just practical," Carter replied. "I don't want to have to carry your sorry ass through this pyramid. And keeping you alive was purely motivated self-interest. I still need your help, remember?"

Nathan nodded. "I remember. Even so, thank you."

Carter snorted a laugh. "Nathan Clynes saying 'thank you?'. It seems that miracles do happen."

The scientist scowled at him, but Carina stepped up to smooth over the rough edges of their still fractious relationship.

"Perhaps he's not a monster after all?" she said, shooting the scientist a smile, which he was powerless not to return. It seemed that his XO had a hold on Nathan. "After all, he did cure me of the Aternien virus and saved my life."

"Motivated self-interest again," Carter said, unkindly. "Don't be fooled."

It was true that Nathan's serum had cured Carina of the Aternien virus, but the scientist had only done so to save his own skin. Ordinarily, pointing this out would have caused Nathan to fire off a string of insults, but the man remained unusually humble.

"Well, since I'm here, and alive, perhaps we should continue on inside?" Nathan said, pressing the crook into the pit of his arm and resting on it. It turned out to be the perfect size. "If Markus modelled this temple on the Great Pyramid of Giza, as I suspect he would have, there will be an ascending passage that leads to a grand gallery and finally the god-king's chamber."

Carina nodded and held out her comp-slate for everyone to see. It was busy compiling a map of the pyramid's interior based on scans that TOBY was actively conducting.

"Unlike this structure, the Pyramid of Khufu in Giza was actually cramped on the inside, but Nathan is right that there are many similarities in terms of the internal layouts."

She highlighted three areas in particular. "I can certainly see what looks like the king's chamber toward the middle of the pyramid, and the equivalent of a queen's chamber and a subterranean chamber too, though their purposes are likely different here."

Carter wasn't a particularly superstitious man, but the thought of descending into the crypts of the Aternien palace gave him chills, which were exacerbated by the cold wind that was whipping through the still open doorway.

"Let's head to the king's chamber before any more Anubi decide to rear their jackal heads," Carter said, inviting Carina to take the lead, since she clearly understood more about the layout of the pyramid than he did.

Carina set a brisk pace, keen to discover more, while Cai dallied a little on account of the fact that he was scanning everything in sight and discussing his observations with TOBY. Brodie picked up the rear, keeping a wary eye on Nathan like a police detective scrutinizing a murder suspect.

"Do you know about the curse of the Pharaohs, from ancient Egypt on Terra Prime?" Carina said, after they had been walking steadily downhill for several minutes.

Carter glanced across to her and a familiar elven smirk curled her lips, which meant that his XO was attempting to alleviate her boredom by messing with him.

"No, and I don't want to know," he replied, hoping to cut the conversation short. Naturally, his XO ignored him.

"According to legend, anyone who disturbed the tomb of an Ancient Egyptian Pharaoh would suffer misfortune or death," Carina continued, speaking as if she were telling a bedtime story to a rapt, if slightly terrified, young audience.

Carter snorted. "Superstitious nonsense."

His XO smiled, perhaps realizing she'd hooked her fish.

"You might think so, but hundreds of years ago, in 1922 on the old Earth Calendar, a British archaeologist and namesake of yours called Howard Carter discovered the tomb of King Tutankhamun." She flashed her eyes at him, trying to draw attention to the dangerous connotations of the discovery, though Carter had never heard of Tutankhamun or any other Egyptian king or god, besides those the Aterniens had named their Solar Barques in honor of. "But Howard Carter ignored the warning and entered the tomb anyway," Carina continued, ramping up the level of theatre in her voice. "Soon after, several people connected with the find died, suddenly, under mysterious circumstances…"

Carter raised an eyebrow at his XO, but this was mostly on account of her bad acting, rather than because of what she was telling him. "Coincidence, pure and simple," he replied, unmoved by her attempt to spook him.

Carina shrugged. "Perhaps, but legend says that the tombs of the ancient pharaoh were inscribed with warnings to deter potential robbers, like us, and caution them of the dire consequences should they enter."

Carter snorted, derisively. "You're an intelligence officer, Carina, but nothing of what you've just told me counts as intelligent."

"Suit yourself," she replied, still teasing. "But since you're unafraid, you can go first." Carina reduced her pace just as the descending passage leveled off into a grand hallway, at the end of which were the tunnels leading up to the king's chamber, and down into the bowels of the pyramid.

Carter felt a shiver rush down his spine, but they were now so deep inside the structure that the cold wind couldn't possibly have reached him. "Let's run some scans here," he said. He'd done his best to make it sound like the delay was merely on account of necessary due diligence, rather than because he'd gotten cold feet. However, his XO's continued smirk told him that Carina knew she'd won.

Cai and TOBY then breezed past them both and began to analyze a mural that occupied almost the entire west wall of the hallway. Thanks to his XO's ghost stories, Carter hadn't noticed it, but now it was impossible to miss. Following his Master Operator, he moved through the corridor and tried to make sense of the image, but the stylized visual language was alien to him. It blended hieroglyphs with images of Aterniens and other creatures, all depicted with their bodies facing forward, but feet, legs and heads turned to the side, in the same twisted perspective that ancient Egyptian artists employed. He felt sure that it told a story, though it was not one he could interpret.

"What do you make of this, Cai?" he asked his Master Operator, who was enraptured by the mural.

"It is fascinating…" Cai replied, drawing upon the data that TOBY had recovered from the library to decipher the mural. "I believe I can translate it and interpret its meaning. Please give me a minute or two."

Carter nodded then folded his arms across his chest and waited. He glimpsed Carina further along the wall, still smirking, and her story of ancient curses invaded his thoughts again.

"Cai, did you notice if there were any inscriptions on the entrance to the pyramid?" Carter asked his Master Operator, keeping his voice low so that Carina wouldn't overhear. "Nothing that maybe warned trespassers not to enter?"

Cai's eyes widened a touch and his mouth puckered,

though Carter wasn't sure if that was a result of his question, or just because of his intense concentration.

"Yes, sir, there were some inscriptions," Cai finally replied, after an agonizing delay.

"What did they say?" Carter asked, tightening his grip on his own body.

Cai stopped working on his comp-slate and turned to him. The man's expression was blank, like a priest rising to the pulpit, about to give a somber sermon. "The inscriptions said, 'All ye who enter should not listen to Major Larsen, or else be made a fool of'…"

There was the snort of a laugher from his XO, who quickly looked away to hide her mirth, so instead Carter scowled at his Master Operator, who was also smirking.

"I think I preferred it when you were a humorless S.O.B.," Carter remarked, feeling every inch the fool he'd been made out to be.

"My apologies, sir," Cai said, though he didn't sound especially apologetic. "However, I have managed to translate the mural, if you'd like to hear its meaning."

"I would," Carter grunted. "Its real meaning, though, not some horseshit story about ancient curses."

Carina sidled up next to him, slapped him on the back and winked, then waited patiently for Cai to explain the mural. As someone who had invested considerable time studying Aternien culture, she was understandably curious.

"In short, sir, this mural depicts an Aternien rise to power," Cai began, starting at the leftmost edge of the painting. "It describes the awakening of the god-king on Terra Prime, and the persecution he suffered at the hands of fearful, lesser minds." They moved along the mural as Cai spoke. "Here we see early Aterniens being vilified and persecuted on Earth, and the subsequent troubles that led to their exile to this world." Carter studied the images of this period of history, which were made to look like Aternus was leading a revolt against a corrupt dictatorship. "This section covers the first Aternien war, with the Union represented as aggressors who continued to trespass on sacred Aternien territory, leaving the god-king no choice but to defend his people." Cai pointed to a sword nestled in a sea of stars. "That, I believe, is the Galatine, or one of the other Longswords."

Carter huffed. "Well, aren't we honored."

"Not really, I'm afraid," Cai replied, in an ominous tone. "We are described as infidels; a bastard race made by lesser beings to murder their own kind and halt the great march of ascendency."

"Jeez…" Carina cut in, surprised by the ferocity of the language used. "If that's the case, why is Markus Aternus so obsessed with you? He seems to want to reconcile with the Longsword officers, not strike you down with wrathful vengeance, like this would suggest."

"That is actually explained here," Cai said, ushering them further along the mural. "After the armistice at the end of the war, Aternus displays his divine mercy by proclaiming a path to ascendancy for all who were wronged and betrayed by the lesser human beings. I believe that is why Markus Aternus sought to convert the surviving Longsword crew."

"Well, his plan worked, to a degree," Carter admitted, thinking of Damien Morrow and his cohort. He looked toward the end of the mural and saw what looked like an exploding star. "So, how does this fairytale actually end?"

Cai moved to the end of the wall and waited for the

others to catch up.

"Here we see New Aternus in the century between the armistice and what is effectively now," Cai continued, recounting the story in a scholarly manner. "We can see them assembling their grand army and unleashing it upon the Terran worlds, where they reclaim their lost lands and vanquish those who wronged them. This flash is Terra Prime, burning like a supernova."

Carter scowled and Carina physically shuddered.

"Does that mean Aternus plans to nuke Terra Prime, or worse?" he asked.

Cai shrugged, but it was Nathan who surprised them all by providing the answer.

"This was Markus' vision of the future long before the uprising or the war," Nathan said. The man was resting against the wall opposite. He looked pale and sickly but appeared to have been following every word Cai had spoken. "He knew that one day there would be reckoning. He foresaw all of this."

"Just how old are you, anyway?" Carina asked. "To have known Markus personally, you must be even older than Carter."

"Yes, but the difference is that I look it." Nathan laughed then coughed bitterly for several seconds, straining against the crook in order to stay on his feet. Carter listened to the man's heart and could hear it growing weaker by the second.

"Nathan was experimenting with ways to extend human longevity at the same time Markus was developing his neuromorphic brain," Carter explained. "Though as you can see, Nathan was somewhat less successful."

The scientist glowered at him. "I'm still here, aren't I?"

Nathan then hobbled over to the mural and rested his hand on the depiction of Terra Prime as a nuclear fireball. "You never knew Markus, but I did," Nathan continued. "He never wanted a war with humans, he was genuinely trying to better the species, just as I was. But the Union turned against him and forced him to defend his people and his way of life. He accepted exile in good faith, to spare further bloodshed, but once he learned that this god-awful world was to be the Aternien's home, he was furious. He knew there would never be peaceful coexistence, because the humans would not allow it. The only way that his people would survive was by turning Terra Prime into a raging inferno of hellfire. That's what you see here. This was Markus when he was young and wrathful, but the god-king you are facing now is far more insidious."

"You make it sound like the Aterniens were justified in waging war on the Union?" Carina said.

"Perhaps they were, and perhaps they still are," Nathan replied, wistfully. "Certainly, humanity is not blameless."

Carter grunted under his breath and rubbed his beard. Nathan's recounting of history was surprisingly unbiased, and his assessment of Markus Aternus was hard to refute, since he knew the man before he was a god. He also knew that bitterness had a habit of clinging to a person's insides, like a cancer. In his soul, Markus was still human, and bent on revenge.

"Enough of the past," Carter said, turning away from the mural, which told them nothing helpful. "It no longer matters why Markus Aternus is waging war, only that he is, and that we have to stop him."

Carter led them out of the hallway to where two new passageways branched off, one sloping steeply upward to the king's chamber, and the other leading down. He didn't consider the lower passage even for a second and had begun heading up when Cai called out to him.

"Sir, I am detecting strong energy readings from the lower chamber," the Master Operator reported. "Conversely, I am measuring nothing from the king's chamber, and have indeterminate readings from the middle chamber, or what would have been the queen's chamber in the Khufu pyramid."

Carter pressed his hands to his hips. He knew what his Master Operator was implying, but still hoped he was wrong. Thanks to his XO, he didn't like the idea of entering the pyramid's lower tombs.

"What's your suggestion, Cai?" Carter asked.

"We should explore the lower chamber first, since it has power, then work our way up," Cai said, proving him right.

"What's the matter, scared of a few ancient mummies?" Carina teased.

"If you're so fearless then you go first," he hit back, hands still on hips.

"Okay, I will…"

Carina drew her sidearm then marched down the passageway toward the lower chamber. Cai and TOBY followed, clearly enthused by the idea of making a discovery, then Brodie shoved Nathan on, though with less force than usual, on account of the scientist's fragile and worsening state. Carter reluctantly followed, feeling the air temperature drop sharply the lower they descended. The passageway seemed to stretch on endlessly into the darkness before finally levelling off and widening into a ballroom-sized chamber. Carter stopped and looked around the space, which was entirely featureless, apart from what appeared to be a crypt on the far wall. It was marked by an elaborate golden arch, twenty meters high at its apex, and covered in Aternien hieroglyphs, including the Ankh of Aternus. Two golden statues stood guard to either side, and it was the statues that gave Carter pause.

"Cai, scan those statues and make sure they're not about to leap out of the wall and kill us," Carter said, pointing at the golden figures, which had jackal heads, like the Anubi warriors. "Everyone, hold position here until we know it's safe to proceed."

His Master Operator and TOBY got to work, while the others waited anxiously for the results. Even Brodie seemed ill-at-ease, though out of them all, his XO was most relaxed.

"Whatever this place is, I'd say it's important," Carina said, staring at the crypt entrance with wonder rather than fear. "The Ankh of Aternus isn't used lightly."

Carter nodded and returned to stroking his beard. He was trying to listen to his senses, but his body was already so amped up that it was hard to detect the subtle changes that might indicate hidden dangers ahead. It was like trying to isolate the sound of an individual voice in a crowded room.

"The statues are just that, sir," Cai reported. "Statues, and nothing more."

Carter grunted an acknowledgement but the report didn't give him much comfort. Carina was correct that the Ankh of Aternus signified that the crypt was important but he was unsure how it would help them locate New Aternus. In the end, the only way to find out was to explore inside.

"Cai, Brodie, you're with me," Carter said, making his decision. "Let's crack this thing open and see what lies beyond."

SIXTEEN
THE MIDDLE CHAMBER

THE CRYPT PROVED to be far more difficult to crack than Carter had expected. Even the lapis lazuli keystone that Monique had given to him had proved unhelpful. Cai had expanded the key analogy to include the fact that not all keys unlocked all doors. It seemed that despite being a high-rank in the Aternien hierarchy, even Overseers lacked sufficient clearance to access the space beyond the crypt door. To Carina and Cai, this had reinforced the notion that whatever lay beyond was important enough to warrant their efforts. Carter had agreed, though he remained cautious. His XO's stories of Egyptian curses may have been fantastical nonsense, but he couldn't shake the feeling that some doors were best left unopened.

"I think I've found a weakness in the structure," Brodie said. His Master-at-arms and Master Operator had been collaborating on the best way to force entry into the crypt. "With the right gear, I think I can blast a hole in this wall large enough for us all to fit through."

"How long will it take to get this gear from the Galatine?" Carter asked. He was keenly aware that the longer they remained on Old Aternus, the more likely it was they'd be discovered.

"Everything I need is already on the shuttle, MC," Brodie said, with a mildly cocky swagger. "I figured there was a high possibility I'd need to blow something up, so I provisioned accordingly."

Carter smiled. In the short time that his Master-at-arms had been back, Brodie had employed gun and sword to devastating effect, but the man's true talent was demolitions.

"Good thinking, Brodie," Carter replied. "Coordinate with HARPER and have him bring over what you need."

"Won't setting off a massive explosion inside the pyramid draw attention to us?" Carina asked. "The last thing we need is a dozen more Anubi or Destroyer Immortals trapping us down here."

"I actually believe that the confrontation with the Anubi Royal Guardians at the pyramid entrance could have been avoided," Cai said.

"I'm going to need you to explain that," Carter replied, rubbing one of many still aching wounds that the Anubi had given him.

"Remember that the Anubi and destroyers are automatons, programmed to respond to threats," Cai continued. "The Anubi at the entrance challenged us numerous times, but I did not think to use what I had learned in the library to translate their words. If I had at the time, I would have known they were effectively asking for identification."

Carter scowled at this Master Operator. "So, you're

saying that if we'd presented the Overseer's lapis lazuli then they'd have just left us alone?"

"There is a little more to it than that, but in effect, yes," Cai answered, and Carter felt like a fool. *The best kind of fight is the one you avoid...* "I would have needed to respond with a vocal command too, but I can now achieve that via my comp-slate."

Carter noticed that he wasn't the only one feeling slightly foolish. Nathan had been listening, his hand pressed to his chest, which had been cracked open like an egg by the Chief Anubi's flail.

"Can you ensure all our comp-slates are programmed with these appropriate responses?" Carter asked, twiddling the blue keystone in his jacket pocket. "I'd like to get out of here with at least some of my new battle uniform intact."

"Already done, sir," Cai replied, with gracious professionalism.

"In that case, I think we should do some exploring," Carina cut in. Carter looked at her like she was mad, but his XO explained her reasoning. "Look, even if we break through this door, we don't know that the crypt contains what we need, so while Brodie, Cai and HARPER are working down here, it makes sense for us to explore other avenues."

Carter couldn't argue with his XO's logic. "Fine, let's check out the middle 'queen's chamber' first," he suggested, turning on his heels and heading for the exit. In truth, he welcomed any excuse to leave the cold, dark lower chamber. "Then if that's a bust, we take a look at the god-king's personal quarters."

Carina joined him but soon he was aware of another set

of footsteps behind them and he glanced over his shoulder to see Nathan in hot pursuit.

"Hell no, you stay here, where Brodie can keep an eye on you," Carter said, holding out a hand to the scientist like a police officer stopping traffic.

"I'm long past causing you any trouble," Nathan replied. The man sounded sincere and, even more remarkably, somewhat penitent. "I'm no use down here, but maybe I can be of help to you still."

Carter narrowed his eyes at the scientist. "What's your angle, Nathan? You don't offer help for free."

"I'm curious, of course," Nathan admitted. "That is why I'm here, after all. To learn everything that I can about Aternien ascension technology."

"You're here because I didn't give you a choice."

The scientist's nostrils flared and for a moment the old, vengeful and conniving Nathan Clynes stood in front of him. "You know what I mean," Nathan replied, clearly struggling to rein in his natural tendency toward spitting insults and abuse.

"Fine, but if you drop behind then you're on your own," Carter said. In retrospect, he'd rather have Nathan in his sights than left behind, where he could scheme and plot to his heart's content.

"Don't worry, I'll watch him," Carina said, waving Nathan forward with the barrel of her energy pistol. "Besides, he probably has a much better idea of what we're looking for than we do."

"That's not really much of a compliment, though, is it?" the scientist hit back, shuffling forward at Carina's behest. "All you people know about Aterniens comes from Union history, which is a one-sided version of events to say the least."

Carter could have responded but he was tired of quarrelling with the scientist, and so allowed him the last word so that they could ascend the lower passageway in silence. Despite the man's injuries and deteriorating body, Nathan's movements were not severely encumbered, thanks partly to the makeshift walking stick Carter had fashioned for him. Once back in the entrance chamber, where the mural foretold Markus Aternus' vision of the future, they were soon heading up again. In contrast to the cold, dark lower chamber, the higher they climbed the more resplendent their surroundings became. The horizontal passageway leading to the middle chamber was a hundred meters above ground level and lit by iridescent lamps, which created a warming, golden glow. Unlike the lower passageway, it was also decorated with Aternien hieroglyphs, embossed in golden metal. Carter still understood barely anything of their written language, but he observed that many of the images represented scenes of ascension. They all followed a common theme, where a human being, stooped over and depicted as a fragile, pitiful creature, passed through a sort of gateway, and became reborn as a majestic, formidable Aternien.

"Would you look at this place…" Nathan whispered, marveling at the drawings. The man's clammy, sickly skin was bathed in the lustrous glow from the Aternien metal, making him seem less at death's door. "Look at everything Markus achieved, despite the odds."

"You really do admire him, don't you?" Carina said. The question was asked with genuine interest, rather than scornful derision.

"I admire what he has achieved," Nathan replied, a touch acerbically. "He was persecuted and left with no choice but to fight for his way of life. Then he was sent to this festering fuckhole of a planet, where humanity fully expected him to fail, and for his post-human society to die out." Nathan stopped and gestured to their opulent surroundings. "And look at what he achieved, in spite of you. You wrote him off, then forgot about him, and now Markus Aternus is on the cusp of superseding humanity as the dominant form of life in the galaxy." He turned back to Carina with inquisitorial eyes. "How could anyone not admire a feat such as that?"

"I think you forget which side you were on, Nathan," Rose cut in. "You helped the Union to fight Markus, and because of the Longsword program, you're probably more responsible for what happened to the Aterniens than any single person in history."

"That's bullshit, and you know it," Nathan snapped back. "The war had already begun before I was drafted in to help. By then the damage had been done."

An awkward silence persisted between them while Carter and Nathan glowered at each other, though neither had the energy to continue the argument, since it was as old as they were. Major Larsen was the one to finally break the impasse.

"Why do you hate humanity so much, anyway?" his XO then asked, again with honest curiosity. "And don't give me the same old spiel about the Union taking advantage of you, because I don't buy it. Like Carter said, you knew exactly what you were getting into when you signed up."

"Oh, I don't hate humanity, my dear Major," Nathan replied, offering her a thin-lipped smile. "But all species must evolve to survive. My life's work revolved around helping humanity to take that next step, in a way that people could accept. Markus went too far, too fast. He didn't foresee that people would revolt against the idea of simply existing as human consciousness inside a synthetic shell."

The scientist suddenly stopped, and twisted his body so that he could point at Carter with the Aternien crook.

"What I created was a bridge between human and Aternien," Nathan continued, suddenly entirely wrapped up in his own ego. "My creations are still flesh and bone, but stronger, faster, more intelligent and impossibly long-lived." He paused to admire Carter with a sort of begrudging reverie. "Behold, my crowning achievement," the scientist said, without any hint of irony. "Your belligerent commander is the next evolution of humankind, but even this the Union rejected." He sighed heavily and shook his head, then met Carina's eyes. "If a species will not evolve, Major Larsen, then it must die. This is the way of all life."

It was quite a speech, and Carter admitted to being surprised by how eloquently and persuasively Nathan had made his argument. In a sense, the scientist was defending him and his fellow Longsword officers – even standing up for him. Yet, still there was a strong undercurrent of resentment, and it was this that made Nathan dangerous and unpredictable. He begrudged what he had given to others, because he could not have it for himself.

"For what it's worth, I think you're right," Carina said.

Carter and Nathan turned to her, both looking like she'd just slapped them around the side of the face with a wet salmon.

"What the hell are you talking about?" Carter snapped.

"He's right," Carina repeated, this time with a shrug. "Humanity does need to evolve, but just because people weren't ready a hundred or so years ago, it doesn't mean they won't ever be ready. Evolution takes time, and maybe you were just rushing it."

"Evolution doesn't always take time," the scientist replied, setting off again towards the middle chamber. "Sometimes outside influences force nature's hand. For example, sixty-six million years ago, an asteroid almost ten miles in diameter hit Terra Prime, or earth as it then was, and caused an extinction event of biblical proportions. Today, the hand of a different god is at work, and the outcome will be even more catastrophic, and life changing."

Carter snorted and shook his head at the man, though since Nathan had his back to him, the scientist didn't see his scornful look.

"That's a hell of a way to justify genocide," Carter said. "Maybe you admire this guy a little too much. You sound like one of his damned acolytes."

"I said I admired his achievements, not him," Nathan countered, his tone now insolent and acerbic. "I hate Markus Aternus the man. I hate him for being everything I am not."

With that, Nathan surged ahead, a dark cloud following his every painful step. Carter let him go, partly because he was a little taken aback at the man's frankness. Considering the scientist's planet-sized ego, Carter hadn't expected Nathan to have been so self-aware. It took him and Major Larsen a few minutes to finally catch up, and when they did, they found Clynes on his knees in front of a grand monument. At first, he thought that the man had collapsed due to his injuries, and the stress of the nano-machine infusion, but Nathan's eyes were wide and bright, and shimmering with tears, like he was experiencing an epiphany.

"I don't believe it…" Nathan said in low, reverent voice, like someone speaking in church. "It can't be…"

Carter scowled at the man then again looked at the monument, which was seemingly the cause of Nathan's sudden catatonia. It resembled an Egyptian burial mask, set inside a frame from which wires and conduits sprouted like the roots of a tree. In all it stood ten meters tall and was mounted on a dull, steel-colored dais, which contained what appeared to be a control console. Carter looked more closely and was astonished to find that the keyboard used English characters, rather than Aternien hieroglyphs.

"What is this thing?" Carina asked, while cautiously approaching the object. "The exterior section looks Aternien, but the core components are definitely Union tech."

"Not just Union tech, but pre-war Union tech," Carter clarified. He had an unsettling feeling that he knew what the device was. "Don't touch it. This thing could be dangerous."

Nathan laughed, though it wasn't a mocking sound, but one that came from the heart and spoke of joy and wonderment.

"It is not dangerous, my dear commander," the scientist said, using the crook to push himself up, before staggering closer to the object, still enraptured by it. "This is an ascendancy conduit. In fact, it is the original ascendancy conduit; the device that Markus Aternus built with his own hands on Terra Prime to transfer his mind to a neuromorphic brain."

Carina suddenly backed away from the object, fearful that it might suck her consciousness out through her nose and deposit it into a microchip.

"And look!" Nathan added. His hands were placed around a perfectly smooth, spherical object, no larger than a grapefruit. "These are pre-formatted neuromorphic brains." He laughed again, breathlessly, then turned to Carter. "Do you know what this means?"

"Yes, I know what it means," Carter grunted. He could feel his senses starting to elevate, giving him further warning of the implications of their discovery. "It means that you've finally found a way to ascend."

SEVENTEEN
THE CRYPT

CARTER WATCHED Nathan pore over the ascension conduit with the fervor of a tortured artist working on his masterpiece. There wasn't an inch of the device that the scientist hadn't scrutinized, and the fact that the conduit remained completely inactive throughout did not seem to deter him.

"At least we've found a way to occupy his time that doesn't involve him being an insufferable asshole to us and the crew," Carina commented.

"Perhaps, but I'm not sure what good can come of this," Carter replied. The uneasy sensation he was feeling still troubled him. "I know that we lured Nathan here with the promise of discovering something exactly like that device, but I didn't expect we'd actually find it."

His comp-slate chimed, and Carter raised his forearm to see that his Master-at-arms was calling. "This is Carter, go ahead, Brodie."

"I think we're ready down here, MC," the Master-at-arms said. "I figured you wouldn't want to miss the fireworks."

"Thank you, Brodie, we'll be down in ten," Carter replied.

"Understood. Did you find anything else interesting on your travels?"

Carter grunted a laugh. "You could say that, but I'll fill both of you in when we return."

"You got it, MC," the Master-at-arms replied, before closing the channel.

"I don't rate our chances of being able to extricate Mr. Clynes from this chamber," Carina said, watching the scientist climb onto the ascension conduit in order to peer into the inner workings, balancing precariously on one foot in the process.

Carter's tone was firm. "He's coming, whether he likes it or not."

Marching over to the device, Carter maneuvered around the object until he was in Nathan's field of view. The scientist noted his arrival but continued his forensic examination of the technological marvel.

"This was adapted to run on Aternien power technology, but the base device is Union hardware," Nathan said, mistaking Carter for someone who gave a damn. "I believe that we could rig it up to a portable supply and get it working."

"Later, Nathan, right now we're needed back in the lower chamber," Carter said. He figured he'd try asking nicely to begin with, on the off-chance the scientist would be cooperative.

"You go ahead, I'll be right here," Nathan replied, head buried inside the machine.

"I'm not leaving you alone, so climb down or I'll drag you down," he demanded. Carter credited patience amongst his roster of talents, but Nathan Clynes had used up all of his good will a long time ago.

Nathan pulled his head out of the device, and shot him a condescending, reproving look. "Commander, this is the most significant archeological discovery of all time," the scientist began. Carter thought that was an exaggeration, but he let it slide. "This is the key to immortality. It is more important than anything else."

"Maybe to you, Nathan, but it's not why we're here…"

"It's exactly why we're here!" the scientist cut in. Carter hated being talked over, and anger flared up inside him. "We're here to save humanity, and this is how we'll do it. You can't defeat the Aterniens, but with this, the Union can become just like them. Then, as equals, a peace could be achieved."

Carter took a step closer, and Nathan retreated from him, correctly guessing that he intended to grab his leg and yank him forcibly off the machine. He let out a frustrated growl and pressed his hands to his hips.

"Nathan, I swear to God that if you make me come up there, you won't like the results," Carter said, surprising himself with his restraint. "If we strike out in the lower chamber, and if we have time, I promise we'll come back. And maybe I'll even sort out a portable generator to power this thing. But, right now, I need you to get down."

Nathan considered this but the man was not oblivious to the fact that Carter had lied to him before.

"How can I trust you?"

"You don't have a choice," Carter grunted. "But since I screwed you over by bringing you to Old Aternus in the first place, you have my word that we'll come back."

The scientist remained out of arm's reach for several

more seconds, then finally relented. "Okay, but you'd better not be fucking with me again, Carter, or…"

"Or what?" Carter barked, cutting Nathan off mid-sentence.

Nathan scowled and bit back what he was about to say, which was no doubt an insult or a threat, or both. Instead, the man smiled and replied, "Or I'll move from my little planet to the forest moon of Terra Nine. I hear there are some lovely cabins in the woods out there."

Carter felt a shiver race down his spine. Of all the threats Nathan could have made, the promise of becoming his next-door neighbor was one of the most chilling.

"In that case, you can be one hundred and ten per cent assured that I'll keep my word," Carter replied, with feeling.

The descent to the lower cavern was quicker and easier than the climb to the middle chamber, simply on account of the beneficial effect of gravity, which helped Nathan to maintain a steady pace. The scientist was mercifully silent for the duration too, though Carter could see that Nathan's mind was racing at the possibilities of what he'd discovered. The drop in temperature and light level as they progressed to the lower chamber was as unwelcome as it had been the first time he'd entered, but the sight of the bright yellow labor bot helped to lift his mood.

"Hello, boss," HARPER said, with a cheerful wave.

"Hello HARPER," Carter replied, greeting him with a nod, since waves were not really his style. "How's Taylor?"

"He is currently charging and running through a full diagnostic cycle, but I believe he will be fine," the bot replied.

Carter grunted and nodded again, then his attention was drawn to Brodie and Cai, who were hustling away from the crypt entrance, covered in dust. Through the archway, he could see the explosive device, part buried in the stone floor and fixed to the left hand, lower corner of the crypt entrance.

"I suggest we stand back for this," Brodie said, directing them to the opposite far corner of the room, out of sight of the explosives he'd planted. "This will kick pretty hard."

Carter checked that everyone was assembled, then nodded to his Master-at-arms. "Blow it…"

In the confines of the subterranean chamber, the explosion was deafening, and it shook the floor and walls like an earthquake. Dust rained down over their heads, causing Carina and Nathan to cough and wheeze, though Carter was largely unaffected, owing to particulate filters in his nose and airways. As the dust settled, he crept out of their hiding place and saw that the controlled explosion had successfully torn open a fissure in the heavy crypt door. However, it wasn't quite large enough to fit through without dropping to a crawl.

"Brodie, Cai, HARPER, give me a hand with this," Carter said.

Stepping up to the fissure, Carter grabbed a firm handhold and waited for the others to find a solid purchase of their own. Once everyone was locked in, Carter took the strain.

"On three, everyone pull…"

Aternien metal was unfeasibly durable, but with three augmented Longsword officers, each stronger than a silverback gorilla, plus HARPER, whose strength exceeded even that, the door folded back like putty in their hands.

"That's enough, you've got it," Carina called out, once the opening was wide enough to fit even HARPER's robust frame through without needing to duck.

Carter dusted down his hands and noticed that Aternien hieroglyphs were debossed into his flesh from the pressure of holding the door so tightly. He shook them out to pump some blood back into his throbbing fingers, then stepped in front of the opening. Freezing cold air oozed out, but it was sterile and clean, quite unlike the musky smell of death and decay that he'd expected to discover inside a crypt.

"HARPER, give us some light, please," Carter said to the labor bot, who was usefully equipped with floodlights.

"Yes, boss," the machine replied, before stepping through the opening and filling the crypt with harsh, white light.

The sudden burst of luminescence caused Carter to squint and shield his face with his hands, and though his eyes quickly adjusted, he still wasn't sure what he was seeing. Inside the crypt were rows and rows of rectangular boxes, all fixed up to an elaborate system of wires and conduits. He moved further inside, and the temperature dropped to below freezing, causing his breath to fog like his lungs were on fire. Power transformers hummed softly on the four walls of the hundred-meter-wide cavern, feeding energy to each of the boxes, through the elaborate arrangement of cables and conduits. In the dead center of the room was another, much larger box, set above the rest on a golden dais, every inch of which was covered in Aternien hieroglyphs.

"Is this some sort of cold storage facility?" Carter wondered out loud. "A place where Aternus preserved artefacts that he couldn't take with him in the exodus?"

"I think you're half-way right," Carina replied. She had stopped beside one of the rectangular boxes close to the entrance and was wiping a layer of frost from the smooth, Aternien metal lid.

"What have you found?" Carter asked, weaving his way through the mass of other boxes to reach his XO, and waving Cai over at the same time.

"I think these are sarcophaguses," Carina said, as Carter arrived by her side. "Look at the inscriptions on the lid. There's the image of a face engraved in the metal, alongside a string of hieroglyphs, and the Ankh of Aternus."

Cai arrived and ran his gaze across the string of Aternien letters, studying the lid with the scrupulous concentration of an academic. TOBY hovered over his shoulder and began bleeping softly into Cai's ear. Cai responded in kind, as if the two of them were exchanging their professional opinions on a new research paper.

"Can you translate these inscriptions?" Carter asked his Master Operator.

"I believe so, sir," Cai replied, setting to work on his comp-slate.

Carter and Carina waited in the cold, as Master Operator and bot worked to decipher the writings. Then Cai's eyes opened a touch wider with surprise.

"This casket contains the body of a human female, called Kiara Singh," Cai explained. "It identifies her as an 'Associate of Aternus' and an 'Ascension Architect'." He pointed to a particular string of hieroglyphs below the engraved image of her face. "These symbols denote that she is an elder member of the Aternien Royal Court."

"Surely you mean *was* a member of the Aternien Royal Court?" Carter asked.

Cai shook his head. "No, sir, this woman is not dead." The bombshell shook Carter even harder than Brodie's controlled detonation had done. "And these are not sarcophaguses, at least not in the strictest sense, but stasis pods."

"What the hell, Cai?" Carter hit back. "You're saying that she's still *alive* in there?"

Cai nodded, and he appeared to be as surprised as Carter was. He rubbed his ruffled brow then looked at the engraving on the casket lid, studying the woman's serene, peaceful expression, which had been carved with exquisite skill and detail. She was clearly important, which made it all the more puzzling that her hibernating body had been interred in a crypt on a planet that the Aterniens had abandoned long ago.

"Get this, Kiara Singh is listed in the Union citizen database," Carina cut in. "And you'll never guess who she is."

"You're right, so just tell me," Carter grunted. He didn't like mysteries and was even less fond of guessing games.

"She worked for the Aternus Corporation as a software engineer," Carina went on, for once ignoring his grouchiness. "She's credited as being part of the team that worked on the neuromorphic brain project."

"This casket contains someone called Wyatt Park," Cai called out. His Master Operator had moved to an adjacent stasis chamber. "He is also in the Union database, as a former employee of the Aternus Corporation."

"Let me guess, he worked on the neuromorphic brain project too?" Carter said.

Cai nodded. "Yes, but as an electronics engineer." He then gestured to the other caskets immediately surrounding him. "And these are similar. All contain people from the Aternus Corporation, all of whom were responsible for key aspects of the technology that directly contributed to the birth of the Aternien race."

Carter was beginning to understand what they'd discovered, but he was no clearer about why Markus Aternus had filled the crypt with people who had worked for him, back when the man was still human.

"I don't fucking believe it…"

The words echoed around the chamber, taking on an unearthly resonance, but Carter knew it was Nathan speaking, even discounting the obvious clue of his foul language. Carter turned away from Kiara Singh and saw the scientist on the dais, beside the large casket in the center of the crypt.

"What have you found?" Carter asked.

"See for yourself," Nathan said, gesturing to the casket with an open hand.

Carter worked his way to the dais with Carina and Cai close behind, then climbed onto the ornate golden platform. The casket in the center was different to those surrounding it, and was fitted with a clear, crystal glass lid, beneath which was an actual sarcophagus that could have been plucked from an Egyptian pyramid on Terra Prime. Unlike those relics, however, the sarcophagus inside the central casket was in perfect condition. A funeral mask covered the head section of the coffin, fashioned from gleaming gold, with shimmering adornments of lapis lazuli, quartz, obsidian and turquoise glass.

"What am I looking at, Nathan?" Carter asked. The occupier of the casket was clearly important, but beyond the familiar Ankh symbol, there were no other markings.

The scientist recoiled with surprise. "Do you not see it?"

Carter bit down a growl and stared Nathan dead in the eyes. "Just tell me."

"This isn't the body of just anyone, Commander Rose," Nathan said, his voice trembling with excitement. "This is the human body of Markus Aternus himself. And he's still alive."

EIGHTEEN
A HIGH PRICE TO PAY

WITHIN ONLY A FEW minutes of Nathan making his fanciful claim, Cai had confirmed it. The sarcophagus, or stasis chamber as it actually was, did contain the preserved human body of Markus Aternus, and the man was indeed alive. Since then, Cai and Major Larsen had gone on to identify other key figures of the Aternien Empire. Those of the highest rank and status were entombed closest to Aternus' sarcophagus, which included his most loyal advisers in the Aternus Corporation, and even members of his close family.

Those toward the outer edges of the chamber were of lower status, such as Kiara Singh and Wyatt Park, but what they all had in common was a notable contribution to the success of the neuromorphic brain project, and the later transfer of Markus Aternus to his first synthetic body. Kiara, for example, had made a breakthrough in the code that governed the transfer of memory from organic to neuromorphic brains. Wyatt, on the other hand, had designed a new type of Resistive Random-Access Memory device that offered the ideal synaptic plasticity characteristics, yet consumed a fraction of the power of earlier devices.

Most importantly of all, however, besides the presence of the god-king himself, were the High Overseers – the commanders of the Royal Court Khopesh Destroyers – and the captain of the Solar Barque Senuset, and Carter's former nemesis, the Grand Vizier. He was more than a little disappointed to find out that the Vizier had at one time been Aternus' lawyer, and that his real name was Dwight Sanderson. However, lifting the veil of mystery that had surrounded the nobles at the heart of the Royal Court did nothing to diminish the risks that they still posed to humanity.

"There are three hundred and forty-three stasis chambers in total, though forty-eight are non-viable, and the bodies they contain are dead," Cai reported, returning to Carter after completing his thorough analysis of the crypt.

"I guess some sort of failure rate over time is to be expected," Carina commented, though Cai shook his head.

"Based on my analysis of the remains, the inactive chambers were already non-viable prior to arriving in this crypt," Cai explained. "But given how far the Aterniens had to travel to reach this planet, that is not surprising."

Carter grunted an acknowledged. "It's a miracle this number survived the journey, which suggests the hibernation technology is highly sophisticated."

Cai nodded. "It is equipment that was banned after the Aternien Act, but the funerary masks are a new addition that I have never seen or even conceived of before."

"You mean that the masks are not just decorative in nature?" Carina asked.

Cai shook his head. "They are brain regulation devices. I'm not clear on their precise function, but they appear to keep the minds of the hosts in a state similar to R.E.M. sleep, which is when people dream."

"So, they're conscious?" Carter asked.

"Not exactly, nor are they in the sort of deep stasis that we'd typically associate with a technology such as this."

"It's to keep their souls alive," Nathan said, still peering into the bejeweled eyes of the Aternus funerary mask. "Markus was obsessed with the soul, and considered it beyond the realms of science, in the same way people view God as beyond our ability to understand."

The scientist then tapped the glass lid of the casket with his index finger, producing a musical chime, like someone preparing to offer a toast at a wedding reception.

"This actually explains a lot, though," Nathan continued, still tapping the glass. "Given how obsessed Markus was about preserving the soul, I could never understand why that fucker murdered himself." He shrugged. "Looks like he never did."

"What do you mean he murdered himself?" Carter asked. "Didn't the original Markus Aternus commit suicide?"

"That's what it says on the official record of death, yes," Nathan replied. "But that was after a complex legal battle, which was all kept hush-hush and away from the press. In truth, the ascended version of Markus Aternus abducted and killed his human self, though the case was thrown out on a technicality."

"That's insane," Carina said. "How did he manage to swing that?"

Nathan smiled then pointed to the stasis casket containing the body of Dwight Sanderson. "Ask your friend the Grand Vizier, since it was his doing. The evidence of guilt was compelling too, so it's somewhat ironic to learn that the original, human Markus Aternus is alive after all."

Carina laughed and shook her head. "I guess that explains why Dwight is such a bigwig in the new Empire."

Carter rubbed his face, massaging his eyes and the bridge of his nose. They'd uncovered a lot in a short of space of time but were still no closer to understanding why the crypt existed.

"So let me get this straight," Carter grunted, his hands now pressed firmly to his hips. "Markus ascends then murders himself, but actually doesn't, and instead squirrels away his body in the basement of a pyramid thousands of light years from Terra Prime, along with three-hundred plus of his bosom pals, in order to preserve their souls." Carter shrugged. "Why?"

"Simple superstition, of course," Nathan replied, as if the answer were obvious. "For a man of science, Markus was a deeply superstitious man, who was obsessed with the mythos of many ancient cultures, not just the Egyptians, whom he romanticized most of all."

Carter still wasn't following the logic. "So, this is all just some sort of giant rabbit's foot? A coping mechanism for his irrational mind?"

"No, I think it's more than that," Nathan said. For some reason, he appeared to be enjoying himself. "Markus often talked about the soul being immutable and almost magical in nature; something that could not be replicated. As such, while he could transfer his consciousness and memories to a neuromorphic brain, for his soul to persist, his original host mind had to be preserved." The scientist laughed. "I assumed that he must have solved that problem, or changed his perception, but this crypt proves that he didn't."

Carter was beginning to understand, and with that understanding came a dramatic shift in the importance of what they'd discovered. If what Nathan said was true, then Markus was not merely storing his original body and mind for posterity, but in order to preserve the integrity of his very soul. It was a safety net, and Carter intended to yank it out from beneath the god-king's exalted feet.

"All this makes it sound like Markus didn't completely buy into the idea of full transference," Carina said. "It's like he wasn't certain that his synthetic self was genuine."

"Quite correct, my dear Major," Nathan replied, jollier than Carter had ever seen him. "Markus was brilliant, but like many great geniuses, he was also deeply flawed. It seems that he believed his synthetic self was tied to the original host soul, like two quantum-entangled particles. Should his original soul perish then the 'copy' would be just that – a fake." He laughed again. "This crypt is like the attic where Dorian Gray hid his portrait to keep it safe."

The analogies that the scientist had spouted went over Carter's head, but it was clear that Nathan viewed the crypt as an admission of failure, or at the very least, weakness. That Markus Aternus had not fully trusted his ascension device to transfer the essence of life itself seemed to amuse and comfort the scientist, as if the lessening of the man's stature somehow elevated his own.

"But this is all hokum, right?" Carina asked. "There's

nothing tangible to the idea that the original soul has to survive?"

"Of course not, it's irrational nonsense," Nathan scoffed.

Carter thought for a moment, rubbing his beard in order to help him concentrate. Nathan was correct that the Crypt was a weakness, and one that he felt sure he could exploit, if only he could figure out how.

"Why didn't they take these bodies with them, when they moved to New Aternus?" Carina asked, coming up with another insightful question.

Nathan shrugged. "Who knows what runs through the mind of an eccentric genius," he replied, in a cavalier manner. "But my guess is that Markus was too afraid to move them again, given that more than fourteen percent of these chambers didn't survive the initial journey. Safer to entomb them here, under guard." The scientist then pointed to Carter's right jacket pocket. "Think about it. If it wasn't for that Aternien skeleton keystone you somehow managed to acquire, you wouldn't have even reached orbit of this planet, never mind landed, or opened the door to this pyramid. The bodies were quite safe here, or at least they should have been."

Carter nodded, more to himself than in response to what Nathan had said, though the scientist had proved surprisingly helpful, for once. He now knew what they had to do, but it wouldn't be an easy task.

"Brodie, Cai, HARPER, I need you to move these caskets into the Galatine's hold and rig up a mechanism to keep them powered up and active," Carter said. "We don't need all of them. Just Aternus, the Grand Vizier and the High Overseers will do."

His officers and honorary chief engineer all

acknowledged the order and immediately set to work. Carina soon sidled up beside him, a quizzical expression furrowing her brow.

"You think we can use the bodies as leverage?" she asked. There was no judgment inferred, just simple curiosity.

"If Nathan is right then holding the people in these stasis chambers hostage should be enough to get the god-king's attention," Carter replied. "Quite how much leverage it will give us, I'm not sure, but if Aternus truly believes that his immortal soul is dependent on the survival of his host mind, I'm hoping he'll be motivated to negotiate. It might even be enough to get the bastard to the table for peace talks."

The almost imperceptible lifting of his XO's eyebrow suggested that she considered the probability of negotiation to be slim at best, but she didn't shoot down his suggestion. Nathan, however, was more scathing.

"Leverage is planting a planet-killing bomb on a world populated by billions, not carrying around a musty old coffin," the scientist sneered. His sudden change of tone was striking, and Carter suspected it was not without good reason. "Bodies in stasis aren't what you came for, Commander. The location of New Aternus is."

Carter could tell the man was angling for something, and he let it play out. "You're right that it's not what we came for, but I'll take any amount of leverage I can get, over nothing at all."

"What if I can give you what you want?" Nathan said. "What if I can give you the location of New Aternus? Then you can destroy the Soul Crypt and take away their immortality, just as you planned. That, along with these caskets, is *real* leverage."

Carter folded his arms across his chest and scowled at the

scientist. "I thought you had no interest in helping us to take down Markus Aternus and his empire?"

"I didn't, until I came here," Nathan replied. "Now I want something more, and I'm willing to give you everything you want to get it."

"You're asking me to help you 'ascend'?" Carter said, and Nathan nodded and smiled. "But how does that get us New Aternus?"

Nathan struggled to climb down from the dais that was supporting the sarcophagus of Markus Aternus, and Carina instinctively went to help him. To Carter's surprise, the scientist let her, and also allowed Carina to help him closer. The man was looking frailer by the minute, he realized, which explained his willingness to compromise. When you were staring death in the face, principles could not hope to stand against the human will to live.

"The body I built, the one you amusingly called Nathan 2.0, was designed to be compatible with the Aternien neuromorphic brain interface," Nathan continued, resting on his crook and looking Carter squarely in the eyes, appealing to him on a human level. "The brains we saw in the middle chamber are pre-formatted to Markus Aternus' personal specification. They were his 'spares' as it were." He leaned in closer, and the man's breath smelled like rotting flesh. "With the Aternien brain installed into the body of Nathan 2.0, I will be able to ascend. And then I will have access to everything."

"What do you mean, everything?" Carter asked. He needed specifics, not vague promises.

Nathan smiled. "Everything you need is stored in the god-king's personal archives. I can not only give you the location of New Aternus, but also the exact position and specifications of the Soul Crypt, and how to destroy it." The man leaned closer still, and the heat of his deathly breath was almost unbearable, yet Carter needed to hear what was said. "I can give you the means to win this war, Master Commander Rose," Nathan whispered. "All I ask in return is immortality."

NINETEEN
MIND TO MIND

CARTER PICKED up the portable power generator that Nathan needed to activate the ascension conduit and began carrying it over to the device. HARPER had dropped it off earlier, before returning to make the final shuttle run back to the Galatine with the caskets containing the human bodies of the High Overseers, Grand Vizier and Markus Aternus himself. Brodie, Taylor and Cai's gopher, TOBY, had gone with the labor bot, while Cai remained to assist Nathan. They were currently absorbed with the task of bypassing the ascension conduit's Aternien input stage so they could rig up the generator to the original machine that Markus Aternus had designed and built, before the man was a god.

Carter set down the generator then backed away to rejoin Major Larsen, who was also observing Nathan and Cai work. He was still deeply conflicted about whether to go ahead with the plan or not, but Nathan had successfully sowed the seeds of doubt in his mind. He simply wasn't certain that holding the hibernating bodies of Markus Aternus and other senior Royal Court members hostage would provide him with enough sway to end the war. He needed the hostages as his ace in the hole, not his only play, and that meant continuing with the original strategy of destroying the Soul Crypt on New Aternus. And to do that, regrettably, he'd had acquiesce to the scientist's terms.

"Are you sure about this?" Carina asked, practically biting her nails as she watched Nathan apply the finishing touches to the power input terminal. "Nathan has hardly proved to be trustworthy. What's to stop him from reneging on our agreement as soon as he gets what he wants?"

Carter had already given this some considerable thought. The truth was, he could think of only one thing that would stop Nathan from double-crossing them after attaining his new body, and that was the threat of Carter immediately taking it away.

"He'll give us what we need," Carter replied, choosing not to spell out his plan in all the gory details. "I won't take no for an answer."

His XO's eyes flicked across to him, and he could tell that her mind was racing with a dozen different possible interpretations of his answer. From her somewhat alarmed expression, he figured most of them were fairly close to the mark.

"Okay, but I hope that in the process of usurping one god-king, we're not merely creating another," she said.

Carter sincerely hoped that this was not an ominous portent for what the future might hold, but he wasn't blind to the possibility. Nathan may have hated Markus Aternus out of rabid jealousy for his rival's achievements, but he aspired to be everything that Aternus was. The difference between them was that Nathan wasn't shackled by superstition, and that made him potentially even more dangerous.

"I hope so too, Carina," Carter replied, resting his hand on the pommel of his plasma cutlass, and hoping that it would not become necessary to use it.

"Sir, we're ready over here," Cai called out.

Carter nodded then sucked in a deep breath. "Okay, start it up."

Cai activated the power generator and the control console began booting up for the first time since the Aternien exodus. Nathan was momentarily awed by this success until he saw Cai operating the console and raced over to him, as if the Master Operator were about to input nuclear launch codes and blow them all to hell.

"No, not like that!" Nathan snapped, muscling in and taking over the configuration process. "This must be done precisely, or we risk overloading the transfer matrix and frying the neuromorphic brain."

Had Nathan barged his way in on him the way the scientist had done to Cai, Carter would have broken the man's already mangled nose. His Master Operator, however, was a far more tolerant man, and graciously allowed Nathan to take over. While they were working, Carter inspected the ascension conduit in more detail. He hadn't noticed at first, but the device had been designed to look like a human head, wearing an elaborate crown or mask, not that dissimilar to the funerary mask that was keeping the original body of Markus Aternus alive. The head section was open from top to bottom, like a clamshell, and inside sat the body of Nathan 2.0. The head of the synthetic body was also flipped open around its circumference, just above the ears, like a boiled egg. Inside was the fabled Aternus Neuromorphic

Brain, the greatest scientific achievement in human history, and the cause of humanity's current woes.

The device also contained another seat, though it was set off to the right-hand side of the ascension conduit and lacked any of the Egyptian-inspired finery of the primary machine. In fact, Carter thought it looked like an electric chair, from the period of human history when the very worst criminals were condemned to death by electrocution. It was a simple, wooden-framed seat, with an apparatus that clamped over the occupant's head, again not unlike an electric chair. Carter couldn't help but note the symbolism, since the ascension conduit did effectively end the life of the original host human by transferring their consciousness to a synthetic brain. The difference was that while an electric chair killed it host, Markus had kept the bodies of the very first ascended human beings on-ice in a permanent dreamlike state.

Suddenly, there was a weighty thump as relays switched and energy was fed into the core matrix of the ascension conduit. For several seconds, nothing happened, but Nathan did not appear concerned. Then the machine lit up and hummed into life. Blue stones, similar to the lapis lazuli that Monique Dubois had given to Carter, sparkled all across the surface of the mask-like structure, while the Aternien metal cladding began to glow as if it had suddenly become hot. Meanwhile, the original machine buried beneath the showy Aternien exterior remained a dull, lifeless steel-grey lump of metal.

Nathan hustled away from the control console and stepped up to the body of Nathan 2.0, carefully closing the lid of its flipped-open cranium. He then jumped down, almost falling flat on his face in the process due to his eagerness and began configuring the ascension machine for the transfer. The scientist worked methodically for several minutes, before executing a final command, then running to the electric chair, barely taking a breath between actions.

"Please, lift the mask and place it over my head," Nathan said, breathing heavily and looking even more sickly-pale than ever.

Carter nodded to Cai and his Master Operator did the honors, while Nathan waited, his restless legs bouncing up and down, while his fingers drummed his thighs.

"Hurry, this stage of the process is time-critical," Nathan said, not even trying to hide the irritation in his voice.

Cai again managed to remain calm, but continued to work at the same pace, refusing to be pressured by the scientist into going faster and potentially making a mistake. Before long, the cranial attachment was securely clamped over Nathan's head and face, covering everything but the man's mouth. It was a hideous affair, with wires sprouting from the top, and crude metal plates clamping the device to Nathan's cranium. If he hadn't known better, Carter would have thought it a medieval torture device, rather than a mechanism through which the man's mind would be transported into a new body.

"We're ready on this end," Cai said.

The Master Operator stepped away from Nathan, who had stopped drumming on his thighs, and was now gripping the wooden arms of the chair. These were scratched and dented, like an antique piece of furniture that had been carelessly moved from house to house over a period of centuries.

"I have already programmed the transfer sequence,"

Nathan said, his voice trembling. "All you have to do is hit the 'Enter' key, and the process will begin."

Cai again looked to him for confirmation, and Carter sighed heavily, rubbing his beard. His senses were telling him that there was risk in what they were about to do, but he didn't need augmented powers of awareness to know that.

"What are you waiting for?" Nathan cried. "Do it now!"

Carter sucked in a deep breath then made his decision. He nodded to Cai, and the Master Operator initiated the mind transference process. The two sections of the ascension conduit clamped shut with a hiss, like a steam locomotive waiting on a station platform. The thrum and whine of the generator began to build, and the glow from the Aternien metal became dazzling. Suddenly, pulses of golden energy coursed between the conduit and the simple chair that Nathan sat in. LEDs on the cranial attachment pulsed like malfunctioning fairy lights, and he saw the scientist's body stiffen, and his hands grip the arms of the chair, as if he were being executed. Then Nathan screamed and the harrowing cry took Carter's breath away and caused Carina to jolt back in surprise and grab his arm. The scientist's fingers bent into claws, and the man's nails dug more grooves into the wood, as his screams continued.

Carina watched, mouth agape, while Cai's expression remained impassive and studious, as if observing the process from a purely academic perspective. After another thirty seconds of agonizing torture for Nathan, the machine finally shut down, and the head-section cracked open again, billowing steam like a factory chimney. Wasting no time, Carter drew his cutlass and climbed onto the ascension conduit, before holding the blade of the weapon to Nathan 2.0's throat. Cai went to the wooden chair, and removed the cranial apparatus from the original Nathan, before checking for a pulse. His officer nodded, confirming that the scientist was still alive, if barely. Then the eyes of the synthetic Nathan opened, and the mannequin-like body sucked in a frantic gulp of air, as if Carter had just pulled a suffocating bag off the man's head. For several seconds the new Nathan Clynes remained frozen, breathing so heavily that he was on the verge of hyperventilating, despite the fact the synthetic being had no functional need to breathe at all. Then, all of a sudden, Nathan 2.0 was overcome with a tranquil calm, and the body stopped breathing completely.

"It worked," Nathan 2.0 said. The man's perfect mouth turned up into a smile. "It worked! I have ascended!" Nathan 2.0 tried to climb out of the seat inside the machine, then felt the edge of Carter's cutlass against the synthetic skin on his neck. "What the fuck are you doing?" he snapped. "Get that thing away from me!"

"Not until you give me what you promised," Carter replied, his tone firm, but measured. There was no need for more excessive threats, not yet.

"I can't do that sat in here, can I?" Nathan 2.0 barked. The strong new body appeared to have also amplified the man's bad attitude. "What you need is in the King's Chamber. So, take that fucking sword away from my throat, and let's get you what you want."

Carter looked at his XO, and she drew her energy pistol and aimed it at the synthetic body. Carter then stepped down off the conduit but kept his cutlass in his hand. Nathan 2.0 glowered at Carter for a couple more seconds, before rising to his feet. At first, his body was trembling, like a newborn fawn taking its first uncertain steps, but the unsteadiness quickly passed. Then Nathan stepped down from the ascension conduit, back straight and chest puffed out like a king about to address his court for the first time.

"How do you feel?" Carina asked, pistol still aimed at the new man's chest.

"I feel like your prisoner," Nathan replied, petulantly. The synthetic man flexed his arms and shoulders, and rolled his head from side to side, before closing his eyes and laughing. However, this was not a typical Nathan Clynes laugh, full of scorn and condemnation, but an uninhibited laugh of unadulterated joy and relief. The man then fixed his bright new eyes onto Carina and smiled, warmly.

"But to answer your question, my dear Major, I feel alive," Nathan said, his words exultant and airy, like a man who had just experienced enlightenment. "It's been so long that I'd forgotten what it was like to feel young and strong, as if no force in the universe could stand against me." The scientist closed his hand into a fist and stared at it, like it was a weapon of mass destruction. "It is intoxicating, Major Larsen. The power. The knowledge. The access… It's all there for the taking."

If Carter's senses had been ambiguous about the risks of creating Nathan 2.0 before, they were crystal clear now. However, what was done was done, and what mattered was getting what he was promised.

"I'm sure this is all very exciting for you, Nathan, but let's move," Carter said, inching closer, blade still poised to strike.

"You can sheath your weapon, Carter," Nathan said. "Unlike you, I am a man of my word." Carter noted the more openly disrespecting tone, a sure sign that Nathan 2.0 no longer feared him, as the frail human version of the scientist had done. "Follow me, I know the way," the man added, smiling.

Nathan 2.0 was about to lead them out of the middle chamber, when the painful groans and wheezes of his original human body made him stop. Cai helped organic Nathan out of the chair and supported him as the man hobbled toward the transcended version of himself.

"Did it work?" Nathan said, his voice gravelly and weak. "Are you… me?"

"Of course, it worked," Nathan 2.0 snapped. "I programmed the process myself, remember?"

Nathan smiled and nodded. "You're right of course," he replied, somewhat deferentially. "So, how does it feel?"

Nathan 2.0 rolled his pristine new eyes. "I already explained how it felt, but you were too busy being weak and pathetic over there," he snapped, speaking to his old self as if the man were an imbecile and an annoyance. "It's not my fault you're decrepit and frail."

Carter considered this an odd thing to say, since it was entirely Nathan's fault that his body was in the condition it was in. It was like Nathan 2.0 had already detached himself from his former life and considered himself distinct from it.

"I'm sorry, the process just took a lot out of me, that's all," the organic Nathan said, holding up his hand to his other self, apologetically. "We can talk about it later."

Nathan 2.0's razor edged stare then softened. The new man approached his old self and placed his arm around Nathan's shoulders. Organic Nathan sagged under the weight of his synthetic self's strong metal frame.

"Of course, we'll talk later," Nathan 2.0 replied, leading the man toward the exit. "You've had an ordeal and need to recover."

Organic Nathan laughed. "Yes, I have. We should compare notes, to understand the process from both sides of…"

Suddenly, Nathan 2.0 grabbed his former self and savagely wrenched his head, snapping the vertebrae in his neck with a sickening crunch. He held the man for a few seconds as the body spasmed and convulsed, the tossed the dead mass of flesh aside like it was garbage.

"What the hell!" Carina cried, backing away from the synthetic human.

It all happened so suddenly that even Carter's senses hadn't managed to alert him, yet within a second, he was behind Nathan 2.0, with his cutlass again pressed to the man's neck. Cai had also drawn his sword and energized the blade ready to attack if necessary.

"Stay where you are," Carter growled, poised to flick the switch on his cutlass and remove Nathan 2.0's head.

"I did what had to be done," Nathan said, sounding unrepentant and even a little bored. "It wouldn't have come as a surprise to him. We both knew that once ascended, the other could not live."

"Just shut up for a goddam second!" Carter snapped. He met Carina's gaze and nodded to the body on the floor. "Check him…"

Carina dropped to her knees beside the body of Nathan Clynes and felt for a pulse, but it was obvious he was dead. The man's head was twisted almost a full one-eighty degrees, and his eyes were bulging out of their sockets.

"I intend to keep my word, Carter," Nathan continued. "You gave me what I wanted, and I will repay the favor. So lower the sword, since we both know you won't strike."

Carter could have dispatched Nathan 2.0 in a heartbeat,

but the galling fact of the matter was that the scientist was right. They'd gone this far, and he had to see it through.

"Move, Nathan," Carter said, using the tip of his cutlass to prod the man in the back. "And don't think that shiny new body of yours makes you my equal. If you cross me, I will kill you."

Nathan turned around and the two men squared off. In the scientist's new form, Nathan was as tall as Carter, as fast as Carter, and arguably just as strong, and the imperious look in the man's synthetic eyes told him he knew this all too well.

"I know I'm not your equal, Master Commander Rose," Nathan said, with a calm, measured delivery that matched his new body's poise. The synthetic man then smiled. "I'm so much more than you are now."

TWENTY
DEAD ENDS

CARTER FOLLOWED Nathan through the Grand Gallery and into the king's chamber, which was situated in the exact center of the pyramid. Major Larsen and Cai were still with him, which he considered to be sufficient backup against one man, even if that man was a newly-ascended super-being with the dangerous-intellect of a depraved genius.

The Grand Gallery had been impressive enough, with its cavernous ceilings, decorated with bejeweled Aternien art, and golden walls lined with statues of Markus Aternus and other Royal Court nobles, but the chamber was on a whole other level. It was like entering a grand opera house, where no expense had been spared to make it the most resplendent place in the universe. Tall pillars in gold and lapis lazuli blue held up another impossibly high ceiling, into which was cut an enormous, ankh-shaped window that allowed what little natural light there was from the gloomy planet to filter inside. There were yet more statues and works of art, all inspired by the ancient Egyptian culture that Markus

Aternus admired most. Then, at the rear of the chamber, across a mirror-polished stone floor, and set in front of a vast window which opened into an Eden-like indoor garden, was a set of a golden steps that led to a throne. Carter could quite imagine the god-king sat there, in front of another giant Ankh, plotting the end of humankind.

"You have to admit that Markus has style," Nathan said, sashaying into the chamber as if he owned the place. "Though, it's a little ostentatious and showy for my tastes," he added, perhaps realizing that he'd inadvertently complimented his rival, and quickly correcting this mistake with a snide remark.

"The garden to the rear of the throne makes me think of the 'Island of Creation'," Carina said. She had been speaking to Carter, but thanks to his new ears, Nathan picked up on everything that was said, and he chose to answer instead.

"Quite right, my dear Major," Nathan said, somehow making the compliment sound condescending. "There is an Egyptian creation myth in which the god, Atum, emerged from the primordial sea of chaos and climbed onto an islet, known as the 'Mound of Creation', from which he created the world and all its inhabitants."

Carter snorted. "I don't know about style, but Markus certainly had delusions of grandeur, that's for damned sure."

Nathan stopped and turned to face him. Carter didn't sense any immediate threat from the man, but he still patted the flat of his cutlass into the palm of his left hand, just to remind the scientist he was wielding it.

"Markus wasn't deluded, Carter, at least not about his aspirations," Nathan said, continuing to be eye-wateringly patronizing. "It's no surprise that he built his own version of the 'Garden of Creation'. In Egyptian mythos, it symbolized the beginning of the world. Order, emerging from chaos." He closed his hand into a fist and shook it. "It represents the power of gods to shape the universe to their will, which is exactly what Markus Aternus has achieved."

"He hasn't achieved it yet," Carter grunted, tiring of the man's pompous lecturing. "Now keep going. I want that information."

Nathan sighed and lowered his hands to his side, though they were still balled into fists. "You should speak to me with more respect," he hissed. "I made you what you are but make no mistake, I am your better now."

"You're still the same self-centered asshole you always were," Carter hit back. "The only change is that now your body is strong." He took a step closer, willing the man to make a move. "But make no mistake, either. I will end you if you step out of line."

The two men continued to stare into each other's eyes for a few more seconds, neither blinking, then Nathan smiled, and huffed a laugh.

"As intriguing as it may be to test that assumption, Master Commander, I have no interest in fighting you," he replied. "I am, and always have been, a man of science, and I won't waste my energies on lesser minds than mine."

With that, he turned and resumed his stately procession toward the throne. Carter followed closely behind, but not so close that the scientist could get the jump on him. Carina and Cai had fanned out to the sides of the vast chamber, both aiming energy pistols at Nathan, and neither one taking their eyes off him for a second. Then the scientist ascended the golden staircase and planted himself on the throne. Carter followed, expecting the man to activate a computer console or other data device, but Nathan simply sat there, soaking in the atmosphere of the spellbinding chamber.

"We're not here so that you can play god-king," Carter said, feeling angry and embarrassed that the man was so effortlessly able to wind him up. "Get my data, before I separate that fancy new head from your fancy new shoulders."

"You really are starting to bore me, Carter," Nathan replied, regarding him like one of his subjects. "But if the delectable Major Larsen will check her comp-slate, you'll discover that I have already given you everything you need."

Carter scowled then glanced over to Carina, who was already accessing her device. Her fingers flashed across the screen for a few seconds then she nodded.

"It looks like it's all here."

"Of course, it's all there," Nathan spat. "What do you take me for?"

Carter descended the golden stairs two at a time and hurried to his XO's side, so that he could also check her comp-slate. Cai arrived a few moments later, but it seemed that his device had not received a similar upload. Carter looked at his own comp-slate, and it too had not received the data.

"Major Larsen will be able to copy the information to your other devices, if that's what you're worried about," Nathan said, correctly perceiving why he and Cai looked a little flustered. "You can't expect me to do everything for you."

"It looks like it's all here, sir," Cai said, quickly assessing the data that Carina had just sent over. "We have the coordinates, and even the jump parameters. Plus, there is what appears to be a detailed map of New Aternus City, including the location of the Soul Crypt and its schematics."

"What about the transponder identification, so we can approach New Aternus without their planetary defenses turning us to atoms?" Carter asked.

"That's here too," Cai replied, nodding appreciatively. "And there's an interface plug-in that will allow me to reprogram the Lapis Lazuli with High Overseer clearance. Using that, I can tie the stone into our ship's systems, and make us appear indistinguishable from a Royal Court Khopesh Destroyer."

"A little more plausible than rocking up as the Kagem-ni, don't you agree?" Nathan said, still sitting on the throne, but now with his legs crossed. "That might have worked here, but not at New Aternus. They know the Kagem-ni was destroyed, so pretending to be that particular Solar Barque would have ended your little adventure very quickly."

Carter stepped away from Cai and Carina and looked up at Nathan, on his perch. The man had been true to his word, and more, but instead of comforting him, this actually made him suspicious.

"You could have withheld that piece of information and let us jump to New Aternus with the Senuset's transponder still active," Carter said. "But instead of allowing us to warp to our deaths, you're actually helping us. Why?"

The scientist laughed; except this time, it was the spiteful, derisory laugh that Carter knew so well. It was the sound of the old Nathan, and his senses immediately shot to high alert.

"I enjoy pointing out other people's failings, as you well know, but the truth is that it really doesn't matter what I give you, because you're never going to reach New Aternus."

Nathan grinned while idly running his finger along the exquisite arm of the throne. "And before you ask, the reason you'll never reach it, is because you're going to die here. All of you."

Carter cursed under his breath then engaged his cutlass and stormed toward the throne, but before he could even set foot on the bottom step, he walked into an energy barrier that knocked him back like a sudden gust of wind. The blast of energy scrambled his thoughts and he lost balance, toppling in an ungainly manner, and landing hard on his back.

"I wouldn't do that again, if I were you," Nathan said. "Unless you want to get cooked, of course."

Suddenly there were hands underneath his body, lifting him up, but Carter's head was still spinning, and he could smell scorched flesh. Touching a hand to the side of his face, he felt the firm ridges of fresh plasma burns.

"Carter, can you hear me?" Carina said, her words distant, like she was speaking through a long tube.

"I'm fine," Carter replied, or at least those were the words he thought he spoke. In truth, he couldn't even hear the sound of his own voice clearly.

There was a brief stab of pain, which was numbed just as quickly, then his head cleared as if it had been dunked into a barrel of ice-cold water. He saw Cai returning a nano-stim capsule to his belt, then peering down at his officer's comp-slate, which was running a bio-scan.

"Ten percent dose, sir, nothing dangerous," Cai was quick to add, knowing that Carter had given himself a stim only hours previously. "Just enough to counteract the effects of the energy field."

Carter nodded his thanks to his Master Operator then

drew his 57-EX revolver and aimed it at Nathan, who was still on the throne, reveling in Carter's downfall.

"Weapons," Carter grunted, taking several paces back to get a cleaner shot at the scientist's head. Cai and Carina both aimed their pistols at the same target. "Fire!"

The report of his revolver drowned out the fizz of the energy pistols, but the onslaught of weapons fire was repelled by the energy barrier, just as effortlessly as Carter had been. He emptied the spent cartridges, loaded five more, and fired again, with the same effect. Nathan was secure in his castle, and worst of all, Carter had put him there.

"You can't stay on that throne forever, Nathan," Carter called out. "Come down and we'll talk about this."

The scientist snorted. "Oh, so now you want to talk? What happened to cutting my head off?" He gestured to the revolver in Carter's hand. "Or shooting it off, for that matter."

"Nathan, this isn't a game," Carter growled. "You're meddling with powers you don't understand."

"That's where you're wrong!" Nathan roared, suddenly springing off his throne and advancing to the edge of the raised dais. "I understand everything, Carter. Everything that Markus Aternus knew, I know. This pyramid and this city are now mine, and you are trespassing. The sentence for that crime is death."

The sound of heavy marching feet, stomping in perfect time, began to drum into the chamber from the Grand Gallery outside, then fourteen Anubi Royal Guardians trooped into the king's chamber and energized their flails.

"Cai, we need another way out of this room," Carter said, hastily reloading his revolver again. He knew that fourteen of the powerful Aternien warriors was more than he, Cai and Carina could handle alone.

Cai worked his comp-slate then shook his head. "There are no other exits that I can see, but there may be a way to reach the south passageways through the Garden of Creation."

"Then let's move!"

The sound of Nathan Clynes laughing followed them as they ran past the throne, and headed for the garden, giving the steps a wide berth to avoid being blasted by the energy barrier.

"Where are you going, Carter?" the scientist called out, sounding unhinged. "You can't get away, but you're welcome to try. My Anubi will hunt you down then bring me your heads!"

Sections of the wall to either side of the king's chamber dropped into the floor, and two Destroyer Immortals were activated. Both stomped out of their sentry posts and immediately turned their glowing eyes to Carter and the others, before clattering after them on their trio of sharp, scorpion-like legs. Every augment Carter possessed powered up to maximum, and every chemical stimulant that his bio-engineered body could produce rushed into his bloodstream. At that moment, he could have a wrestled a kaiju to a standstill, but what was coming for them was even more deadly, and he wasn't fool enough to think he had a chance in hell against the Aternien automatons.

"It's too high!" Carina called out.

She was trying to scramble up the wall to reach the lip of the window that led inside the garden, but it was ten meters above her, and the wall was as smooth as glass.

"Get ready to grab on!" Carter said, gripping Carina by her hips.

"Grab on to what?…"

Her question went unanswered as Carter launched his XO into the air like a rocket. Her arms and legs flailed wildly and she screamed, but through a mixture of good fortune and keen reactions, she caught the lip and managed to drag herself onto the ledge. Carter and Cai then also leaped to the exit, their hyper-dense muscles propelling them like springboards. Both judged the jump with perfect accuracy, and landed beside Carina, who was shaking from the shock of being thrown into the air.

"Cai and I will drop first, then you jump," Carter said, as particle blasts from the Anubi's crooks flashed past.

"Don't you have a parachute or something?" Carina replied, trying to mask her fear with humor, but her body and voice were still trembling.

"I'll catch you; just jump," Carter said. The ten meter drop on the other side was cushioned by the soft grass inside the Garden of Creation, which had somehow been meticulously maintained, despite the occupants of the city having left a long time ago. He backed away from the wall and looked up to see Carina peering down at him. "Jump!" he called up to her. "It's okay, I'll catch you!"

Carina nodded then he saw her take a deep breath and prepare to make the leap, but before she stepped off the ledge, a particle blast thumped into her back, and sent her flying. Carter tried to compensate, but he knew that he wasn't quite going to make it in time. In desperation, he jumped backward, as if making a reverse dive into a swimming pool and managed to scoop his XO into his arms. Moments later, he landed with the full force of her body smashing down on him. He figured he must have blacked out for a second or two, because when his eyes focused again, Cai and Carina were pulling him up by his wrists. Cai plucked the nano-stim from his belt, but Carter waved him off. However bad he was feeling at that moment, another hit from a stim would make him feel ten times worse.

"You should play outfield with hands like that," Carina said.

She was trying to smile, but she was still shaking from adrenalin, and her face was also cut and crazed from being tossed into the undergrowth of the Aternien garden, after rebounding off his chest.

"You're forgetting that I hate games," Carter said, cradling his chest and sides. He figured that he had more broken ribs than intact ones, but he could breathe fine, and he could still run. Then he heard the sound of metal hands clawing against the metal wall, and he could sense that the Anubi were coming. "Keep moving," Carter said, turning into the garden and wading through the lush, tall grasses.

Their progress was swift, but the Anubi were hot on their heels. From their elevated vantage on the window, the warriors rained down particle fire, forcing them to take cover behind trees and ornamental rock structures. With their targets out of sight, the Anubi threw themselves off the ledge and continued their pursuit, like rabid hounds. Carter, Cai and Major Larsen ran hard, finding a patch of neatly mown lawn and picking up speed, but the sound of the Destroyer Immortals dragging their colossal frames over the ledge put paid to any notion that the worst was behind them. The animal-like fighting machines hurled themselves forward, and ploughed through the garden, bulldozing trees, rocks and ornate, Egyptian-inspired garden structures out of their path with terrifying ease.

"Cai, tell me there's a door back here," Carter said, dragging Carina off the ground after she stumbled and fell in a patch of denser grasses.

His Master Operator was silent as he scanned while continuing to run. Because of his plain spoken, plain-faced demeanor, Cai was never an easy man to read, but Carter could tell that he had not found a way out, even before the man announced it to them.

"There is no exit, sir," Cai said, suddenly stopping and drawing his sword. "We have no choice but to fight."

Carter gritted his teeth then drew and energized his cutlass, before sliding his 57-EX out of its holster and offering it to Major Larsen. "Make every shot count," he said, trying to instill within her – and himself – the belief that they were not finished yet.

Carina took the weapon the blew out a shaky sigh, before smiling. "You know, I've always wanted one of these."

Carter grunted a laugh. "Well, I guess today is your lucky day."

With them cornered, the Anubi and the Destroyer Immortals slowed their advance and tightened up their formation. Then Nathan Clynes appeared through a bed of blue iris flowers that seemed to have been genetically modified to reach heights of two meters or more. The Anubi formed an honor guard then began spinning their flails. This created a protective shield that Carter knew could repel any attempts on their part to shoot the man dead.

"At least you get to die in this place of beauty," Nathan said, examining one of the irises as if he were merely taking a Sunday stroll in the park. "After your lifetime of sacrifice, you perhaps deserve that at least."

"You can go to hell, Nathan," Carter grunted. There was no sense trying to negotiate with the man. He'd lost, and they both knew it. "If you're going to kill us then just do it, and let's get this over with."

"As you wish," the scientist replied. The man seemed not to care one way or another whether they lived or died. It was like Carter was beneath him, a lower form of life. Nathan then raised a hand, and the Anubi aimed their crooks.

"We got further than I expected," Carina said. She then took Carter's hand and interlocked her fingers with his. "I don't regret a single second. I want you to know that."

Carter nodded then turned to his Master Operator. More than his own life, he regretted being the cause of Cai's death, because unlike him, Cai would leave people behind; people who loved him.

"I'm sorry, Cai," Carter said.

"I am not, sir," the man replied. "I am proud to do my duty and to serve with you one last time."

"Are you all done?" Nathan said, plucking an iris from its stem and breathing in its scent.

Nathan's casual disregard for their lives was sickening, and also the last straw. In that moment, Carter made a choice to die with his sword held high, rather than be gunned down like a prisoner of war. Summoning all his strength and speed, he released Carina's hand and charged. In the blink of an eye, he was almost within striking distance, and the Anubi could not react fast enough to stop him. He smashed though the shield wall of spinning flails, taking crushing blows to the shoulder as he did so, then plunged the cutlass into Nathan's gut. The man staggered back and pulled the weapon from his synthetic flesh, before cradling the wound, eyes wide and mouth agape. Then Nathan turned to Carter, anger and indignation replacing shock and fear.

"Kill him!" Nathan roared, before staggering into the long grasses and tall flowers. "Kill them all!" his voice came again, this time reverberating off the walls of the garden with the commanding resonance of a church organ.

The next thing Carter knew, he had been beaten to the soft, sweet-smelling grass with energized flails. From the flat of his back he saw four Anubi standing above him, ready to mash his body to a pulp. He could hear Cai and Carina screaming at the top of their lungs for the warriors to stop, but Carter had made his peace, and waited for the end to come.

It didn't.

An explosion ripped open the end wall of the garden and the Anubi were hit by the flying debris and driven back. Carter managed to scramble out from beneath their flails then energy blasts flashed above his head, and the guardians were blown to pieces in a savage barrage of cannon fire. The Destroyer Immortals charged, howling like wild beasts, but were obliterated a split-second later by another precise and devastating volley of energy. Carter didn't know for how long he remained on his back in the cool grasses of the Garden of Creation, listening to the crackling fires of the burning Aternien automatons, but he didn't dare move for fear of stirring whatever had just annihilated the automatons. Suddenly, Carina and Cai scrambled to his side and dropped to a crouch, eyes fixed on a point behind him, where the wall had been blasted open.

"Carter, get up," Carina whispered, still looking into the distance. "We've got company…"

Carter turned over and, with great effort, managed to push himself to his knees. His back hurt like hell, and he knew that bones were broken, but he couldn't worry about his injuries at that moment, because an Aternien Griffin-class Combat Interceptor was hovering toward them, through the chasm in the pyramid wall. A loading ramp opened from beneath the craft's belly, and the ship began to descend until the end of the ramp burrowed a few inches deep into the soft garden soil. A figure emerged, dressed in a black cloak, with the hood pulled up over her head, concealing her face, but Carter could see glowing eyes through the veil of darkness. They were eyes that he'd seen before. The woman then stepped off the ramp and threw back her hood.

"Hello, Master Commander Rose," said Monique Dubois.

TWENTY-ONE
A LIFE DEBT REPAID

CARTER LISTENED TO HIS SENSES, which though clouded because of the pain that was beginning to overwhelm his sensation blockers, did not climb sharply at the sight of the former Overseer, Monique Dubois. That told him that, contrary to the violent method of her arrival, she was not a threat, at least not to them.

"You are probably wondering why I am here," Monique said, walking toward Carter. She was unarmed, or at least not armed with her usual war spear.

"You could say that, Monique," Carter replied, in what was likely the greatest understatement in human history. "But if you're looking for another duel, I'm afraid I'm not at my best."

On Venture Terminal, Monique had helped Carter only in order to secure a fight to the death; a duel which she had intended to lose, in order to escape from the dishonor of failing her god-king, Markus Aternus. However, Carter had refused to kill her, and instead had set her free. He hadn't expected to see the woman again, least of all in the Pyramid of Aternus on her former home world.

"I have no wish to fight you," Monique replied.

"That's good." He managed a weak laugh then propped himself up by stabbing his cutlass into the ground and using it as a crutch. "Because right now I can barely stand."

The former Overseer continued to draw closer, and Cai stepped between them, sword in hand. At the same time, Major Larsen flanked Monique, and aimed Carter's 57-EX revolver at the back of the Aternien woman's head.

"It's okay people, if she'd wanted to kill us, she would have atomized us with that Griffin combat interceptor," Carter said. He indicated to his officers to stand down, and reluctantly, both did.

As an Overseer, Monique Dubois had caused them a world of problems, and it was difficult to view her as anything other than their enemy. However, at that moment, there was nothing remotely threatening about the Aternien warrior. In fact, she appeared calm and peaceful. The former Overseer was looking around the Garden of Creation with the reverie of a Christian seeing the Church of the Holy Sepulchre, or a follower of Judaism visiting the West Wall in Jerusalem.

"Do you know that I never saw this garden before now?" Monique said, enraptured by the space. "Nor was I ever permitted entry into the king's chamber, either here or on New Aternus. Those are privileges reserved only for members of the Royal Court." She laughed. At one time, this would have sounded alien coming from her lips, but now it was as natural as breathing. "It is ironic that, only after my exile, do I finally get to see this sacred place."

Carter was fascinated by the former Overseer, not only in

terms of how she'd serendipitously saved their lives, but in how much she had changed from the iron-clad warrior of the Empire he'd first met on a barren world inside the Piazzi asteroid field. However, they were still in a bad situation, and he didn't have time to indulge whatever it was the Overseer wanted him for.

"Not that I'm ungrateful for you saving my ass, but why are you here, if not to challenge me again?" Carter asked.

"I do not really know," Monique answered, her voice drifting away like pollen in the wind, as she continued to enjoy the garden. "After our last encounter, I found myself lost and without purpose for the first time in my life. Since then, I have been searching, and my search led me back here, to you."

Carter frowned, though even this simple action made his face hurt.

"So, you're telling me that it's just an incredible co-incidence that you happened to blow through the wall of this pyramid, just at the right time to save our skins?"

The question snapped Monique out of her contemplative trance, and she took another step closer to him, so that they were no more than an arm's length apart. It was the closest he'd come to his former adversary, without them trying to kill each other.

"It is no coincidence that I am here," Monique admitted. "When we last spoke, you said that you were giving me the freedom to choose my own path, but that path is not yet open to me, not until my debt is paid. I have been tracking you, watching for an opportunity to repay that obligation, though this is the last place in the galaxy I expected to end up."

"You don't owe me anything, Monique," Carter said. "I didn't spare your life, just so you could be indebted to me."

"That is not how it works, Commander." She spent a moment looking around the garden again, before her eyes returned to his. "I may no longer be part of the Empire, but I am still Aternien, and as you know, our society borrows elements from some ancient Earth cultures, in particular ancient Egypt. We have a concept known as *ma'at*. It is our belief in the importance of harmony and order in the universe. Right now, I am in chaos, and until I find balance, I will never truly be free."

"And you believe that repaying your debt to me will allow you to achieve the balance you seek?" Carter asked, and Monique nodded.

Carter couldn't deny that having her on his team, even temporarily, would be an enormous boost to their chances of getting off Old Aternus alive. However, he was painfully – quite literally, given his current condition – aware that she had already saved his life. To ask more of her would be dishonest.

"You've already helped me enough, Monique, not only by saving us here, but by giving me the lapis lazuli keystone." Carter sighed; aware he was turning away much needed backup. "I'd say that your debt is already paid."

The former Overseer was surprised. "So, you are releasing me?"

Carter smiled and nodded. "You can't lose what you didn't know you had in the first place."

Monique considered his words for a moment, then bowed her head, even taking her eyes off him as a mark of trust and respect. "Then I will take my leave."

She turned her back on Carter and began walking to her

Griffin-class combat interceptor. She was about to pull up her hood and ascend the ramp, when something caused her to stop and look back.

"When I broke through the wall, I saw Anubi Guardians and Destroyer Immortals, but there was someone else too – a man," Monique said. "When I looked at this man, I recognized that part of him was Aternien, but he was also something else. I cannot explain it."

"He's called Nathan Clynes," Carter said, ruing the fact that his desperate attack had not been enough to kill the newly-ascended scientist. "He used the Ascension Conduit in the middle chamber to transfer his consciousness to an Aternien neuromorphic brain. The body he made himself."

Monique's expression shifted from confusion to fear, another emotion he was unaccustomed to seeing on the face of an Aternien, and yet more proof that she was changed.

"This brain that he used, was it alongside the Ascension Conduit?" Monique asked.

"Yes," Carter grunted, and an ominous sense of foreboding swept over him.

"Those were experimental designs, which were superseded and left behind because they were of no further use to the Empire, along with the original Ascension Conduit," the former Overseer explained. "They are unstable, and even dangerous, especially after so long left inactive."

Carter gestured to the wrecked Destroyer Immortals and the bodies of the broken Anubi. "I think it's fair to say that the new Nathan Clynes has been acting a little erratically…"

"It is far more than that," Monique replied, pacing back toward him. "Without intricate adjustments, the mind of anyone who transfers into one of those brains will begin to suffer wild delusions, and dangerous personality defects. Only Markus Aternus himself was capable of making such minute alterations. This Nathan Clynes you speak of could not possibly have understood the risk he was taking."

"I'd say he was desperate," Carter replied, which was the truth. Even if the scientist had known the risks, he doubted it would have stopped the man from proceeding.

"There is more," Monique said, and Carter had a sickening feeling that he already knew what she was going to say. "Those brains were intended only for Markus Aternus. By transferring his soul into them, Nathan Clynes has access to everything on this world that still functions. In effect, he has the power of a god."

Carter sighed and looked at his XO. The scenario that Carina had predicted had come to pass, and it was worse than either of them could have imagined.

"We have to stop him," Carter said, turning back to the former Overseer. "I know I said your debt to me is paid, and it is, but I could really use your help in this." He hobbled closer, still using his sword as a crutch, then held out his hand. "So, as one solider to another, I'm asking for your help. Not because you have to, but because you choose to."

Monique looked at Carter's outstretched hand, and the perfect Aternien skin on her brow furrowed, as if she was trying to access her oldest memories and remember what the gesture meant. Then she clasped her hand around Carter's forearm, and he tightened his grip around hers, and they shook.

"I will help you, Master Commander Rose," Monique said. She looked at Cai and Major Larsen. "I will help you all."

Suddenly, Carter's legs gave way and he started to fall,

but Monique caught him before he hit the ground, and hauled him back to his feet. Cai and Carina were at his side a moment later, and both threw an arm over their shoulders to support him.

"First, your injuries must be treated," Monique said, stepping back and allowing his officers to take the strain.

Carter nodded then removed a nano-stim from his belt but hesitated. He knew that anything more than forty percent would be dangerous, and potentially fatal. Yet, he also knew that forty percent wouldn't be enough to heal the critical injuries that were killing him more rapidly than his body could self-repair. Reluctantly, he turned the stim to eighty percent, and pressed the injector to his neck. However, before he could depress the plunger, Monique snapped the device out of his hand, and tossed it over her shoulder, like an empty snack packet.

"What the hell are you doing, lady?" Carina snapped. If she hadn't been supporting his sizable mass at the moment, Carter wouldn't have put it past his XO to have popped Monique in the mouth. "If he doesn't get that stim, he'll die!"

"If he administers those crude nano-machines, he will still die," the former Overseer replied, coolly. "The only difference is that his death will be agonizing, and slow."

"Do you have a better idea?" Carter asked. At that moment, he was willing to try prayer, but he was hoping that the Aternien had something more physical in mind. Then, ironically as if in answer to his appeal, Monique nodded, and gestured for them to follow her.

"Come with me," she said, heading back to her ship. "There is a way."

Monique led them inside the combat interceptor, which

was little different to the layout of a Union ship, ignoring the golden accents and Aternien hieroglyphics that were used in place of English-language characters. The former Overseer hadn't explained where they were going, but the journey turned out to be remarkably swift. She simply piloted the craft across the garden, and into the king's chamber, setting the interceptor down in front of the throne, with its guns aimed at the exit into the Grand Gallery. Despite the brief transit, by the time Cai and Carina had helped him down the ramp of the Aternien craft, he was weaker than ever. Carter was no stranger to injury, and during the first war he had even sustained what would have been a critical wound, even for an augmented Longsword officer such as himself. The difference at that time was that he had access to the Galatine's specially-configured medical bay, and the ship's Master Medic, Rosalie Moss. Isolated on a foreign planet, without access to either of those advantages, his chances were not good, and everyone knew it.

"Carry him to the throne," Monique said, running up the stairs ahead of them. She then abruptly stopped half-way and stretched out her hand to Carter. "My lapis lazuli – the keystone – do you still have it?"

Carter nodded then tried to fish the stone out of his jacket pocket, but his coordination was shot, and he simply fumbled around in the general area, unable to locate it. Carina stepped in, and thrust her hand into his pocket, causing Carter to gasp with pain as she inadvertently punched his ruptured kidney. A moment later the stone was in her hand, then flying through the air as she tossed it to Monique, who caught it delicately between thumb and forefinger. The former Overseer continued to race up the steps, as the lapis lazuli glowed in her hand, like a bottled firefly. Then, when she reached the dais and opened her hand again, the stone was gone, absorbed into her body like sunlight.

"Set him down on the throne," Monique said. The Aternien caressed her fingers across the right arm of the golden seat, with the elegance of a concert pianist. Hieroglyphs flashed into life as she did so, fading to nothing a moment later, despite the fact that the arm had appeared smooth and featureless prior to her touch. At the same time, Cai and Major Larsen set Carter down, and he flopped into the throne, striking his head on the unforgiving metal back of the regal seat, and causing yet more pain to shoot through his body.

"No offence, but I hope you're not about to turn me into one of you," Carter wheezed, struggling to keep his eyes open. Blood soaked his uniform, spilling out of his body more quickly than his bio-engineered bone marrow could replace.

"Nothing so dramatic," Monique replied. "But while our synthetic bodies are hardy and resistant to decay, they are not immune to it. To ensure that we remain pristine, we use a form of nano-regenerative therapy, not dissimilar to your nano-stims, but without the debilitating side-effects."

Carter coughed a laugh. "If I'd known that a century ago, I might have signed up to join you golden bastards."

Carina laughed and even Cai cracked a smile, both appreciating his gallows humor. It simply wouldn't do to meet his end, grimly contemplating his life and regrets. If he was going to die, he'd die the way he'd lived – on his terms, for better or worse.

"Step back, please," Monique said.

Carina and Cai did as they were instructed, then

Monique entered a final sequence into the arm of the throne, before also stepping away. Then a pyramid-shaped object began to descend from the high ceiling directly above where he was seated, and a beam of golden light erupted from the tip, like a laser. At first, the beam struck only the top of his head, before expanding to envelop the entire throne. Carter had no idea how it must have appeared to the others, watching from the outside, but engulfed in the stream of energy, he imagined it was like being inside a womb. He was protected, fed and warm, and entirely oblivious to anything that was happening beyond his golden cocoon. As he waited, held in place by a mysterious force, he could feel life returning to his body. Organs were repaired, nerves regrown, and bones fused back together, and all without any of the agonizing pain that came with a nano-stim injection. On the contrary, it was blissful, like standing under a hot shower in a steam-filled bathroom, then looking up into the flowing water and allowing it to massage your face and soothe away your aches and pains. Then the beam shut off, and it was like being awakened from a deep sleep by your bedside alarm blaring an ungodly screech at maximum volume. Carter gripped the arms of the chair, molding them beneath his grasp as if the Aternien metal was soft clay. He took a breath of air, and his chest no longer hurt. He felt no pain at all. In fact, he'd never felt stronger in his entire life.

"Monique, name your price, but I have to have one of these," Carter said, standing up from the throne and feeling ten-feet tall.

"I will have a word with the god-king, when I next see him," Monique replied.

Carter looked at her in disbelief, as did Cai and Carina.

Then his XO burst out laughing and jostled the Aternien on the shoulder.

"You just told a joke!" Carina said, still jostling the Overseer, who appeared too shocked by the sudden physical contact to do anything other than allow it. "There's hope for you yet, Monique," she added, finally pulling away.

Suddenly, the pyramid shook, and the mood altered like a changing wind. Carter checked his comp-slate and detected an energy surge coming from the very top of the giant structure. Monique darted to his side and adjusted the scan readings to clear up the signal, her expression becoming more urgent by the second.

"Nathan Clynes is attempting to escape," Monique said, rushing down the steps toward her vessel. "Quickly, we do not have much time."

They all piled into the compact Griffin-class interceptor, and Monique steered the vessel back across the garden, before punching out into the open, through the same hole that she'd blasted into the wall. She established some distance from the structure, then looped around and aimed the nose of the craft at the golden summit of the great pyramid. At the same time, the diamond-tip detached from the main structure, and began rocketing skyward, flames roaring from an engine that had been concealed in its base.

"That is an Abydos," Monique said, answering the question Carter was about to ask. "It is – it was – Markus Aternus' personal yacht."

"Is it jump capable?" Carter asked, as Monique climbed in pursuit of the craft, but the interceptor lacked the thrust to keep pace with it. "If it is, we have to shoot it down before Nathan can go to warp. It's too dangerous to let him loose with that brain in his head."

Monique nodded then activated the targeting systems, and a golden reticule lit up over the top of the pyramid-shaped vessel, which was getting smaller by the second. She rested her thumbs on the triggers and fired, sending shards of particle energy tearing through the dark, rain-soaked sky, but the blasts of energy hit only empty air. The Abydos had already jumped.

TWENTY-TWO
PLAN OF ATTACK

THE ENTRY RAMP of the Griffin-class Combat Interceptor hit the deck inside the Galatine's shuttle bay, and Carter stepped off the Aternien vessel and onto more familiar terrain. Major Larsen and Cai followed soon after, then Monique Dubois also alighted. Brodie Kaur was waiting in the shuttle bay, and Carter could see the man's hulking muscles twitch as their former enemy walked freely aboard the Union's most powerful warship. However, a quick look from him told his Master-at-arms that all was well, and Brodie took no action.

"Thanks for the lift," Carter said, as the Griffin's loading ramp closed, and the shuttle bay's conveyor system began to maneuver the craft onto the vacant launch pad, next to Cai's shuttle. "And thanks for fixing me up too. I'd say that more than makes us even. In fact, I owe you a debt, so if ever you find your *ma'at* out of balance again, feel free to look me up."

Monique smiled and bowed her head. "Thank you, Master Commander."

"Call me Carter," he replied, gently squeezing her shoulder. "After all, we're friends now, right?"

Monique considered this then smiled and nodded. "Yes, I believe we are."

"So, what will you do now?" Major Larsen asked.

It was a good question, Carter thought. After all, he doubted there were many opportunities within the Union of Nine for a former Aternien Overseer. Given that a century of ingrained fear and suspicion of posthumans still affected his relationship with 'normies', as Kendra Castle liked to call regular humans, he couldn't see Monique being accepted, at least not any time soon. And nor could she go back to the Empire.

"I will remain here, on Old Aternus," Monique said. It sounded like she'd already given the matter some thought. "It was my home once before and it can be again. Perhaps, it may even become a refuge for Aterniens, like me, who find their *ma'at* out of balance. Certainly, if you succeed in your campaign against the god-king, a great many will question his divinity."

"Many, like you?" Carter asked. He was curious to learn just how much Monique had changed, and she considered her answer carefully, before responding.

"It will take me some time to reconcile my beliefs, but it is safe to say that I no longer aspire to the Aternien Royal Court," the former Overseer replied. "Where that leaves me right now, I cannot say."

"It leaves you free to do whatever you want," Carter said, confidently. "And maybe that makes you even more special than Markus Aternus." He smiled. "Just don't let it go to your head. We don't need a god-queen, as well as a god-king."

Monique raised a perfect eyebrow. "I hadn't considered that possibility, so thank you for suggesting it."

Carina laughed. "See? She's a natural bullshit-artist, just like me!"

"No-one does it at well as you, Major," Carter grunted, shooting her a disproving look.

Monique then offered Carter her hand, and they clasped wrists, just as they had done in the Garden of Creation inside the Pyramid of Aternus.

"Goodbye, Carter," Monique said.

"Goodbye, Monique," he replied, their grip still firm.

The former Overseer then offered her hand to Carina, but instead of shaking hands, she pulled the Aternien woman in for an embrace. Monique froze and tensed up, but Carina didn't relax her grip and soon the former Overseer relaxed into the hold, and finally reciprocated the hug.

"You saved us, and helped us when you didn't have to," Carina said, drawing back. "In my book, that makes you okay."

Monique bowed her head. "I never imagined that I would ever say this to a human, but I think you are 'okay' too, Carina Larsen."

"Take care of yourself, Monique," Carina said, slapping her shoulder and unbalancing her for a moment.

"And you also, Carina."

The Aternien stepped back two paces, then bowed to them both. It seemed that she was about to turn and leave, but Carter could sense there was still something on Monique's mind.

"Assuming you still intend to destroy the Soul Crypt, you should know that it is shielded against any form of attack," Monique said. "To end Aternien immortality, you will first need to destroy its source of power. Look North of the Great City, to a reservoir, and there you will find what you need."

"Thank you again, but I hope that by telling us this, you aren't compromising your oath?" Carter replied.

"Believe me, I am not doing you any favors by encouraging this course of action," Monique said. She paused, appearing deep in thought. "But what the god-king is doing is wrong. We are not so unalike, you and I. And in time, perhaps all Aterniens will realize this."

Carter bowed, taking his eyes off Monique as a mark of trust and respect; the same respect that she had shown him. Then the Aternien boarded her Griffin-class interceptor, and Carter nodded to Brodie, who operated the controls to lower the craft into the launch tube. The upper bay door closed and the lights went green.

"Aternien combat interceptor, you are clear to launch," Brodie said, over the comm channel.

"Acknowledged, Galatine, I am clear to launch," the Aternien replied on the same channel. "Our bond is immortal. Our bond is forever. Farewell."

The outer shuttle bay door opened and the sleek Aternien craft raced out of the launch tunnel, then arced around the Galatine and set a course toward Old Aternus. Carter and Carina watched on the screens inside the bay, until the ship was nothing more than a dot. Then it was gone.

Carter's comp-slate chimed and he saw it was his Master Operator calling. Cai had gone straight from the shuttle bay to the briefing room to start planning their attack on New Aternus. He figured that the man had already made significant headway, given that he'd not stopped working on his comp-slate during their entire return journey from the planet to the Longsword.

"Carter here, what's your status, Cai?"

"I believe I have a strategy, sir," the Master Operator replied, proving Carter correct. "If you are available now, I can give you a short briefing."

"Brodie, the major and I will there in a few minutes," Carter replied. "Ask Amaya to join us too, I want her to double-check Nathan's jump parameters, to make sure the slippery eel hasn't programmed a course into the middle of a black hole."

"Copy that, sir, Cai replied. "I would suggest also inviting HARPER, so he can provide input on our engine and Soliton warp drive status. The jump to New Aternus will need to be completed with absolute precision, so as to arrive at an allotted junction point."

"Agreed, ask him to join," Carter said. "And I hope this briefing will also include what the hell 'junction points' are," he added, conscious that this was the first time he'd ever heard the phrase.

"I will explain everything, sir," the Master Operator replied. "Cai, out."

Brodie locked down the shuttle bay control systems then joined him and Major Larsen as they entered the long central corridor, headed toward the briefing room.

"Speaking of Nathan, do you think he'd alert Markus to what we're planning?" Carina asked, as they walked.

Carter had wondered about this too, but the truth was he didn't have an answer for his XO. Nathan was unpredictable at the best of times but considering what Monique had said about the fragile condition of the neuromorphic brain inside Nathan 2.0's head, and the fact the ascension process had likely not been perfectly configured, he was even less sure what the scientist would or would not do.

"We'll have to go ahead, assuming he hasn't alerted the Aterniens," Carter said, which wasn't so much an answer to Carina's question, as an answer to the follow up question of what they do next. "But if we warp into Aternien space and find a thousand Khopesh Destroyers aiming their cannons at us, then I figure it will be pretty clear he talked."

Carina snorted a laugh. "So, I guess we're flying on a wing and a prayer?"

"It certainly looks that way," Carter admitted. "But the greater the risk, the greater the reward. The Soul Crypt is a prize too valuable to ignore."

Carter reached the door to the briefing room first, and it opened as he approached. Cai, Amaya and HARPER were already inside, standing around the briefing table, above which was a holo image of a planet that he assumed was New Aternus.

"Let's have it, Cai," Carter said, bustling to the head of the table. "How do we pull this off, and live to tell the tale?"

His Master Operator jumped into gear and worked the comp-slate built into the briefing table. The holographic planet vanished and was replaced by a three-dimensional star map. One in particular was highlighted, and there was something oddly familiar about it and the surrounding stars, Carter thought.

"Thanks to the information Nathan provided, we now know that New Aternus is located on a planet close to a star named Alnilam," the Master Operator began. "As viewed from Terra Prime, this is the central star of Orion's Belt, in the constellation Orion."

"I thought that configuration of stars looked familiar,"

Carina commented, evidently thinking the same thing as Carter.

"Alnilam is a blue supergiant, approximately 2,000 light-years from Terra Prime, and one of the brightest stars in the Terra Prime sky," Cai continued. "Prior to the establishment of the colony worlds, the Union sent out thousands of unmanned probes to search for habitable worlds. However, that region was never considered, since there were literally thousands of better options."

"Smart," Carter grunted. "Aternus knew we'd never go looking out there, so he could hide in plain sight."

Cai nodded. "The brightness of the star also makes it difficult for warp-based telescopes to observe that area of space, which helps to keep New Aternus concealed from view."

"There's another reason why they chose Orion's belt," Carina cut in, and all eyes turned to her. As their resident Aternien expert, she could often provide insight the others lacked. "The ancient Egyptians associated Orion with the god Osiris, who amongst other things was the god of fertility and resurrection."

Carter grunted a laugh. "I can see why he might choose to base New Aternus out there. It fits with the god king's ideals."

The Master Operator worked the comp-slate again, and the holographic image of the planet Carter had seen upon first entering the briefing room replaced the star map.

"This is New Aternus," Cai continued. "Other than its location, what's interesting about this planet is that, unlike Old Aternus, it cannot sustain human life. This not only means it would be of a zero interest to the Union, but it also protects it from potential retaliatory strikes. Instigating a ground invasion would be challenging, to say the least, without breathable air."

"Okay, so they don't want us to pay a visit; that's understandable," Carter said, keen to move on to the crux of the briefing. "But we're coming anyway, and I need to know how to strike our target and get away again without the Galatine being atomized in the process."

Cai nodded then replaced the image of the planet with an image of an Aternien city, not dissimilar to one they'd recently left on Old Aternus, but considerably larger.

"This is New Aternus City, which alone is home to eighty million Aterniens," the Master Operator went on. "It is only one of many such cities, but it has the distinction of being the location of the new Pyramid of Aternus."

The image zoomed in and the structure was revealed in exquisite detail. It was even more stunning than the pyramid on Old Aternus and looked like it had been made from solid gold, adorned with bright blue jewels that must have been the size of paving slabs. The image then swept North and focused on another structure that was equally as grand as the pyramid of Aternus, which in itself was an indication of its importance. The second building was built in a hexagon shape and towered hundreds of meters above the golden roads that ran through the gleaming city. Each face of the hexagon was split into hundreds of pyramid-shaped sections, as if the building was constructed from tens or hundreds of thousands of smaller building blocks, like the interlocking plastic construction toys that children played with. Most striking of all, however, was the face built into the front of the building, which itself was over two hundred meters tall, and immediately recognizable as the visage of Markus Aternus, the god-king.

"I take it that's the Soul Crypt?" Carter said, asking the question, even though it seemed obvious.

"Yes, sir, that is our target," Cai replied.

"It's certainly big," Brodie spoke up. The Master-at-arms had been quietly taking in all the information, but all he really cared about was what he needed to shoot at, and how much firepower he'd need to deploy in order to destroy his target. "So long as we can get close enough, it won't be hard to hit."

Carter nodded. "First, we need to take out the shield that protects the crypt from exactly the kind of bombardment we're planning."

Cai worked the controls, and the image panned out and moved further North, beyond the city limits. The reservoir that Monique had told them about was exactly where it was supposed to be, and in the center was a manufactured island that housed a vast reactor complex. Unlike the structures in the city, however, it was unassuming to look at, lacking the regal splendor of the pyramids and Soul Crypt.

"Are we sure that's the power source?" Brodie asked. "It doesn't look like much."

"I'd say that's the point," Carter replied. "They didn't want to paint a crosshair on this thing, so they built it away from the city, and made it look as ordinary as possible. If it weren't for Monique's tip-off, I don't think any of us would have considered this a potential target."

Carter waited to see if anyone challenged his assumption, paying particular attention to his XO, whom he fully expected to make a wise-ass remark. However, to his surprise and delight, she was keeping a lid on her bullshit-artistry, at least for the moment.

"Amaya, what about the jump parameters that Nathan

gave us?" Carter asked. He was satisfied that they had their targets; now he needed to know if they could make it to New Aternus in one piece.

"The parameters check out, skipper, though I've made a few refinements," the Master Navigator replied. "There isn't much more I can do, though, since the entry points into the New Aternus system are strictly governed. If we jump in too far out of position, a thousand big guns will spoil our day in pretty short order."

Carter remembered Cai talking about "junction points", and he figured that this was what his Master Navigator was referring to. As if he'd read his mind, the Master Operator quickly jumped in to the clarify this point.

"What Amaya is referring to are the set locations within the orbital sphere of New Aternus that are permitted entry points into the system," Cai explained. "They are referred to as junction points, but essentially, they are gateways. So long as we arrive exactly within a junction point, we should be able to progress without attracting any attention. To the automatons guarding these gateways, the Galatine will simply appear as a Khopesh-class Destroyer."

Carter nodded and rubbed his silver beard, remembering how Nathan had advised against them impersonating the Solar Barque Kagem-ni, since the weapons platforms surrounding New Aternus would recognize that vessel had been destroyed during the first war, blowing their cover in an instant. For all the trouble the scientist had caused them, he had at least proved useful in some respects.

"And are we in fit shape to make this jump?" Carter asked, directing the question to the bright-yellow labor bot. "I'm conscious that we took a pounding on the way in, and that the Galatine isn't in the best shape."

"The Galatine is functioning at ninety-two percent efficiency," HARPER replied, sounding proud to be able to announce this. "I have focused on ensuring that weapons, shields, and engines are in perfect working order. We are all set to jump."

"This is good, and it will get us through the door, but once we start tearing through the atmosphere and blowing stuff up, the Aterniens will come after us with everything they've got," Carter said. "We might be able to pull off destroying the Soul Crypt, but we'd never make it out alive. And, I don't know about all of you, but I'd very much rather make it out alive."

The room was in silent agreement, then Carina smiled and snapped her fingers.

"You have the look of a woman with an idea?" Carter said, casting his XO a sideways glance, while stroking his beard.

"What we need is a distraction," Carina said. "And I'm thinking that a few hundred Union warships dropping in unannounced might just do the trick."

Carter smiled. "If we only we knew someone who was closely related to the Flag Admiral of the Fleet, and who had her ear…"

Carina smiled and flashed her eyes. "If only…"

TWENTY-THREE
THE BRIEFING

THE GALATINE COMPLETED the long jump back to Terra Prime, and Carter felt the pulsating beat of their Soliton warp drive rapidly diminish to nothing. Ahead of them was Station Alpha, the beating heart of Union military operations, and their next destination. Warships ranging from diminutive corvettes to leviathan battlecruisers were swarming around the outpost like bees around a hive, and hundreds more vessels loomed in orbit of the planet, or in patrols clustered nearby. It was the largest concentration of ships that Carter could ever remember seeing at Terra Prime, even during the height of the first conflict. Through a combination of cunning strategy and military might, the Aterniens had brought the war to humanity's doorstep, and they were on the verge of smashing their way in.

"Jump complete, all systems nominal," Amaya called out.

"Cai, is our transponder reading correctly?" Carter asked his Master Operator. "I don't want Admiral Krantz thinking we're the Solar Barque Kagem-ni, or a Khopesh destroyer, and sending an entire fleet to gun us down."

"I was also concerned about that, so rest assured I am transmitting our Union ID," Cai replied, swiftly setting his mind at ease. "I have also transmitted our request to dock at Station Alpha, and to meet with Admiral Krantz at her earliest convenience."

Carter grunted his appreciation of Cai's efficiency, then allowed himself to relax back into his chair. However, while his body was at ease, his mind was far from calm. He knew he was about to ask a lot of the admiral, perhaps more than he could reasonably expect her to give, but he needed to make his case as watertight as possible. Wars could be won or lost in a single engagement, and his senses told him that they were about to get their chance. It might be their last.

"Amaya, make our way to Station Alpha, best possible speed," Carter said.

"Aye, sir, main engines engaged," his Master Navigator replied.

The Galatine's thunderous propulsion system drove them forward, but they hadn't gone far before a message came through from Station Alpha. Carter saw it flash up on the comp-slate built into his chair, and noted that it was encrypted, and on a secure channel.

"Message from Admiral Krantz directly, sir," Cai reported. "She orders us to hold position and prepare for her arrival."

Carter frowned. "Where is she arriving from?" The tactical console and his comp-slate both chirruped, but JACAB was ahead of the game, and pre-empted Carter's upcoming request by projecting an image of the new vessel from his holo emitters. He recognized it at once as an ambassador-class executive shuttle – Admiral Krantz's preferred mode of travel, outside of her battlecruiser, the Dauntless.

"A shuttle just launched from Station Alpha, and is on an intercept course," Brodie confirmed. "It's not broadcasting a transponder ID, and there was also no flight plan logged with the station, but it's coming in hot. If I didn't know any differently, I'd say Amaya was flying that thing."

The Master Navigator swiveled her seat to face the tactical station. "Is that a compliment or a criticism? I can't tell."

Brodie smiled. "I suppose it's a bit of a both. Your driving was always a little sporty for my tastes."

Amaya snorted. "A big strong guy like you should be able to handle a little speed."

"Hey, I can handle it," the Master-at-arms hit back. Even the slightest challenge would have Brodie beating his chest like an ape. "I just prefer to cruise, is all."

Amaya smiled. "That's cute. My grandma also liked to cruise…"

The competitive interplay between Brodie and Amaya had always been a staple part of life on the Galatine, and as much as Carter enjoyed seeing them at it again, they had more important matters to handle.

"Why don't you agree to disagree on this occasion," Carter cut in, before his Master-at-arms could fire back a retort. "Amaya, all stop. Brodie, prepared the shuttle bay for an arrival."

"Aye, aye, skipper," Amaya replied, playfully scowling at Brodie.

"You got it MC," Brodie added, returning Amaya's scowl with a pouty frown.

While his officers got to work, Carter turned to his XO. "Are you ready for this?" he asked, keenly aware of his own apprehension. "We need your aunt's buy in, or we're sunk before we even set sail."

Carina smiled. "Hell no, I'm not ready, but it'll be fine. You have more sway with Clara Krantz than I think you realize."

"Let's hope so," Carter grunted. He got out of his seat and his XO rose alongside him. "Brodie, once the admiral has docked, please escort her to the briefing room." He then looked around the bridge at his other officers. "I need everyone in there, including HARPER."

There was another swift round of acknowledgements, then Carter headed off the bridge to make the short walk to the briefing room. Cai and Amaya followed shortly after, and the hulking seven-foot frame of HARPER stomped in a few minutes later, nodding and waving to everyone as he ducked under the doorframe. The bot and his officers took up position to his rear, ready to snap to attention as soon as the admiral arrived. While they waited, Carter noticed that Major Larsen was anxiously drumming her fingers on her thighs, which normally would have driven him to distraction. However, his mind was similarly preoccupied, working up variations of what he might say to Krantz, while also trying to predict how she'd respond, and the questions she might ask. The admiral had demonstrated on numerous occasions that she wasn't afraid to make tough calls, but he also knew that his next request overshadowed anything he'd asked of Krantz before, and he genuinely wasn't sure if she'd go for it. Finally, after what seemed like an age, the door opened and Admiral Krantz walked in. Everyone came to attention, including HARPER, who did so a little belatedly, since he was still getting used to Union military protocol.

"At ease, people," Krantz said.

The admiral hauled herself to the briefing table and dropped heavily into one of the waiting chairs. There were dark circles around her eyes and she looked physically exhausted, as if she hadn't slept for days. She then rolled up the right sleeve of her uniform, and Carter winced at the sight of dozens of puncture marks, left over from the test device that determined human from Aternien infiltrator.

"It's okay, Admiral, I think we can take it on trust that you're who you say you are," Carter said, as Krantz removed a testing device from a stow on her belt.

"Protocol is protocol," Krantz replied, pressing the device to an area of less perforated skin, and squeezing the trigger. There was a hiss and thud, like a crossbow firing, and Krantz physically flinched, clenching her teeth together as the needle sampled her bone and bone marrow. A few moments later, the device registered a negative result, proving what Carter had already known; she was human.

"I can't wait for the tech boffins to come up with a version of this thing that doesn't hurt like a sonofabitch," Krantz added, replacing the device onto her belt. "And don't worry about you and your officers; if I can't trust you to be who you say you are, then we really are screwed."

"I'll do it still," Major Larsen said.

She unhooked the device from her aunt's belt, and the admiral protested fleetingly, but she was too tired to put up a real fight. Carina then rolled up her sleeve and took a sample. Like Admiral Krantz, she flinched as the needle penetrated her bone, and Carter heard the sharp intake of breath that accompanied the brief, but intense stab of pain.

"Oh good, I'm human," Carina said, handing the device back to her aunt. "After being locked up, unconscious, in Nathan Clynes' dungeon for several days, it's actually quite comforting to have it confirmed."

The mention of Clynes did not go unnoticed by Admiral Krantz, and Carter could tell she was parking questions about the fate of the scientist for later. However, Nathan was not the reason he'd asked to meet her, and she was perceptive enough to realize this.

"I read your report, Commander Rose," Krantz began, crossing her legs and placing her hands delicately on her knee. "I read it three times, in fact, since I didn't believe it the first two times, and honestly, I was still unsure after the third."

"I realize it's a lot to take in," Carter said. He didn't want to add anything further yet, until he'd gauged the admiral's mood.

"A lot to take in, you say?" Krantz laughed, weakly. "For quite some time, I got stuck at the part where you found the original human body of Markus Aternus, still alive and in stasis in the bowels of a great pyramid. I didn't think you could top that, until I read how you helped Nathan Clynes to 'ascend' to a new body, using a neuromorphic brain intended for the god-king himself. Then I read the part how you were rescued from certain death by a former Aternien Overseer, who then magically healed you, only for 'Nathan 2.0', as your report charmingly describes him, to warp into the unknown in a golden, pyramid-shaped spacecraft."

Carter winced, as if he too had been stabbed with Admiral Krantz's detection device. "When you put it like that it does sound a little far-fetched," he admitted, sheepishly. "But we at least got what we went for. The location of New Aternus, and the information we need to destroy the Soul Crypt."

Krantz was silent for a time, staring intensely at him, as if attempting to read his thoughts through the gateway of his own eyes. Like himself, Carter suspected the admiral was running through a thousand possible scenarios for why he'd asked to meet, though he figured she'd already correctly guessed some time ago.

"I need a drink," Krantz said, looking for a trolley or drinks counter in the briefing room, but the Galatine was not stocked with such excesses.

"I'm afraid we can't help you there, Admiral," Carter said. "Though there might be something in the stores."

HARPER then stepped out of the corner of the room, and Krantz almost fell backward off her chair as the yellow machine stomped toward her. It seemed that in her brain-addled state, she hadn't noticed the bot upon first entering the room.

"Who the hell are you?" the admiral demanded.

"I am HARPER," the bot replied, a little crestfallen that his approach had been met with such an aggressive response. "I am, in effect, the ship's new engineer."

"We recruited him on Gliese 832-e, at the same time we picked up Major Larsen," Carter explained. He considered going into more detail, but it would simply have opened up a can of large and particularly wriggly worms. "It's probably best we don't go into it here."

Krantz cocked an eyebrow at Carter but took his advice and didn't pursue the matter any further. HARPER then proceeded to open a vault-like compartment in his abdomen, and remove a stainless-steel hip flask, which he offered to the admiral.

"What's this?" Krantz asked. She opened the cap and sniffed the contents. "Smells like moonshine."

"I distilled it myself on Gliese 832-e from a tall, perennial grass akin to sugarcane," HARPER replied. "Nathan made me carry it around, in case he needed 'a quick tipple'. He used to call it, 'Good shit', which I understood to mean it was pleasurable to drink."

Krantz shrugged, wiped the neck of the flask on her tunic, then took a swig from the cannister. Carter understood that the admiral liked a drink every now and again, but the content of the hip flask took her breath away.

"He was right," Krantz said, barely managing to wheeze out the words. "It is good shit."

HARPER couldn't physically smile, though the subtle alteration in the tint and flicker of his eyes suggested the bot was pleased with the review. Krantz then replaced the cap on the flask, and set it onto the briefing table, though still within easy reach, should the need take her again. The powerful alien liquor appeared to have given her courage enough to ask the 64,000-dollar question.

"Okay, Commander, what is it that you need?" Krantz asked.

"I need five hundred ships," Carter replied, choosing to get to the point, without any preamble, while the effects of the liquor persisted. To his surprise, Krantz did not recoil at hearing this number, so he continued with his request at flank speed. "This armada will warp into the vicinity of New Aternus, beyond the range of its defense grid, and draw the enemy out. At the same time, the Galatine will jump into orbit of the planet, arriving at a pre-defined junction point, and posing as a Khopesh-class destroyer. Taking advantage of your distraction, we will then proceed planetside, destroy the Soul Crypt's power source, thus rendering the crypt's shield inoperable, and destroy the target. If all goes to plan, we'll be in and out again, before Markus Aternus can even say, 'immortal'."

He could have given a more detailed briefing, making use of the holo emitter in the table, and that remained an option, but he wanted to place all his cards on the table first, and hope the admiral believed he had a winning hand. For several painful seconds, she said nothing, while drumming her fingers on the table in the same irritating manner that her niece was partial to doing.

"While you've been away, the Aterniens have been conducting constant hit and run attacks, destroying our planetary defenses, and whittling down our forces one ship at a time," Krantz said. She sounded angry, though it wasn't anger directed at him. "They don't sleep, and they don't stop. Already, half of our personnel are running on fumes, and the other half isn't far behind. We're in a bad way, Commander, and already it's touch-and-go whether we can still repel an invasion force from striking Terra Prime and landing a bio-genic weapon." She stopped tapping on the table and pushed herself out of the chair. "And you're asking me for five-hundred ships?

"I am, Admiral," Carter replied. He had expected to meet resistance and was prepared to fight it. "This could be our last chance to change the direction of this war. Our only chance."

Krantz sighed and rubbed her eyes, which only served to make them look puffier and more bloodshot.

"You don't even know for sure that this target exists," Krantz continued, now more exasperated than angry. "And even if it does, you don't know for sure that destroying the

Soul Crypt will be enough to bring Aternus to the negotiating table."

"I appreciate that, but I asked the former Overseer, Monique Dubois, if destroying the crypt would make Aternus think twice, and she said, 'More than you could possibly know…'."

"And you trust this Aternien?" Krantz hit back.

Carter nodded. There was no doubt in his mind. "Yes, Admiral. We've been through a lot together."

Krantz blew out a heavy sigh and shook her head, then snatched the hip flask, and took another long draw from it.

"I know it's a risk, Admiral, but I wouldn't be here if I didn't think it was the only way."

"You're asking me to send more than half of our remaining defense fleet into the heart of enemy territory, on the word of a former Aternien officer and traitor."

Carter resisted the urge to snap back a reply, knowing that it would only escalate into an argument. And when you argue with an admiral, you invariably lose. Instead, he sucked in a deep breath, and chose a different approach. One he hoped would hammer the message home.

"Admiral, you said it yourself; the fleet is in bad shape," Carter said, speaking calmly. "The Aterniens won't stop. They'll come at us again, and again, and again, until eventually, probably sooner than we realize, they will break through. And if that happens, we lose everything." He took a step closer to Krantz, who didn't take her eyes off him for a second. "And I don't know about you, but I don't like losing."

Krantz sighed and shook her head again, though this time she wasn't questioning the sanity of Carter's plan, but the wisdom of her own decision. He could see it in her eyes; he'd won her over.

"The president will never go for this, and the senate would debate it until the Aterniens stormed the Capitol building, put them all against the wall, and shot them dead," Krantz said. She then shrugged. "But what the hell, we're going to do it, anyway."

Carter felt a rush of excitement that was so powerful, he thought his blood was about to boil inside his veins. Krantz took another swig from the flask then handed it back to HARPER.

"I knew I'd live to regret bringing you out of mothballs," the admiral said, merciless as ever. However, Carter was not offended. Quite the contrary.

"Admiral, if you do live to regret this, then it means we'll have succeeded."

Krantz snorted a laugh then headed for the door. "Give me two hours, Commander, and you will have your invasion force …"

TWENTY-FOUR
STRIKE BACK, STRIKE HARD

THE FINAL TASKFORCE joined Krantz's invasion fleet, and Carter marveled at how rapidly the admiral had managed to amass the five-hundred and twenty-two ships that were dominating space ahead of the Galatine. In all, it had taken her less than two hours to assemble the armada, a herculean feat in itself. However, the speed at which she'd mustered the fighting force wasn't merely for the sake of efficiency. She had to act before word spread to less cooperative members of the senate, who would quickly move to quash the plan, and remove the admiral from her post. She was committing career suicide by ordering an invasion without approval of the senate, or even the commander-in-chief, but Carter had to believed that history would prove Clara Krantz – and himself – right.

"Message from the flagship," Brodie said from the tactical station. "All ships are in position and beginning a phased jump to New Aternus."

"Acknowledge the message, Brodie," Carter replied, as the first Union vessels began to disappear from the viewscreen, headed in the direction of Orion's belt. "Amaya, once the last ships have jumped away, wait two minutes then execute our warp to the junction point."

"Aye, aye, skipper," the Master Navigator replied.

"Sir, Dauntless actual wants to speak with you," Brodie added.

Carter pushed himself out of his seat and stood tall. "Put her on the screen."

Admiral Krantz appeared on the bridge of the Union Battlecruiser Dauntless. In the background, Carter could see that the ship was a hive of activity, and he could almost feel the crew's nervous energy through the screen.

"We jump in sixty seconds, so I wanted to make sure you're all set," Krantz asked.

"We're ready, Admiral," Carter replied, ensuring there was no ambiguity in the tone of his voice. "I don't know how you managed to swing this, but color me impressed."

"Let's just say I was creative in how I presented the facts," Krantz replied. Had it been Carina speaking those words, it would have been done with a roguish smile, but the admiral was never less-than ice-cold and serious. "If this goes South, then it's my ass on the line, but at least I did something. I'd rather be damned for trying than for doing nothing."

"You'll get no argument from me, Admiral. And for what it's worth, thank you."

Krantz nodded. "See you on the other side, Master Commander."

The channel was closed, then within seconds the Dauntless and its task force were gone, along with three-quarters of the fleet. The time for action was fast approaching, but Carter felt none of the flutters in his gut that might have plagued the 'normie' human officers. In fact, he felt a rush of excitement flowing through his body. This was their chance to strike back at their enemy, and strike hard, and he intended to do just that.

"The last ships are away," Brodie announced.

"Aternien transponder is live and transmitting," Cai added. "To anyone looking, we are now a Khopesh-class Destroyer."

"Warp countdown has begun," Amaya chimed in. "T-minus one-twenty seconds until we jump."

For Carter, the waiting was the worst part, when two minutes could feel like two hours. Many captains filled such silences with unnecessary bluff and bluster, and while he wasn't the sort of commander to give rousing speeches, on this occasion, he made an exception. What they were about to attempt was beyond audacious, bordering on foolhardy, and it was up to him to make the impossible sound like just another day on the job.

"Admiral Krantz has done her part, and now it's time to do ours," Carter began, turning to face his officers. "Amaya will jump us squarely inside our designated junction, and to the Aterniens, we'll appear just like one of them. No-one will be looking closely at us, because by the time we arrive, all hell will have broken loose. From there, it's simple. We punch through the atmosphere, using our plasma shield to protect us, then fly fast and low, straight at New Aternus City. We hit the power generator to the North and blow it sky high, then launch everything we've got at the Soul Crypt, and get the hell out of Dodge, before they know what's hit them."

There was a resounding chorus of "Aye sir!", which sent electricity racing down his spine. If he needed any reassurance that the Galatine was ready, he'd just gotten it, and then some. Suddenly, an alert rang out and Carter turned to his Master Navigator.

"That's our cue, Amaya," Carter said. "Punch it."

The pulsating thrum of the soliton warp drive rose to a crescendo, then the Galatine fell through a hole in spacetime, and was transported two thousand light years in the blink of an eye. New stars appeared, along with a rusty orange planet, whose methane-dominant atmosphere was thick with volcanic activity. White ice caps at the poles provided some much-needed contrast, like a light dusting of sugar on top of a ginger pudding.

"Jump complete, we're in the junction and dead-on target," the Master Navigator reported.

"Well done, Amaya, maintain course and speed," Carter replied. "Let's not attract any unwanted attention."

"Sir, the Union fleet is in position, beyond range of the planetary defense grid, just as planned," Brodie added. "I'm reading one-four-seven Aternien warships on an intercept course with them and closing fast."

"How many does that leave still in orbit of the planet?" Carter asked.

"Zero, sir," Brodie replied. There was more than a touch of amusement in the Master-at-arms' reply, and Carter couldn't blame him.

"A hundred and forty-seven ships are all they have stationed at New Aternus?" Major Larsen asked, surprised.

Brodie shrugged and nodded. "It looks that way, ma'am. Seems to me that they never expected us to find this place."

"Don't pop the champagne corks yet, we still have a long way to go," Carter cut in, and as if to reinforce that point, the tactical station chimed an alert.

—

Forty-nine of the ships headed for the Union fleet are going to pass right by us," Brodie said. "And I mean close. Close enough that if they looked out a window, they'd realize pretty quick that we're not a Khopesh destroyer."

"Let's see them," Carter said, hustling back to his seat.

JACAB obliged by projecting a tactical holo map of the Aternien taskforce relative to their position, while Brodie updated the main display to put the lead ship front and center on the view screen. His Master-at-arms hadn't been exaggerating; the closest ship in the task force was projected to pass within a hundred meters of the Galatine.

"Should we change course to avoid them?" Carina asked.

"Negative, hold course and speed," Carter ordered, quick to dispel any notion that they would flinch first. "To them, we're just another Aternien. If they're doing their jobs, they'll be focused on Krantz's fleet, not us."

Carina's fingers began to drum on the arm of her chair as the Aternien taskforce drew closer, and the magnification on the view screen steadily dropped to a 1:1 ratio. A shudder ran through the deck as the Galatine was buffeted by the engine wake of forty-nine powerful enemy destroyers, but they all slipped past without so much as a scanning beam looking in their direction.

"See, piece of cake," Carina said, before blowing out a sigh of relief.

"That's one hurdle overcome, but we still need to get past the Star Cannons," Carter said.

Brodie updated the viewscreen, and JACAB updated his tactical map, but whichever version Carter looked at, it was bad news.

"There must be about a billion Star Cannons between us and the planet," Carina said, as her drumming intensified.

"Brodie, can you give me a number that's a little more precise than the major's unhelpful estimate?" Carter asked, drawing an irked sideways glance from his XO.

The Master-at-arms worked his console, processing the positions and capabilities of the hundreds of Star Cannons that were within potential striking range of the Galatine. Carter had thought that the defense grid protecting Old Aternus had been bordering on excessive, but it paled in comparison to the network of orbital particle cannons defending their new home planet. It was clear that the godking was not taking any chances.

"We'll pass within immediate weapons range of twenty-eight Star Cannons on our current course," Brodie reported. "But these weapons platforms are updated designs, and we don't know how fast they can move. If our cover is blown, we could be surrounded by upwards of three hundred big guns before we reach atmosphere."

Carter nodded, but was careful not to show any emotion, other than steely determination and unyielding confidence.

"Steady as she goes, Amaya," Carter said. "But be ready to floor it."

"Aye, aye, skipper," the Master Navigator replied. Like himself, if Amaya was in any way concerned – and he'd be surprised if she wasn't – then she wasn't showing it.

"Brodie, make sure the shield is charged and ready," Carter added. It would soon be time for them to make their run, and he wanted to be certain they were prepared.

"You got it, MC. Shield charged and ready to deploy, on your command."

Carter turned to HARPER, at the engineering stations at the rear of the bridge.

"Mister HARPER, steal power from wherever you can, but keep our shield up, is that understood?"

"Yes, boss, perfectly understood," the bot replied. HARPER's iron mask couldn't show fear or anxiety, but the nervous twiddling of the bot's bright yellow fingers, as if he were playing an invisible piano, gave Carter a window into the machine's thoughts.

"You'll do fine, HARPER."

Unlike his other officers, the labor bot had yet to experience shipborne combat, and he knew that a few simple words of calm reassurance could go a long way. It was a shame that such techniques no longer worked on hardened veterans like himself. For Carter, the burden of taking his crew into battle, knowing they might not return, weighed heavier each time.

"Three minutes until we reach atmosphere, at present speed," Amaya reported.

"Star cannons are holding position," Brodie added. "Our cover is still solid."

The tension in the man's voice was palpable. It was like winning a bid at an auction and waiting with bated breath for the hammer to drop, praying that no-one snuck in at the last second with a higher offer.

More alerts chimed, and this time it was Cai who was first to report. "Warp signatures detected," the Master Operator said. "It's a sizable distortion. I'd estimate hundreds of ships."

"Location?" Carter asked.

"The distortion is forming beyond the junction points, close to the Union fleet," Cai replied. "They're coming through now…"

The tactical station went haywire as a seemingly never-ending stream of Aternien warships blinked into existence.

"I'm reading seven-hundred Aternien vessels, and climbing," Brodie announced. "Nine hundred… twelve hundred…" There was a pause, but Carter's sincere hope that his officer's report had ended was soon quashed. "Seventeen hundred ships, sir, including the Solar Barques Senuset and Mesek-tet, all on an intercept course for the Union fleet."

"If the Mesek-tet is here, it's a sure bet the god-king is here too," Carina said.

Carter also understood the significance of the god-king's sun ship leading the enemy armada. It meant that Markus Aternus intended to show no mercy. The Union had dared invade his sacred territory, and the gloves had come off. Carter suppressed an urge to curse, fighting to maintain the persona of calm confidence, despite the crushing news, and turned to his officer.

"How long before they're within optimal weapons range of the Union fleet?"

Brodie ran a quick calculation then looked at Carter with dead eyes, his expression drawn and cheerless. "Ten minutes, sir, at present speed."

Carter nodded to acknowledge his officer then faced front, back straight and chest broad. "Then we'll be done in nine," he replied. "Amaya, when I give the order, I'll need you to fly this ship as hard and as fast as you possibly can."

Amaya managed a smile. "I thought you'd never ask."

Another alert chimed from the tactical console and Brodie reported it with extra urgency. "Sir, a star cannon has moved out of formation and is heading toward us." The view screen added an image of the orbital weapon inset on the screen.

"We're being scanned," Cai added.

"Not yet..." Carter said. He could sense that all eyes were on him.

"Weapons lock," Brodie called out. "The Star Cannon is preparing to fire!"

"Now, Amaya!" Carter growled, closing his hand into a fist and shaking it at the rusty orange planet on the screen.

The engines kicked into full burn and the Galatine accelerated harder than the compensators could adjust for. Carter staggered his stance, but remained standing, as if he were a figurehead on the bow of an ancient sailing ship, urging the vessel on through hazardous seas. Then the deck shook as particle blasts thumped into their hull.

"Direct hit," Brodie said. "Armor is holding. No damage."

"Ready plasma shield, on Amaya's command," Carter said.

"Plasma shield on Amaya's command, aye," Brodie answered. "Sir, we have forty-nine Star Cannons converging on our position... Belay that, three-four-three cannons, inbound and within weapons range in twenty seconds."

"Thirty seconds to atmosphere!" Amaya added, raising her voice to a shout to be heard over the roar of the engines.

"Increase speed, all ahead flank!" Carter answered leaning into his stance and trying to will the ship to go faster.

More particle blasts hammered the Galatine, but their armor absorbed the shots and their progress was not slowed. The planet now consumed the view ahead, and Carter returned to his seat, knowing that they were about to run headlong into a storm that even he couldn't weather while still standing.

"Plasma shield engaged!" Amaya called out, as the Longsword-class vessel hit the atmosphere of New Aternus at a velocity that would have reduced any other ship to molten slag. "We're entering the atmosphere."

The second part of his Master Navigator's announcement was unnecessary, since it felt like the Galatine had just crashed headlong into another ship. Outside visibility was reduced to zero, as the plasma inferno surrounding the ship battled against the inferno raging beyond it.

"Ventral armor is ablating!" Brodie yelled, hands gripped around his console, which was shaking so violently that panels were cracking and the metal frame was becoming distorted. "Roll us over, Amaya, and do it fast!"

The Master Navigator responded instantly, rolling the ship to pit their dorsal armor against the furnace that was threatening to overwhelm their shield.

"Thirteen seconds to maximum hull stress," Cai Cooper shouted, his voice barely audible over the tumultuous roar of looming destruction.

"Hold your course!" Carter called out. "The Galatine can take it."

Carina was working her console, fingers fumbling and making mistakes as savage jolts shook her body and forced her to re-enter commands. Then she spun around and looked at HARPER, who had anchored himself to the deck with mag-locks.

"HARPER, give us a twenty-percent boost to the main engines for three seconds, on my mark!" Carina yelled.

Carter frowned, but the look on his XO's face screamed, 'trust me,' and he did.

"HARPER, now!"

The jolt of additional engine power was barely noticeable above the seismic forces that were already ravaging the ship, but Carter felt the ship accelerate.

"Exceeding maximum hull stress," Cai called out. "Attempting to compensate."

No sooner had Cai cried out the words that the Galatine punched through the wall of fire like a cannonball smashing through a burning portcullis.

"Shield disengaged," Brodie said, no longer needing to shout his voice hoarse.

"Damage report," Carter commanded.

Carina analyzed the readings on her seat's comp-slate, shaking her head the whole time. "There are a lot of systems in the red, but the ones we need most are still functioning," his XO replied. "We can still fly, we can still shoot, and we can still jump away."

It was hardly a comprehensive report, but he had to admit that Carina had told him everything he needed to know.

"Commence attack run," Carter called out, and his officers all replied with a crisp, "yes, sir!".

Amaya pulled the Galatine out of the suicide dive at the last possible moment and levelled off barely fifty meters above the liquid methane oceans of the alien planet, kicking up a wave of spray in their wake as tall as a tidal wave. The Master Navigator then accelerated hard, punching through the sound barrier eight times, then nine, then ten, while flying completely on manual control, relying on her unique neural connection to the ship's sensors to see the way ahead.

"Target in sight," Brodie announced. "Weapons locked and ready to fire."

The view screen displayed the Soul Crypt's dedicated power source, which was located on a manufactured island with the obelisk-like fusion reactor complex in the dead center. Carter noted that its structural design was different to what they'd seen in the pyramid archives on Old Aternus. It wasn't different enough to rule out a positive ID, but it was different enough that he found himself massaging the wiry bristles on his chin, contemplating what it might mean for phase two of their assault.

"Weapons away!" Brodie reported.

A furious volley of cannon and plasma fire surged toward the power plant and utterly obliterated the entire complex in a single, devastating strike. The reactor exploded so violently that the detonation might have been mistaken for an atom-bomb, but the Galatine had already raced past, and Amaya was steering them toward their primary target.

"That got the Aternien's attention, alright," Carina said, eyes fixed to her screens. "We have Griffin-class Interceptors inbound."

"How many?" Carter grunted. Carina's eyes grew wide, and he raised a hand to stop her from answering. "Never mind, I get the idea."

"Sir, the city's defenses are trying to target us," Brodie announced.

"Trying, or succeeding?" Carter replied, curious how his Master-at-arms had worded the statement.

"Trying and failing," Brodie said, the corner of his mouth turned up into a smile. "Our crazy-ass pilot is flying so low they can't get a lock on us."

Carter nodded, and considered asking, "how low?", but in the same way that he preferred not knowing how many interceptors were chasing them down, he figured ignorance was bliss.

"We're ninety seconds out from the city," Carina cut in. "Brodie, tell me you've IDed the Soul Crypt?"

The smile vanished from Brodie's face, and instead he winced. "I think so…"

"I need you to *know* so, mister," Carter hit back. "We only get one shot at this."

Brodie shook his head. "No structure in the city exactly matches the schematics from the pyramid," his Master-at-arms explained. "But there are three that are close."

"Put them on-screen."

Carter and Carina both jumped to their feet and cursed at the same time. There were three structures on the view screen, and the chilling reality was that any one of them could have been the Soul Crypt.

TWENTY-FIVE
THREE OF A KIND

THE CLOCK WAS TICKING and Carter was acutely aware that it couldn't be reset. They didn't have time to attack all three possible Soul Crypts, which meant they had to pick one, and hope they chose wisely.

"Cai, can you identify which of those three structures is the Soul Crypt?" Carter asked his Master Operator.

"Negative, sir," Cai replied. It was obvious he'd already run the analysis. "Sensors can't penetrate inside, and since we destroyed the power source that generates the crypts' shields, they are all equally unprotected."

Carter cursed under his breath. Had they scanned the city first, they might have learned which structure was the Soul Crypt, simply by virtue of the fact the energy signature of its shield would have illuminated it like a lightbulb.

"Sixty seconds to target," Brodie called out.

"I've reduced speed as much as I can," Amaya added, "But if I go any slower, the Interceptors will overrun us before we can escape."

Carter turned to his XO. Without any hard evidence to go on, they had to take a guess, and as the ship's resident Aternien expert, there was no-one better placed than Carina Larsen to make the call, whether she liked it or not.

"It's your call, Carina," Carter said, shocking the woman into silence. "Any of us would just be making a guess, but at least yours is an educated case."

Carina knew better than to debate the point; they simply didn't have the time. Carter had passed her the ball, and she had to run with it.

"Cai, is there any logical order to the position of the three structures?" Carina asked. "As in an order of priority, or an obvious progression?"

Cai frowned and his fingers flashed across his console, while TOBY chattered in his ear at the same time.

"Thirty seconds to target," Brodie warned, his voice low but no less urgent.

All eyes were now on Cai. Carina hadn't given him much to work with, but if anyone could find an answer, it was his Master Operator.

"Yes," Cai called out, breathless with anticipation. "The relative positions of the three structures correlate to the pyramids of Giza, in what was Egypt on Terra Prime."

Carina clapped her hands together and the snap was like a gunshot going off in Carter's ear.

"Target the third structure in the progression!" Carina said.

Carter nodded and turned to his Master-at-arms. "Do it!"

Amaya banked toward the new target and Brodie locked on. Dozens of particle blasts were flashing over the top of the ship, but Carter knew that as soon as they began to climb again, they'd take a hammering. First, they had to strike their target.

"Weapons away!" Brodie said, as the Galatine shuddered from the kick-back of every gun, cannon and missile silo firing in perfect harmony.

"Climbing now!" Amaya added, pulling the Galatine into a steep ascent.

The Aternien structure was hit, and a colossal explosion rocked New Aternus City, destroying nearby structures and producing a powerful shockwave that extended for several hundred meters, wrecking everything in its path.

"We're taking heavy fire!" Brodie said, as the city's surviving defense platforms bombarded them with particle blasts. "Our shield is gone, and we have hull breaches on deck five, sections G-to-K. They're hammering our belly, MC."

"Amaya, we're in your hands now," Carter called to his pilot. "Show me what you can do."

"Aye, aye, skipper…"

Amaya was already throwing the ship into a chain of wild, gravitationally-assisted maneuvers, while constantly rolling the Galatine to disperse the incoming fire across as much of the ship's area as possible. Even so, they were still taking hits, and their armor was failing. Then the planet's rusty atmosphere began to thin and the particle blasts grew fewer and less intense, and within seconds they were back into space.

"Spin up the Soliton drive, and warp us out of here, before the Star Cannons make mincemeat out of us," Carter ordered. "And get me Admiral Krantz on the horn."

His officers acknowledged the orders, then Krantz

appeared on the viewscreen. The bridge of the Dauntless was on fire, and Carter could see at least three dead crewmembers in the background. The admiral herself was also bleeding, and her uniform was scorched black on her right shoulder, where an exploding console or burning debris had struck her. She had her hand clasped over the wound, fingers gripping tightly to her burned flesh, as if she were stopping her arm from falling off.

"Mission accomplished, Admiral, get the hell out of here," Carter said, getting straight to the point.

"It's about damned time, Commander," Krantz answered, coming across like a mother scolding her teenage son for getting home late. "See you at Station Alpha."

The channel cut off, and immediately Carter could see the Union fleet maneuvering to retreat. Of the five hundred and twenty ships that had arrived at New Aternus, only a hundred and fifty remained.

"Sir, we're being boarded!" Brodie's announcement was like a hammer blow to the side of his head. "It looks like the Aternien reinforcements deployed breaching pods in orbit, like a damned minefield, and we just flew straight through it."

"Lock down and secure all critical systems and prepare to repel boarders," Carter answered. Then to his Master Navigator, he added, "Amaya, how long before we can jump?"

"Sixty seconds, skipper," Amaya replied. "I have the boarding pods on my screen, and I can avoid the rest until we jump, along with the star cannons."

Carter grunted an acknowledgement then drew his cutlass. He was about to gather his officers to mount the defense of the Galatine, when a notification chimed from all stations.

"Sir, we have an incoming message," Cai reported. "It's from the Mesek-tet. Markus Aternus is demanding to speak with you."

Carter raised an eyebrow and halted his exit from the bridge. This was an opportunity he didn't want to miss.

"Something tells me that we hit the right target," Carina commented.

Carter nodded. "Let's find out." He turned to Brodie. "Route Aternus to the main screen, then take Cai and Taylor and get after our intruders."

"Sir, I would also like to help defend the ship," HARPER cut in.

Carter looked at the bot, recalling how formidable the machine had been in hand-to-hand combat.

"Request approved, but stay in once piece, Mister HARPER," Carter said, aiming a stern finger at the yellow bot. "We're in a sorry state, and I need you to keep us together."

"Yes, boss. You can count on me."

Brodie and his gopher, Taylor, led the charge, followed by Cai and HARPER. Carter was itching to get into single combat himself, but first there was another duty to perform; he had an audience with a king. Tapping the comp-slate in his chair, Carter finally answered the incoming hail, and the face of Markus Aternus filled the viewscreen.

"I was prepared to be merciful," Aternus began. Far from serene and godlike, the synthetic man's face and long golden chin projected wrathful hatred toward Carter. "I was even prepared to forgive your slights and allow you to ascend.

But now you have violated not one of my sacred cities, but two, and murdered the souls of billions of my children."

Carter cast his XO a sideways glance. She was smiling, and for good reason. The god-king had just confirmed that her choice had been correct. The Soul Crypt was no more.

"I'd watch your tone, Your Majesty," Carter snarled. "Now that you can't be reborn, dead means dead."

Aternus' glowing blue eyes flashed brighter than laser light. "You fool!" the god-king roared, his voice thundering as if it were being projected through a megaphone. "I can build a new crypt within days. You've done nothing but anger a god, and in return, you will receive a god's vengeance. Remember that when you walk the charred streets of Terra Prime's once great cities. Remember, and know that humanity suffered because of you."

The channel was shut off at the source, and Carter felt a shiver run down his spine. Doubt crept into his mind, and he wondered if he'd just made a terrible mistake. Aternus had believed that his actions in using a bio-genic virus to kill human populations was somehow benevolent and merciful. Now, Carter feared that he'd just unleased the full might of the god-king's wrath.

"The Aterniens are leaving in droves," Major Larsen said. She was back in her chair, analyzing readings from her comp-slate. "That includes the Mesek-tet and Senuset. I don't have Cai's skill with this sort of thing, but I'd say the warp signature is the inverse of what we used to reach New Aternus." She stopped at look Carter in the eyes. "They're going after Terra Prime."

Carter tightened his grip around the handle of his sword. "Amaya, get us home. I have a bad feeling about this."

"Aye, aye, skipper, warping in ten seconds…" Amaya replied.

Carter headed for the door. "You have the bridge, Major," he grunted, before flipping the switch to send plasma coursing along the blade of his cutlass.

"Hey, don't you need my help?" Carina asked, hurrying after him, energy pistol in hand.

Carter turned to her and the look on his face stopped her dead, as if he were a gorgon that had turned her to stone.

"Not this time, Carina, I need you here," he answered. "Once we're back at Terra Prime, regroup with the fleet and prepare for battle. I'll be back soon."

Carter stormed off the bridge, cutlass casting flickering shadows on the austere walls of the Longsword-class battleship. He might have angered a god, but Markus Aternus had made him furious too. His plan to stop the god-king had failed but he still had an ace up his sleeve. They just had to survive long enough for him to play it.

"Sir, we have thirty Immortals contained in the cargo bay," Brodie said, over the comm system built into Carter's battle uniform. He could hear the fighting in the background. "But a squad has broken through and is heading for the bridge."

"How many?" Carter grunted, secretly hoping the number was high.

"Ten, sir, including a warden. I'm on my way to help."

"Negative, you, Cai and HARPER deal with the intruders in the hold. I'll handle the rest…"

It was part of Brodie's job to ensure the safety of his commanding officer, but they'd fought side-by-side enough times that his Master-at-arms knew when to push back, and when to acquiesce without argument. This was one of those times.

"You got it, MC," Brodie replied. "I'll see you on the bridge."

The stomp of Aternien feet grew louder, and the squad of Immortals marched out from a junction and turned sharply toward his position on the long central corridor. The Aternien warriors didn't flinch and didn't stop, and neither did Carter. Expanding his buckler, he charged at them, blocking shots from their particle rifles, and allowing his battle uniform to soak up the blasts he'd couldn't shield against. Accelerating, he ran up the side of the wall and threw himself at the Immortals, thrusting his cutlass through the neck of the lead warrior and severing it clean off. He landed deftly and spun around, whirling his blade through the front ranks and cutting down two more.

A blast thumped into his gut, but the pain was numbed and Carter responded by thrusting his cutlass through the chest of the Aternien warrior that had shot him. He disengaged the blade to keep his cutlass lodged inside the body of the fighter, then used the Immortal as a shield, maneuvering the warrior like a puppet on a stick. Particle blasts began to disintegrate his Aternien shield, but he only needed the Immortal's synthetic body to hold firm for a few more seconds. Drawing his 57-EX revolver from its holster, he aimed and squeezed off five shots in quick succession. Each bullet smashed through the eye socket of an individual Immortal, before bursting out of the backs of their heads, destroying their neuromorphic brains in the process. Then he slid the body off his sword, re-engaged the plasma edge, and faced off against the Warden, who was the only remaining warrior from the squad of ten. The Aternien 'sergeant' hesitated, and Carter could sense the Warden's fear as he marched toward the warrior, sword and buckler held ready.

Does he already know that the Soul Crypt is gone? Carter wondered. *Does he know that when he falls at the edge of my sword, dead really means dead?"* In the end, it didn't matter to him. The Warden had invaded his ship, and threatened his crew, and the Aternien would pay the price.

He swung his cutlass and the Warden parried with the energized bayonet attached to his plasma rifle, but the blow knocked the warrior backward. Carter drove on, hacking and slashing, and forcing the Warden to parry with increasing frenzy. Then in his anger he overreached, and the Warden counterattacked, stabbing the bayonet into his side. Carter gritted his teeth and growled, before grabbing the barrel of the weapon and squeezing it flat. The Warden fired and the weapon exploded in the Aternien's hand, blowing the warrior's arms off below the elbows. The Warden staggered back, looking at its stumps in confusion and disbelief. Carter removed the bayonet from his flesh then grabbed the warden's neck and pulled the Aternien closer.

"This is the end for you, Warden of Aternus," Carter growled, and he could see the mortal terror in the man's vivid blue eyes. "Aternus is not immortal, and neither are you." He drove the bayonet into the base of the Aternien's skull, severing the synthetic man's soul block in half, and causing the light to leave the Warden's eyes, forever.

"We dealt with the intruders in the hold." Brodie's voice came through strong and clear. "What's your status, MC?"

"I'm done here too," Carter grunted, tossing the Warden

to the deck, followed by the bayonet, with a crisp clatter. "Head to the cargo hold and guard the casket of Markus Aternus," he added, already on his way back to the bridge. "We have one more chance to end this."

Brodie acknowledged the command and closed the link, then Carter stepped back onto the bridge, under the curious gaze of Major Larsen.

"Everything okay?" Carina asked.

She was looking at the multiple new holes in his uniform with a mix of confusion and concern, since there was no visible damage to the exposed skin beneath. To Carter's surprise, his wounds had already completely healed. He didn't know what restorative energy Monique Dubois had exposed him to when he had sat on the Aternien throne, but it seemed that its effects were long-lasting.

"Never better, Major," Carter answered, straightening his jacket. "Report."

"The Aternien armada is here, and they look pissed," Carina replied. Carter allowed the curse; in this case, it was merited. "Aternus must have called in his forces from all over the galaxy. I'm reading more than three-thousands ship, including both Solar Barques. It's an invasion force."

Carter shook his head. "No, they don't intend to invade. They mean to raze every town and city on Terra Prime to the ground."

All stations chimed an alert, and Carter saw that Admiral Krantz was calling. He put her through directly, since there was no time to waste.

"Commander, you told me that destroying the Soul Crypt would make Aternus think twice," Krantz said, visibility angry. "Instead, all we've done is write our own death certificates."

"It's not over yet, Admiral. There's still something Aternus doesn't know."

Krantz's bloodshot eyes narrowed. "Whatever you're going to do, Commander, do it fast. We can't hope to repel a force of this size, but if I have to, I'll die trying."

"It won't come to that," Carter insisted. "I need to make another call. I'll let you know how it goes."

"Do that, Commander," Krantz replied. "I'm not going anywhere…"

The image of the admiral was replaced by a magnified view of the Solar Barque, Mesek-tet. It was leading the armada with the Senuset on its wing, and the seven Royal Court Khopesh Destroyers close behind.

"Hail him," Carter said to his XO.

Carina nodded then executed the command. The Mesek-tet responded promptly.

"That was quick," Carina commented. "I guess he's keen to rub our noses in it."

"We'll see about that," Carter answered. "On screen."

The god-king appeared larger than life, the synthetic man's eyes still glowing as hot and as furious as twin suns.

"Are you here to beg for your life?" Aternus hissed. "If so, you are wasting your time."

"Just shut up for a second and listen," Carter snapped, and the insult seemed to stun the god-king into temporary submission. "Maybe losing the Soul Crypt wasn't enough to reign you in, but I have something else of yours that I think you'll care more about."

Carter nodded to Carina, and she added Brodie to the conversation. The image of his Master-at-arms standing next to the stasis pod of the original Markus Aternus was being transmitted in perfect fidelity by Taylor. He watched as the god-king's eyes flashed wide with surprise. Synthetic or not, the man could not hide his still-human emotions.

"That is a trick," Aternus roared.

Carter shook his head. "I assure you, it's not. We found your body, and the body of your old lawyer, Dwight the Grand Vizier, plus the High Overseers, and even your human family, in the lower chamber of your former palace on Old Aternus."

Carter paused to let this sink in, but it was clear that he'd captured the god-king's undivided attention.

"What do you want?" Aternus replied, the words seeping through clenched, solid gold teeth.

A jolt of electricity raced through Carter's body. *I have him… Finally, I have him.*

"One, you turn that armada around, and send them back to New Aternus, right now," Carter answered, beginning his demands. "Two, you cease all hostilities against Union targets. And three, you and I meet immediately at the Diplomatic Outpost on the demarcation line to discuss terms for a permanent ceasefire."

"Those demands are absurd!" Aternus roared, his voice rattling the deck of the Galatine.

Carter held his nerve and folded his arms tightly across his chest.

"You'd rather I just pull the plug on your caskets, and eject them into space?"

He could have said more, but his senses told him that he'd done enough. Now it was up to the god-king to decide whether the sanctity of his immortal soul was more important than prosecuting his murderous objectives.

"I agree," Aternus replied, the words rumbling like thunder.

The channel closed and Carter was left reeling. His gambit had paid off, and just in time.

"The Aternien armada is leaving," Carina said, scarcely able to believe her own words. "The two Solar Barques, and the seven Royal Court escorts are preparing to warp. It looks like they're heading to the demarcation line, just as you told them."

Carter nodded. "Then we're still in the game." A thought then occurred to him, one that had been at the back of his mind ever since the attack on New Aternus, but that he'd not yet had chance to voice.

"Just how did you know for us to attack the third of the three possible Soul Crypts?" Carter asked his XO.

Carina smiled. It looked like she'd been waiting for an opportunity to explain her reasoning. "The number three played a major role in Egyptian mythology and culture, so when Cai confirmed that the three crypt-like buildings were built in a progression, like the Giza pyramids, I knew which one to hit," she began. "Ancient Egyptians believed there were three stages of the afterlife: death, judgment, and eternal life. And if the Soul Crypt isn't a manifestation of Eternal Life, I don't know what is.

Carter huffed his appreciation. "You're a damned genius, do you know that?"

His XO's smile grew broader. "I do, but it's about time you figured it out too." A notification chimed from the tactical and operations console, and she rushed over to check the station. "Surprise, surprise, the admiral is on the line for you," his XO said.

Carter managed a muted laugh. He figured he'd earned one.

"Ask her to give me sixty seconds, so I can take her call

in the briefing room," Carter replied. He was about to walk away when another thought occurred to him. "Oh, and make sure Brodie doesn't flush the bodies of the dead Immortals out of the airlock just yet. I have a plan for them."

Carina scrunched up her nose at him. "That's dark, but okay..."

TWENTY-SIX
A DARK REFLECTION

BY THE TIME the Galatine arrived at the Diplomatic Outpost, the Mesek-tet was already docked to the Aternien side of the space station. The Senuset and the Royal Court ships were holding position a few kilometers away, but their weapons were powered down.

"It's a good job we also brought some backup," Carina commented, noting the arrival of the Battlecruiser Dauntless at the head of Admiral Krantz's taskforce. "Though, if this turns into a fight, we're still vastly outgunned."

Carter agreed with his XO's assessment but had a feeling that it wouldn't come to that. To make sure, he'd already prepared a contingency plan.

"Amaya, dock us to the Union side of the Diplomatic Outpost, but be ready to break the connection and run if things turn ugly."

Amaya acknowledged the command in her customary manner, then Carter opened a channel to HARPER in the cargo hold.

"Mister HARPER, are we good to go down there?" Carter asked the labor bot.

"Yes, boss, we're ready here," the machine replied.

Carter nodded. "Good, we're on our way."

According to Brodie, the labor bot had acquitted itself with distinction in the defense of the ship. Using a plasma-edged fire axe that the bot had taken from an emergency equipment cabinet while en-route to the cargo hold, HARPER had taken out almost half of the Immortals by himself. Brodie had brutally hacked down most of the rest with his energized claymore, while Cai harassed and distracted the enemy to make it easier for the two big hitters to do their thing. As much as he missed Kendra, he was glad that her post had been filled by someone that could do justice to the role, and her memory.

"Cai, the ship is yours while we're gone," Carter said, aiming a finger at his Master Operator, before leading Carina and Brodie toward the ship's cargo hold.

No-one spoke a word en-route. They had already gone over the plan again and again, and no-one was left under any illusion as to what came next. This was to be their final gambit, and if it didn't work then all they could do was stand their ground and fight till the end.

At least we'll go down with our heads held high, Carter thought, as he entered the cargo area and found HARPER waiting for him. *If anything is written of us in the years to come, at least it could say that.*

"The stasis chambers you requested are ready to ship out," HARPER said. "To be clear, we have the sarcophaguses of Markus Aternus, the Grand Vizier, and the seven High Overseers." The bot was standing in front of a stack of sarcophaguses, which were piled onto anti-grav loader /

unloader platforms. They were all hooked up to a series of portable generators, which ensured that the stasis systems were active, and that the occupants of the pods remained in hibernation.

"That should be enough," Carter grunted. "They might not give a damn about the others, but I'd bet my ship that they care a whole hell of a lot about their own immortal souls."

Carina looked less than convinced by his statement, but she also looked more than ready to find out, one way or another. Carter led the party to the docking area and unlocked the hatch. It swung open with a gentle hiss to reveal the access corridor that led inside the Union section of the diplomatic outpost. He did not have happy memories of the place. During their last visit, the Grand Vizier had double-crossed then tried to kill them, and given a chance, Carter expected that his old adversary would do so again.

"Wait here," Carter said to his Master-at-arms. "If I need you. Or more likely, *when* I need you, I'll be in contact over comms."

"You got it, MC," Brodie said, standing guard outside the hatch, plasma sub-gun in hand.

Carter continued to lead, with Major Larsen at his side and HARPER bringing up the rear, using his considerable size and strength to maneuver the stacked sarcophaguses into the grand meeting chamber. Markus Aternus was already there, standing even taller than HARPER, and projecting an even more dominating presence. The ruler of the Aterniens had an ethereal, almost magical aura, and was magnificent to behold, like a golden statue carved by the greatest masters of the Italian renaissance.

The Grand Vizier stood slightly behind and to the side of

his king. As the commander of the Solar Barque, Senuset, during the first war, the Vizier had killed countless millions, even before he'd led the latest campaign against humanity. Men, women, children, babies… it made no difference to the Vizier. A human was a human to him, no more significant than a germ. Behind the Vizier were the High Overseers, the seven most senior members of the Aternien Royal Court. All of them had played a pivotal role in the Aternus Corporation, and had been amongst the first to ascend, along with Markus Aternus and the Vizier. Carter suddenly found himself thinking about Monique Dubois, the Overseer who had so desperately wanted to become a member of this elite inner circle. He couldn't understand why, and if Monique could see the High Overseers now, he believed that she would think as he did. To Carter, they looked pathetic and ridiculous in their royal finery and unnaturally modified bodies. For people supposedly at the forefront of human evolution, they were ridiculous to look at.

"Take the stasis chambers to the north end of the room and set them on the divider between the Aternien and Union sides," Carter said to HARPER, and the bot nodded and obliged.

Carter approached the location where the table had once stood, before he'd been forced to use it as a shield to protect himself and Carina against the cowardly ambush that the Grand Vizier had instigated, during their first meeting at the station. That event had set the war in motion, and Carter hoped that the diplomatic chamber would also prove to be the venue where the war ended. The table now lay melted and destroyed in the Union half of the chamber, which itself had seen better days. None of it mattered, though, because Carter figured that the 'negotiations' would be short.

"There you go," Carter grunted, pointing to the sarcophaguses. "Just as we agreed."

The Grand Vizier glided across the room to the stacked stasis chambers and went immediately to the casket containing the human body of Markus Aternus. He smoothed the condensation off the glass to check that the funeral mask was still in place, then dropped down and bowed to Markus Aternus.

"The body is intact and the funeral mask is operating within expected tolerances," the Vizier said, returning to his god-king's side. "These power supplies are crude but sufficient, and stasis has been maintained."

Markus Aternus appeared satisfied with the report and returned his glowing blue eyes to Carter, before pointing a ring-heavy finger at Major Larsen.

"Remove the human from my presence," Aternus snarled. "It is an insult to have brought her."

"It's an insult to speak to her that way," Carter snapped back, instantly riled up. "God-king or not, don't do it again." Carter was about to add, "…or else I'll slice your head off your shoulders," but he figured that since he was on a diplomatic mission, it was better to hold back.

"It is unwise to threaten a god," Aternus said, now glowering at Carina, though to her credit, she stood tall and glared right back at the god-king, without flinching. "And it is also pointless," Aternus added, focusing back on Carter. "There is a vault inside the Mesek-tet that stores my soul. For all your endeavors, you have failed to endanger my existence."

Carter pointed to the sarcophaguses. "I tend to disagree."

Markus Aternus said nothing, and Carter suppressed the

urge to smile, despite knowing that he had the Aternien leader in a bind.

"I suggest we cut to the chase, Your Majesty," Carter added, keen to keep the meeting short and to the point. "I give you the sarcophaguses, and you agree to cease all hostilities against humankind, now and forever."

Markus Aternus considered the question, not because it required any great amount of thought on his part, but because it was regal to keep the lesser party waiting.

"If I agree, it is on the condition that humanity never again trespasses into Aternien territory, either Old Aternus or New, or any system we inhabit from this day forth."

Carter nodded. "Agreed."

The god-king regarded him skeptically. "Your meagre rank does not grant you the authority to make such a treaty."

"Actually, I do have the authority," Carter answered.

Carina handed him a folder containing a sealed hardcopy document, and Carter offered it to Markus. The Vizier darted forward and intercepted the folder, like a soldier diving on a grenade to protect innocent civilians, then opened it and read the contents.

"This document grants Master Commander Carter Rose the power to treat on behalf of the Union of Nine, as if he were the President himself," the Grand Vizier announced, summarizing the contents. "The authorization stamp encoded into this manuscript is valid. The Commander is correct. Any bargain struck here is binding."

Markus Aternus offered the slightest nod of acceptance, and the Vizier bowed and handed the folder to one of the High Overseers.

"Then you have my word as a god that we will honor the terms of this treaty."

The god-king removed a pendant in the shape of the Ankh of Aternus from around his neck. Hieroglyphs began to glow on the golden metal as the king held it in his powerful hand, then passed it to the Grand Vizier.

"This is to symbolize our treaty," the Vizier added. "By accepting the Ankh, the agreement is binding." The Grand Vizier sashayed closer then offered the pendant to Carter. He took it without question, and additional hieroglyphs lit up on the surface, and were burned into the metal.

"It is done," Markus Aternus said.

Carter bowed his head to the god-king and gestured to the caskets. "Then they're all yours…"

The door leading to the Aternien docking section thudded open and twenty-eight Anubi Royal Guardians marched in, two-by-two. Carter almost reached for his weapons, but managed to restrain the urge, and instead watched with rising fear as twenty-one of the Anubi broke formation and formed an honor guard in front of the god-king. The remaining seven wasted no time in hauling the sarcophaguses away, and everyone waited in absolute silence, until the grav platforms had been removed from the meeting room. At the exact same moment the door thudded shut, Carter's comp-slate chimed an incoming message from Cai Cooper aboard the Galatine.

"Sir, three-hundred and forty-three Khopesh-class Destroyers just jumped in behind the Royal Court ships," his Master Operator announced, calmly. "I await your instructions."

"Thank you, Cai, but stand by for now," Carter replied,

before closing the channel and calmly lowering his wrist to his side.

Suddenly, the Anubi guardians adopted fighting stances, and the synchronized stomp of their feet on the deck sounded like an army on the march. The guardians spun their flails to form an impenetrable shield in front of Markus Aternus, and the god-king smiled.

"Did you truly believe I would capitulate so easily?" Aternus said. "A god does not treat with a mortal. How easily you are deceived."

"I was thinking the same thing," Carter said, returning the Aternien's smile. He then raised his arm and tapped his comp-slate. "Brodie, you're up."

Brodie marched into the room with another man, who was following anxiously behind and to his side. The figure remained in shadow for a time, until he drew close enough to the center of the chamber to be illuminated by the overhead lights. The face of the god-king suddenly lost all its radiant elegance and beauty, and instead became twisted and afraid. The man who had entered the room was Markus Aternus.

"What is the meaning of this?" The Grand Vizier roared, stepping out from behind the whirling shield of energized flails. "Is this some kind of trick?"

"It's no trick," Carter grunted. "We swapped out the contents of the sarcophaguses you just hauled away with the bodies of Immortals who boarded my ship. The funereal mask was very helpful at concealing Aternus' true identity."

The human Markus Aternus staggered forward and grabbed Carter's forearm for support. The man was frail because of his long years in stasis, though it was not hibernation sickness that had caused Aternus' legs to weaken, but the sight of what he had become.

"No, no, no!" Aternus said, growing more distraught with each cry that escaped his chapped, thin lips. "This is not what I wanted. This is not the future I worked so hard to make possible."

Human Markus released Carter's arm then edged closer to the god-king, and the Aternien backed away, terrified at the sight of his organic self – his mortal soul.

"Stand down!" the god-king shouted, commanding the Anubi to stay their flails and return to a guard formation at his rear. "No one hurt this man! No-one is to touch him!"

The human Aternus continued to hobble toward his ascended form. Carter had never seen so much anguish in the eyes of a single soul before. He almost felt sorry for the man.

"I wanted humanity to take its next evolutionary step together, as a species, not for you to create another race!" Aternus said, despairing at what the god-king had done. "I wanted to create a future for all people, but instead you became a tyrant and a murderer!"

"Your ideals were naïve!" the god-king countered. "You have no idea what happened after you were put to rest. You have no idea how I was treated!"

Human Aternus shook his head. "I know enough. I know of the millions upon millions you have killed. The commander showed me what you…" he paused and shook his head again, "…what I have become."

"You fool!" the god-king snapped, stepping toward his human self, and towering over his mortal frame. "I remember our ideals, and what we wanted to achieve, but it was a dream, nothing more! Humans feared us, hated us and drove us away. If you had experienced the shame, the humiliation, the intolerance that I had to endure, you would have done the same thing!"

"No!" the man yelled with surprising force. "Your choices are not mine!" The original Markus paused for a moment to regain his breath and his composure, body trembling with outrage. "You are not me. You are not Markus Aternus. You're an imposter. A copy! A flawed creation, borne out of my arrogance!"

The god-king roared, and his eyes flared like supernovae. Then he grabbed Markus Aternus around the throat and with another maddened cry of rage, drove his hand into the man's chest and crushed his heart like an egg. Markus yelped, but the sound was feeble, like his body. Blood gushed onto the ground, coating the god king's arm, and painting his golden skin red. The sudden realization of what he'd done struck him like a plasma blast, and he pulled his hand out of the man's flesh, but it was already too late. Markus Aternus was dead, and the god-king's mortal soul had been destroyed.

TWENTY-SEVEN
THE RECKONING

THE GRAND VIZIER ran to the body of Markus and fell down at his side, prostrated as if in prayer. The Aternien's quivering hands hovered just above the body, as if the Vizier were afraid to touch the blood-soaked, mortal flesh of his god-king.

"What have you done?!" the Grand Vizier said, gasping the words to his god-king, who had staggered away from the murdered body, deep in shock. "Without him you are nothing. You are without a soul!"

The Vizier's accusation roused the god-king from his traumatized, catatonic state, and Aternus' eyes gleamed hot once again.

"I am Markus Aternus!" the god-king replied, attempting to regain his regal posture, though despite his efforts Aternus was still cowering, as if the weight of his actions were pressing down on him.

"No…" the Vizier gasped. "Markus Aternus is dead." The Aternien second-in-command finally managed to lay his hands on the body of the man he once knew. "His vital essence has departed his body, and his heart has been destroyed, and can no longer be weighed." The Vizier looked at Aternus, and it was as if his glowing eyes were filled with sparkling tears. "You have condemned yourself."

"No, I am your god and your king…" Aternus said, his voice shaking as he took faltering steps backwards, blood-soaked hands unsteady at his sides. "You will obey!"

The Grand Vizier climbed to his feet, and Carter watched as the seven High Overseers gathered behind him. Aternus, still hunched over and trembling, shook his head in disbelief.

"You are no longer our king, and you are certainly not a god," the Vizier announced. "You are nothing more than an imitation. Because of what you have done, the soul of our great visionary leader, Markus Aternus, has been condemned to an eternity of restlessness."

Suddenly, Aternus snatched a crook from one of the Anubi guardians and aimed it at the Grand Vizier. "You will obey me!" Aternus cried, brandishing the weapon like a madman. "I created you! I created all of you!" he roared, waving the crook at the High Overseers too. "If it were not for me, you would already be dead. I am Markus Aternus, and I command you to obey!"

The Grand Vizier was unmoved and the High Overseers remained at his side. Then, with a single nod in the direction of the Anubi Royal Guardians, the warriors that had once been the god-king's sworn protectors, snatched the crook from Aternus and seized his arms and legs, holding him in a vice-like grip that not even Carter would have able to break free from.

"No, you can't do this!" Aternus cried, as the Grand Vizier and the High Overseers drew long, golden blades and stalked closer. "I am your father! I am your…"

The last word was stolen in a gulp of shock, as the most senior members of the Aternien Royal Court plunged their energized daggers into the god-king's chest and stomach, melting through his scale armor like a hot knife though wax.

"Stop!" Aternus pleaded. "Please, I beg you!"

All pretense of his regal persona was gone, and all that remained was a terrified man, trapped in a synthetic body and mind, who was for the first time in his exceptionally long life grasping the reality that he was about to die.

Finally, the Anubi released him, and Aternus fell to the ground, his body ruined by knife strikes, his once perfect face ripped and torn, like old leather. Aternus curled into a fetal position, and feebly pulled his golden cloak over his head so that no-one could see his ravaged features. Then the Grand Vizier knelt behind him and drove his blade into the back of the god-king's head, prizing the soul block from his skull. Aternus' body immediately froze, like a machine that had been turned off. The Grand Vizier rose to his feet and crushed the soul block in his hand, before scattering the remains over the body at his feet.

"It is done," the Grand Vizier said, turning to the High Overseers. "By my command, the false god will not be reanimated. The organic body of Markus Aternus will be mummified and interred in the temple of Aternus, there to be remembered for all time." He gestured to the broken figure at his feet. "Dispose of this as you see fit."

The High Overseers all nodded their obedience, then without a single look cast in the direction of Carter, Carina or the others, they grabbed the arms of the former god-king, and dragged the body out of the meeting chamber, like a dead animal killed on a hunt. Soon, only the Grand Vizier and the Anubi that were now under his command, remained in the room. Carter studied his old adversary's eyes, which were tinged with sadness, but above all filled with anger and resentment. He could see that the Vizier wanted to kill him, but something was holding the Aternien back, and Carter knew exactly what it was.

"Think very carefully about your next move," Carter said. His time as spectator was over; now it was his chance to command the meeting to its conclusion. "I still have your body, the bodies of the High Overseers, and all of the critical inner circle. And before you get any stupid ideas about storming my ship to seize them, you should know they are safely locked away, a very long way from here."

For some time, the Grand Vizier simply stood there, glowing eyes fixed onto him. Carter could sense the de-facto leader of the Aternien Empire was running through dozens, perhaps even hundreds of scenarios in his mind for how he could kill Carter and still recover his mortal soul, but the truth was it was checkmate. Carter had him, and the Grand Vizier had no choice but to concede.

"What do you want from me?" the Vizier said.

"You already know my terms," Carter replied. "But now I have your mortal souls as leverage. I'll keep the stasis pods active, and your souls alive, on the condition that you leave and never come back."

The urge to fight was ingrained into the commander of the Senuset. The Vizier was not a politician, but a warrior, and Carter had disarmed him and taken away his power.

Hate coursed through the Aternien's synthetic body, but he was helpless to refuse.

"You will have your peace," the Vizier growled. The Aternien then aimed a finger at Carter like a gun, and it took everything he had not to grab the Vizier's hand and snap it off. "But know this, you cannot keep those sarcophaguses hidden from me forever. One day, perhaps when you are long dead, I will recover our mortal souls. And then there will be a reckoning."

Carter passed the center line and squared off against the Grand Vizier, effectively encroaching onto Aternien territory. The Anubi snapped into action and energized their flails, but the Vizier raised a hand to stop them.

"No, fall back!" the Vizier commanded, and the Anubi obeyed, lowering their weapons and marching ten paces back in a triangular formation. "You must not hurt this man. The survival of my soul depends upon it."

Carter smiled at the Vizier, then grabbed his neck and pulled him close. Words choked in the man's mouth, but the Anubi Royal Guardians, under orders not to intervene, remained stationary.

"We know where your planet is now, and we'll be watching," Carter said, whispering the words into the Vizier's ear. "And know this too. When the day of reckoning comes, I'll still be here, waiting. And you and I will finish what we started a century ago."

With that, Carter pulled the Vizier into a choke hold and squeezed with all his considerable might until the Aternien's head was wrenched from his body, which thudded to the deck in a crumpled heap. Still, the Anubi did not respond, and now it was Carter's turn to command them.

"Here, take this," Carter said, tossing the Vizier's head to the Chief Anubi, who caught it deftly, and tucked it under its arms. "Plug him into a new body, and make sure he remembers what I told him. Make sure he remembers what happens to those who cross blades with a longsword."

TWENTY-EIGHT
THE END GAME

MASTER COMMANDER ROSE stood at the window in the conference room on Station Alpha, arms folded tightly across his chest. Beyond the glass, docked to one of the station's upper pylons, was the Union Longsword Galatine. It had seen better days, but it had also looked worse. What mattered, however, was that – like himself – it was still fighting. The door to the conference room opened and Major Larsen walked in, follow by Brodie, Amaya, and Cai. HARPER and the gophers, TOBY, JACAB and Taylor, had remained on the ship as a skeleton crew, of sorts, overseeing the repair operations.

"I wonder what's happening out there," Carina said, stopping at his side and also folding her arms so that their shoulders were almost touching.

"I'm sure JACAB has everything under control," Carter replied. "And HARPER will bang the Galatine back together in no time."

Carina smiled. "I didn't mean the Galatine, I'm not worried about her." She pointed toward the constellation

Orion in the far distance, and in particular the middle star of Orion's belt. "I meant I wonder what's happening on New Aternus."

Carter had given that some thought too and the answer was that no-one could know for sure, but he would have certainly loved to have been a fly on the wall in the pyramid of Aternus at that very moment.

"Their god-king is dead, so their cities will be in turmoil," Carter replied, hazarding a guess. "I don't know if Aterniens grieve but most will be shaken to the core. Maybe they will accept the Grand Vizier as their new leader but I wouldn't be surprised if there was deep unrest, even a civil war."

Carina nodded. "Let's hope so. It will keep the bastards busy for a time. Too busy to bother with us." She sighed then cast Carter a sideways glance. "And I'm sure that Aterniens experience grief, regret and even remorse. Just look at Monique Dubois. If she can change then perhaps the rest of them can too, in time."

Carter grunted an acknowledgement. "It must be nice to be young and optimistic. Life beat the optimism out of me a long time ago."

"That's a cartload of horseshit, Carter, and you know it," Carina snorted with derision, and he looked at her wide-eyed. "If you didn't still have hope then you would have stayed locked up in your cabin on the forest moon of Terra Nine, and never gotten involved." Carter was about to argue the point, but his XO didn't let him get a word in edgeways. "And you can save that bull about 'duty' and 'honor' too. There's more to you than duty. I can see that, even if you can't."

Carter was blown away and didn't know how to

respond. Then the door opened again and Admiral Clara Krantz walked in, removing the opportunity for him to answer back. He snapped to attention, along with the other officers but Krantz was quick to dispel any notion of formality.

"For pity's sake, stand at ease," Krantz said. Carter noted that she looked more rested, and less browbeaten than the last time he'd seen her. "I think we've earned a bit of downtime, don't you?"

A steward wheeled in a trolley that was stacked with drinks, including coffee, along with pastries and neatly-cut sandwiches. The smell of the coffee, in particular, attracted Carina like a moth to a flame.

"Now we're talking," she said, helping herself to the first cup, before the steward had even finished locking the wheels of the trolley in place. "I don't know what the Galatine had in its stores, but it sure as hell wasn't coffee."

"That muddy sludge is all the same to me," Carter answered, gruffly.

Brodie was also quick to attend the trolley, and began stacking pastries onto a plate, like he was playing a game of Jenga in reverse. Cai was more reserved and precise in his selection of finger sandwiches, while Amaya focused on a contradictory collection of sweet treats and fresh fruit. Carter left them all to it. He wasn't hungry or thirsty, even though he felt oddly empty inside.

"To say that that every man, woman and child in the Union owes you their gratitude doesn't really cut it, Commander," Krantz said. She had skipped the trolley in favor of speaking to him by the window. "There aren't the words to describe the debt that humanity owes to the crew of the Longsword Galatine. And there's no way I can adequately express my personal thanks and admiration for what you've done."

"I was just doing my duty, Admiral," Carter said. It was gruff and terse response, given the heartfelt nature of the admiral's opening statement, but he didn't feel particularly special.

"You've done far more than that," Krantz replied, firmly, not allowing Carter to brush off her commendation so easily. "You've given humanity a future, and a much-needed kick up the ass. You should be proud of yourself and of your crew."

"I am proud of them admiral, Carter said, this time also speaking from the heart. "But they're much more than my crew. They're the closest thing I have to family."

Carter suddenly realized why he was feeling so downtrodden, despite their astounding victory over the Aterniens. The end of the war, and his assignment aboard the Galatine, meant that he and his officers would soon go their separate ways again. He shoved that thought to the back of his mind and decided to distract himself by requesting an updated briefing from the admiral.

"Did the Union scientists manage to replicate Nathan's serum?" Carter asked, painfully aware that there were still billions at risk of dying from the spread of the Aternien biogenic virus.

"It's fair to say that it has proven a challenge to reproduce, but I'm confident that a recent breakthrough will allow us to swiftly ramp-up production," Krantz replied. "We already have tens of thousands of doses arriving in the most affected regions, and millions more en-route. Even so, it will not be enough to save everyone."

Carter drew in a sharp intake of breath and let it out slowly. The news was as good as he could have expected.

"You may also be interested to learn that as soon as the Aterniens withdrew from Union space, dozens of senior officers and government officials turned up dead, or rather 'deactivated'," the admiral added. "They were all imposters. It was like someone had just flipped a switch and turned them off."

Carter nodded. This was good news in a broad sense, though not for the loved ones of the people who had been copied, because it meant that those officers and officials had been murdered.

"I'd continue to scan anyone in a position of importance or with potential access to sensitive data," Carter replied, focusing on what they could still affect. "The Grand Vizier was truthful when he said he'd never give up the search for the sarcophaguses. Deactivating some of the Imposters may simply be an attempt to lull us into a false sense of security."

Krantz's posture stiffened and her body language suggested that she was fully aware of the ongoing security risks. "Only a handful of people know the location of the Aternien stasis chambers, and we are devising a plan to ensure their safety," she replied. "To that end, we've extended an invite to the Aterniens to meet every three months at the Diplomatic Outpost, so we can prove that we're keeping the sarcophaguses active and in good condition. This time, I'm sure they will actually come."

Major Larsen then sidled up beside her aunt, coffee cup in hand. She had been close enough to catch the gist of the conversation. "A regular meeting also provides an opportunity for diplomacy, and maybe even a more lasting peace, based on trust," his XO added.

Carter smiled at her. "There's the sunny optimism of youth, again."

Carina scowled but it was a good-natured scowl; playful, rather than peevish.

"I have also sent recon vessels to the outposts the Aterniens seized at the beginning of all this," Krantz went on. She had gotten into her flow and was recounting everything she thought Carter might need or want to know. "The outposts were all abandoned, and there's no sign of the Aterniens anywhere in Union space. It looks like your threat to destroy their mortal souls had the desired effect."

"We shouldn't count on that threat as our only line of defense, Admiral," Carter replied. More than any of them, he was aware of how the Union's complacency had gotten them into the mess in the first place. "We still need to ramp up our defensive capabilities."

Krantz might have taken offence at a Master Commander telling an admiral what she should be doing, but the end of hostilities had trimmed her frayed edges, at least a little.

"I have spoken to the president already, and the ban on technological development will be eased." The admiral seemed to enjoy Carter's shocked expression, as she announced this. "There will still need to be checks and balances in place, so that we don't create another Markus Aternus or Nathan Clynes, but we can't afford to handicap ourselves, as we have done in the past. We need to be ready, should the Aterniens turn aggressors again."

"Speaking of Nathan, have there been any sightings of the pyramid ship, the Abydos?" Carina asked.

Admiral Krantz shook her head aggressively. This was clearly a sore point, Carter realized. "I sent a scout ship to Gliese 832-e, but it was clear that Nathan had already been there," the admiral said. "His underground complex had been ransacked, but we don't know what he took, since we have no idea what he had stored there in the first place." She shrugged. "Either way, he appears to be gone."

"He'll be back," Carter grunted, feeling his muscles tense up. "Hopefully not for a long time but something tells me we haven't seen the last of Nathan Clynes."

A lieutenant entered the room and approached the admiral. She excused herself to speak to him then nodded to the young woman and returned.

"I'm afraid I must go, I have a meeting with other senior officers," Krantz explained.

"Hopefully, not your court martial hearing?" Carter asked, only half-joking.

Krantz gave him a rare wry smile. "Not on this occasion, but I'm afraid that is coming. I accept the consequences of my actions, whatever they may be."

Carter felt suddenly angry. "They wouldn't dare," he growled.

"I have faith that the favorable outcome of my actions will weigh in my favor, but there is no question that I broke the chain of command," Krantz answered, seemingly reconciled to her fate.

Carter grunted again. Krantz may have been prepared to accept the judgement of her peers and superiors, but he was not.

"If they do lock you up then you have my word that I'll break you out of jail," Carter said, sternly.

Carina laughed and gave Carter a knowing wink. However, she quickly realized that she had misunderstood him entirely.

"You're serious?" Carina asked.

"When am I ever not serious?" Carter grunted in reply.

Carina glanced at the admiral, who curiously didn't react by ordering Carter not to do anything so foolish, and returned to her coffee cup, looking more than a little awkward.

"I must go, but I'll catch up with you all a little later on, once the dust has settled," Krantz said, swiftly moving the subject on.

Carter nodded and was about to check out the refreshments trolley, when Krantz caught him by the sleeve of his uniform and held him back.

"I'd like a moment with the commander in private, before I leave," Krantz said.

Carter stayed put, and Major Larsen excused herself. The admiral waited until they were alone, and out of earshot of the others, before continuing. She looked earnest, as if she were about to give him some bad news, but he couldn't have been more wrong.

"Commander, assuming I retain my position, I intend to restart the Longsword program."

Carter was unable to hide his shock. "I'm not so sure that's a great idea, Admiral, given what happened with Damien Morrow and the other turncoats."

"As you know better than anyone, the original Longswords were selected in a hurry, and in the Union's haste, certain personality defects were overlooked," Krantz said, unmoved by his initial objection. "For the new program, we can be selective, and refine the procedures so that they aren't quite as medieval as the experience you had to endure."

Carter grunted, but he still wasn't convinced. "The trials must still be rigorous. Candidate officers have to want it badly enough, and be tough enough, to endure extreme hardship and struggle, both physical and mental." He then shrugged, acquiescing a little. "But you are correct that there are better ways to achieve this than what I and the others were subjected to."

Krantz nodded. "I bow to your superior knowledge. And to that end, I want to promote you, and make you the head of the new Longsword division. I want you to recruit and train the next generation."

Carter was staggered again, and his initial reaction was to resist, though he couldn't explain why, even to himself.

"Admiral, I put this uniform back on to deal with the Aterniens, and I've fulfilled my obligations. Now it's time for me to go home." He glanced across to Brodie, Cai and Amaya, who were still enjoying the refreshment trolley, and each other's company. "Perhaps ask Brodie, he'd make an excellent commandant. They all would."

"My hope is that your officers will accept positions as veteran instructors," Krantz replied. It was clear that this wasn't just some random idea that she'd had. It was fully formed in the admiral's mind. "And I also believe that having you back in the military system, in a visible position of authority, will help to overcome the old fears and prejudices about post-humans. That's something we're long overdue tackling."

"I think people are now more fearful of post-humans than ever," Carter countered. He felt bad for continuing to react so negatively, but he couldn't simply ignore his own feelings on the matter.

"It's Aterniens that people fear, not you," Krantz replied, giving as good as she got. "You are perhaps unaware of the lasting impression you have made on people. The chatter throughout the fleet, and on the Union worlds, is that you're humanity's knight in shining armor."

Carter huffed a laugh. "Perhaps Lieutenant Ozek has something to do with that."

His thoughts wandered to the young officer he'd met aboard Venture Terminal and was again struck by her bravery and professionalism under the most extreme circumstances.

"She'd actually make for a fine Longsword candidate," Carter continued. He then nodded subtly toward Major Larsen. "As would your niece."

"Then accept the promotion, Commander," Krantz said, eagerly. It was like she was fishing, and Carter had just nibbled on the bait.

"Promoted to what?" Carter asked, admittedly growing more curious, and interested. He then flashed his piercing eyes at Krantz. "Master Admiral has a nice ring to it…"

"Don't get ahead of yourself, *Commander*," Krantz answered, and Carter was struck by how easily her icy stare and tone could disarm him. "I was thinking a new position and new rank would be in order. My idea was 'Master General'. Still reporting to me, of course."

"Of course," Carter repeated. He wouldn't have had it any other way. He then sighed, blowing out his cheeks in the process, and pressed his hands to his hips. "Can you at least give me some time to think on it?"

"Certainly," Krantz replied, seemingly satisfied that she'd hooked her fish. "Go home, Commander. No-one has earned it more. I'll be in touch."

They shook hands, then Carter saluted the admiral, and she departed with the lieutenant to attend what he expected to be a long string of meetings, culminating in her own court martial. Anger again flared inside him at the prospect of vindictive politicians trying to influence those proceedings, and to have Krantz removed and replaced with a more 'malleable' officer.

"What was that all about?" Carina asked, slinking up beside him. "Does she want to pin another hundred medals on your chest?"

Carter laughed. "Actually, she wanted to promote me."

"Well, congrats, you sly old bastard!" Carina cried, thumping his chest with genuine zeal, though Carter met her enthusiasm with an aggravated scowl. "You must hold the record for the longest amount of time in service, before reaching admiral."

"General, actually, and I haven't said I'll take the job yet."

Carina looked blown away. Carter imagined it was similar to how he'd looked when Admiral Krantz had offered him the job.

"Why the hell not?" Carina snapped. "I mean, what else are you going to do? Go back to your cabin in the woods and hunt 'death hogs'? What were those beasts called again?"

"Morsapri," Carter grunted. "And they taste better than military meal packs."

Carina scowled at him, and he decided to quickly change the subject.

"What about you, Major?" Carter asked. "What's your next move?"

Carina shrugged. "Back to my old job, I guess, though my desk in military intelligence is never going to hold a candle to my time on the Galatine. I know it sounds bad, but in some ways, I don't want this to end."

Carter understood her meaning completely. "The

Galatine is so much more than a crew. It's a family, and you're a part of that family now."

Carina pulled a face. "That sounds incestuous…"

"No, it doesn't, you weirdo," Carter snorted. "Besides, if your aunt has her way, then you might be in line for something more exciting."

Carina's eyes lit up. "Ooh, what do you know?"

Carter grinned and flashed his eyes, then mimicked the action of zipping up his lips, as if it were a state secret he couldn't reveal, under pain of death. Carina, however, was not dissuaded.

"I'll get it out of you sooner or later," she told him. "You're no good at keeping secrets, at least from me."

Carter huffed and looked offended. "I have no idea what you mean. I'm literally a mystery wrapped inside an enigma."

Carina laughed freely, and slapped him on the chest again, much to his continued annoyance. Then her name was paged over the station intercom, and her face fell, knowing that their time together was rapidly coming to a close.

"Duty calls," Carina sighed, then she grabbed the sleeve of his jacket and tugged on it gently. "Don't leave till I clock off, okay? I want to say goodbye before we both ship out."

Carter nodded and replied with a noncommittal grunt, then offered Carina his hand, but instead she pulled him in for a hug. He was hesitant at first, but finally loosened into it. It was bittersweet, like saying farewell to a family member after a long-overdue reunion, and it simply reminded him how he detested goodbyes.

"Take care of yourself, Carter," Carina said, after they separated. "Don't be a stranger."

"You too, Carina," Carter replied, with a strained smile.

Then Major Carina Larsen walked out of the room, and Carter watched her go for a few seconds, before turning his thoughts to what came next for him. He was already booked on a transport back to the forest moon of Terra Nine, and it departed in an hour, long before he'd get a chance to see Carina again. He considered changing his ticket, but Carter was never one to put off what had to be done.

It's better this way, he told himself. *It's better for all of us.*

Master Commander Rose then left the conference room, taking one final look at his crew – his family – then turned along the corridor and headed to the transport terminal, and to the ship that would finally take him home.

TWENTY-NINE
YOUNG AGAIN

CARTER PULLED up outside his log cabin, deep inside one of the many woodlands on the forest moon of Terra Nine and allowed the burbling V8 engine in his truck to idle for a few seconds, before switching off the ignition. The cabin looked just as he'd left it, untouched by thieves or Aternien bombs, though not everyone on the forest moon had been so lucky. The devastation he'd witnessed as his transport shuttle had come into land made it clear that the moon had been hit hard. No doubt, the Aterniens had thinned its already scant population further, he mused.

He opened the door of his truck, which creaked like the rusted lid of an ammo container, and jumped out onto the stony ground. He was struck by the recognizable sights, sounds and smells of his home. Everything from the long and complex trills and whistles of the leafhopper finch, as it skipped from tree to tree, to the throaty growl of the morsapri 'death hogs' was as familiar as an old pair of shoes. It couldn't have been more different to what he'd grown accustomed to on the Galatine. Despite the idyllic peace and tranquility of the setting, he found himself missing the thrum of starship engines and the fizz of his plasma cutlass being ignited.

At least I can still listen to that whenever I want to, Carter thought, glancing at the sword, which was resting on the back seat of the cab.

Suddenly, his senses heightened and his eyes snapped to the tree line, where a morsapri was watching him, breath fogging the air like steam billowing from a kettle.

"If I were you, I'd run," Carter grunted to the beast. "Unless you want to be dinner?" The morsapri appeared to hear him, and the death hog turned tail and vanished into the undergrowth. Carter snorted a laugh. "Smart animal. I guess we both live to fight another day."

Carter grabbed his bag off the passenger seat then slammed the truck door shut and headed for his cabin. The crunch underfoot seemed unnaturally loud after the soft clacks of his battle uniform boots on deck plates, but they soon gave way to the rhythmic tap of heels striking hardwood, as he climbed the steps of his porch. Then he saw that his front door was ajar and he froze. For some reason, his senses hadn't alerted him to any danger, but then the sudden appearance of the morsapri had already put him at an elevated level.

Carter slowly set down his bag and considered returning to the truck for his sword, but if there was still an intruder in his cabin, they would have heard his approach. Instead, he picked up a shovel that was resting against the wall and held it ready in one hand, while easing open the door with the other. He pushed through and darted inside, ready to strike down the thief who had unwisely chosen to steal from him. Instead, he found

Carina Larsen lounging in his armchair, in front of a made-up, but unlit fire.

"Digging for buried treasure?" Carina asked, in her smoothly sarcastic manner.

Carter set the shovel down and pressed his hands to his hips. "What the hell are you doing here?"

"Nice to see you too," Carina replied, with a notch more sarcasm. "I tried to build and light a fire, but honestly, I have no idea what I'm doing. I think I scorched your rug a bit."

Carter looked at his morsapri-pelt rug and saw that Carina had not merely scorched it but burned a hole in it six inches wide. "You're supposed to set fire to the wood, not my cabin," he grunted.

"Well, duh," Carina snapped. She was clearly angry with him, and the reason for that was obvious. He'd skipped out on her, despite her request that they meet again before either of them left Station Alpha. However, her presence in his cabin begged another critical question.

"How did you get here before me?" Carter asked. "Do you have a personal soliton warp drive?"

"In a manner of speaking," Carina said, her tone softening a little. "There are certain advantages to being the niece of the Fleet Admiral, one of which is being able to borrow her shuttle." She pushed herself out of the well-worn leather armchair and moved to the window, pulling back the curtains a little to see outside. "I figured I was due some leave and thought, where better than the cold, rain-sodden, and hog-infested woods of Terra Nine's Forest Moon?"

Carter huffed a laugh. "It is lovely at this time of year."

He'd expected Carina to return his smile, but instead she folded her arms in a classic defensive posture and glowered at him.

"Why did you just run out on me like that?" she asked, obviously hurt by his actions, which he immediately regretted. "Was it all really just duty to you? You didn't care about me at all?"

"Of course, I do, Carina," Carter replied, shamefaced. "But I've been through this before, remember? It was hard enough to have my crew and family broken up once, but for it to happen again… Well, let's just say I wasn't ready to face that."

"But you don't have to," Carina countered. She'd clearly prepared what she was going to say during the shuttle journey to Terra Nine. "Why not just take the job that my aunt offered you? That way, you can keep everyone together."

"Sure, until this president, or the next, or the senate, or even the military top brass decides that we're too much trouble," Carter said. He sighed and rubbed his beard, which was needing a trim again. "It's not the first time I've been promised the earth, only to have it all taken away from me. It happened after the last war, when public opinion swung against us. Then it was more politically expedient to sweep us under the rug."

Carina stepped forward, her eyes imploring him to reconsider. "It won't be like that this time. My aunt won't allow it."

"Assuming she keeps her job," Carter grunted, well aware that if the admiral's court martial went badly then Admiral Krantz would be out on her ear too.

"She's not going anywhere," Carina said, waving her hand in a dismissive gesture. "Every general, admiral, colonel, captain and anyone in between is in her corner, and the president is too smart to put the 'victorious admiral' on the block. They already convened a special tribunal, which will conclude that Admiral Clara Krantz acted in the best traditions of the Navy, and in the interests of the Union, blah, blah, blah. Honestly, it's probably already over by now."

"Well, shit, really?" Carter said, stuck for anything more eloquent to say.

"Really," Carina replied, and Carter could tell that she was stone cold serious. "So, are you going to take this job or not? Master General has a pretty nice ring to it."

He could tell that Carina wasn't going to take no for an answer, and he suspected that her aunt wouldn't either. If he looked up the word 'stubborn' in the dictionary, he felt sure the entry would read, "Fleet Admiral Clara Krantz".

"If I do take the job then I'll need some recruits," Carter said, testing the water.

Carina nodded agreeably, but with a nonchalance that suggested she knew exactly where Carter was going with his line of questioning.

"That's true," she replied, wearing a contemplative expression that was very obviously forced. "Do you have any potential candidates lined up?"

"One or two people immediately spring to mind," Carter replied, continuing to play along.

Carina maintained her air of thoughtfulness for a few more seconds, before she couldn't keep up the façade any longer, and grinned.

"How about you tell me all about it over a beer?" she asked, her eyes sparkling with a dangerous mischief. "Maybe we can get drunk and have another bar fight!"

Carter grunted a laugh. "I can't get drunk, but the fighting part I can definitely do."

Carina sprang at him, and for a moment, Carter thought he was going to be subjected to another hug. Instead, she hooked her arm through his, and guided him swiftly out of the door. He pulled it shut behind them, and it felt like closure, in more ways than one. The last time he'd walked away from his cabin, it was to be drawn back into a world he resented for abandoning him. Now, it felt like he was embarking on a new part of his life – a life that he thought had been over long ago.

Carter Rose started the engine of his truck and pulled onto the dirt track road that led into town. It was a path he'd trodden many times before, but on this occasion, there was so much more ahead of him than a backwater town with a bar that served warm beer and over-salty snacks. Ahead of him was a fresh start, and a future with purpose.

He glanced across at Carina Larsen, and she smiled back at him, full of youth, ambition and hope. Before he'd met her, he'd had none of those things. Now a fire was burning inside him that couldn't be quelled. Carter Rose was a hundred and seventy-two years old and had experienced more than most people would have done in a dozen lifetimes. Yet in that moment, he realized something profound. He realized that he felt young again.

The end.

EPILOGUE
THE ABYDOS

FIRES BURNED in the streets of New Aternus City, just as they burned in the streets of dozens of metropolises all across the Aternien home world. Their society had been torn apart by the death of their divine leader, Markus Aternus, a being who was believed to be eternal and all-knowing, but who had instead proved to be as vulnerable as a mere mortal.

Some chose to follow the Grand Vizier, who offered stability and a continuation of the Aternien way of life, but with his soul imprisoned by the humans, he was weak and afraid. A veritable recluse, the Vizier locked himself away in his palatial country retreat, beyond the city limits, and beyond sight of the Aternien people.

Some chose to believe that Markus Aternus would return, while others saw the collapse of their empire and religion as a sign that they were being punished for abandoning their human origins. Tens of thousands fled, taking to the stars in all directions, some even choosing to return to Old Aternus, and adopt the old ways, before the greed and fanaticism of the god-king drove them to war. Others waited, hoping for a sign that would show them the way forward, and reward their faith.

Then one day, under the flickering light of burning buildings, an Abydos descended from the sky and landed atop the great Pyramid of Aternus. Its occupant claimed he was the god-king reborn, possessing the mind of Aternus, but the soul of another. A pure soul. One that could not be swayed or corrupted by humans.

The occupant of the Abydos was a post-human named Nathan Clynes. And the Aterniens flocked to his side in droves.

CONTINUE THE STORY

Thank you so much for reading The Aternien Wars, part one. Book six, **Master General,** releases June 2024 on Amazon. Pre-order now!

https://geni.us/MasterGeneral

ALSO BY G J OGDEN

LATEST:

Hero of Metalhaven

Sa'Nerra Universe

Omega Taskforce

Descendants of War

Scavenger Universe

Star Scavengers

Star Guardians

Standalone series

The Contingency War series

Darkspace Renegade series

The Planetsider

G J Ogden's newsletter: Click here to sign-up

ABOUT THE AUTHOR

At school, I was asked to write down the jobs I wanted to do as a "grown up". Number one was astronaut and number two was a PC games journalist. I only managed to achieve one of those goals (I'll let you guess which), but these two very different career options still neatly sum up my lifelong interests in science, space, and the unknown.

School also steered me in the direction of a science-focused education over literature and writing, which influenced my decision to study physics at Manchester University. What this degree taught me is that I didn't like studying physics and instead enjoyed writing, which is why you're reading this book! The lesson? School can't tell you who you are.

When not writing, I enjoy spending time with my family, walking in the British countryside, and indulging in as much Sci-Fi as possible.

Printed in Great Britain
by Amazon